ALSO BY HAN ONG

Fixer Chao

THE
DISINHERITED

THE

DISINHERITED

Han Ong

FARRAR, STRAUS AND GIROUX

NEW YORK

Farrar, Straus and Giroux
19 Union Square West, New York 10003

Library of Congress Cataloging-in-Publication Data
Ong, Han.
  The disinherited / Han Ong.
    p. cm.
  ISBN-13: 978-0-374-28075-8
  ISBN-10: 0-374-28075-4 (alk. paper)
    1. Inheritance and succession—Fiction.   2. Americans—Philippines—
Fiction.   3. Manila (Philippines)—Fiction.   4. Children of the rich—
Fiction.   5. Filipino Americans—Fiction.   6. Fathers—Death—Fiction.
7. Philanthropists—Fiction.   I. Title.

PS3565N58D57 2004
813'.6—dc22

                                                        2004040566

Designed by Cassandra J. Pappas

www.fsgbooks.com

1 3 5 7 9 10 8 6 4 2

For advice and support, and for help big and small, the author thanks:

Susan Bergholz
John Glusman
Ralph Peña
Angel Velasco Shaw
Natsuko Ohama
and the MacArthur Foundation

PART ONE

Under the Philippines

I T WAS NOT A GOOD DAY for a funeral procession. Temperature: ninety-two at one p.m. and expected to rise to a hundred and ten before day's end.

As bad as the day was, the hour was even worse. Twenty minutes of walking and they had yet to get to EDSA. It was a city where the cars seemed to multiply daily, making gloomy the prospect of even the most superficial kind of progress.

Glossy black Mercedes-Benz hearse bedecked with flowers. On the car's roof was rigged a blown-up black-and-white studio photograph of Jesus Caracera taken when he was in his forties, at the height of his good looks and good fortune, living a continent away. His mug, the procession's masthead, smiled smugly and with a twinge of comic superiority at the poverty all around. On the antennae sticking up from the right fender hung two small flags: one American, the other Filipino. The procession moved so slowly that they remained limp.

The legendary Caraceras, whose empire had been built on sugar. Jesus Caracera had passed away in America and was returning to take his place among his family. He was the widely admired figurehead of a pedigreed family whose name could be found in nearly every household and restaurant in Luzon and Visayas: boxes and sacks of sugar to season cups of Sanka or Nescafé or Klim or to make flan with; to dip the sticky rice *suman* in; to throw into a hot skillet along with butter creating the powdered milk confection *pulburon* or the harder *pastillas*—both popular Christmas treats; to roll the sour tamarind seeds *sampaloc* in. For decades the family had been vital to the well-being of the nation in the tiniest, most momentous ways.

Flanking the vehicle on one side was forty-four-year-old Roger Caracera, the dead man's youngest and, up until a few days ago, estranged child; and on the other Roger's sister, Socorro, the famous pediatrician, who was crying, being consoled and supported by the eldest, Roberto.

The sky was an uninterrupted sheet of aluminum. Below it lay an expanse of asphalt and concrete convecting the heat from the ground up. Some of the women in the procession, noticed Roger Caracera, perhaps due to poverty, though more likely and more disturbingly, with a sense of voluntary, punitive penitence, were marching barefoot. He felt shamed by the extravagance of their display—wailing, hitting their chests, making of the long trip to the cemetery a walk on hot coals. It was as if for them a hero, long missed and much needed, had finally returned and they were pouring out all the energies and hopes accumulated during a lifetime of waiting.

Finally they turned a corner and came down EDSA, the thoroughfare whose full, marvelous name was Epifanio de los Santos Avenue. *Epiphany of the saints.* It hung there like an aspiration that had failed to materialize, an advertisement for dashed hopes.

The thoroughfare had been chosen by Mrs. Amador Caracera (Caracera's aunt-in-law, married to the youngest living Caracera uncle) because it was one of the city's most heavily trafficked areas. Surprising Caracera, the procession, headed by two policemen on motorbikes, turned out to be two blocks long. On their way to Quezon City's Kalayaan Cemetery, they attracted onlookers who were made equal parts reverent and resentful of such a vulgar display of wealth.

The choosing of the cemetery, which was not where Jesus Caracera's father and grandfather were buried (they were in Negros, the province where the sugar business once thrived but which consideration no longer seemed apt for the succeeding generations), was also left to Mrs. Amador Caracera. She reigned, alongside a handful of women, as a prime scene-shaker and -maker in Manila, and therefore, when she said of securing a lot (managed not without a little difficulty, seeing as everything had long ago been booked "full to eternity") at Kalayaan Cemetery (where the textiles tycoon Jorge "Bongbong" Sanchez and the real estate magnate Claudio Araneta III, among other luminaries, were buried) that it was "the only thing to do," it was understood by the family, including the three children of Jesus Caracera, that she knew whereof she spoke. So Kalayaan it would be, the name meaning Freedom. In Manila, it was apparent that to attain freedom you had to have a shitload of money.

Exacerbating the heat, Roberto, Socorro and he were dressed, head to foot, in black. He had neglected to bring anything from New York and had to have a suit specially ordered from a family tailor, a spindly Chinese man who worked out of a decrepit shop in Ongpin, amid the bun and noodle shops, and movie houses, and temples, where another cacophonous Chinese that was different from New York Chinese was spoken.

Because of the glaring sunlight, the three were also wearing sunglasses. Caracera had cried all the tears he would ever cry over this episode and wore his glasses as a shield.

The members of the immediate family were required by the official "couturier" of the family (a flaming queen by the name of Fabian the Fabulous, again picked by Mrs. Amador Caracera) to wear sashes in which the family name was spelled out in gold dust. These were secured by, for the men, a pin depicting the family coat of arms—a triangular mishmash of the Philippine and Spanish flags with a white dove over three sugarcanes in the middle; and, for the women, diamond brooches that were family heirlooms and that had been held in trust for just such an occasion. The brooch Socorro was wearing was valued at over a million pesos, which may have helped to explain the worried glances Mrs. Amador Caracera occasionally threw her niece-in-law's way.

Caracera had been required to get a haircut. He and his brother had their hair "styled" by another of the gay men that surrounded Mrs. Amador Caracera like drones around a queen. (Mrs. Amador Caracera, fittingly enough, had an Imelda-like beehive piled atop her head.) For

Caracera and his brother, having their hair "styled" essentially meant allowing a more-than-generous amount of pomade (which smelled faintly of sampaguita flowers) to be run through their hair, and then having the hair combed back to affect a severe look that made them appear to be wearing helmets. Walking down EDSA with their pomaded hair, sweating foreheads and sunglasses, the brothers achieved masks of celebritylike glare.

Because of this, there were whispers all around them that, try as hard as he might, Caracera could not ignore. Asking whether they were indeed part of a movie shoot, and if they were, where had they hidden the cameras?

Rosaries dangled freely from all the women's hands, someone was leading the group in prayer and response, they were now thick into what seemed like the hundredth Hail Mary, images of whom dangled at the end of necklaces and bracelets and medals and were even emblazoned on the fans used by the women at the back, that he referred to as the "gallery," so that they became transformed into rainbows. The prayers kept time with the steps as the procession was smoothly guided by the two cops who had been specially compensated to provide pomp and protection.

Flanking the funeral line on either side, recurring at intervals of a hundred yards, were pairs of cops, and at the tail end, protecting it from the onrush of impatient, resentful traffic—which was made to slow down and diverted into one narrow lane running alongside the procession—were three more cops. All in all, thirteen policemen waylaid from regular duty to help stage-manage Mrs. Amador Caracera's lavish display of the family's imperviousness to death and tragedy.

Jesus Caracera, in death as in life, was a Filipino bigtimer, on a par with slain senators and prematurely dead movie stars in being thought worthy of a procession down one of the city's main arteries. The only challenger to, the only refuter of this monarch's authority being the man directly behind the police escorts, standing to the left of the hearse, the other side taken up by his siblings; a man who had been ogled all afternoon long, starting at the church services, by the women in the balcony and even by the matriarchs to his back who should've known better, and by his relatives among whom he was a dark star famed for truancy and dissoluteness. He'd hoped to be a writer, something the dead man had strongly disapproved of. Perhaps this had made him want to become a writer even more. His delinquency could then be seen as a path paved on the way toward Art. But when asked if he'd published anything in America, he'd been shockingly candid, confessing to being an "utter failure." At church he had been obliged to take off his reflective glasses and he'd compensated by bowing his head at all times, knowing that it might suggest burdensome grief to some. But as soon as the services were over and he'd moved to the front, along with Roberto and four of the Caracera cousins, to bear the coffin to the hearse, back had gone the glasses over his eyes, to seal his icy view of the surroundings.

The smell of the pomade clashing with the sweetness of the corsaged hearse was beginning to make him feel pukey.

> Hail Mary full of grace
> the Lord is with you
> Blessed are you among women
> and blessed is the fruit of your womb Jesus . . .

He mouthed the words for the first time. They had no meaning, only so many steps to climb until he could, just for a moment, get above his head, away from the smell, away from the sun gripping him at the back of the neck (was that a breeze? at this late hour?), away from the sight of a naked little girl at the side of the road who seemed to be eating a plastic bag, and away from his father who continued to smile benignly at everything that crossed his path, up and away, reaching which, he felt a woozy relaxation that made him have to right himself, and once more, back he plunged into his body, his sight wrested from where it had peacefully observed their heads from on high, just so many bobbing black orbs in a curious dance routine (a brunette sea! what an oddity after so many years in America!). Once again, he took into view the miraculously dry backs of the cops guiding them, one of whom was corpulent in a manner to suggest prosperity beyond what a cop's salary would provide, and to the side, his brother and sister, who continued to grieve, and farther still, nearly left behind but not quite, the sliver of the naked girl still chewing on her plastic bag like a small goat and just as thin, still staring dumbly at all of them.

He turned his neck to crack it. The gremlin, which had for the moment moved from his chest to his shoulders, slipped off.

Mrs. Amador Caracera asked the driver to lower the windows and turn the air-conditioning up. She moved closer to an open window, futilely seeking relief from the heat.

The police escorts slowed down. From this Roger Caracera knew that they were near their destination. Suddenly, in the middle of Metro Manila, where even the sidewalks and the road dividers were taken up by the rough assemblages called home by the indigent, there was only a blissful emptiness. A reigning quiet. This seemed the direct product of costly policing. The procession caused unseen birds high up in the trees on both sides of the road to twitter, panicked squeak-squeaks like the sound of sneakers darting across concrete. For a moment Caracera thought that a tennis court was nearby. (Tennis! Its method of solitude against solitude perfectly distilling his own way in life, with his family. Strange, to be recalled to it on the day his father was being laid to rest. It was Jesus Caracera who had first encouraged him to take up the game, to uphold, to perpetuate the tastes and traditions of their class. Because of this, he had refused to play along.)

Soon they had the high gated entrance of Kalayaan in view. Many people, the cops included, made the sign of the cross. He felt obliged to follow.

They passed the entrance and slowed down some more. Mrs. Amador Caracera left her husband's side to confer with the police, who clearly did not know where to head. The expanse of the cemetery spread out on both sides of them, offering no clues. Mrs. Amador Caracera went in search of the manager or a groundskeeper. In the meantime, the procession was forced to come to a halt, the tail end still outside the gate. Information was relayed backward to make sure that nobody panicked unnecessarily.

The silence around them was a startling contrast to the hellishness of the gauntlet through which they had passed, as if they had finally made it to paradise after an arduous trial which involved having to face the staring judgment and malign wishes of cadaverlike thousands, knowing they more than deserved it because to honor one man's death they had gone to an extravagance horrendously contemptuous of those left behind. Caracera looked and saw that the cemetery was chillingly quiet.

Socorro wouldn't stop crying. It had been Roberto's job all afternoon to comfort her. Soon, Caracera feared, it would be his. At least, he thought, Socorro's grief had the benefit of quelling her normally whiny voice and turning her constantly status-assessing gaze inward, to confront her inability to measure up to the role of devoted daughter. She and Roberto had been criticized for not accompanying the coffin to the Philippines and she'd known that nothing she could say, not even the fact that she had given herself and her home over to take care of the dying man in his final days, would change the relatives' minds. Socorro's tears Caracera understood to be as much for herself as for the man about to be laid to rest.

The priest who had presided at the services, taking advantage of the interruption, came up to say a few words to Socorro. Caracera couldn't hear what was being said but was sure that words from his homily were being recycled; sentiments about how the man was "now with our beloved Father," which seemed to Caracera to be based on a laughably ignorant (perhaps willfully so) assumption about the dead man's character. How much had the family donated to be able to get a mass for Jesus Caracera at the cathedral, one of the oldest and grandest in Manila?

The phalanx holding up the rear kept up their Hail Marys.

Amador Caracera stood glumly by himself near the back of the hearse, an officially childless old man (his only son, a druggie, banished from the family) awaiting the return of the Mrs., who was known by the entire city to be the force in the marriage and who, just like in her role as a prime hierarchical arbiter of Manila, had sealed the fate of a social liability (never mind that he was her child) by not only turning her back on and closing her doors to him but asking everyone she knew to do so as well.

Caracera caught a glimpse of himself in the hearse: the upturned nose (his mother's), the voluptuous mouth framed by the chin with a tendency toward jowliness (his father's; the imprint of both men's fondness for drink), the perpetually pushed-together brows and the lined forehead (his own innovation, which he wiped). It was the first time the handkerchief was being put to use all afternoon long. It had seemed pointless earlier to keep fighting the heat and he'd allowed his pants and his armpits to turn into maps. Also he felt it had behooved him to exhibit an unkemptness that would stand in for the sorrow he couldn't manifest.

Roberto looked at his brother, looked away.

Yet another Hail Mary begun. For the first time it occurred to Caracera to wonder, Who are all these women? He knew they could not all be relations. The possibility that they were being paid by Mrs. Amador Caracera to give the proceedings needed bulk fluttered through his mind. The whole thing—wake, reception, church services, funeral procession, interment at Kalayaan—with so many outstretched hands awaiting payment before his father had even been lowered into the ground, began to be movielike in another way: a daunting budget that he guessed easily topped a couple of million pesos.

The fans kept snapping back and forth, though because of the ample shade thrown by the acacias that stood at the sides of the cemetery lane like slouching sentries it had grown noticeably cooler. The rosaries continued to click, on to the next bead, on to the next Hail Mary.

All right all right, Caracera thought, trying hard to restrain himself from crossing the border into speech, this woman's full of grace— we've already established that! Let's move on!

Perhaps the women had not been paid by Mrs. Amador Caracera at all, but had simply been magnetized by the sight of death so available. They'd drawn near with an unacknowledged desire to follow the dead man to his grave, envious of his imminent return to the place their faith had been preparing them for since childhood: Jesus Caracera would soon sit at the right hand of the Father, while they had to wait years more. If only the Second Coming would hasten . . .

General Douglas MacArthur, a man who promised to return and did indeed, in October 1944, return, was the secular incarnation of Jesus Christ, who'd made the same promise but had yet to make good on it. The general, it occurred to Caracera, was revered as a symbolic foretaste of the great Liberation about to occur and urgently longed for. Perhaps that was truly why they, the entire procession, were celebrities for the day: not for the pomp, the flamboyance, the money molded by riveting bad taste, but because the image of them galvanized the hopes of an entire city, an entire nation, a whole culture in which death was the central hub around which everything turned. Death-besotted. Death-longing. People weighted with lives that were the clearest argument for forgetfulness via religion: the ability to see this penurious time as nothing more than a gauzy veil layered over the true picture: a pastoral scene where it was always dawn, the hours before the lacerating sun gathered its full strength. They couldn't wait to cut through the cheesecloth uncertainty of this life to get at the reward of ease waiting behind it.

Thinking of this, it occurred to Caracera that Harvey Keitel, who was in Manila shooting a movie in which he'd been cast as the legendary, beloved general, was no Jesus Christ. He smiled.

What had been a momentary glitch was now threatening to turn into a full-fledged snafu. Where was Mrs. Amador Caracera? Socorro took a break from grief to try on a new expression, of panic. Everything's all right, Roberto assured her.

It would not be a Filipino ceremony, thought Caracera with great dispassion, without at least a couple of farcical elements curling around the edges, about to overturn things.

At the open casket ceremony two days ago, an elegant, middle-aged beauty dressed to the nines in what Mrs. Amador Caracera called "*McCall's*-pattern Chanel" had clicked angrily toward the coffin in high heels ("pure Marikina," Mrs. Amador Caracera had added in case the first comment had failed to do the job). Everyone had held their breath. Whispers had spread quickly, though no one would tell the children who the woman was. However, it was clear from the way she confronted Jesus Caracera, with a widow's sense of interrupted entitlement mixed with the indignation of a spurned mistress, that her relationship with the dead man had been deeply amorous, lengthy and unremunerative.

Caracera had been made more curious than anything by the sight of the woman. Finally here was a phantom from the treasure chest of Jesus Caracera's hidden life come to confront them. One among many who had been wronged by the supposedly respectable family. She had begun, to Caracera's great thrill, to bang on the coffin, as if hoping by her hot-bloodedness to stir the man into a belated dialogue. And more thrillingly, the lid of the coffin had come crashing down, making a sound like a drunk at the piano. Quickly, before the drama could escalate, Mrs. Amador Caracera had ordered two of the Caracera cousins (recent college graduates who wanted to go to the States to "explore options") to hustle the woman, kicking and screaming, out of the hall. They tackled the poor woman with a complete disregard for how ridiculous they looked—one of them using an armlock around her waist and the other yanking her by the outstretched arms. Caracera had thought of them as twin henchmen who had found their true calling: no use going abroad when they were already in the bosom of their life's vocation, bouncers entrusted to keep sanitized the Caracera name. And boy, did it need sanitizing.

Finally, to the procession's audible relief, Mrs. Amador Caracera came back with a short man wearing a straw hat. Seeing the procession and the priest, the man took off his hat and gave a bow. He motioned to the policemen to follow him.

Now he was leading everyone, and the rustle of resuming activity was like a collective letting-out of breath. Mrs. Amador Caracera, taking her husband by the arm, hustled them closer to the front, whispering all the while. Caracera caught something about the owners from whom the family had negotiated to buy the site on which Jesus Caracera's mausoleum would eventually be built. Seeing by the obvious costliness of the day's proceedings that the Caraceras could afford more than they'd initially vouchsafed (news traveled fast in the city), the owners had decided at the last minute to up their asking price.

This had caused some confusion with the people who had loaned the plot into which Jesus Caracera would momentarily be interred. The loaners were friends of Mrs. Amador Caracera, specifically a Mrs. M with whom Mrs. Amador Caracera played mah-jongg. The loan, it was understood by both parties, was to be for six months, and six months only. (It was hoped by everyone that Mr. M, in whose name the plot had been registered, would not inconvenience plans by dying during the allotted six-month period.) And then Jesus Caracera's coffin would be taken out of the temporary plot and transferred to its final resting place in the projected crypt for which designs had already been drawn up by a highly respected Chinese architect. This man had built a faithful following among wealthy Chinese Filipinos whose custom it was to outfit their dead down to the last extravagance, hoping to inspire the afterlife to a similar treatment.

Mr. and Mrs. M, it turned out, having heard that the sellers of the mausoleum plot were possibly reneging, had called the cemetery to put a freeze on their loan. It had taken Mrs. Amador Caracera several minutes of cajoling and reassuring and, when all else failed, threatening, over her cell phone, first to Mrs. M, then to her husband, to finally let things proceed as planned.

The man with the straw hat, who might've been trying to fill in the hole already dug when the procession had entered, led the family to the site: extravagant, beribboned floral tributes bookended folding chairs set up for the family, and at the north end of the grave was a lectern for the priest. The grave was bordered by flowers whose edges were already starting to shrivel and turn brown.

The hearse stopped. The pallbearers once more lifting the coffin onto their shoulders. Each man was mindful of his footing on the grass. Mrs. Amador Caracera and one of the other wives stayed behind to organize the rest of the crowd. They were asked to stay on the lane, to leave a proper, respectful distance between themselves, mere spectators, and the family, whose grief, being superstars', required witness to complete it. The poor women obliged with the meekness of sheep. They stopped their prayers and waited for the activities to commence.

The men rested the coffin on top of the mechanical contraption that would lower it into the ground. The gold fixtures on it caught the light. Caracera headed for the back row, standing next to cousins, whose names he'd forgotten. One was a young high school girl who was so shy she had never been able to look him in the eye. The other was a businessman in his thirties who was beginning to go bald and who, to the consternation of his mother, remained unmarried. (Was he gay? worried the family.) Caracera left Socorro and Roberto seated in front. His aunt-in-law turned around, looking for him. He avoided her eyes. She clearly wanted him, for the sake of keeping to the geometry of her plans, to sit with his siblings: the three children facing the priest and the coffin, and by whose actions God could adjudge the successfulness of the dead man's life and either grant him entry into or bar him from the gates of heaven.

Roberto and Socorro, sitting next to an empty chair, didn't bother turning around. They knew their brother better than anyone and would not be drafted into one more futile exchange with him.

The priest began to speak.

Mrs. Amador Caracera, despite her grave demeanor, seemed to have a twinkle of pride in her eyes. So it occurred to Caracera, who did not begrudge the woman her sense of accomplishment. A logistical night-mare had been handled with great panache. For a few minutes it had seemed as if things would not go smoothly after all. But they had. All thanks to the hawkish watchfulness and attention to detail of Mrs. Amador Caracera, who had singularly, it seemed, contrived an occasion the majesty of which was in inverse proportion to the worth of the man being honored.

Exhaustion was finally catching up with Caracera. And what better conduit to sleep than the words of the priest, a man clearly in love with the sound of his own voice, and filled with the conviction of his eulogy's baublelike ability to distract from the sorrow at hand? There was more talk about the afterlife, which unfortunately did not carry past where the family sat and therefore missed its true audience, the gallery that had gathered a few yards away as if at the theater. For those women, as for most of the people they had passed along EDSA, the afterlife was the only thing which made their life worth living.

Caracera closed his eyes. He was shielded by his glasses. Still, if anyone were to catch on, he wouldn't care.

It had been a long day for everyone, and longer still for him, who, as soon as he'd arrived six days ago, had been required by his official responsibility (being the dead man's son and therefore a kind of host) to answer any question asked of him by people who had either known him as a child (though the traffic did not flow the other way) or who'd known his father. Mainly what was wanted from him were inconse-quential details he hadn't thought about in a long time, such as where he lived; what did he do for a living and was that what he'd dreamt of doing when he was a boy growing up in the Philippines (he was an "utter failure," he admitted with the same pleasure in degradation that, more than anything, impelled his return to this country); was he mar-ried or was he entertaining any plans of getting married soon (*hopefully he wasn't gay?*); and was he only here for his father's funeral or could he stay longer to reacquaint himself with the home he knew only from a period of boyhood ignorance?

No, he'd always replied politely to the last question, he had responsibilities awaiting him in New York and couldn't stay. To which they would always respond with unconcealed disappointment, as at a child's bad grades.

The truth, the habit of truth, was completely exhausting.

The last thought he had before drifting off to sleep was occasioned by the sight of the beautiful long purple stole that hung over the priest's shoulders, gold crosses embroidered at both ends like anchors hanging near the ground. He cackled to himself, without a doubt as to the value of the piece of cloth: vow of poverty indeed!

A minute later he was awakened by the shrieking of his sister, who had to be restrained from causing harm to herself and to those around her as the coffin was lowered into the ground. He rushed forward instinctively to take the place of an aged uncle and, with Roberto on the other side, formed both wall and cushion for Socorro.

Seeing her brother at her side for the first time that day, she collapsed into his chest, sobbing, Papa's gone Roger he's gone and he's never coming back.

I know, replied Caracera, feeling her hit out at him. I know, he kept repeating.

He saw that Mrs. Amador Caracera was pleased that he was finally taking his rightful position. She even gave a small smile, nodding at him.

CHAPTER 2

HAT CARACERA CHOSE during the heady American time that was his own to call, freed from the supervision of relatives in the Philippines, as well as the vigilance of Jesus Christ, were pursuits that in his mind were meant to correct the imbalance caused by his schooling and his churchgoing. Instead of compulsory goodness, the new regimen of his San Francisco adolescence would be compulsory delinquency. So he'd hung out with junior hoodlums whose badness consisted mainly of listening to loud music on the streets. They'd enjoyed congregating in public places to advertise their gangness, and had mostly harassed women and other boys younger than themselves, shaking the latter down for money. They'd branched out into spray-painting walls with epithets and curses that widened the audience for their apathy and disdain, and had graduated, at their boldest, to making away with the contents of mailboxes that they'd jigged open with screwdrivers, box cutters or ice picks. They'd clearly been on the path to long stints in jail.

But Caracera had bailed before that could happen. Mr. Caracera had forced the issue by threatening to fly him back to the Philippines. He had no overwhelming positive feeling about America, and therefore saw no benefits to be deprived of. Still, the Philippines, being the land of Jesus, Inc., would guarantee him a life of automaton guilt and obedience.

But the main consideration he'd had to weigh was whether he preferred to live with his father (or near his father or, better yet, *in the vicinity of* his father, whose absenteeism was proving, in his adolescence, to be a boon) or with his mother back in the Philippines.

He didn't dislike his mother. He didn't like her either. The Ice Queen, their father had called her, first jokingly, and then with bitter resignation. About her Caracera felt a shruggishness not unfriendly, and which, because it was the same coolness she herself radiated, seemed to have the poetic balance of a natural order. If she'd needed help, he would help, no question about it. If she'd approached him . . . But he knew she would never do such a thing. Knew that she would brush off any attempt at charity. He even believed that she didn't make any effort to track her children down in the States. Had perhaps felt of their being kidnapped a relief that went beyond her characteristic enervation. To this woman, the children were distasteful reminders of her life's failure. She'd come to the Philippines as a Peace Corps volunteer, intending to do good for a great number of people. ("This country attracts all sorts of crackpots—visionaries, missionaries or, in your mother's case, fashionaries," Jesus Caracera had said, encouraging the children to laugh at their mother's rants against the "failed promise of the Philippines.") Teresa Caracera hadn't planned on marriage to a playboy, giving birth to his spoiled, awful children and extending the line of a decrepit dynasty.

So Caracera had pacified his father by playing at goodness, which consisted mainly of redirecting his transgressive tendencies toward the girls and women he noticed were paying him close attention, seemingly wherever he went in San Francisco. At the library, the young students had peered up shyly from their books. At the grocery store, the checkout girls had slowed down their transactions to be able to flirt, asking him how old he was, did he go to school, did he have a girlfriend, what did he like to do, what ambitions did he have, and making of his face, as they listened to his furtive but slowly-gaining-in-confidence lies, sectioned traps where their eyes lovingly lingered: he felt all Eyes, or all Mouth, or sometimes One Big Nose. The women had been no better. He'd expected age to have equipped them with ways more devious than obvious, but they too had looked at each part of his face with girlish transfixedness; approving of each, he felt, but not really sure what they thought of the sum of those parts. Perhaps his beauty was such that it was better handled broken down into bits. Or perhaps they were only responding to the Frankenstein aspect of his origins, trying to tease out a history and lineage from the grouping of incompatible components. Filipino and Spanish and a little German and English and blah blah, he would say. Blah blah: a favorite phrase of his mother's which he had unthinkingly been parroting since childhood. A term meant to convey disdain for the unsaid things that seemed to comprise so much of their lives. He was Filipino and blah blah. His mother and father were not divorced, but they were blah blah. He had not been in touch with either his older brother or older sister for years because, well, he had nothing in common with them and you know how those things go, it was so much blah blah.

Sex, then, had replaced delinquency, which was itself a replacement. For religion—that font into which he'd poured his boyish ardor, following the example of his family.

But eventually, he'd discovered his country's faith to have been comprised of tissue upon tissue of lies—all engineered to correct human nature (that was to say, sexual nature). The bedrock of Jesus, Inc., was the hatred of human beings *as they were,* and he'd learned it without meaning to by making a contrast of the erection in his hand, which had always felt unwrong, against the legislative rumbles of the Bible that came during scenes replicating his actions but which were called "sins" instead of actions, rumbles which were like far-off roars echoing, Wrong wrong wrong, having to him the sound but not the matter of a real storm. The characters risen from the Bible to condemn him were the ancestors of the spinsterish Filipino instructors and Filipino priests who taught him. These men and women always looked twisted with excessive sacrifice and had a sourness that was like the taint of so much putrescent flesh. Putrescence: there, he'd taken a word from the Bible and had turned it against itself.

He'd liked his dick. What was wrong with that? He didn't know where he'd gotten the wherewithal to forge ahead with this challenge to his Catholic legacy.

And he'd liked the things to which his hard-on pointed. They'd felt natural. Uncleanness part of nature.

He'd liked the way women's nakedness looked. Built to be entered. Wanting to be entered. He'd liked when they gave themselves, in ways ranging from wholehearted to regretful (but only playacting at such so he wouldn't think them too easy). He had specially enjoyed recalling their earlier demureness, their obscuring primness when he finally had them pinned below him, his body imprisoned by the panicked, beseeching embraces of their skinny arms and legs. He'd loved the moaners, and the nonmoaners. The latter with their tightly shut eyes, inside which they seemed to be tabulating the costs to their souls of what they had not only agreed to, but had actively encouraged. He'd loved the fact that they were willing to hazard God's punishment—just as he had. He'd seen all the irreconcilable things in the world, all the paradoxes—beauty and disgust, pleasure and pain, sin and sacrifice, and on and on—fused into *one* thing which rendered all the contradictory components ridiculous and inconsequential, a skewer of light on which their bodies hung, impaled and writhing. Afterward they were restored to the sadness, the clarity, of their daily lives—joy *or* gloom, courage *or* cowardice, regret *or* rejoicing. He'd loved even that sadness, that postcoital tang in the mouth of acrid smoke trailing from a fire put out inside the loins, the heart, the skull. It had been drunk-making.

What else? He'd loved committing adultery with adulterous wives, whose unhappiness was evident in anything not having to do with sex. He'd remembered sex with these women as a zone of forgetfulness for them, and had felt a little less excited knowing that he was performing an act of charity, but they'd seemed to blossom under his care and in their eyes a version of him as someone whole, someone equipped with answers and solutions, had stared back at him, and he'd found the image, being a lie, sexy.

He'd gotten crabs more than a few times. He didn't love that. But he'd escaped the other, severer punishments.

He'd fallen in love, which he'd loved, up to a point. And then he'd come to contrast the small elisions and untruths of romance against the cleansing candor suffusing sex, and had further been provided with three successive and close-at-hand portraits of the doomy joke of companionship in the form of his parents and the quick (seemingly too quick) marriages of his brother and sister, and so had come to pitch his tent away from the possibility of being like the rest of the world. Of being a unit.

Cut adrift, he'd floated from bed to bed. At the end, he had only his own. On which, two decades and a new city later, he lay alone night after night, all desire wrung out of him, moved by his recollections to marvel only at the athleticism of someone who could not have been him, whose energies, passions, single-mindedness, whose lust (for life as well) had left not even embers to suggest the same body, the same person tenanted at one end by a youthful spirit and at the current terminus by that spirit exhausted, resting: no, they were two entirely different people. Lust? What was that? As if to underline his incorporeal state, above him floated the pale unflecked whiteness of his New York ceiling, which was like the sky, and which separated him from a neighbor, the quietest man on earth, whom Caracera knew to be above him on no evidence other than his belief.

CHAPTER 3

T HE PRODIGAL SON'S TRIP from New York had been without incident and he was now sitting outside.

His sister's and his brother's faces, with their racially indistinct looks, were perfect matches for his own. Were they white? had asked the various classmates and acquaintances of their question-filled youths. No, not really. Meaning, not fully. White and some other. Catching sight of their father, the enquirers would nod. Yes, of course. White and brown. But brown as in what? Latin? Asian, yes? What part of Asia?

Years later, in this antiseptic environment, red carpet at his feet, polished mahogany ceiling gridded, leather furniture, the books lining one wall serving as advertisements for a lifetime of being involved in the right things, Caracera felt for the first time in a long time the privilege of being at home. His face had precedents.

He'd never, in his wanderings during his familial absence, encountered anyone with the same look, and so had been confirmed about being set off from the rest of the world. When his brother and sister had walked up to him at the San Francisco airport terminal earlier that day, though he'd been shocked by how old and tired they'd appeared despite his having been prepared for them to look that way, he'd been more shocked, in fact repulsed, to discover how their faces were a thievery of his cherished individuality. Only later, in the car driving into the city, when all the preliminary small talk had been used up and they were all pretending to find the landscape outside the windows riveting, had he realized that it was a good thing. For the moment a weight had seemed to lift from the top of his lungs. The gremlin whose seat it was, confused by the sudden emergence of two others who so resembled the man it'd been assigned to haunt, assigned to, if not goad into action, then at the very least kill with the weight of guilt, had scampered off to collect its wits. He'd felt the instant peace of legibility, like a bottle aligned with mates in a row.

The wealth of the sister's home was the same wealth of their childhood in the Philippines and which had remained unabated during their relocation to San Francisco. The sister and the brother had made of their lives tunnels through which this wealth could travel into the present. There was something subterranean, something untouched by sunlight in the way their faces hung, the way they covered up with clothes emblazoned indiscreetly with the logos of luxury, and specially in the way they formed their words, betraying too much time spent rehearsing for the right, casual effect. You'd think it would be him evidencing this quality of prolonged malnourishment, but even he had to agree with his siblings when they'd expressed shock (and was that dismay?) at his improved appearance.

They'd been shocked as well when he'd told them that he taught at Columbia. He'd purposely let the name dangle in the air, and didn't elaborate on his course, that he was still only an "adjunct," hoping they wouldn't inquire further. Roberto had looked away, and Socorro had pursed her lips.

Now his brother stepped into the room where he sat waiting with Socorro. Denisa says hi, Roberto told Caracera.

His nephew and niece, Denisa and Roberto's children, were twenty and twenty-one, respectively. Polite, obedient, altogether exemplary. Giving their parents no headaches. He didn't look forward to meeting them.

His brother sat down next to his sister, the two facing him.

Socorro began by saying, Be nice when you talk to him.

Caracera thought it wiser not to reply.

And we'd like, added Roberto, while you're here, to meet the lawyer to talk about Papa's estate. All three of us together.

I don't want anything, Caracera said.

Socorro looked away. She seemed to be thinking: You might not have been given anything. She looked back. When you talk to Papa, don't tell him what you just told us. If you don't want anything, fine. But don't tell him that. It'd be like a slap to him.

What about Mama? asked Caracera.

You haven't heard? his brother asked, looking at Socorro, whom he'd expected to have filled Caracera in.

She's dead? he asked without emotion.

Socorro shook her head. She looked exactly like their mother. She's in an asylum.

Asylum? You mean . . . ?

Nobody would answer him. What do you mean? he asked again. A *mental* hospital?

Mandaluyong, replied Socorro, bowing her head.

Papa knows this? he asked.

Of course, she replied.

The lawyer told me— began Roberto.

Socorro looked up.

—that he knows for a fact that Papa has left enough for Mama's indefinite care in Mandaluyong. Until she dies.

They expect her to die in there? he asked.

Don't be naive, Socorro said. If you're in Mandaluyong you're too far gone. She, like Roger, spoke in a tone without a trace of feeling.

Did Socorro and Roberto verify the legitimacy of the diagnosis? Hadn't it occurred to them that Teresa Caracera's husband and her husband's family might've arranged for her internment? Of course they would want to get rid of her, with her exhibitionistic unhappiness, her vocal disgust for the family whose wealth, whose sense of disproportionate *noblesse oblige* she viewed as one kind of illness crippling the country she had grown to hate—in which she would now be imprisoned forever. The other illness was Catholicism.

He'd grown to believe the very same things, distancing himself over the years from both.

Why hadn't they told him about Teresa's condition? Surely this was important enough to breach his estrangement for? He was her child, even if he himself didn't think of it that way. In him, her anger and disgust seeped into the next generation. They'd known that he would've fought their decision.

But would he have? Wasn't Teresa part of the past he had chosen to avert his gaze from? And wasn't he, Roger Caracera—with his spoiled behavior, his laziness, his drinking, his promiscuity—the very spitting image of his father, a man she had happily cut out of her life with her coldness, her ceremonious disregard?

The mother in a mental institution. The father hooked up to tubes two rooms down. The son, an outcast, returning to perform a final rite. He thought of himself in the third person, with a detachment exactly like narrating his story to himself. By this remove, he hoped to effect the proper combination of graduation and reduction that would deliver him from the trap of emotion. Mother. Father. Son. The classic elements were in place, though the son was no woolly-haired errant schoolboy but a tired forty-four-year-old with his instincts for apology decimated, with no desire to be, or gift for being, forgiven. Still, the story was comforting. Yes. A comfort, sharp points converging toward a resolution. Not sad at all.

CHAPTER 4

HE MAN, surprising his children, had made a stipulation for his will to be read in the old Caracera home in Manila, which was still standing and which a husband-and-wife team from the province of Samar—in Caracera's memory stick figures, who must certainly be all bones by now—had been taking care of for the last thirty-odd years.

This made compulsory the return of all three Caracera children, who, uprooted in adolescence and dissuaded from ever returning, never thought the day would come. The man's diatribes against the Philippines had been dictates against the children's mother, everyone had understood. And as they forgot about their mother, they also cast aside the Philippines. The man knew this and had intended to make up for the success of his campaign with the edict that all three children return to Manila, where he would be buried, or forfeit monies and assets coming to them.

For years he had vacillated between being buried in Manila, his boyhood playground, and Madrid, his playboyground, and finally San Francisco, where his playing, courtesy of a wild junior whose mimicry of the father was indistinguishable from mockery, had decisively ground to a halt. It was here that, confronting the heartbreak of this child, he had finally become a father. In later years, it seemed more and more likely that he would go with San Francisco, a place that, having chosen it himself, he had been forced to defend with a passion which was a reverse image of his hatred of the children's mother.

Shockingly late in life, regret for uprooting his children, for his injunctions against their return, had come upon him. It had been a secret he'd kept well, expressed only to the lawyer who had faxed the children upon news of the man's demise. This lawyer, named Miguel Santos, would be awaiting them at the Caracera house, which was, as he was writing, being prepared for their return. In his note he'd said that separating the children from the "place of their origin"—he had decided to skip over the word "homeland"—had been considered by their father his greatest failure as a parent. Jesus Caracera could see, in the offhand choices, in certain off-guard moments in the lives of the successful children, Socorro and Roberto, a kind of listlessness, an airy unfixedness which must certainly have at its root their very sudden dislocation. As for the last child, Roger, there was no doubt that his rebellion owed to a personality wrested in midformation. From the grave, Jesus Caracera would make sure to fulfill the didactic directives of fatherhood which he had left untouched while alive. The children were to be encouraged to turn the occasion of their father's death and burial into an opportunity for "self-reflection" and "reconnection."

Caracera wasn't sure which was the greater tragedy. Socorro's ceaseless sobbing and her refusal to allow the corpse to be dragged out of her home; Roberto's paralysis, surrendering all decisions to the lawyer, Miguel Santos, and, closer at hand, to the surprisingly assured younger brother—these were votes for the overwhelming tragedy of the death of a flawed and belatedly cherished man.

However, for Caracera, the usurping tragedy was the man's late-in-life sunniness. How could this sour citizen for whom alcohol had been like water believe the fates of his children to be anything less than settled, and settled by him, his long, patient tutorial, aided by generous dollops of corporal punishment? How could a three-week stay in a place like the Philippines, the renowned Third World, for crying out loud, which, even before their father's regime of drunken, curse-flecked homilies and teachings they hadn't felt any strong attachment to, how could a return, now, at this point in time, with their lives more than half lived, reverse that? Death was a great joker and this was merely one of its attempts at comedy. Caracera had the cumbersome sobriety to recognize this even amid a flurry of distraction in Socorro's household. Doctors and all the necessary people involved with death had come and gone, leaving in their wake a quiet like a magnification of their father's absenteeism during their childhood. Except this time that calm would remain undisturbed for a long time to come. There would be no more abashed hellos on the doorstep ending a capricious disappearance, no more attempts at seducing the children with gifts brought back from an undisclosed land, no more fanciful tales of adventures undertaken for the benefit of the children which he couldn't go into and which they would only be able to understand when they were much older anyway. In short, no more of the noisy cooing lies they had once been such gullible sponges for and which, in their adulthoods, they had used as a foundation for their dealings with the world: always suspicious, ever on the lookout in the next person's eyes, the curl of the lips, for an attempt to single them out as marks. In Caracera's case, this had helped lay the groundwork for his subsequent disavowal of his faith, in whose Father he had come to see an echo of the one who doled out punishments and enticements in random sequence which he now understood to be drink-begotten but which, while he was under the man's spell, had simply been part of the going definition of a law: primal and without reason. Like religion—like grammar, as an English teacher at St. Jude Catholic School, where he went from five to seventeen, used to say—his father's rule was "just something you have to accept." He had awoken to his father's and then his father's faith's duplicities and then began to steel himself by making of the space between his body and the world a barrier that he was determined nothing—but sex, for a time—would breach.

Faxes and phone calls arrived from all over the world, as well as cards and flowers, turning battlefieldlike Socorro's living and dining rooms, where they were all heaped haphazardly on tables and chairs while from above the chandeliers looked on like crystallized explosions of artillery fire, incongruously celebratory and optimistic.

They came from far-flung Caraceras and friends of the Caraceras, all of whom were not-so-secretly longing for the occasion of a funeral to make public their obsequiousness even now, after the family name had acquired a cobwebby aura of lightless relevance, of having once been at the center of things. Their name was, as it were, running on the gas fumes of past conquests. That it was still running at all was a bewildering phenomenon that even the sight of Socorro's house, and of Roberto's lordly house too, where Caracera had eventually gone to pay his respects to the wife and his nephew and niece, had not seemed adequate proof of. The niece and nephew had been trotted out and dressed like china figurines but which constriction did not appear to be unnatural to them, and he had seen his appearance on the scene as of an audience member before whom a contest between Roberto and Socorro was being elaborately played out—a competition as to who was the richer, the more successful, the more typically Caraceran. Perhaps Socorro had sent her children away because they weren't at an age compliant enough to be Mommy's shiny, quiet props as Roberto's children had been for him.

Even as various tubes were being disconnected from the dead man, the bedsheet pulled over his head, the metal guardrails at the sides of the bed taken down, a rosary removed from his clutch—a ritual nobody but Caracera would authorize because everyone was afraid of its meaning—he had been thinking many ungenerous thoughts about Roberto, Socorro, thoughts that had to do with their oneupmanship even in grief. Also, ungenerous thoughts about the dead man. Wasn't it just perfect that a man who had lived his life with such remorselessness now clutched the rosary as if he deserved its powers of sanction, its life-giving guarantee? Mostly Caracera was filled with ungenerous thoughts about himself, unmoved when the proper behavior ought to be a tearful, public remonstrance against God for foreshortening the time in which he could make up for his years of absence by an energetic vengeance of filial piety. He was still his old self and would not be swept underneath a tide of emotion. He was emptied of all feeling but a bone-deep exhaustion. He would prolong it by postponing sleep and immersing himself instead in the post-death activities (festivities, he tagged them, as the floral tributes piling up around Socorro's house began to acquire a rotten sugary scent that became, as the days advanced, the complement of Jesus Caracera's banishment from this life). By prolonging this exhaustion he hoped to make it something like a

new skin, something which, being part of himself, he could not remember a time when it had not been there. Sleep needed to be de-
layed, and through its treacherous duration, every fiber of his body
needed to reroute the current away from his brain and heart, potential
repositories for haunting by a dead father, and toward the muscles, the
eyes, bones, hands, legs, feet—things made dead by the effort required
to keep up with the embalmer, the family lawyer, the travel agencies,
and the stationers (from whom three hundred standard cards reading in
gold ink were ordered).

> We, Roberto, Socorro and Roger, the
> grieving children of our beloved,
> recently deceased father
> JESUS CARACERA
> thank you for thinking of us in this
> our time of need

Was it only a few days ago that he had, having seen the dying man
for the first time in years and having further not hesitated a second to
take the open palm directed at him, moving at once to the dying man's
side, been crying openly, unashamedly, almost, he would even have to
say, operatically? Had that been a performance then? No. He'd been
crying without self-consciousness as only an animal, recognizing in
another animal's clear physical suffering a kinesthetic corollary, can.
He'd wanted, more than anything, for the man's pain to be put to an
end. No matter that it had struck Caracera that the man was finally
being let in on a portion of the torture he himself had inflicted on others; on them, the children, bent to the specifications of his iron-fisted
will, cowardly, indolent, cursed with perpetual unsureness; on their
mother, whom he had ceased to love after she had exhibited an inde-
pendence of mind unsuitably masculine to him; on various employees
of the Caracera concern whom he'd delighted in humbling, hectoring
over, harassing, hugging but in a way that suggested the handling of
owned goods, so that the children came to regard themselves lucky in
comparison.

Caracera'd cried, wishing all the time for death to arrive, to release
the man from the wrinkled envelope of his kingship. To stop him from

dribbling out, along with the saliva running down both sides of the mouth which Socorro had kept tamping down with a handkerchief until the man, convinced that he was being suffocated, had shouted for her to stop, his murmurs and ululations of what sounded like regret. These were complemented by a doglike keening that he would stretch the last word of a sentence into, as well as the slow batting of the eyelids as if they were typewriter keys intent on the spelling out of an important message.

Miraculously, twenty minutes into Caracera's first interview in nearly two dozen years with the man he had tried all his adult life to run away from, the man expired, his head dropping to one side, where the curtained windows were and away from where his children were standing.

And Caracera realized—even without Roberto having to say "See? He was waiting for you before he would go"—that he, Roger Caracera, was really nobody less than the Angel of Death.

CHAPTER 5

T HEY'D BEEN IN THE SKY for six hours now. Each passing o'clock was one more number shifted into the plus column of his sacrificial log. The lights were dimmed in the
cabin, just so many necessary points to be able to guide you to the
bathroom, and a few bright stars showing where readers of books or
peerers into laptops sat.

He couldn't sleep. Relief would not come. Not until they—his father and he—had landed at Aquino International. Until he made sure
that the body had not been violated. Even the slightest bump might
disarrange the corpse's sealed mouth into a frown or a gasp waiting
to communicate to relatives what the man thought of Caracera's
guardianship—yet one more failure to add to lore; but this time incur-
ring not the usual absentminded disbelief or chuckling tolerance but,
more properly, rage at the elder siblings: what were Roberto and Socorro thinking, entrusting the care of their father's body, this most serious of tasks, to someone they knew to be reprobate and unrepentant?
Didn't they know that people never changed? Or couldn't they see
that Roger Caracera had already surpassed that point in life when
transformation was still possible? Then, of course, they would go into

that most assured of screeds: living in America being one long process of corruption, and now here as proof they had the withered, vestigial limbs of the remaining highest branches of the Caracera family tree— the three children of Jesus Caracera. His marital wranglings and the economic sacrifice of his decision to immigrate had come to naught.

Not that Caracera considered it his duty to defend his American-ness. Certainly he felt no sense of being beholden to anything.

HARVEY KEITEL WAS on the very flight they were on, himself en route to the Philippines.

He was about to shoot a movie financed by Twentieth Century Fox called *Fiesta of the Damned*, based on the very successful book of the same name which recounted the final events leading up to the rescue of Americans and Filipinos who, having survived the Death March to Bataan, had been interned by the Japanese in POW camps. His costars, variously on their way or awaiting Mr. Keitel's appearance in Manila, were John Travolta, Robert de Niro, Samuel L. Jackson, James Caan and Bert Convy. This was the fifth production in as many months to be shot in the Philippines, the others also based on bestselling accounts and regurgitating, as *Fiesta of the Damned* hoped to, one more episode of World War Two by which could be memorialized a peak period of American manhood, filled with decisive action unencumbered by fem-inine ambiguity.

Direction would be courtesy of a twenty-three-year-old kid genius best known as an acolyte, and archival overseer of the films, of the late Stanley Kubrick and who, until *Fiesta of the Damned*, had largely been known as a semantics-besotted film theorist published in the pages of *Sight and Sound* and *Cahiers du Cinema*. He was also a quarter Filipino and had cast the aging Filipino superstar Nora Aunor and the new-comer matinee idol Arsenio "Paduy" Macapagal in sizable supporting roles in the interests of flushing the Philippines out of the narrative and historical background into, well, if not exactly the foreground, then the *"ummm, sea level and not sunken like buried treasure."* Miss Aunor and Mr. Macapagal would be playing a mother and son caught in the maws of the Japanese-American conflict, the former an unwilling whore to the Japs and the latter a messenger between the insurgent anti-Jap native forces and the American army who, through the course of the story, is caught and forces his beloved mother to trade her freedom for his life. Until they are rescued near the end by men led by Harvey Keitel playing General Douglas MacArthur.

Any of the information not available through the gossip that passed down to him from first class and which was further augmented by the friendly stewardesses could be found in the in-flight magazine in an article bearing the title: "Philippines: Hot Hot Hot!" Besides its comprehensive coverage of the recent popularity of the Philippines as a Hollywood outpost, this article was pocked again and again by the mystery-giving phrase "jungles of the Philippines." Repeatedly, even when he was forced by a sudden seething that was a compound of bitter humor and voluptuous horror to read no further and only skim the article, the phrase kept snagging his eyes. Its reference point, the center from which it radiated, turned out to be the rerelease in the upcoming year of the "cinematic masterpiece" *Apocalypse Now*, this time with half an hour of extra footage and newly retitled *Apocalypse Now Redux*.

The film had been shot "in the jungles of the Philippines." During production there had been "delays exacerbated by storms in the jungles of the Philippines." Martin Sheen, one of the principals, suffered a "heart attack in the middle of the jungles." Budget overruns costing "enough to transform the jungles into whole cities." Cast and crew "stranded in the jungles of the Philippines." "Beautiful and treacherous Philippine jungles." Marlon Brando finding "a counterpart to his beloved Polynesia in the jungles of the Philippines." "Napalm dropped on the jungles of the Philippines." "Conradian habitats of the provinces of the Philippines": reading which, he imagined whole acreages of trees like an endless expanse of paper towels having to sop up a steady stream from the cut veins of American guilt. Had he seen the movie?

Yes. He remembered now. He'd been on coke and speed at the time. And the movie had kept fucking with his high. His drug-induced phantasmagoria, initially placid, had gotten weirder and weirder. At its most unbearable it had produced an identity panic: who was he? was he the white American shooting the gooks in the boat or was he the gooks? He'd gone having heard it was a great movie to trip on, much like *2001: A Space Odyssey* and that Disney movie with Mickey Mouse as Merlin the Magician had been for previous generations. And instead he'd been rewarded with the debut of the gremlin that had, from that moment on, taken up residence directly over his lungs, sitting on his chest with the sole intention of crushing the breath out of him. He'd laughed at it for failing to do its job until realizing, years later when it still remained there above each exhalation, that it was a patient creature and would be willing to wait however long it took for its mission to be fulfilled.

He wished that he'd been clean then so that he could've retained any images of the "jungles of the Philippines," and thus be better prepared for the nebulous zone to which he was headed, a place that was to him at best an accidental filigree on the surface of the earth. He knew, of course, that Manila, where he would be spending his days, was far from a jungle, but had no memory from which to draw even the most inconclusive picture and, what was worse, was certain that he would, after having been spoiled by San Francisco and New York, succumb to using the same imagery that he had regarded with such suspicion in "Philippines: Hot Hot Hot!" He was sure, knowing well his lack of fortitude, that he would, made aghast by the place, turn into the newest shiny exemplar off the assembly line of the Ugly American.

Looking up from the magazine, he saw the man seated next to him flashing a smile. It turned out that he was among the crew headed for the *Fiesta of the Damned* set in Manila. They shook hands and Caracera managed to finagle an invitation to the shooting.

A MAN SPOKE to a young girl in tones of boasting. He was on his way to an island off the Sulu Sea to collect a treasure recently recovered from the waters nearby. It was a gold kris—a ceremonial Moro sword with twin serrated edges and whose handle was mother-of-pearl encrusted with precious stones; it had been among the treasures plundered by the Japanese during the Second World War and which had sunk on ships en route to the Emperor.

A stewardess was speaking to the companion of a Swiss man asleep in a window seat and over whom the companion had placed a self-brought wool blanket. By the solicitous way the stewardess was referring to the sleeping man, Caracera got an idea that the man might be ill, and sure enough, he heard the companion talk of the Philippines as being among the most psychically active places on earth and of its population as having the highest concentration of people with psychic powers, such as ESP and, more pertinent to the discussion at hand, faith healing. First, said the companion, they would spend a few days in Manila, finalizing contacts and arrangements, before they traveled to Banaue, where a faith healer would preside over the sleeping man's ravaged body. And then, if even that didn't work, said the companion, who gave off a humorous sense of recognizing that because they were desperate they ought to be prepared for anything, they would return to Manila to St. Jude Church—the patron saint of lost causes—where they would sponsor a mass in the dying man's name. And if that didn't work, they would fly to Lourdes, France, to bathe in the miraculous spring waters. Of course, added the companion, she hoped the saints would overlook the fact that they weren't really Catholic and didn't believe in the Pope. Or, for that matter, in Jesus Christ. Again she shrugged, as if to say that if it finally came down to that . . .

Two old women were speaking to each other in a language he knew to be Tagalog but which, save for a few stray bits and pieces that didn't seem to connect at all, he was unable to understand. By the tone of their voices he supposed they were reminiscing about lives in the Philippines that would shortly be resumed.

His father too would be going home.

In his sister's San Francisco home, in the shadowed smallness of that room, with the curtained windows that seemed to him like a last attempt to delay judgment, he'd felt, just as he was sure his father had, hidden from the world. He'd felt free. To cry, making a fool of himself. All the time he'd been squeezing the dying man's hand. Again and again, like trying to pass his own blood into the man's body. Through osmosis or will or hope, through a compound of all three, raise the man's level of life to a few more days, weeks, months. At the same time he'd been hoping that the man's suffering would soon come to an end. While Socorro, standing on the other side, had been narrating a happy story of Caracera's progress for Jesus Caracera's benefit.

Roger's teaching at Columbia, she'd said.

I'm teaching at Columbia, he'd repeated to Jesus Caracera. On the man's face following the news Caracera thought he could discern a struggling comprehension, a numinous feeling trying but unable to focus itself into relief.

He's teaching writing, she'd said.

I teach writing, he'd followed again.

Isn't that great? she'd asked the father.

The father had nodded, had seemed to nod.

I have many students, he'd continued, through tears. I teach Tuesday, Wednesday and Thursday. I've been teaching since 1995. For five years. And some of my students have gone on to publish stories in— well, you wouldn't recognize the magazines and journals—

Socorro had encouraged him to name them nonetheless.

Well, let's see— Squeeze of the palm. Ummm. Squeeze of the palm. *The New Yorker*—

The New Yorker, that's great, that's a famous magazine, cooed Socorro. She had been holding on to the father's other hand and at the same time trying to fan out on his forehead phantom hairs of his lost youth.

—*Harper's*—

That's another famous magazine.

—*Paris Review*—

See that? she'd asked the man. Roger's done good. He's helping people.

Socorro had been smiling at him the whole time. Perhaps she'd known that he was lying but had chosen instead to focus on the comfort he was providing, like a blessed source of light in the cavelike room.

He'd continued. The names had gotten more obscure so that Socorro had been made to give up her role as echo.

His tears had continued throughout his cataloguing. And then it had been the man's turn.

His animal sounds, pitiful and which failed to communicate anything but the cumulative weariness of waiting for death. Ooo-ooo's and ahhh-ahhh's, drunken monkey sounds. Die now please, Caracera had kept thinking all throughout, never letting go of the man's hand.

Socorro had kept nodding, repeating over and over, Of course. But Caracera knew that even she could not have understood what the man was trying to impart.

Jesus Caracera had been crying, and so they'd assumed that he shared in the entire room's desire to foreclose on his death with, if not exactly happy, then peaceful, resolved, calm, grown-up signatures. But for all they knew, his tears could've been tears of impotent rage. Of wanting, but not having the facility, to indict Caracera for his crimes, to foretell what awaited the younger man on his own deathbed.

At the time the man was dying, they had been slow to realize just what was going on. And even after they had, their panic, though mounting and peppered with convincing exhalations, even from the atheist younger brother, of the name of God, had felt only obligatory, part of the fulfillment to the last of a filial duty. They had known that he was going to die very soon, and he had died. They'd known there was no bringing him back. Neither he nor they really wanted him to come back. Except perhaps Socorro—for whom the demonstration of proper grief, which included the very vocal exhortation for the body's resuscitation, was more important than the practical consideration that the man's pain would inevitably be lengthened should this occur.

At the time it happened, death had seemed to him unfathomably stupid. One last burp, one last inchoate grunt, one last saliva drip—and that was your final moment. Your whole life of struggling—and then no more struggle. No meaning deeper than physics—body in motion will inevitably turn into body at rest. Similar laws as those governing objects. You were therefore no better than an object. Did he really need one more proof of the enduring futility of life?

Most of the passengers got off in Tokyo. Alongside the few who remained, including himself and his father (which he triple-checked with the Narita personnel), and, he guessed but did not see, Mr. Keitel, were newly added sightseers, white and Asian, but no blacks; a raft of Japanese schoolchildren accompanied by two elderly teachers, a man to oversee the boys and for the girls a spinster straight out of Barbara Pym, with her sweater and pleated skirt, hair pulled tight into a severe bun, eyeglasses, and caressing her thin lips, a constant hint that she was suppressing naughty, ungenerous comments about what she saw

around her; and a bevy of Fat-Assed Fucks. All men, all white, all giant. They were all, to judge by their accents, Australian, scattered
throughout the cabin, a few clumped in dozens, others duoed and tri-
oed, clearly united by a singular purpose which, seeing the stewardesses look on with dismay and lip-bitten disapproval, he thought he
understood but did not want to put into so many words. His father's
coffin was only four—and counting—hours away from the hands, the
festive grief of the Caracera clan and outlying branches. He would be
the deliverer to this group of the excuse for their gathering. He would
be the Prodigal Son made good. He would, like Harvey Keitel in a
penultimate scene in *Fiesta of the Damned*, tell them: *I have returned.*

He marveled at the sudden significance in his life—and in the lives
of countless others, all of them suspended in the anxiety of getting
there—of this strange, passed-over name: the Philippines. Now it was
at the center of his sights. The dot at the center of the map of the
world, into which his father would go, swallowed forever. He kept picturing it seen from above. God's-eye view. As if he were a bird unsure
of alighting. Forced himself to see it, burning and burning, a bright
cone of roiling activity, as at the tip of a volcano. All of this was in direct avoidance of the hullabaloo being raised by the Fat-Assed, Fat-
Bellied Fucks who, all around him, were visibly fingering and passing
around, accompanied by guffaws of comradeship, pictures of Filipino
women, some of them barely women, in fact, girls, thin as sticks and
flat as boards, and also passing around lists and guidebooks filled with
the names of their contacts, of bars and nightclubs and "hotels," some
of which were highlighted by red stars placed alongside the margins,
whose clear significance he tried to eradicate from his mind by thinking of his name, Roger Caracera; his function, as proxy of the missing
Roberto and Socorro, as conveyor of the coffin that sat below (or
above? or to the side of?) them; and his significance beyond being an
attendee at a funeral, which, reaching him from across the seemingly
vast distance of the cabin's din that the stewardesses tried unsuccess-
fully to shush, came across as: nothing nothing nothing. But which
frequency, cut into by the men's drunken celebration, came through as:
nothing disgusting nothing nothing disgusting nothing disgusting disgusting disgusting . . . This disgust for the beery Australians and what
he knew to be their mental pictures of the Philippines as one big

whorehouse—a place, he hastened to remind himself, he had no right to feel protective about—was so consuming that he was surprised to hear a message from the cockpit saying that their trip had been expedited by a little over half an hour and that they would soon be arriving in Manila and would they please put on their seat belts and turn off all electronic equipment in preparation for landing.

CHAPTER 6

THE PASAY OFFICE of the lawyers Miguel Santos and Miguel Santos, Jr., who were the executors of the last will and testament of the late Jesus Caracera, occupied half the second floor of the private residence of the elder Santos. It was a large, shady room, with windows on three sides out of which could be seen a profusion of green, swaying in the wind. The main desk was parallel to the south window, where the elder Santos sat with his back to it.

All the windows had metal guards on the outside, and the windowpanes, which were the kind that slid open and shut, were made of capiz shells filling in wood latticework.

The coffee tables on which the various family members had rested their cups of coffee and saucers had capiz-shell tops protected by sheets of glass. Between the capiz and the glass were imprisoned a smattering of photographs showing the Santoses with various personages and celebrities—some even recognizable to the American children, for example, the movie actor George Hamilton. He was photographed at one of Imelda's various parties thrown on the occasion of the first Manila International Film Festival in 1981. He was posing gamely, if stiffly, with the elder Santos in front of a cheap-looking white lattice bedecked with what looked like plastic leaves and blossoms. Santos, on the other hand, who was only shoulder-high to Hamilton, had one arm around Hamilton's waist and was clutching in the manner of someone making away with a precious souvenir. The smile splitting open the lawyer's face and the crinkled slits of both eyes, in each of which the flash had deposited a tiny star, were signs of a bright future anticipated. George Hamilton, Imelda: it was almost certain that Santos would see his stock rise soon after, his fledgling business putting down roots in the fertile soil of such rarefied company.

The building was erected in the time of the Spaniards. Red tiles sloped in a gentle decline on the roof and, though blanched by centuries of baking sun, still provided a distinct contrast to the encircling treetops. Vertical beams were put up a dozen years ago on the south side to help shore up the wood-paneled walls.

The floors on the first story were mahogany, dark and shiny. However, the stairs leading from the ground floor to the second were of a lighter-shaded wood, replacements put in when one of the original steps had given out, causing the elder Santos to be hospitalized for a week for a broken ankle.

The whole house squeaked with each footstep, tiny mice sounds that thrilled Caracera, except for the new steps, which did not give under their treads. Ascending the stairs, it had occurred to Caracera that they were leaving behind the falsely rustic facade and entering into the true, beating, modern heart of the house, and that the enterprise they were about to undertake would soon expose the steel in Santos & Santos (revealing why his father had chosen them).

But when he'd stepped onto the second-floor landing, again the floorboards had creaked, again the decor was in keeping with the rest of the house, and he'd felt as if a guided tour of a colonial-style dwelling would segue painlessly and smoothly into the Old World ritual of the will-reading, which would be, after all, courtly and free of intrigue.

Two potted dwarf palms flanked the window in front of which Mr. Santos sat.

His son stood to one side of him, also facing the family. His son's hands were behind his back. From the way he stood and from his silence, the son gave Caracera an idea that his function was largely symbolic, being one more bodyguard in this culture that required such signposts of economic ascendancy.

Caracera looked to Roberto, whose true face seemed to be behind a piece of opaque glass. There was no clearer sign of the burden imposed by the environment they had suddenly found themselves in than in Roberto and Socorro's being unable to marshal enough energy to go past the walls of their hotel on more than a few occasions. They seemed stayed by a hand that was more than just the censure of the relatives or the grief required by Jesus' death.

In this trip they had come upon a secondary occasion for mourning: they'd been in their twenties when their father had uprooted them, and so even more than Caracera had been made to contemplate the great what-might-have-been of lives in this country. Returning here, they had had to ask themselves if it was possible that they'd been hijacked from their true destinies.

Besides Socorro and Roberto, those gathered included, in order of the age of the men: Mr. and Mrs. Eulalio Caracera, Mr. and Mrs. Rodrigo Caracera, Mr. and Mrs. Casimiro Caracera and Mr. and Mrs. Amador Caracera. In all, thirteen people. Chairs had been gathered from the rest of the rooms to accommodate everyone and yet there was no mismatch. Fastidiousness was the strongest character trait evinced by the Santoses' arrangement.

If the furniture, the coffee they had made for their guests (specially imported from Brazil!), the handsomeness of both Santoses' attires— barong Tagalogs with fronts denuded of any embroidery, seeming to presage no complications about to follow—were to be believed, the Caraceras were in safe hands. Should there be anything unpleasant in the dead man's missive, the lawyers would be sure to glaze it over with a tranquilizing civility that was part of what they were being paid for.

A dog barked. For the first time Santos Jr. spoke. He said that there was a neighborhood stray on the loose and that it seemed to always dodge the animal control department and so the neighborhood, in an organized and easily unanimous effort, had put out some poison by the garbage bins where the creature was known to rummage. He revealed this with a smile on his face, oblivious to the possibility that an urchin could chance upon it.

Caracera tried to put out the thought of one of the beggar children lying dead on the street, his mouth a whirlpool of foam and spit.

Suddenly Eulalio Caracera, the eldest of the remaining Caraceras, coughed. He had recently had surgery on his lungs to harvest polyps cultivated from a lifetime of smoking. His wife patted him on the back, easing phlegm.

The cough was taken by Santos Jr. to have the power of a starting gun. Does anyone need anything before we begin? he asked, looking around.

No one stirred.

Thank you very much for coming today, Santos Sr. began, taking in the assembled.

He looked down at the sheaf of papers between his hands and slowly began to read.

I, the undersigned, Jesus Consuelo Rodriguez Caracera, hereby assign the firm of Santos & Santos of Pasay City, Manila, on this day, July 17, 1997, as the executor of my last will and testament.

The brothers looked variously at the ceiling or above each other's heads, as if to get the best possible reception for the dead man's voice. None of them were as handsome or as successful as the deceased had been, and the black shirts, pants and shoes hanging on their withered frames only added to their subordinate status. The wives were fanning themselves. Predicted rains had yet to fall but in the meantime the moisture saturating the atmosphere caused them to break out in tacky sweat. Thank God for the disguise of their black dresses, which were less severe versions of what they had on on the day of the funeral.

I certify that I am of sound mind and judgment and that the terms of my will are final. They are as follows—

Santos Sr. looked up, enough to take in that the dead man's three children were all looking away from him: the girl to her left, as if at an invisible bird which had alighted on her shoulder; the older boy over Santos Sr.'s head and out the window; the younger boy, who'd disrespectfully kept his sunglasses on, down at his feet. He resumed reading:

Number one. The disbursement of the total monetary value of my estate which amounts to 2.5 million U.S. dollars—Santos didn't look up but could hear a turn in the air, as if somebody had speeded up their inhalations.

The amount had been a disappointment to the dead man, and now to his family.

100,000 dollars each to my brothers Eulalio, Rodrigo, Casimiro, Amador, to spend or invest or disburse in any way they see fit; the money going to their wives or their children or to a charity of their choosing in the event of their deaths. Or in the event of the deaths of the natural heirs and in the further event that no charity had been chosen by these heirs, the money is to go to one of the organizations listed under separate cover, the endowment to be named for the deceased brother.

Santos Sr. paused, using the excuse of having to adjust his glasses to steal a look at the dead man's brothers and their wives. Having had ample experience, he could distinguish between authentic calmness and uneasy stoicism, and he believed it a symptom of how trusted and beloved (and feared?) Jesus Caracera had been in life (and continued to be) that nobody was now evincing anything but the most respectful of silences. Ready to move on, he was stopped at the last minute by Mrs. Eulalio Caracera, whose husband had initiated the proceedings with his impatient cough. Mrs. Eulalio Caracera had an arm raised and everyone, except for Roger Caracera, had turned to look.

Yes, Celeste? Santos Sr. asked.

What are these organizations that are mentioned in the will? she asked, at the same time fingering a small gold crucifix that hung on a chain around her neck.

The ones under separate cover?

Yes. She nodded.

You will all be provided copies of those before leaving today, Jr. replied. They're simply suggestions should, as the will states, something happen and the money hasn't been given away.

Celeste Caracera didn't seem satisfied with the answer but was not about to say anything else.

Jr. canvassed the room. Saw no further questions. Nodded to his father.

250,000 dollars each to my two oldest children, Roberto and Socorro— Did Santos Sr. hear an involuntary groan from the youngest, knowing himself to be shut out of the will? Or was it from one of the other two, in commiseration with their disinherited brother? He went on: *—again* *to spend or invest or distribute in whichever way they see fit, without any encumbrances; however, the undersigned would like to state his desire for some part of this money to be put to use for traveling between the primary residence of aforementioned children in the United States and—it is hoped—their second home, the Caracera residence in Makati, Metro Manila.* Santos Sr. looked up to say: More about the residence in Makati in a minute.

The relatives gathered were all trying not to look at the youngest son of the dead man, whose head remained bowed, his feet newly crossed one over the other.

To my youngest son, Santos Sr. read, with the expert prolonging of the performer he became in such situations, and he could hear a rustle of evident surprise, or perhaps preparatory primness in the event that what was coming was an admonishment from the grave, a slap the dead man had been unable to administer in life. Santos Sr. felt he had to start over. *To my youngest son,* he repeated, *Roger Caracera, who, it must be admitted, has shown little proof of deserving my love, and even less proof of being equipped to deal with the business of life, and it should be understood that the following bequest is being given in the spirit of wanting to help him repair this fundamental inadequacy and not, as my two older children might be misled to believe, favoritism: to Roger Caracera, I, the undersigned, being of sound mind and judgment, leave 500,000 dollars, again to spend or invest or distribute in any way he may see fit—*

A loud groan filled the room. Santos Sr. looked up to see the man who'd inherited half a million dollars appearing as if he'd been stabbed, his body pushed back.

Roger? Socorro asked, not so frightened that she didn't register the embarrassment her brother was causing her in front of the family yet again.

Another animal sound escaped from the man's mouth. And he bowed his head like he was going to vomit.

Mrs. Amador Caracera stood up. To her credit, she was neither nonplussed, as were the other wives, nor irritated, as were Roger's uncles: who could've believed that the overwhelming sensation they would be made to feel for someone who'd just come into five hundred grand was—disgust?

Sit back, Mrs. Amador Caracera ordered her nephew-in-law, at the same time positioning his head on the seat so that he was looking at the ceiling. Then she gave the okay to Santos Jr. to fetch a glass of water.

The aunts looked at the lawyer in commiseration, having to forbear this unnecessarily maudlin performance. From day one of Roger's return, they'd been struggling to overcome their prejudicial, un-Christian view of him as a stranger: unknown, unknowable and perhaps not worth the trouble to get to know. They had been placed in the perverse position of elders having to pay courtesy to a junior whose bereavement demanded respect (although there had been no evidence of such bereavement until today) and whose first appearance among the children of the dead man had conferred upon him the immediate status of someone representative, a second Jesus Caracera, as it were.

Again Eulalio coughed.

Celeste looked to the lawyer, beseeching him to disregard the theatrics and proceed. Can't you see my husband hasn't much longer to live? said her expression.

Everything about her, thought the lawyer, spoke of the impacted rage of being married to a powerless brother, more to be pitied than feared. And even after the banishment of Jesus Caracera's wife to an insane asylum, when the mantle of female authority ought to have descended on her, the clan's senior wife, her position had been usurped by the more beautiful and more astute youngest sister-in-law, Mrs. Amador Caracera.

He was thankful for the reappearance of his son, who rushed to Caracera with a glass of water. Here drink this, Jr. said.

Caracera drank because everyone was looking to him to reassure them.

Only after Mrs. Amador Caracera returned to her seat did Santos Sr. take up where he left off: —to spend or invest or distribute in any way he may see fit, again without any encumbrances, and again, with the hopes, as with his older siblings, that a portion of the money may be put to use for traveling between the United States and Manila, to the Caracera residence in Makati.

With great difficulty, Caracera tried to look at the lawyer as he read. Though no one was staring at him outright, except for the junior Santos, who shot him intermittent looks not unclouded by contempt, he knew that he was the room's sun, its glaring center, about whose presence you were aware even without having to turn in its direction.

Number two. With regards to the residence in Makati, I, the undersigned, designate my three children, Roberto, Socorro and Roger Caracera as the rightful heirs of this property, which encompasses, aside from the main residence, the adjoining 6,000 square meters (1.5 acres), which cumulative value is estimated, on July 17, 1997, to be 45 million pesos. With the following prohibitions and encumbrances: 1. They are prohibited from selling the property. 2. They must, between the three of them, take charge of the upkeep of and improvements to the property—the cost not to come from their allotted bequests, but from estate monies specifically allocated for such purposes. (More about that in a minute.) *3. They may assign proxies of their choosing to take care of the property; the proxies to send a detailed annual report to the three of them, as well as to Santos & Santos, who will act as watchguards and scouts for the three owners. It is understood, however, that final authority on all matters regarding the property shall fall to the three co-owners. 3b. Should any disagreement arise between the three owners, Santos & Santos will act as the last resort before legal arbitration. 3c. Should repairs and lawsuits arise from the incompetence and negligence of the proxies for the management of the property, the cost of repairs and legal costs will automatically devolve to the three owners. 4. The children born and yet to be born of Roberto, Socorro and Roger must at least once in their lifetime return to the Philippines and spend no less than 30 days (in one visit or cumulatively through several visits) in the Makati residence. Should this last condition not be met during the lifetime of any of my three children, the property will automatically transfer to the heirs of my brothers, who will be charged with the upkeep of, and improvements to, the property, the cost to be borne by estate monies. 4b. Responsibilities for the property are to be shared equally by the inheriting parties. 4c. Santos & Santos will be the last resort in the event of disputes among said parties before legal arbitration.*

Number three. The remainder of the cash value of the estate, which amounts to 1.1 million U.S. dollars, to be held in an account to accrue interest. This sum and the subsequent interests are for the following: 1. As mentioned, specially allocated funds for the upkeep of and renovations to (if necessary) the Makati residence. 2. The care of Mrs. Teresa Caracera at St. Mary the Immaculate Hospital in Mandaluyong, Metro Manila; and all doctors' and nurses' fees that attend to such care; the duration to last the lifetime of Mrs. Teresa Caracera. 3. Provisions for the subsequent hospitalization of Mrs. Teresa Caracera, the location of which may or may not be St. Mary the Immaculate (to be decided by Santos & Santos, to whom I leave the details of her care); as well as provisions for her funeral and burial in a plot in Malate that is being held in reserve. 4. For one-fifth of the real estate taxes and one-fifth of the maintenance and personnel costs relating to the family estate in Negros (burdens shared by my brothers Eulalio, Rodrigo, Casimiro, Amador) until such time as the owner of the property (Eulalio) or his heirs choose to divest themselves of said property . . .

Caracera was prepared to sit where he was for hours, listening without understanding but giving to his expression the crystal alertness of someone newly elected to a position of leadership, if not in letter then at least in spirit. But before he knew it, the basso buzz from Santos Sr. faded and in its place, after a brief silence, came the multiple rustlings of his relatives getting up, heading to him but trying not to seem as if they were doing so.

He put on a weak smile. Socorro and Roberto stood behind him. The Santoses were moving to the group.

Caracera shook his uncles' hands. He was embraced by each of his aunts. Already the currying for favor had started. From the handshakes and hugs, he tried to determine who was the neediest. It turned out to be Celeste Caracera, who clung to him with a newfound familiarity. Too bad, thought Caracera, that, as in all things, she had been beaten to the punch by Mrs. Amador Caracera, who had helped him in regaining his composure earlier.

The lawyers milled around, talking to the uncles, to Roberto. Socorro stood silently and gave the impression of suffering those who spoke to her and specially those who touched her as they did so. She was ready to go, waiting for Roberto to tie things up.

Finally, the Santoses had their moment with Caracera. The elder Santos shook Caracera's hand, asking if he was all right. Caracera replied that he'd been shocked by his father's bequest. The elder Santos said that of course he shouldn't be shocked. Jesus Caracera loved his youngest son, about that Caracera now had incontrovertible proof. There was nothing more satisfying than a father's love, as he himself well knew, saying which he put an arm around his son and drew him near them.

The junior Santos asked Caracera for his bank account number.

Roberto and Socorro had already given theirs. Caracera, unthinking, gave the needed information.

Outside the Santos residence, the cars were waiting, six humming engines and six open doors lending to the courtyard and sidewalk an impression of something momentous transpiring, or perhaps, more accurately, an interlude between something momentous just concluded and something even more important following in its wake, the participants about to be whisked away to separate quarters where, once repaired, they would devise stratagems to right the balance in their favor. To some of the drivers who had been in the family employ for decades, it always seemed as if their employers were in perpetual states of grievance. So it seemed to be the case again when the men and women in black reappeared outside the lawyer's home, briefly milling about to exchange last pleasantries before stepping through the doors being held open for them.

It took a while but finally the courtyard and sidewalk were peaceful again. Santos Jr. wondered aloud whether the stray dog had finally bitten the dust. His father said that he hoped so. He couldn't stand another night of a yelping and baying that seemed unsettlingly sad— haunted, he would even say.

They began to discuss the afternoon's proceedings, which they concluded had been a success. In the middle of the elder Santos's wondering at the significance of Roger Caracera's behavior and his appearance, thunder sounded in the sky, causing both men to look up. The father remarked that perhaps Manila was finally no longer under its protective star, and that the predicted typhoons would soon alight. Then both men went inside.

CHAPTER 7

HREE KLIEG LIGHTS SHONE the diffuse light of an
overcast, rainy day with the help of paper filters—exactly the
kind of day outside the Manila Hotel.

At the center of the lit area was the door to a room and surrounding it a little patch of wall and corridor. But whatever scene was supposed to be enacted there had been temporarily postponed while
various technicians wearing the Hawaiian shirts and cargo shorts of a
perpetual lunch break/vacation futzed and fumbled with the various
metal boxes and wires and bulbs and hinged pieces of equipment that
were omnipresent and imposing, as at a scene of a scientific experiment, so that Caracera came to understand, implicitly, that the entire
moviemaking process was about the mastery of gadgetry and that art,
if it happened, would at best be on the sly. These men moved their
pieces of equipment noisily, in a way that made clear their control of
the set. Among them was the guy who'd invited Caracera to watch the
day's shooting, but who had not taken notice of his guest sitting in a
corner on a canvas chair with a backrest that read Craft Services.

Taking advantage of the break, the young director was busying
himself with the press. HBO had a camera crew waiting. So did PBS.

Meanwhile, Twentieth Century Fox had also sent their own camera team and they were now being treated to some serious disquisition by the young man who, to his credit, did not look overwhelmed. He answered questions with sweeping hand gestures like a majordomo indicating all that he sat on and smoothly controlled. It occurred to Caracera that the boy must know that the interview footage—along with the dailies—would be screened for his bosses and so had to act up to his role as, in effect, overseer of a budget in the tens of millions. Surely they were looking for some reason to fire him and he would not let them have the satisfaction? Surely his age and relative lack of experience had been a source of worry to them from the very beginning? Perhaps he'd gotten on the helm through the backing of one of the stars—who'd hoped that the young man's relationship with Kubrick would be roughly tantamount to the passing of the torch of genius to this generation; and who, furthermore, never having had the chance to work with the master, would get the chance now, at least by association?

Art was one thing, however; economics and accounting, another. The boy was trying to overcome the undeniable physical fact of his boyishness with a lowered voice and an assurance to his bosses that they were all on the same track and that the movie he would deliver would be one long action sequence; however, this message was couched in counterproductive vocabulary that would be sure to send the executives back on the lot after their eject buttons. The young man talked of things being "perspectival" and "unmediated by the tangle of cerebration and sophistry," and of the episode being depicted in the movie as an "opportunity for the reinstatement of a kind of headlong and heedless trajectory that had its apotheosis in the fifties, say, with the movies of men like Ford and Fuller."

Seated on both sides of Caracera were people with tape recorders and steno pads, awaiting their turn. In the meantime they were brushing up on questions they intended to ask and on background notes for the production, which they'd been provided by a female assistant. Caracera had one too. He'd been mistaken for one of them and had been handed a sheaf of these notes, which he now went over lazily.

He expected, for some reason, to find the phrase "jungles of the Philippines" in these notes and was surprised to be told instead of how the production had had to choose between Vietnam and the Philippines for its location. The Vietnamese, Caracera figured, were trying to return the favor for *Apocalypse Now*, in which the Philippines had been chosen to stand in for their country.

So the Vietnamese government had offered free accommodations and other incentives to woo the production. The burgeoning Vietnamese tourist trade desired the further boost of a Hollywood connection. But in the end, the Philippines had been where four of the last five Asian-themed U.S. movies were shot, and on the strength of that recommendation had won out.

This seemed the only thing of interest to be gleaned from the notes, which were otherwise filled with biographies of the personnel involved, a plot synopsis and a brief historical sketch of U.S. intervention in the Philippines—culminating in a jingoistic defense of American foreign policy, which seemed to Caracera more wishful and nostalgic than anything.

Suddenly the journalists who had been busy scribbling into their pads looked up.

Activity was again starting up. This was indicated by the sudden hush, as if a machine whose job it was to create an enveloping blanket of noise had broken down. It was the same kind of silence, awed and a little fearful, that ought to be followed by the entrance of a dignitary. Keitel, perhaps, or his cohorts. But the white actors dressed in military garb were not known to any of the people Caracera was grouped with. With them, walking several steps behind and apart, were Filipinos. Only after they too stepped into the hot ring of the lights, which were being turned up, was it understood that they were actors, needed for the resuming shot. Managing their movements was a Filipino AD wearing an overlarge T-shirt that read, MADONNA LIVE! ON HBO, above low-slung, wide-hemmed black jeans. He gave the impression of having not much to do and was making up for it as visibly as he could.

Names were called out. A bunch of phrases, including "Quiet on the set." Then came the young ringleader, conferring with his director of photography in a loud technicalese.

The actors were arranged by the AD to flank the doorway where the camera was pointed. Military men and some Filipino comrades, it looked like, waiting for the general to finish up with his Filipina beauty—who, if his history lessons sufficed, Caracera remembered to have been the gift from a grateful nation to the victorious liberator.

Not once did the director check up on his actors. Instead, his style was to have the AD yell "Action" for him, and then look not at the live scene but rather at its magnetized ghost in a monitor that flickered in front of where he sat and which was attached to the camera through a series of wires snaking on the floor.

Not once were the Filipino actors heard to utter anything until near the end, and only one of them actually opened his mouth: "Yes, boss."

The scene was ordered "Cut!" by the same assistant. Once more, the director and DP were seen to consult. Once more, "Action!"

Turning to the screen this second time, where the image literally flickered and pulsed, and the actors were rendered bluish, Caracera noticed an X mark at the very center and, to demarcate the edges of the film frame, a square drawn in a thin line that reminded Caracera of a spiderweb. Again and again, the scene was reenacted. Not once was the camera moved for another angle. What was so special about the scene—which involved the military men conferring with each other, waiting for the general to finish with his native paramour? Unable to wait any longer, they finally entrust the sentinel's duty to one of the three Filipino men, before leaving to attend to other matters. The curious sameness of scene after scene, during which breaks the director did not offer a single adjustment, owed to an obsessiveness Caracera found hard to account for. Perfectionism, to be traced back to the young director's apprenticeship with the notoriously exact Kubrick?

Two of the three Filipinos—the ones with no lines—were positioned to the rightmost side, so that their bodies jutted outside the excluding web.

"Yes, boss." Yet again. "Yes, boss."

Could this be what the overflow of pride in the Filipino press regarding a new, strengthened amity between this country and the U.S. was about—exemplified by this fifth in what was hoped would be an ongoing series of movies? "Yes, boss."

Yet again the scene was replayed. The white soldiers conferring, and while they did, the Filipinos—were they actually Allies? could they be hotel staff?—waited. Waited for the one line.

"Yes, boss."

It had only taken him a few short days to be reacquainted with the overwhelming humility of the countrymen around him. Had they no pride? They evinced a palpable quality of Catholic prostration that he had long since surpassed.

Around him the Filipino journalists, preparing questions for the director, gave no sign of understanding.

"Yes, boss." Jungles of the Philippines.

Nobody but he seemed to see beyond the words, through them.

Here he sat, back in the land of infinite shadow, the land of arrested development, back in childhood.

CHAPTER 8

TERESA CARACERA WAS a beautiful woman. Absolutely gorgeous. This was a fact everyone agreed on, even till the bitter end, when another consensus was reached: she was also very insane.

Her face had . . . rigor. The angled planes. The cheekbones sheared as if from a rock face, jutting gloriously. The nose, which specially in profile could be seen to tilt up—a feature her beauteous daughter Socorro and her youngest son, the problem boy Roger, had inherited; and which seemed, as it had their mother's, to mark their characters. The girl, from adolescence, turned her nose up at every suitor who dared cross the family threshold; and the boy, perhaps in a futile attempt to endear himself to Teresa, mimicked her tastes and opinions, which often ran in the direction of disappointment, of a high mind let down by petty concerns, mostly having to do with money.

Her beauty was specially surpassing when she was surrounded by her peers—those women who were the mothers of Roberto and Socorro and Roger's classmates, as well as the wives of the men with whom her husband did business. These men understood the value of a showpiece by their sides and had chosen their spouses wisely, picking from among the plentiful field of Filipina beauty queens and almost-beauty queens. At parties, Teresa Caracera, wearing no makeup except for a bright moist slash of lip balm, made a mockery of these beauties' considered presentations. There was something almost mannish in Teresa Caracera's appearance during these times, as if, by refusing to be enslaved by the hours-long preparations for winning the men's approbation, she had designated herself their equal. Really, her virtuousness seemed untoward and had a bedrock of disdain and self-satisfaction that her husband should try to curb or he would find himself cut out of many party invitations in the future.

When listening to these women at the parties, Teresa Caracera had an unmistakable look of superiority, forbearance, although not a word of criticism was heard from her during, or after, in front of her children. Nearly always, however, something negative would be said to them on a variety of other subjects by their mother; so often that they'd been forced to consider the possibility that they had been created for the sole purpose of providing an audience for her screeds, to keep her company during these convulsions when everyone else had been successfully driven away.

Besides lip balm, the one concession to femininity, to vanity of this famously unvain woman whose beauty seemed oddly heightened by abnegation and asceticism, was a dab of L'Air du Temps by Nina Ricci, one on each side of her neck, just below the ears. The first bottle she ever owned was a gift from a friend visiting from Europe. At that time, she was already a mother of two, and the present had perhaps been chosen with an eye toward lifting her out of some presumed midlife doldrums and recalling her to happier times. It was the same scent she used to swipe from her mother's bedroom vanity, slapping it on her elbows and at the back of her neck before going out on secret rendezvous with boys. Those had been reckless, carefree times and it was hoped that the perfume might work restorative, rejuvenating powers for the woman whose joy for life had been sapped by motherhood. That was what the friend had believed, although there could not have been two better-behaved children anywhere.

Roberto and Socorro, temperamentally alike, had emerged from the womb quiet and considerate, with the sophisticated ability to sense that they'd been born into a war zone, along with an adult sense of complicity. Without having to be told, their first instinct was to never ask questions, but rather suppress them, or allow them to be overtaken by consuming small talk. In this way they formed a family whose happiness, because always precarious, was a small miracle. L'Air du Temps, which their mother began to wear when Roberto was five and Socorro three, would forever call up, in each child's mind, the blessed interlude before the birth of their brother. That event would not only cause their paradise to be intruded upon but would finally break their mother's back. After Roger, she would never be quite the same. There was an appreciable increase in the theatricality and the authenticity of her bitterness after Roger. Not that she hadn't meant all the negative things she'd said before. But this time, there seemed in her sermons and her lengthy proclamations an attempt to extinguish in her audience the very life and vitality that had been extinguished in her. Her children would pay.

Specially when Teresa was in the front seat of the family Mercedes, next to the driver (she herself never drove), with the windows open and the wind streaming through, she could be counted upon to hold forth. The front passenger seat was her favorite podium. The windows of the car were often ordered rolled down to remove the barrier between the children and the "disappointment and penury of the Philippines." When it was the children's father driving, Teresa could be seen to slouch close to the window, hugging the door. When it was one of the family drivers, the view from the back showed the chasm between the two bodies much abbreviated.

The wind would make of Teresa Caracera's coral-teardrop earrings agitated insects, at the same time that it caused to be permeated all throughout the car the stunning scent of L'Air du Temps. What an anomalous combination: the perfume and the punditry. One meant to seduce, the other to repel.

Look, children, she would say, pointing out the window. Look at the poor boys and girls begging on the streets.

She would never refer to Socorro or Roberto or Roger by name during these times. Children, she would say, even if there was only one of them in the car with her, accompanying her to the family club or to have tea in one of the fancy hotel restaurants, where Teresa would go to check out the European visitors and scoff at their naïveté, their ignorance in choosing the Philippines as a vacation spot.

On the way there, she would point out the street urchins. Look children, the poor boys and girls. Look at their clothes. See how many holes there are? Some of them aren't even wearing shoes. Look! Don't turn your head away, Socorro!

Their mother's English was an instrument that seemed honed for this very purpose. A British accent overrode her native Spanish rhythms, courtesy of a private school education that provided exacting English tutors. The words came out of her mouth like spit bullets, blunt, punishing. The very same delivery that made her Tagalog stiff and awkward, liable to provoke laughter from the family maids and drivers, and from the Filipino mothers of the children's classmates.

Look, Socorro!

Why did it seem as if her mother picked on her all the time? The boys, at least, had extended moments of respite.

Look how little separates you from those children over there. They have to beg to make a living. Or steal. Or some of the girls have to—

Mama!

The whole world isn't just you and your precious schoolmates talking about your little crushes and what to wear and what lipstick to try and what diets to go on.

I know that.

Do you? Look!

What do you want me to do?

How fortunate you are, don't you know! What are you going to do with such fortune? Are you going to become just like your aunts—beauty, beauty, beauty? You'd think they only had one word in their vocabulary! No, two! Shopping! Disgusting!

I'm not like them! And, she would've liked to add, I'm not like you either. More and more, she was afraid of turning into her mother, in whose face could be seen what the young girl had to look forward to—the role of a natural aristocrat, to whom the tribute of ease and being taken care of was owed. By shirking such tribute—leaving the bosom of her wealthy Madrid family to come to the provinces of the Philippines to minister to the natives, eschewing dreaded bourgeois comfort for the bone-crunching hard work that was the realization of a blueprint of youthful idealism—Teresa Caracera had caused to be twisted the machinery of her fate, condemning her to an unhappiness of which she, in the end, was the sole architect. This was the main lesson Socorro learned from her mother: Do not become like that woman. What else, along with that beautiful face, might have been passed from mother to daughter? It was a fear that would guide Socorro all throughout her life, making her at once acquiescent when their father decided that they would leave the Philippines for San Francisco, to live in a house he had already bought and had had furnished. Roberto and Socorro would switch to colleges abroad and would have to start their lives over. Relief was the paramount feeling for her. The severing amounted to a quarantine. No longer close enough to be infected by their mother, she, Socorro, could be guaranteed a fate of her own. The face might be the same, but her life, her character would not be similarly distinguished, extinguished.

Bahala na: roughly translated, What will be will be. It was what their mother often said as she pointed to the unfortunate men and women and children that the family Mercedes passed by. (Did their mother always ask for the driver to skirt the periphery of the city slums for their benefit?) *Bahala na* was an enduring slogan of these beggars and slum dwellers, and mimicking them in her stiff European accent—Bah!-*hall*-ah Nah!—their mother wanted to laugh not only at them but, more damningly, at herself. These poor creatures were echoes of the country folk who had refused to be swayed by her pragmatic Peace Corps wisdom, choosing instead the mystical enslavement of God's benevolence. How could she have hoped to engineer any positive change in a country which continually excused its poverty, its lack of education, its deplorable standard of living, its history of willing subjugation (first to conquerors Spanish, Japanese and American; and more recently to a string of despots, highlighted by the twenty-year reign of Ferdinand Marcos) using the wisdom of *Bahala na,* which essentially said that all these things would not be happening if God had not willed for them to happen, or that God would ultimately take care of things as He saw fit?

Misfortune could be corrected by hard work, by remedies practical, such as education, and medical. This was what she, what the Peace

Corps had to offer. Part of this doctrine involved preaching birth control, which she did. Couldn't the natives see that their standard of living was brought low by siring more mouths than they could reasonably feed? Couldn't they see themselves as part of a larger structure matching each mouth with a finite quantity of natural resources growing more finite as out of each mouth came even more hungry, devouring mouths?

But for these people—whom Teresa called "*the* Filipinos" with commensurate gestures of hand (as if about to conduct an orchestra) and face (lips pulled down into a major frown)—there was no bigger view possible except for a vision of themselves as ants under the dominion of a God who looked with equanimity at their helplessness. By doing nothing, He had as good as made a decree to sanctify such hardships as necessary. *Bahala na.*

L'Air du Temps and *Bahala na.* The war between their mother's residual instinct for pleasure and the punitive didacticism she had settled on as her life's mission.

Really, it was too much to be recalled to those episodes now, thought Socorro, who was on her way to St. Mary the Immaculate. Would she have the courage to go in? Socorro hadn't decided.

In front of her sat the driver next to an empty seat. Maybe that was what had started her reminiscing. The heat seemed to be seeping into the car, although she could feel the air conditioner blasting furiously at her feet and at her back. She felt dizzy. The grim scene outside was of another of the city's famous traffic jams. At least the driver assigned to squire her around did not commit the mistake of trying to make small talk.

Manila exhausted her. The vertiginous sweep of the past in the line of the horizon; the faces of her relatives; the chipped concrete of the sidewalks and of graffiti-scarred overpasses. Her own face was thrown back at her from the mirrors, the pool of the Manila Hotel, and now in the windows of the car, a face that seemed transformed in some essential, untraceable way, as if the scenery had wanted to demonstrate its undimmed power over her, turning her once more into a dreaded Filipino, with Filipino superstitions, Filipino backwardness. It was as if these traits were carried in the humidity and had seeped into her skin, infecting. Her past was in the way the palm trees with their heat-withered fronds swayed in the gathering winds; in the ping-ping-*ting* of the recent rains on the rooftops of the houses and businesses; in the smiles of the street urchins all of whom believed her to be the solution, at least for the day, to their problems; in the reckless jeepneys with their appliqués of drag-queeny, fiesta-fever color—everything was a reminder, though truthfully, nothing from her past was still standing. The world of her girlhood had long been taken over by new, younger tenants. Her Manila all but dissipated. Except perhaps for the family residence in Makati—a museum attesting to bygone days of unhappiness she had no desire to revisit. It was she, along with Roberto, who had asked for the will reading to be conducted in the lawyers' offices. And it was she who chose the Manila Hotel to stay in. It had been years, decades even, since the hotel had been chic, but it still retained a sentimental value for her.

It was to the hotel that her father would often take her—and only her—for *merienda*, leaving her to loll around the pool and watch as a succession of pop stars, and local and American movie stars, got in and out. To this day she could see the dazzlingly blue chlorinated water, made that way by the offsetting whiteness of the pool. Needless to say, the years had done their work—both to her and the hotel—and the pool was no longer the same magical place.

She eventually realized, of course, that her father had simply brought her along to be a decoy while he conducted his various affairs in one of the hotel's lavishly furnished rooms—preferably in the shady, discreet back. But she was her father's girl, more than anything, and would remain loyal. Never mind that he had, by providing so meagerly for her after his death, essentially repudiated her love, her efforts for him. Who had given her house over for his care during his last days? Who had made sure that he should be reunited with his prodigal son so that his death would be peaceful, relinquishing? Had he not considered his grandchildren, Socorro's three children?

It was clear that her father could only read one kind of signature: the acid etching of disrespect, and not the careful cursive of her and Roberto's obedience, a thing so fluid and smooth as to have been as good as invisible.

And hadn't her brother claimed not to want anything from the dead man? Where was his famous renunciation?

Still, she had to acknowledge: Roger was a bum. His job at Columbia had been more than a surprise; it had been downright shocking, as if a fish had sprouted legs and grown a nose with which to breathe. The new Columbia Roger was an evolutionary anomaly that would not survive long on its own, it would need all the financial oxygen their dead father could see fit to give. Otherwise, she and Roberto would be required to bail him out—sooner, she expected, rather than later. And for how long would they need to keep up their patronage? His indolence seemed like an indicator of a healthy life span.

Yet, it was that indolence that had won him the prize of their father's love. Perhaps not love. Rescue? That same indolence that on him was indistinguishable from charisma—as witness yesterday's paper. Had her brother seen his mug on the inside pages of the *Metro Manila Register*, right next to the slew of gossip columns? Three-quarter profile. Frosted glasses on. Who the hell did he think he was, Steve McQueen? Caught, per the caption: "at his father's funeral procession along EDSA five days ago." Eyes lowered, as if reading a book placed on the ground. Looking not only properly bereaved, but oddly dignified. "A camera never lies"—bah! A dignified Roger Caracera, that would be the day.

He was not alone in the papers, however. He figured in a double panel. Beside him was the exact same pose by the actor Harvey Keitel, costumed for *Fiesta of the Damned*. Oddly, her brother's expression exactly matched that of Keitel—could it have been manipulated by the paper? Keitel had his sights trained outside the frame, and on his face seemed a sadness occasioned by no less a thing than history.

Said the bumptious caption writer: "Separated at birth? Who is Roger Caracera, American returnee and sugar scion (who's come into a million dollars, we hear!), and who, General Douglas MacArthur, we mean Harvey Keitel, as General Douglas MacArthur in the movie 'Fiesta of the Damned,' currently shooting on location in Manila? In both cases 'I shall return' magically applies—since Mr. Caracera has not been back to our country since leaving as a teenager!"

Two hours ago, her car had been parked outside the Makati residence. In the end, she had decided not to go in. She didn't need to see Roger. Nothing he could say would assuage her fears of his squandering the money. It was his to do with as he chose. And if he should choose foolishly, it would be his own doom he was sealing. Throwing away half a million dollars, he could not expect Socorro or Roberto to help him out. At least this way they were forever absolved from the responsibility of his care and rehabilitation.

An hour later, she was outside the Pasay residence of the lawyer Miguel Santos, whom she had phoned to inquire about her mother, since he was the man designated to supervise her residency at the hospital.

Socorro had verified the name and location of the institution, quickly reassuring the lawyer that she would not be so unwise as to pay the woman a call. At least, not without notifying the family or the hospital staff in advance.

She did not really intend to let him know anything. She didn't require his permission either. Nor the family's, who would be given another reason to disapprove of her. So why had she gone to Pasay, why had she looked up at the second-floor window with such longing?

How could she have expected the lawyer—a faithful family servant if ever there was one—to tell her that her fears, at least in a small part of her heart, were true? That Teresa Caracera had not really been insane at the time of entering St. Mary the Immaculate, but rather had become so as a result of Jesus Caracera's and the family's machinations?

She had not been able to broach the subject over the phone, and in the end found no courage to broach the subject in person and asked the driver to take her away from Pasay.

Teresa Caracera was insane. The family had done right. Yes, Socorro could not be surer. The woman's insanity had its seed in the push-pull between L'Air du Temps and her passenger-side pulpit and, what's more, matched up with the central fact of her: her sense of superiority. She'd been too good for her husband, Socorro's father. Too good for her children. Too good for this country—though hadn't she come here to eradicate that Spanish arrogance, making of it a sacrifice in the sun-baked fields of her Peace Corps assignments? Didn't she want, in the end, to be left with the husk of a body asceticized by the trials of deprivation, the passport of youthful ideals that required the stamp of a Third World locale to complete it? Wasn't that why she'd gone mad? Because she had found herself at the conclusion of her journey not beautiful with purpose and virtue, as she'd intended, as she'd let her prosperous Madrid family, whom she'd shunned, believe, but rather beautiful in a merely ornamental way, serving as the handsome facade of a Manila family whose rapidly declining fortunes had required the services of her looks and pedigree to buoy it up? Hadn't her pride ensured that she could not, in the end, be able to live with such a compromise, a comedown?

Certainly among the causes of her insanity could not be said to be bereavement at the loss of Socorro. Or Roberto and Roger. All of whom she had made no effort to track down after they'd been kidnapped by their father to live in the United States.

The car pulled smoothly up to the sidewalk outside St. Mary the Immaculate. Across the street was the famous WackWack Golf and Country Club.

Beside Socorro on the seat was an envelope of cash—bribes for the hospital staff. She wasn't her father's daughter for nothing.

The driver, as before, sat quietly as she made her decision. He did not turn off the engine, so the air conditioner could continue to run.

Socorro had thought to make up for arriving late in Manila by extending her stay. Now she saw what a mistake it was. What was left for her to go through?

Yes, the idea of a vacation had been welcome. When was the last time she had had one, without the dead weights of her children and husband, much as she loved them?

Who would have thought that being a pediatrician could sand you down to the barest nub so quickly and often? Those children seriously ill had a severity of expression, robotically brave, that was hard to look at day after day. And there was a whole legion of patients who were just as exhausting—afflicted by phantom ailments which could not be localized in any part of the body, as if illness were a liquid that circulated, settling in this, that and many other areas in the course of its capricious journey. These children, it occurred to her, managed a solo performance during which they hijacked, with expert control, the spotlight of parental vigilance.

She was familiar with this strategy, having grown up with Roger. Seeing him again had been a bad omen. She knew it would be. And now her father's meager will, a reproof, was proof.

There was a statue of the Virgin Mary on a pedestal surrounded by a small, immaculately tended garden. Steps led up to sliding glass doors, through which she could make out nothing. Would she go in, or would she, as she had twice before, ask to be driven away, back to the Manila Hotel, where she would ensconce herself until it was time to be driven to the airport, days later?

She looked at the cash beside her, and then she looked at the back of the driver's head. It occurred to her that she didn't even know his name.

CHAPTER 9

IN THE CARACERA HOME in Makati, Roger slept in his boyhood room on the second floor. The caretakers had thought he would want to. Outside were the abundant leaves and thick branches of a calamansi tree, the fruit of which fell to the ground and was collected by the houseboy to make juice. The leaves and branches, still when he'd first arrived, had now begun to scrape at the windows with regularity, vanes announcing the monsoons. Their insistent *krrk-krrk* against the steel guards and their shadows on the walls of his room gave them the same power they had had when he was a boy: giant skeleton fingers endeavoring to claim him for the devil.

His father, wanting to pacify him, had once ordered the tree to be pruned. About the boy it was known that he had an imaginative and artistic nature, perhaps overly so.

It was a rude shock to be recalled to the tenderness of his enemy. Across the tunnel of years his father's act was revealed to be a grand gesture, something which he couldn't have realized then, and which, knowing it now, was weighted with pain: he hadn't deserved it; and his father had been fully justified, in later years, in his rancor against Caracera, forever having to tabulate the costs of such largesse against the meager shows of sentient gratefulness from a boy locked inside the room of his private resentments.

AN UNCLE IN THE PHILIPPINES, whose favorite nephew he'd been, had decided to bequeath him a large sum of money. He'd envisioned himself to be the subject of frequent, disappointed talks which had eventually burned out and been replaced by a thick, cryptlike silence—just this side of having been completely forgotten. So when he'd been informed of this uncle's bequest, he was shocked not only by the fact that he'd been remembered, but, more preposterously, by his having been designated any family member's favorite.

Uncle Eustacio was his father's youngest brother and had lived his whole life in the Philippines.

The family sugar plantation in the province of Negros had long since seen its prime during the reign of the clan's patriarch, Caracera's great-grandfather, slid into a limbo of leeched profits and diminished market control. The business was crippled as much by halfhearted management as it had been by absurdly escalated graft payoffs to local officials well trained to turn a blind eye to the sundry abuses visited on the overworked, underpaid laborers.

The blame fell on Caracera's grandfather, then Jesus Caracera, and, in his turn, Caracera's eldest brother, each of whom had made sure to crush the family business through a combination of lack of acumen and interest (the clan's early success had guaranteed a dynasty of useless playboys). There was a brief moment when Caracera's uncle had been considered for the job. It had been the natural line of progression, after all; but the man was so abjectly unqualified for anything requiring leadership, lacking both the decisiveness and ruthlessness which his predecessors, albeit in diminished quantities, had possessed, that they'd given the post instead to Caracera's brother, the junior by a good two decades. His inexperience had been considered less of a liability than the uncle's benignly somnambulant nature. Still, in the end, the family business had had to be eventually released from the family's hold, sold off to eager competitors.

Uncle Eustacio had been called the family "dreamer"—that was all Caracera remembered of this man. Though what exactly he'd dreamt

of had been a mystery to Caracera. Surely it suggested an artistic nature—but which field of the arts? Had he wanted to be a writer,
painter, composer, movie director? And where would he have gone to
put in oars in these fields?

There had been a brief crisis of conscience before Caracera eventually accepted the money. Sixty thousand dollars. It was not, he ra-
tionalized, the same money that he had, distancing himself from
the shameful family, cut out of his life. It was the money of another outcast—perhaps that was why his Uncle Eustacio had chosen
him.

In two years the sum was frittered away by Caracera. On nothing.
He could never entirely believe in the money's innocence, after all.
Eustacio Caracera was still a Caracera. He might've wanted, using the
money, to change his nephew, turn him back into a member of the
family before it was too late.

Sixty thousand dollars would not change him. Not for the worse
and, conversely, not for the better.

Years later, expecting his estrangement to be met with his father's
posthumous censure—in fact, desiring to be made a fool of in front
of the family, hoping masochistically to hear his name during the
will reading entwined with the zero figure he believed would be
the crowning achievement of his life—he had been dealt a blow.
His father had made him, for the second time in only a few years, a
beneficiary.

He didn't need to return to the Philippines. The great thing about
being an outcast was that, with minimum effort, you could continue to
be one. He'd only wanted to come because he knew he wouldn't get
anything. He'd wanted the family to see that it was all right with him.
In fact, better than all right. He'd prepared a smile that would show
his utter imperviousness to the loss.

EACH MORNING, a different Caracera uncle, usually alone, sometimes accompanied by the wife, and more rarely by one of the cousins,
would come for breakfast, keeping him company. It was thought that
the boy's stoic demeanor concealed a depth of sorrow that, unex-
pressed, would hasten the metastasis of some terminal illness which,

because he was a Caracera, was a distinct possibility in the not-too-distant future.

The uncles were men ravaged by youthful pleasures who had had tumors removed in the last few years and who now hoped to encourage the nephew to break precedent, avail himself while he still could of healthy avenues of expression and guarantee himself an old age free of debilitating pain and worry. Somehow, it was intuited that Roger Caracera, when he chose to express himself, releasing the guilt and sadness he must certainly feel about his estrangement from his father, would select harmful means. Did he go whoring? (This, after they'd ascertained that he wasn't—cross his heart and hope to die—a faggot.) Did he indulge in drugs? Did he drink?

No no, he had nothing, he curtly assured them.

Left with no safe topic to talk about, they conversed volubly and with admiration of Caracera's deceased father. They wanted the young man to know about the man he had wronged by misunderstanding. It had been known, they variously expressed, that Jesus Caracera, and not just because he was the eldest boy in the family, would be the first to die. It had seemed only fitting that someone who burned his candle as vigorously as Jesus did should sooner rather than later run up a bill for his tirelessness. Seen in this way, Jesus Caracera was a man who had deserved his death, having worked hard in this life. His efforts had bought a prosperous life in the United States, where he could rear his three children in the light of utmost respectability. Meanwhile, he returned occasionally to the Philippines to conduct a shadow (Caracera's word) existence and to keep alive the Caracera reputation for generosity and extravagance and philandering—as witness the appearance of the middle-aged beauty at the wake.

But what about Uncle Eustacio? Caracera asked, mentioning the uncle who'd been known as the "dreamer" in the family, the one ousted from the sugar business and who, after his death and out of nowhere, had sent Caracera a tidy inheritance: sixty thousand dollars. He'd been the only family member to have breached the chilling silence of Caracera's twenty-four-year estrangement. Hadn't he been the first brother to die?

As loquacious as they'd been when talking of Jesus, they were just as tight-lipped at the mention of the younger brother.

None of the uncles would talk. None of the aunts either. And as for the cousins, Caracera felt like a recently released felon when around them. They twitched when he approached, and spoke first before he could, scattering winds of diffusing, meaningless chitchat in advance of the poison he was likely to release into the air between them. The irony of it was that Caracera believed himself to be less corrupt than they. With their up-to-the-minute Guccis and Pradas bought on shopping sprees in Milan and Madrid, and their just as up-to-the-minute drug habits, they were more successful copies of the decadent lifestyle that had been attributed to him than even he, who was closer to the source of corruption, was. Though they held jobs in various industries, these seemed to him merely for show, things with which to be occupied while waiting for nighttime and the partying to commence.

Surprisingly, the one who was unafraid to be asked questions about Eustacio Caracera was none other than Uncle Amador, the man who sat through all family functions voiceless and who, for all intents and purposes, with his aura of being missing in action even when at the center of a room, could've been a stuffed prop in a diorama illustrating the decline of the Caracera line.

We don't talk about that, he said forthrightly when his nephew mentioned the youngest brother.

Why not? Caracera asked with an outward show of innocence, though he felt the perverse pleasure of putting a finger on a wound.

A man who'd identified himself as a former employee of his Uncle Eustacio's law firm (not Santos & Santos, surprisingly enough) had called on the Makati residence only the day before. He'd wanted to speak to the "head of the Caracera family—the American." The caretakers, suspicious, had tried to usher him out of the property but he wasn't so easily pushed aside. He told Caracera that he was seeking payment for his continued silence. He had shameful information about Eustacio Caracera, deceased just five years ago. As a bonus, smiled the man, who had the feral calm and intrepid skinniness of a scavenger, here was a tip: Eustacio Caracera, looking for a romantic "partner," had not chosen wisely, earning him the family's eternal censure.

Would this man have approached Caracera unless he'd known about the inheritance from Caracera's father? Thanks to the gossip columnist Dolores Macapagal-Arroyo and her column "Tumors (Truth or Rumor?)" in the *Metro Manila Register*, the whole country knew of the "new sugar scion" visiting from America.

According to her report, Jesus Caracera—known throughout the country as the handsome mestizo face of the family in countless print and TV ads during the seventies and through the mid-eighties, as well as being the introducer of several old Filipino movies for "Caracera Sugar Presents" on Channel 7 on the first Monday of every month from 1974 to 1982—had tearfully reunited with his youngest, estranged child, another handsome playboy in the Caracera mold. As a gift, the dead man had bestowed upon the prodigal son a cool "U.S. one million dollars!" Eager starlets and aspiring beauty queens had been advised to seek out "this new, *unmarried* millionaire!" before he was "snapped up."

Caracera had sent the blackmailer packing. "Partner": he'd heard all he needed to.

Like Jesus Caracera, whose romantic entanglements (or rather, a tiny portion of them) were brought to light at the wake, Eustacio Caracera (or perhaps, more accurately, the Caracera family) was to be revisited by a ghost from the past. Not a fake Chanel-clad mistress, but this time a man. Romantic "partner." What else could so perturb the family, with its constant mania for rooting out potential homosexuality among its ranks?

He removed himself from the family, replied Amador Caracera. That's why we don't talk about him.

If that's your criterion for editing him out of the family history, why are you talking to me? I removed myself from the family too.

You broke from your father, that's a different thing.

I broke with the family. With you. I'm sorry to be unpleasant but that's the truth.

After a silence in which Amador registered the information, he asked, So why'd you come back?

I'm here for the funeral, Caracera replied. And to hear what he had to say, he added, embarrassed to be invoking the will.

I hope you're going to a financial planner when you go back, said Amador, only too aware of this nephew's profligacy. In every generation, a family's clean record was marred by a gleeful vandal. In the case of the Caracera brothers, it had been the youngest, Eustacio.

Do you ever see my mother? asked Caracera.

She hates us, the uncle replied in a tone of gentle bewilderment.

He decided not to fill in the obvious.

Why don't you talk about Uncle Eustacio?

You want to know the truth? He was sick in the head.

What does that mean?

The man is dead. I'm alive. Why don't you ask about me?

He sighed. He respected the man's obstinacy, which matched his own. He respected it even more because it came coated with seeming candor. How do you spend your days, Uncle Amador?

Go to the club, see friends, visit my family. What kind of question is that?

How about church? Caracera asked.

Goes without saying, he replied. At my age it's like insurance, you know.

They both laughed.

The club his uncle referred to was a luxe establishment in Greenbelt that Caracera had gone to at the invitation of some cousins who'd wanted to impress him. All afternoon long, he'd watched as handsome, unctuous tennis instructors with the same brilliantined hairstyle glad-handed handsomely preserved matrons starved for attention from absentee husbands. He'd wondered whether there was a club where the husbands went to seek out young girls, poor and still eager to please, because their wives had already hardened into their ideal selves, cosmetically, morally lacquered and no longer sexually attractive to them—but of course there would be such places. The reputation even carried far abroad, as witness the Australian men who'd come in on the plane with him.

Caracera looked at his Uncle Amador and asked, unable to resist, Where's Uncle Eustacio buried?

The uncle looked. Considered whether or not to say anything. Would this nephew visit the grave? Then finally revealed, In Malate. This was a seedy part of the city that must've been seedier when Eustacio had passed.

Why Malate? Caracera asked.

You know the joke about the rapist who was asked why he raped?

Caracera shook his head.

The rapist replies: Because there was an opening. There was an opening in Malate.

The next day, it was Mrs. Amador Caracera's turn to visit.

You look pretty, he told her as he walked out into the garden, fresh from his early morning run: three and a half miles along Roxas Boulevard, passing the U.S. Embassy and circling the Cultural Center complex on Manila Bay.

Don't be ridiculous, she said, clearly self-conscious of her hair, which she had yet to sculpt into her regular beehive, and of her unmade-up face. Why do you do this? she asked in exasperation. Your uncle has a gym membership that he never uses. You can run there.

I don't like running in air-conditioning. It's not healthy. Besides, there are too many actors in there. One half of the gym primps, the other half ogles. It's disgusting. Everywhere I go I just get reinforced in thinking that this place is one big whorehouse.

She chose to ignore his comment. If you're going to persist in running by yourself so early in the morning—

It's the best time of day, he replied. It was true. Any later than eight, the street urchins would be jogging along with him, begging and yanking at his shorts the entire way.

If you're going to do this silly thing I'll send Ernesto with you. Ernesto was one of the family drivers and bodyguards.

What for?

Don't be perverse. We've told you again and again. There are kidnappers. *Dios ko*, you're a Caracera. Remember that. Irene Caracera was aware of her nephew-in-law's appearance in "Tumors."

What's Ernesto gonna do? Jog? With me?

He'll follow you. In the car.

Now who's being perverse?

You don't know how tough life is here. They hate us. People think kidnapping arises from need of money. But that's not all. It arises from hate. That's what they always forget. How much they hate us. The Caraceras, the Macapagals, the Cojuangcos, the Ayalas, the Rosaleses. Because we have so much and they have nothing. It's not our fault. What we have we've worked for. They should learn the same thing.

Between wanting and having is a long line called effort. Which they're unwilling to walk. So they resort to things like kidnapping. And some-times—like with the eldest son of Nicanor Salvador, the movie star who's now a hotel magnate?—even after they acquire the ransom they still kill the kidnap victim. That's how I know it's really about hate. In a way I admire it. Hate is a strong feeling. And I'm all for strength. That's the one thing about wealth. It softens you. It gets harder and harder to stay strong. Ernesto will go with you. You don't have to know he's there. But he'll be there.

They ate, slowly. Caracera was glad for the distraction of the food.

What happened to Tito Eustacio, Tita Irene?

He's dead. We don't talk about the dead.

I get the feeling even when he was alive nobody wanted to talk about him.

She grew exasperated. Just because you got some money from him doesn't mean he's a saint.

He finally decided to back down from this blind alley of Eustacio Caracera. How do you spend your days?

Excuse me?

What do you do in a day? Today, for example.

She looked at him, trying to decide whether this was a game she was willing to play. Then she said, I'm having breakfast with you.

And after breakfast?

How do you spend *your* days? Besides jogging.

I take a walk.

Around Manila? she asked, shocked.

Around the city, around this house.

You perverse boy! She had an image of Roger striding down the city sidewalks with both arms swinging like a latter-day John Wayne, entirely conspicuous and victimizable. I'm telling you, you do not have carte blanche in this city! Ernesto goes with you. Understand?

Okay, he said, tit for tat. How about you?

She sighed. I go home, then I get ready. For lunch, with my friends. Or sometimes I have appointments with my hairdressers, *manikuristas,* dressmakers—because I try to support the local industry unlike the young people who shop for anything with a foreign label. I'm a woman of a certain age, as they say. Too many foreign labels on me would just be vulgar. She interpreted the look on her nephew-in-law's face: You think it's awful.

I think you're beautiful the way you look right now.

In my *duster*?!

What's a duster?

It's what you wear when you're dusting.

You dust? he asked, shocked and tickled.

Of course not. It's for the heat. It's much cooler.

He asked, Do you go to church?

Your Tito Amador told me you asked him the same question. What's with you and church? Of course we go to church. It's our faith.

Not mine.

What are you saying?

I don't believe.

In God? She stared. Then she discreetly made the sign of the cross. *Naku*, she said, sighing sadly. Roberto and Socorro don't believe either?

They believe in God. As far as I can tell. Do you ever see my mother?

She ignored his question. *Hijo*. She touched him. It's not too late. You can still repent.

No, thank you.

She replied calmly, You're going to hell.

It seems like I've arrived, he said, tossing his hands to indicate his surroundings.

She looked at him with sudden understanding. To you we're all dead, aren't we? As soon as you go back you're never returning. You ask your tito and me how we spend our days not because you're really interested but because—because you have an idea of how bad life here is and how bad the people here can be and you want to be justified in thinking that you and the way you live your life are luckier, more correct, better. Who needs a God when you can be your own? Right?

This seemed to Caracera first preposterous, and then dead-on.

Tell me, continued Mrs. Amador Caracera, when you go running, is it because you want to pass everything quick and not have to stop and look?

What do I need to learn about this place that I don't already know?

What do you know? She ventured a guess: Poverty? She saw the look on his face and knew that she'd been right. Everybody comes here and talks about the poverty. That's so easy.

You want to know what I learned? he asked. He wasn't afraid. She was right: these were people he would never see again.

What.

He turned coward at the last minute.

What? she persisted. I'm not afraid to hear it. I've probably heard worse things in my life.

We're awful, our family. And I'm ashamed. That's what I've learned again.

A moment of silence passed. He couldn't eat. Couldn't look at her. She herself attempted neither. What makes us such bad people? she finally asked. Because we have money? Is that the liberal wisdom of your American upbringing?

He thought of their summer vacations in the Negros hacienda intruded upon by parties seeking an audience with his father—workers' representatives whom his father had listened to as if he were a monarch being regaled by serenaders, before sending them away empty-handed; and on the opposite end of the spectrum, high-ranking officials of the various Marcos-established acronyms whose purpose was to centralize the siphoning of the proceeds from the sugar industry, men who had reversed the usual flow of tribute in his father's life, and meetings with whom always ended with the discreet sliding over, across a table elaborately laid out for afternoon *merienda*, of a cash-fat envelope. Caracera had not only been a frequent witness on the scene, but had been, even more distressingly, a witness to his mother's distressed witness. From her looks he had first gotten the idea that something wrong was going on.

He held silent for a second before unleashing his fury on Irene. He told her about the Negros episodes. Surely she'd heard about them before? He saw that she was stung and reached out an arm to comfort her.

She pulled away. Be consistent, she warned. Hate us if you hate us. Don't spew your hatred at me and expect to be forgiven with a touch. At least your mother was consistent.

A pause. She resumed, What are you going to do with your money? Your *evil* money?

I don't know.

But it makes you bad. That's what you said.

What are you advising me to do?

Advice? Me? she seemed to be saying with her expression.

A poor woman, in a losing match against the truth. A gay brother-in-law; a haranguing, truth-telling, exhibitionistically unhappy, finally insane sister-in-law; and a drug-addicted outcast son. Was he, Caracera, the official fourth outlaw? Apparently the family hadn't yet made the distinction, though they regarded him with a spurious, suspicious bemusement.

Except, perhaps, the gay uncle himself, who, looking around to pass the baton of his willed ostracism and his careful, quiet mutiny, had selected, in his opinion, a natural: sixty thousand dollars as a vote of confidence from one gay man to another. His uncle had looked, and chosen, from among the children of Jesus Caracera (the eldest, most powerful brother, the better to spite the family), a boy who was still, at forty-something, unmarried and, what was more, had sequestered himself from his own immediate family. Surely there were no better signs of the correctness of Eustacio Caracera's hunch? His nephew, the news of whose banishment had reached him all the way from the United States, owed his fame to the same cause as his, Eustacio Caracera's, did: a *bakla,* a lingerer in ill-lit, illicit places, a bachelor whose appetite for aloneness curved his inclinations and turned him reedy with hunger.

The sudden knowledge made Caracera more sad than anything. Sad for, among other things, the fact that he had taken the money under false pretenses, not being gay. But how could he have known?

Why don't you give the money away?

To whom? he asked. You?

She ignored the insult. Go to Negros. Find the sugar workers. It seemed that the twinkle in her eyes was not malice so much as a genuine surprise—matching his—that she should be saying such uncharacteristic, downright blasphemous things.

Wouldn't the sugar workers all be dead? he thought but didn't say.

Go ahead. Rent a plane. Fly over Negros. Throw the money out the window. In fistfuls. It'll be Christmas early this year. Hooray for the good Caracera—the exception!

She hadn't been serious after all. Are you through having your little joke?

How did they get to this place, with him calling up an impromptu tribunal and, more shockingly, with her dropping her silken, famous diplomacy, denuded by anger? Looking at him, she thought, Why hold back now? I could tell the day of the reading how unhappy you were, she said. Are. How unhappy you are. How unhappy the money made you. At first I thought, He's putting on a show, the way he used to do as a boy. He wants us to understand that the money means nothing to him. As opposed to us—all we care about is money. But no. I knew that wasn't it. Then I understood. You've always claimed no one in the family has treated anyone humanely and now someone has. Your father has treated *you* with kindness—there's evidence. So now you feel guilt about this evidence, the money. You can't face the fact that you were wrong. And on top of that you can't face the fact that you don't really deserve the kindness. A bigger kindness than any of your uncles received—all of them loved your father and he loved them all. A bigger kindness than was shown to Roberto and Socorro, who've always been by his side. Do you deserve it, Roger? After what you've done to your father? To us? Putting us through what you did. Your hateful letters—I kept them from the rest of the family, you know. Your Uncle Amador doesn't even know that you think of him as an evil man. He always saw your troubles as a by-product of intelligence. Intelligence without channel, he used to say. He used to say to your cousin—to— She couldn't bring herself to say the name of her disinherited child. To our son. He used to say, If only your troubles were rooted in intelligence maybe something can be done about you yet but— He used to say, There's hope for Roger still. There's hope. How old are you, Roger? Forty-five? Forty-six? Is there still hope? Maybe there isn't. So the money has to be bad. Bad money, like the bad family. She put her fingers to her brows, slowly massaging. For the first time, seeing her look truly old and worn, Caracera understood the arsenal of her hair, her makeup, the shrill, self-congratulatory talk between her and her coterie of admiring young gay men.

Maybe I *will* give it away to the people in Negros, he said.

She raised her head and looked straight at him. If I were you, I wouldn't be in a rush to idealize people just because they don't have any money. Go ahead, give them money. But think about it. Wouldn't that turn them, by your definition, evil?

He looked away.

I see, she said. So long as *you* don't have the money anymore, that's all that matters. Money isn't bad, Roger. How can it be bad? It's just a thing.

A thing, he repeated without conviction.

A bringer of opportunities, Roger. That's why your father gave it to you. So you would be able to change your life.

PART TWO

Finding the Beneficiaries

T HE VILLAPEÑA (or VIP) Club had been proposed as early as 1978. By June of that year a lot in the burgeoningly exclusive subdivision known as Greenbelt had been purchased. By July, initial plans by the much sought-after architectural firm of Avellana and Yap, who specialized in knock-offs of Le Corbusier's International Style and Louis Khan's gnomic structures, were drawn up. The two-story building sitting at the center of the three acre lot would be a departure for the architects, who would now be pillaging from the Mexican/Californian ranch tradition. The roof would be red tile, the walls, if not exactly adobe, then adobe-ish, which meant that they would have the appearance of red stucco. There would be a wraparound balcony overlooking the property on the second floor, which would be echoed in the interior, where a terrace would wrap around and hang over a central courtyard/lobby sitting beneath a sunroof. The landscaping was crucial to maintaining the fiction of living the good life in California (read: lots of trellises, shrub borders and a lawn that stretched from one end of the compound to the other, to rival a cemetery or WackWack), said an accompanying pamphlet which had been printed to solicit members, who would be invited to join only if they were within a certain income bracket. Membership dues would be prohibitive to better sieve out the Manila riffraff.

But dramatically, just as ground was about to be broken, the quorum of five businessmen who were the planners and funders—the textiles tycoon Jorge Sanchez, the real estate magnate Claudio Araneta III, the hotelier Narciso Ponce, the coconut industry oligarch Persefio Mendiola Sing and the former ambassador to France, former Minister of Tourism and close friend of the Marcoses, Edward "Crunchy" Dulce—had found themselves reduced by two, Sing and Dulce having been, with great fanfare, sentenced to prison for crooked business schemes that had come to light. Even Dulce's close ties to the Marcoses had been useless in the face of the overwhelming evidence of his having diverted public monies to purchase two homes in Manila and a hacienda for his mother in Cebu City, where he grew up.

Unable or unwilling to split the financial burdens left by the obsolete partners among them, and unable to recruit new investors willing to overlook the taint of bad money and similar luck that had, in one unforeseen swoop, settled on the project, and further beset by unreal real estate taxes instituted by Imelda Marcos in one of her capricious schemes to divert public interest from the conditions of the poor millions for which she and her husband the President were later to be held responsible, the partners had had no choice but to agree to let in a new partner (and his family) whom they would never have considered before: Rodrigo Caracera, Caracera's grandfather. Only he, it seemed, had been willing to bet that the shadows thrown by the scandal (made worse because the criminals had fallen from high living) would not hang around long enough to keep the club from turning a profit within a year. Or, in the meantime, attract celebrities and their ilk: the *appearance* of profitability foreshadowing the real thing.

Rodrigo Caracera had not only agreed to take on the financial share of the two defunct partners, but had promised to push the club through to the head of the line seeking exemption from Madame Marcos's real estate tax burdens. This he would accomplish through the intercession of the lawyer Miguel Santos, who was rapidly becoming an indispensable Marcos crony.

The formerly déclassé family, with purchase into the VIP Club, had found themselves with a momentary upsurge in importance and glamour, and about their failure in and subsequent disentanglement from the sugar industry, the perception had suddenly changed from its being the tail end of an inevitably tragic and boring soap opera to its being an amusing curve in what might be, after all, an even more enduring saga hewing closer to legend: up, down, and now up again.

Still, Rodrigo Caracera had been given no say as to the layout of the club, to how many tennis courts there would be (five outdoor; one in) and what kind they would be (all hardcourt), or how many swimming pools (three: one Olympic-sized, another heated, both indoors, and a regular-sized one, outdoor), or the possibility of a mini-fairway (rejected at the last moment, since all the founding members, including Rodrigo, had memberships to WackWack), or even the creation of stables and riding grounds (also rejected), or to the various particulars of the landscaping (bougainvillea the presiding flora, because they were perfectly suited to the weather and provided cheap and effective bursts of color and, most importantly, would help create the villaesque atmosphere the architects were aiming for). Rodrigo Caracera was just as glad not to have any choice in the matter. Similarly, about the mascot of the VIP Club—an eagle (Asia's largest, a Philippine *haribon*) holding in one talon a Philippine flag and in the other a clutch of sampaguita blossoms (the national flower), and in its beak a scroll that to this day nobody could be sure what it represented (the Constitution? the club's charter—did it even have such a thing? a piece of paper exempting it from Imelda's tariffs?)—Rodrigo Caracera had not been consulted. Seeing it for the first time during the opening ceremonies he had had nothing to say about it one way or the other, merely clapping along with the assembled crowd, which included his family, who were too baffled by finding themselves at the hot center of Manila life after a long interval of what seemed like banishment and so had forgotten to be grateful.

The club officially opened in June 1980, and was part of the First Lady's groundwork for the Manila International Film Festival. She had hoped that by the festival's inauguration in mid-1981, the city would be steered away from its Third World state of scandalous poverty to become, if not yet the premier city in the East, then at least a template on which such aspirations, having already borne fruit in selected areas, could be legitimately superimposed. At any rate, she would be conducting for her visitors a personal and highly selective tour, in the course of which such places as the VIP Club could be used to extrapolate the success of the presidency.

Now, twenty years later, the VIP Club was in decline. It had had to open its doors not only to the highly suspect nouveau riche, but even worse to the gauche, heavy-treading middle classes, whose capacious flesh seemed the perfect disclaimer of the successful image the club was trying to maintain and seemed, at one point, to effortlessly radiate.

Also it had been subjected by the new board to the further indignity of being made open to the public every Thursday and Sunday, for an entrance fee of five hundred pesos per person per day.

As a final blow, the truly hip and the young had duly moved on to another club—also, inconveniently for the VIP, in Greenbelt—called the Two Seasons, and with them had brought the eye of the press and public, as well as investors in the form of movie stars and the newly minted rich returning from abroad with fancy degrees and small-time successes (mostly in electronics and digital telecommunications) ripe for expansion into the untapped markets of the Philippines and of Southeast Asia.

All along, it had been intuited by those in the know that a club which would accept as part of its founders a family on the wane would sooner or later be dragged down by such an association. Ill luck, being rapacious and opportunistic, absorbed everything put in its path.

Aside from the fact of its diminished status, everything about the VIP Club was much as it had been during its heyday in the mid-eighties, prior to the catapulting of the Marcoses out of power and out of the country. In other words, it had struck more than one observer that it was like a mausoleum standing in honor of bygone days, and that the clientele huddled inside its confines (protected by guard stations and which grounds were patrolled by security men being pulled by Dobermans and rottweilers) were like hibernating bears waiting not just for the end of a long, bitter winter but for the dawning of a new term in the warm sunshine that would never come. Meanwhile, they would pickle themselves with drink, conveying themselves into a comforting state of amnesia.

The Makati village of the Caracera residence, Kalayaan Cemetery, the museum house of Miguel Santos, Sr., and now this place, with its faded, dusty exterior (the red adobe making it look like a giant kiln) and its bougainvillea, which, outmatching the management's budget or energies to prune it, was left to grow wildly, another sign of the club's decline—these places served as pockets of peace, soundproofed booths inside which their members and patrons were shielded from the cries of so much teeming poverty: enter and be lulled. More than in any location Caracera'd been to before, money had a tactile presence in this country. Its power, put plainly, was supernatural. Those who had it not only lived more comfortably but longer; amuletlike, it put its owners out of the reach of the demons of death, whose victims were necessarily from the lower dregs. These poor—as it was understood from the entertaining and grotesque reports in the daily papers that Caracera finally gave up reading—had been lured to their fates by frenzied attempts to remedy their lack through a variety of criminal means always undone by the wrong proportions of courage (too much) to finesse (none at all).

This afternoon, there were not many bears in attendance at the VIP. Rather, the scurrying from court to locker, from locker to pool, from gym machine to gym machine gave the club the atmosphere of a field where squirrels busied themselves at the height of summertime.

The bear contingent was represented solely by a group of Caraceras and relations, who sat along the side of one of the tennis courts. They were spread out over four tables.

At the center of the party sat Roger Caracera. Next to him was the teenage girl at the funeral, his cousin Cielito. She was the youngest child of Celeste and Eulalio Caracera, the surprise fruit of their later years and rumored not to be Eulalio's. Her pretty face suggested a bland openness to imminent corruption by the family wealth. Beside her, the caretaker Segismundo and his wife, both of whom sat hunched and looked pained. Anyone seeing them would conclude that this was part of the overweening humility of being servants.

But really they were suffering the guilt of prospective turncoats, specially the wife, to whom the Makati home's previous owner, Jesus Caracera, had appeared twice since his death, and each time voiceless though menacing. She had yet to report this spectral visitation to anyone but her husband, himself susceptible to belief in the supernatural. And she knew that such an announcement would have to be given hand in hand with her notice.

Beside Segismundo sat the twelve-year-old houseboy Dolphy, named after a famous movie comedian, thirstily sipping his Sarsi. He came to work three days a week, Wednesday, Friday and Saturday, spending Monday, Tuesday and Thursday in school, and having Sunday off to be able to attend mass and have some leisure time. The scheme of keeping the boy in school had been Jesus Caracera's, Caracera was surprised to learn. His father had agreed to keep the boy only if his parents promised not to yank him out of school. He would pay them the equivalent of a whole week's wages regardless of the days the boy missed for being in school, plus a bonus each semester when the boy brought his report card for Jesus Caracera to inspect.

Apprised of this by the caretaker Segismundo, Caracera had felt that his plan for his father's inheritance might not be, after all, as the lawyer Miguel Santos had sneered, a misappropriation but precisely what the man himself would have intended. This streak of charity, being a secret Jesus Caracera had thought to conceal from his family, reminded him of that line from *The Importance of Being Earnest*: "I hope you have not been leading a double life, pretending to be wicked and being really good all the time."

Next to Segismundo and Dolphy was the driver and security guard Ernesto. The man had one hand stuck inside his jacket the whole time. But it was an empty gesture because Caracera and Ernesto had finally reached the point at which interest in Caracera was beginning to die down. This was after a period when, as a result of the successive days of newspaper coverage, they had been vigorous fenders-off.

Two of those Caracera hadn't wanted to fend off or hadn't succeeded in fending off (he still wasn't sure which) sat at the next table, an old classmate from St. Jude's named Benjamin Goyanos and his teenage daughter, Marta. Goyanos was nursing a whiskey and soda, and his daughter a vanilla milkshake that she sucked at insolently. She was resentful at the intrusion of Caracera into their lives, even if, truth be told, the intrusion came from the other way around. It had been Goyanos who, alerted by the write-ups in the papers, had called the Makati residence and, surprising himself, had spoken with the man

he'd last encountered as a boy of seventeen, and whose sudden and un-
explained disappearance from what he and his schoolmates assumed
would be a lifelong acquaintanceship had made Caracera a lasting fix-
ture of all their imaginations, persisting into adulthood.

Caracera chose not to confess that he didn't remember his friend
that well. He had a rough idea, of course, of having once been a boy
in Catholic school shorts, with a regulation haircut and shiny black
patent-leathers, surrounded by peers similarly uniformed, all of them
more or less equally devout, in manners to suggest competition.

Caracera could not believe that the two people who claimed to be
father and daughter were related. Perhaps the gene for destructiveness,
for rebelliousness, thwarted in one generation, exacted its full vengeance in the next. Marta Goyanos was dressed as a punk, complete
with mohawk, streaked green and red, a metal ring through one nos-
tril, and several hoops and jagged pieces of silver up and down the
lobe of one ear. On this hot day, she was wearing all black: a T-shirt
that had what looked like a Satanic pentagram beneath a superimposed
image of a ram's head with its demonic curlicues thrusting out on each
side, and tight, ripped-up black jeans gathered here and there by safety
pins. On her feet were black Doc Martens that looked new, making a
mockery of the fastidious weathering on the other articles.

Goyanos had explained without sadness or apology that he had
had to chaperone his daughter every waking hour of every day, as she
had just been freed from detox for heroin. The prim father certainly
couldn't have missed the look of judgment on Irene and Celeste Caracera's faces when he had walked in with his daughter. The women
flanked the party at each end. Each was busy knitting, and their nee-
dles had, to Caracera, the look of guns not quite taken out of holsters,
each woman being a duelist aware of the tiniest shifts in movement of
the other.

Irene had come in the spirit of concession, wanting Caracera to understand that she didn't resent his low opinion of the family, or perhaps she had come in the spirit of gamesmanship, knowing that
Celeste was accompanying her nephew-in-law to the club and not
wanting that woman to have the monopoly on his affections. Irene sat
a table away, right next to where the punk girl and her forbearing father sat.

Celeste was at the table closest to the courts, next to Caracera's. With her sat her guest, an Italian-American Catholic missionary named Frannie Prusso, whose long, stringy hair and, even after two years in the Philippines, pallid complexion suggested that she'd just emerged from a long slumber at the bottom of a lagoon. Sitting next to her was a thirteen-year-old pipsqueak who looked nothing like her but whom she'd introduced as her daughter, Camelia. The girl blinked so infrequently she recalled the alien awakeness of Japanese comic-book characters, and with that face she greeted every facet of the scene: the tentativeness of the ball's journey across the net; the varying degrees of awkwardness of the players contrasted with the good-natured, almost apologetic ease of their instructors; the sun slicing through the rips in the fabric of their umbrellas (another sign of the VIP Club's deterioration) to diagram sharp splinters on the tables; the avocado shake which she had been curious to try but which had been sitting neglected and sweating to one side. Even to her mother's poisonous yakking, destroying the afternoon's purpose, she gave the same blank look, as much present-minded as faraway, as if those words were the most ordinary thing in the world and there was nothing she could do to stop them. Wasn't she made edgy, as any self-conscious thirteen-year-old would be, by the other guests' clear discomfort at her mother's ceaseless nattering? Perhaps she thought the best way to extricate herself was to demonstrate to the guests by her eerie, mute, precocious ballast, in startling contrast to the woman's declamatory speechifying, that the two of them could not possibly be related, whatever her mother may have said to the contrary.

For the gigantic failure of this country ("not here today, of course, but I mean elsewhere") the missionary woman Frannie Prusso blamed the inadequacy of the population's Catholic applications. The Spanish introducers had not conveyed their religious strictures with the proper astringence and the subsequent centuries saw the resulting dead end, like the stillborn embryo of two incompatible progenitors: God's tenets mixed in with unholy pagan superstitions so that the very face of God Himself should be transmuted into a confusing, whirling, many-headed idol, each head crowned with a ring of fire equally compelling as the warning of hell awaiting those who strayed from the one true path.

You'd think this place was India, she'd said, naming the one place on earth she'd been to that she most detested. Further, she said, the term Third World, kebobbing both India and the Philippines, was a certification of low ranking devised by no less an authority than God: the number had something to do with the distance of the populations from Him.

Frannie Prusso had been loquacious, like someone who believed she was among similar-minded people. Her audience's silence could be interpreted as approval, even quiet applause. Caracera felt like a congregant at a Mass in which she was the sermon speaker, thirsty with vengeance over the unacknowledged injustice of her situation.

Or perhaps she was speaking with the earned bitterness of a burnout.

She'd been saying how she'd lost twenty pounds in two years, as if the Filipinos had been eating away at her flesh as soon as she'd arrived in this country. How was she expected to frighten them into the arms of the Father with tales of Boschian punishment when Boschian punishment was the norm in their lives?

Caracera closed his eyes.

What a poor, recumbent country, he thought, which made him have to open his eyes and take a sip of his calamansi juice. The tartness of the drink was bracing; with it his throat constricted, and his thoughts tautened.

What he was picturing was this: two planes, each bearing an opposing party, each party with plans to use this country for its own ends. But he was neither of these parties. He was outside the story.

Soon these planes were discharging their passengers. Down one staircase: the brothers of the beery, big-bellied Australians who'd been on the same flight as he, clearly participants in a sex tour.

Down the other: Frannie Prusso's reinforcements: stringy, self-abnegating women with a miniature bonfire inside each eye.

Each of these groups saw themselves as proselytizers, as saviors. The Australian men by offering money in exchange for the common commodity of sex. The Frannie Prussos saving the natives not in this life but in the other—the more lasting existence whose punishments, if successfully courted, were tenfold the duration, tenfold the magnitude of the degradation suffered in this life.

Imagine that, above them in the sky at any given moment waited saviors eager to land in this place with the strange, melodious, not-quite-real name: Phil-ip-pines. Intent on the task of conversion: transforming the rowdy, mercurial population (Fil-i-pi-*nos*) into orderly rows, down which aisles the head Australian or the head Frannie would walk, extending a hand over each Filipino and by such an act imparting the virus of their belief. In a matter of seconds, each Filipino's face would reconstitute itself into an exact replica of the Australian's or of Frannie's (Fil-i-pi-*yeses*; "Yes, boss"): a whole acquiescent field stretching into infinity beyond the dip of the horizon, an entire nation adding the sum of their bodies to the force of a single belief: choosing either the salvation from sin, or the salvation *of* sin.

The sky was wallpapered with falling missionaries, like a Magritte, replicated into eternity, holding neither bowler hats nor umbrellas, but instead penises or crucifixes.

He looked at Frannie Prusso, who was exhausted from her talk, to which, gratefully, nobody had responded, not even Caracera. Even in repose she appeared disapproving. So frequently had she needed to emboss that displeasure to suggest the hellfire of a spurned God that the mask was hardening into her true face.

Her thinness too was an illustration of the sternness of God's love—she was there to serve God's will by becoming the most unextraneous picture of His idea of human life that she could think of.

About the tennis, which admittedly wasn't much of a distraction, only the boy Dolphy, the caretaker Segismundo, and occasionally Benjamin Goyanos would applaud a point, during games when the instructors combined classes and had their students play against each other. At intervals the instructors themselves, encouraged by the applause and driven to impatience by the gelatinous fumblings of their students—neither-young-nor-old women who'd intended the game to be nothing more than a larky interval between social engagements—took center stage and competed against one another, ostensibly to demonstrate proper form for the benefit of their students.

Soon, one session was concluded and two new people came on court. A rich, pampered wife trailed by a boy with a crewcut who was dressed in a white polo T-shirt and white shorts. He was among the pool of hitting partners the club provided while the women awaited their instructors.

The wife didn't know how to control her racket and sent the boy to retrieve the ball with doglike avidity. His eye was always on the fuzzy yellow-green ball. His legs, like the Brazilian tennis star Gustavo Kuerten's, seemed mere sticks, the knees bruised grapefruit shapes marring the clean line. And yet, also like Kuerten's, those legs were capable of not just quickness, but grounding power. His feet, shod in worn-out sneakers, were firmly planted on the hard court each time he prepared to take the ball early.

When he lunged to cut off an errant ball and send it back across the net, falling in the process, Caracera felt an appreciative thrill.

How old was the kid? Caracera thought about fifteen. He had dark brown skin that made his costume appear radioactive in contrast, and his teeth, betrayed with each grimace, each self-satisfied grin, were crooked, plaque-ridden. He barely broke a sweat, although the moisture in the air was at an unbearable level. His face was rounded; underneath the spiky, splintery haircut, it looked even more boyish. How could something that looked so tentative produce strokes of such assurance and beauty, and move, when called for, with the linear aggression of a bullet? The staff, Caracera knew from having observed, were supposed to humor the clients, not pound them further into the amateur status that they were painfully trying to crawl out of. Yet the boy was doing exactly that. The youngish wife laughed but the sound spoke of her awareness of being observed. Looking at them, you couldn't help thinking that the microcosm of the Filipino class system which they perfectly embodied was being upended.

The tennis instructor, with his brilliantined hair and his near-perfect smile and his dark skin that (unlike the boy's) was like a cosmetic gloss, arrived. He dismissed the boy, who walked away slowly as if he meant to extend the waiting time of his next appointment. One minute the young wife was sweating with worry and embarrassment, the next she breathed deeply with relief: at last here was someone who, if not her social equal, then would at least understand what her position merited: the constant massaging of her ineptitude so that it became one more bauble bought by money and standing.

What are you thinking of doing while you're here? asked the teenage Cielito Caracera.

What am I thinking of doing with my life? asked Caracera.

She laughed but did not correct him.

I don't know, replied Caracera. And yourself?

Myself what? she asked, though she knew what he meant.

With your life. What are you thinking of doing?

She checked to see if he was joking, saw that he wasn't. I'm thinking of being a nurse.

Where?

In the provinces, Cielito replied. They need nurses there.

Why not be a doctor? Caracera asked her. They need doctors in the provinces too, don't they?

The young girl looked at Caracera, then quickly looked away. She seemed to be deep in thought. Then replied, cobbling words with care: Doctors are— They make a lot of money. I don't know that I can still do what I want if I make a lot of money. Does that make sense?

What is it that you want to do? asked Caracera.

Help people. And if I make money won't I just want to keep making more money? She hazarded a look at Celeste, her mother, half afraid, half challenging.

Ahhh, thought Caracera: the family dilemma, visiting the girl earlier than it had him. He smiled.

To Cielito, it looked as if her cousin was implying that he knew so much more about the way the world worked but had kept himself from saying anything. She felt indignant but kept quiet. At least her mother, to whom Cielito's ambitions were not exactly news, had not responded, starting another quarrel.

They watched the two people on the court, who had started on the gentle, inconsequential task of bunting the ball to each other. The instructor and the wife were standing inside opposing service boxes, each a few feet from the net. From that distance what they did looked like child's play. Then they gradually moved back until both players were stationed at the baseline. The wife evidenced a deftness that surprised Caracera. Under the instructor's mindful guidance, she was blooming, eager to do good to earn more of the handsome teacher's fulsome praise.

The audience was comforted by the spectacle of the ball going back and forth, each bounce seeming a distinct response to the sprinklers around them: *pat-pat, thwop; pat-pat-pat, thwop,* on and on like a drowsing percussion.

Finally Caracera stood up. You wanna go take a walk Ben? he asked Goyanos.

Goyanos looked at his daughter, and then, deciding that she wouldn't get the chance to get into trouble with all these people around her, followed. He turned back to her and said, Behave yourself.

Fuck off, she replied. Not receiving the startled censure she perhaps counted on from the women around her, she slumped farther in her seat.

Is she all right? asked Caracera as they headed indoors for the lobby.

Ever since she was a girl, she's been that way.

Maybe something's wrong with her.

What do you mean?

Physically. Physiologically. Have you ever had her examined?

They had reached the central courtyard, beyond which any number of options presented themselves.

Let's go to the pools, Caracera said. It's cooler in there. He led the way.

You think I should have her looked at? asked Goyanos.

Just a thought. Couldn't hurt.

And then what? Feed her more drugs? That's the way they do things in America, I suppose. She'll outgrow it, Goyanos declared. Besides the real answer, as I see it, is God's love.

Please. Caracera shot him a look. I've had enough of Jesus and his mission for this afternoon.

Goyanos laughed good-naturedly.

Someone was carving a perfect line down the middle of the Olympic-sized pool, over and over again. On both sides of him, people were bobbing in the water with abashed airs, as if, not being as good as the seeming professional, they would be told to get out soon.

That's Federowski, said Goyanos, marveling at the man drawing a white streak in the pool like pulling a thread out of a piece of cloth. He was a half-Polish, half-Filipino basketball superstar playing for the San Miguel team of the PBA.

Do you know Santos & Santos? Caracera asked, as the two found a seat on the benches rising to the back of the wall and which faced, across the pool, a row of frosted glass windows.

Goyanos was himself a lawyer and gave a whistle at the sound of the name. Are they your lawyers?

The family's. They represent all but one uncle of mine. And this uncle's dead. And I'd like to get in touch with his lawyers, just to ask a few questions. Why, for example, his estate doesn't fall to the Santoses' care. Would you be able to find out who these lawyers are for me?

I can try.

Caracera gave his uncle's name. He died in 1995, he told Goyanos. Around that time I got a letter informing me of my uncle's bequest. A letter which, along with its follow-up arriving with the check, he'd subsequently thrown out.

Goyanos tried to instigate some reminiscence about school days. Caracera let Goyanos do all the talking, and when Goyanos was done, feeling partly that he needed to keep up his end, he informed his schoolmate about the sorry state of his family history, about his recent inheritance, about how one plus the other equaled a trip to Negros.

Goyanos perked up. Negros Occidental or Oriental?

Occidental. Bacolod. It's where the family summer estate is. Where the sugar plantations used to be. I mean where they are. They're still there but we have nothing to do with them anymore. Somebody, I forget who, bought us out years ago. Who do I speak to to help arrange a trip? Then he mentioned the idea of doling out financial reparations to the descendants of the Caracera cane cutters.

How would you go about finding these people?

That's why I need help.

Goyanos nodded, a faint smile on his face. Imitation of Christ, he said.

It was entirely possible, thought Caracera, that he'd misheard Goyanos, but in case he hadn't, in case this was one more ploy to drag him into a discussion about their childhood faith, Caracera decided to let it pass.

But Goyanos repeated himself.

This time Caracera couldn't resist. He asked, What's that mean?

Oh, said Goyanos. It's a . . . slogan of mine, you might say. It's just to remind myself of actions to aspire to. Like your—like this thing, going to Negros. Helping people, doing good.

Caracera raised a hand, like one of the Supremes in a stop-in-the-name-of-love gesture.

Goyanos looked.

Good? No, that was not the way he saw it. In his mind, a debt had been incurred. And he was paying it back, that was all.

It was his father's debt. His father, who had done bad. And now it was his father who was the one doing, well, all right, good, trying to reverse himself with his, Jesus Caracera's, own money. Caracera, his son, was only the agent, it was that simple. This was not the product of deep thinking or prolonged consideration but instead its opposite. The speed and intuitiveness by which he'd come to this decision seemed to vouch for its rightness, as if he'd merely tuned in to something long foreordained.

After a moment of silence, Goyanos asked, When were you thinking of going?

By the time they returned to where the gang sat by the tennis courts, it was decided that Goyanos would accompany Caracera to Bacolod next Monday, bringing along with them Marta Goyanos, whom her father would not allow to be by herself or with her equally untrustworthy mother.

The party dispersed with the usual murmurings of thanks and you're-welcomes, the aunts saying what a good, restful afternoon it had been and that perhaps they should do this more often, and in the aunts' homes the next times.

On the way to the parking lot, Caracera espied the boy who had made such sport of the young wife. Standing next to him was the tennis instructor, and next to the instructor, a supervisor. Apparently the wife had told of the boy's misbehavior.

Caracera heard one of the men say to the boy that he was being fired. Characteristically, the boy didn't look repentant, but had a glowering look on his face.

Caracera went up to the men and introduced himself. Told the supervisor that he'd witnessed the scene between the wife and the boy, and said that the boy didn't appear to mean any harm. It was only that he was good and young and therefore didn't know to push down his natural boastfulness. This remark earned a disgusted look from the boy.

Caracera told the men that if they fired the boy they would only have him to answer to. His family were founding members, did they know that?

They were only waiting for his speech to conclude so they could ask him to pose for a picture and to sign autographs.

Excuse me? Caracera asked.

You're Roger Caracera, *the* Roger Caracera?

I'm Roger Caracera, he said with an air of defeat, knowing that they'd seen him in the papers.

The instructor had gone off somewhere and now came back holding a Minolta point-and-shoot with a black strap. Caracera was squeezed between both men, the flash blinded him momentarily and then pieces of paper were being pushed in front of him, along with a fountain pen. Please, sir, the supervisor said.

Caracera, still blinded, dashed off signatures on both pieces of paper.

This means so much to us, said the instructor, who, after reviewing the autograph, shook Caracera's hand vigorously.

And don't worry, sir, assured the supervisor, the boy will stay with us.

All this time the boy had been looking at the three men with an air of being mildly amused and also disgusted. If only to oblige both superiors who were pointedly staring at him, he thanked the man who had come to his rescue. Thank you, sir, he whispered, managing only a faint smile, which was just as well, considering the state of his teeth.

Don't mention it. Caracera asked him what his name was.

Donny, sir.

Donny what?

Donny Osmond Magulay.

He thought the boy was putting him on and had him repeat the name. The same far-fetched words greeted Caracera's ears. I suppose I can guess who you're named after, he joked.

The boy didn't catch the joke and replied, I am named *po* for Donny Osmond the singer.

How old are you? Caracera asked.

Sixteen *po*. Once again the boy inserted the honorific used to converse with elders. Yet, Caracera could tell this arose from no reflexive sense of humility on the boy's part. If anything, the boy used the word grudgingly, earning Caracera's admiration.

Where'd you learn to play like that?

The boy lowered his head, evincing a becoming modesty. Teaching myself *po*.

Really? Caracera couldn't believe it. All that from just practicing by yourself?

And I am watching tapes *po*.

Caracera supposed the boy meant that he watched games televised. Who's your favorite tennis player?

Ah! That's easy *po*! Pete Sampras!

Caracera, not being fond of Sampras, a man of rare defeat, winced. Keep up the good work, he said to the boy in parting.

The two men once again shook his hand, and the supervisor's last words were, Your father was a great man, sir.

For a moment, Caracera considered if this was in fact true, and wondered what the man knew to have made him form such a confident judgment. And then he decided that perhaps by "great," the man had meant "famous."

He called his friend Goyanos the next day, taking pains to point out, before their trip, a possible source of conflict: he was having none of Goyanos's talk, involved or otherwise, about Jesus Christ and the heavenly Father, having come by his antipathy to Christianity through hard-earned trial and error. If this would present any problems to Goyanos, his friend should know sooner rather than later.

Strangely, Goyanos, the devout attender of church services, and the father who entrusted his daughter's recovery to God's care, said that it was no problem at all. He hadn't meant to talk to Caracera about religion and certainly would not bring anything up now that he knew.

Later, Aunt Irene would inform Caracera that Goyanos's wife was famously making a cuckold of him. If not for the humiliation fostered by this infidelity, he would have certainly been the recipient of some other, more serious comeuppance. That was how much his success as a lawyer was resented.

CHAPTER 2

BACOLOD, NEGROS OCCIDENTAL. Hot, humid, tempered by breezes blowing inland from a strait that connected the Visayan and Sulu seas. The beaches, farther south, were about an hour away. The 1993 Ford Explorer was on its way to the local museum showcasing the history of the sugar industry.

Inside was the driver, who came with the rental, a nut-brown middle-aged man named Constancio, "Stan" for short; Goyanos; his daughter Marta, for whom the trip served to paralyze whatever little comprehension had been left her by her recent addiction, and who was dressed, mimicking the look if not entirely the manner of the prototypical lesbian, in an overbig plaid lumberjack shirt and blue jeans ripped at the knees and on the inside of one thigh; and Caracera, who was so riveted by the catalogue of rebel looks (there had also been, once, a black motorcycle jacket and kohl-rimmed eyes) this young girl had adopted to provoke her father and his circle, which included Caracera, that the surprise of finding himself in Negros, his plan spooling a little too quickly, could only take a back seat.

It would not surprise Caracera if at any moment during the ride or subsequently during their stay in Bacolod, Marta Goyanos would suddenly make away with the bowling ball bag which he held next to him. Five million pesos was in it, which had been wired to the largest bank in Bacolod and which they'd picked up as soon as they landed. This was a large gesture of optimism on Caracera's part, as he had no way of knowing whether he would be helped by the person they had come to see. More and more, it looked as if Irene Caracera's joke about renting a plane and throwing the money out the window might be the only recourse he had—just how determined was he to dispose of the money? With it, he'd been able to charter a private jet to Bacolod, to make sure that a full meal as well as some liquor awaited them on board, to hire a driver and car for their entire stay, to pay a seven-and-a-half-percent wire transmission charge at the bank, and if the woman they were about to meet did not change her mind, he would be able, on short notice, to rent a private hacienda for their overnight stay before flying back to Manila. The Caracera mansion was off-limits—the family knew nothing of this trip. With the money too he'd allowed his Aunt Irene to take him shopping, picking up clothes for his extended stay in the Philippines.

Stan the driver pointed the Explorer at a spot in the horizon with determination. There seemed in his silence a kind of negative criticism of the vehicle's occupants, and so the task at hand seemed to be to get rid of them as quickly as possible. Caracera was wearing the black long-sleeved shirt which he'd worn at his father's funeral, and also newly bought black Hugo Boss pants and black Ferragamo leather loafers. His Aunt Irene had picked out the items for him, and besides, he had to keep reminding himself, this way the money dwindled more quickly.

He had drawn the line, however, when she had taken him to the Cartier counter at Rustan's to pick up a replacement for his trustworthy, if dinky, Timex. (When he had been forced to consider giving it up, he had turned it over to read at the back: "Made in the Philippines." The phrase had seemed, more than anything, redundant, as if letters indented in his skin had embossed themselves on the back of the watch face).

There was nothing in their way. They speeded smoothly along, only occasionally feeling a bump, though this could not be from the road—which, though narrow, was paved—but probably because of some suspension problem of the vehicle.

From the bustle of the plaza just outside the airport, where he saw by the bus and jeepney stops, standing either languidly or listlessly, some denim-skirted women with overly made-up faces whom he suspected to be whores (in the middle of the day?); from the first miles of their northward trek to the city of Silay when they were accosted by the blaring of American pop from speakers standing outside "luxury, air-conditioned" restaurants that, by installing a few cheesy bands doing perfect renditions of the same blaring pop hits, billed themselves "supper clubs"; from this same stretch of road where they were greeted by a profusion of new-looking malls and multicolored signs (advertising hair salons, bakeries, Japanese restaurants, noodle shops, *lechonerias*, cafés boasting Internet connections, video stores and a storefront *iglesia* or church trying to temper the march of the city toward Western progress and amorality); from the main road that had taken them to the bank and alongside which signs hawked an animal preserve, a resort, Mt. Kanlaon Nature Park (icons showing a volcano and a tree, along with the photograph of a meek-looking animal and beside it the legend: "Come see the rare bleeding-heart pigeon") and, of course, to their north, sugar plantations that offered tours through grounds and refineries; from the clamor of modern Bacolod (which seemed to be striving to become a second Manila, circa 1990), the driver finally turned onto what he called the "off roads." Here, they were brought back to a time of sleepy antiquity, before the invention of any transportation and where the absence of humans and their noises spoke of an undiscovered or abandoned country.

Stan continued not to say anything. He had showed up at the airport with a sign. Caracera and the Goyanoses had approached him, and he had led unceremoniously to the waiting car, painted an attention-getting orange, with silvery puffs of injury just above the front and back tires on the right side.

My name is Constancio, Stan for short, I will be your dri-ber because you hab requesting it.

That was the only contribution from the man, offered as he climbed into the driver's seat, having waited for everyone to settle in before he'd done so.

That, and the starting vroom, which seemed to suggest that Stan and Caracera were working toward the same goal: get it over and done with.

There were chickens on the side of the road, pecking the dirt along the shallow ditch which separated the road proper from where banana trees manifested with comic and useless irregularity, alongside other trees and bushes and long dried sticklike grass with surprising shoots of green at their bases.

Finally they encountered a car, an old Toyota Corolla, and overtook it, fast enough that Caracera couldn't see who was inside.

Are those tourists? he asked.

There was no reply from the monkish driver.

Do you get a lot of tourists? he asked. Stan?

Again, no reply.

You've been here before, haven't you? asked Goyanos.

As a kid. This all looks strange to me.

For example, he didn't remember if this road was new or old— there must've always been a road here, but had it been pothole-free, or was this a late-in-the-century, post-Marcos upgrade? Or had the Cara- ceras, eager to announce their presence every summer, never taken this back way before?

It's disgusting, said Marta Goyanos.

What is? Caracera asked her. Since he was the one responsible for the trip, every complaint was a complaint directed against him, even if the girl was ostensibly talking to her father.

The poverty.

This was not the first time Caracera had spoken to the girl, but it was the first she had thought it worthwhile to reply. By "poverty" Caracera supposed she was referring to the few natives they'd seen, mostly children dressed in oversized cast-offs (some saying comically: UNICEF), and who stared at them with stunned open mouths; and to the lack of any kind of dwelling except the thatched huts that looked, because of their seeming abandonment, like repositories for goods rather than proper dwellings, and also, glimpsed in the distances, broad

Spanish-colonial houses with exteriors speckled with the impasto of peeling layers of paint. And perhaps she was referring too to their driver, whose inability to hold a conversation might in fact owe not to rudeness but to his limited (if any) schooling, and who had to suffer the indignity of an old age spent catering to curiosity seekers trudging through what Caracera guessed to be his hometown.

This is the provinces, honey, said Goyanos. People here live like this naturally.

She snorted.

They pulled up to a whitewashed bungalow that turned out to be a church. Surprisingly, there were people on the premises. Several provincial women kneeling just inside, beyond the holy water font, clutching their rosaries with mouths atwitch and eyes shut. Also, several white customers who were taking pictures of the women (whose devotions continued unperturbed by the sound of the lens shuttering open and close) and also taking pictures of the surroundings: the holy water font with its basin of polished stone and its stand of dark, oil-stained wood; the cross-hatched wood beams on the ceiling; the crucifix at the back of the altar with its muscular Jesus fashioned roughly of metal and oxidized. The hammy look of sadness on Jesus' face appeared intended for the tourists who, by their documentation, seemed to be encouraging the surroundings to play up to a degree of indefinable falsification. Caracera recognized that he too was among the audience Jesus was playing to.

Hello, he said to the white men and women. They smiled back.

How long have you been here? he asked.

Pardon? they asked back.

He shook his head.

The driver Stan led them through a door at the side of the altar from which they emerged outside to witness, trailed by the French tourists, a mural of a Jesus with eyes whose lids sloped downward, looking unencourageable, and whose robe was like the ropy knots of a muscle, done in livid shades of red underlined with blue. His heart, a burning fist, was surrounded by a cordon of thorns: Keep Away.

Church of Angry Jesus, their driver said, pointing.

Why are we here? Caracera asked, as the shutters sounded around them.

Good question, said Marta, by which she meant to expand the inquiry to include Negros.

Stan didn't answer, and merely led them back to the car. It seemed he had a mistaken idea of their agenda. Caracera told him as soon as they got back in, We're not tourists.

Speak for yourself, said Marta.

I mean, he said to Stan, we're tourists but we're not here to sightsee.

Why am I here? Marta asked. She tapped Caracera on the shoulder. He turned back to look at her. Was this your idea? she asked him. So I could watch you giving money away?

Believe me, said Caracera, I had no part in this.

Hija, you understand why you're here.

Caracera looked at the driver, who seemed determined not to participate.

A carload of loud teenagers passed them going the other way. They struck Caracera as possibly backpacking European ravers, high on X or K or some new consonant that rendered their speech all vowels— Ooooo! Aaaaah! They were likely headed for the beach, being all nearly naked.

Marta gave them a quick look at once envious and contemptuous.

Another few minutes of Stan's eerie quiet—which seemed like a carrying out of a directive from Angry Jesus; why else would Stan have detoured them there, unless it was to make them understand that their trip was being conducted under the watchful eyes of that roiling, sizzling deity?—and they came to a stop. They had pulled into the shadows cast by the straw roof of a hut in front of which stood a middle-aged woman with a red dot in each ear: ruby earrings.

She was the person pinpointed as Caracera's best resource and hope. A Frenchwoman who had been with Médecins sans Frontières and had, after her itinerant group had departed for less hospitable and needier locations, stayed behind to fill a needed hole which few had wanted or thought to address: what were the deposed sugar workers to do to earn a living?

She had, for the last dozen years and with varying degrees of success, been helping to inaugurate new (and untested) industries in Negros Occidental, such as shrimp and fish farming, the introduction of novel crops such as corn and rice and even (foolishly, some said) coffee and installing as owners and managers and workers the various men and (to a lesser degree) women and children (no younger than ten, though) whose entire ways of life had historically been shaped by the sugar industry—up until its precipitous decline. The markets for Philippine sugar had long been usurped by places like Cuba. Now what little cultivation remained of the fields attached to the ancient sugar barons' haciendas seemed symbolic more than practical and profitable. What little employment there was on the remaining sugar fields was unsteady and only for a small window of time, the rest undertaken by modern (and cheaper) machinery. Only a handful of workers were needed to clear a starting patch of field before the mechanized harvesters took over.

Virginie was the Frenchwoman's name. Shaking Caracera's hand, she repeated what she had said to him over the phone: I don't think this is a good idea.

The museum had been started by Virginie and the locals as a gesture of civic pride as well as for the benefit of tourists. Inside, Virginie took her guests through a pasteboard-walled maze, stopping before each picture to explain in her accented English. The stories she told attested to her deep knowledge and almost prickly custodianship of this part of the country and its residents; if she hadn't arrived, who knows but that the history of the sugar industry, paid no more than lip service to by the rest of the country and by historians seeking to flatten the Philippines into a mere map of salient "contributions" (meaning crops) from each province, might evanesce and never be known by future generations?

Here they were, stopped before this black-and-white picture: three sugarcane cutters regarding the camera with wide smiles, their eyes twinkling, as if their livelihoods required none of the heavy labor of lore. Around their necks were rags, which were not scarves but masks traditionally worn over their mouths to keep the insects that proliferated in the fields from getting in, and also over their ears and the sides of their faces to protect them from leaf cuts, and also their noses when the leaves that had been hacked off the canes became smoking bonfires. Virginie told them all this, shaking her head the whole time. It was only to oblige the photographer that the men had pulled down these rags. From this it could be assumed that the photograph had been taken for the Department of Tourism. Virginie also pointed out the padded elbows and knees of the workers, formed too from rags, which had been wound around the joints again and again until the desired thickness had been achieved. This was to protect the men from leaf cuts as well as from the knocking of the stalks against their bodies.

A few steps farther on was a photograph of some cane workers on Cuban fields, migrants from Haiti. They too had the same choking rags, but instead of bundled-up pieces of cloth to protect their joints they had shiny metal caps, making them look like harried, constantly injured roller skaters. The purpose of this picture's proximity to the image of the Filipino cane cutters was to say that everywhere in the world the "blacks" were united by oppression, dispensable cogs in the capitalist machinery.

At some point, Marta left the room. Stan was awaiting the conclusion of the tour so he could drive the three to an empty house Virginie had helped to procure.

Was he tired? Virginie asked after they had gone through the exhibit.

Caracera said he was, but not too tired to discuss his plans with her.

She told him that any discussion would not find her deviating from what she'd already said.

How could the poverty-stricken workers not use financial help?

This was a retread of the phone conversation which had done nothing to dissuade Caracera, and she let her exasperation show on her face. First off, the descendants of the original workers Caracera referred to—the *sacadas*—who toiled the fields during the industry's prime, from roughly the turn of the century to the 1920s and '30s, had dispersed to other locations. They were itinerant by nature and went wherever the work was. The only descendants of those sugar workers remaining in the area were in the handful of graveyards scattered across the countryside. The only act of reparation these people needed was already being undertaken by Virginie. Every year, during All Souls' Day (which celebration she capitulated to as a symbol of goodwill), she paid local children to place sugar cubes on the earth above the graves. This was, of course, a borrowing from the Mexican tradition.

And second, what would Mr. James Smith (as Caracera had introduced himself) gain by offering his money?

In Manila, despite his features, which were clearly not fully white, the citizenry could be intimidated into thinking otherwise by his frosted glasses, his perfect English, his royal, perturbed manner suggesting he'd found himself in an environment far beneath him. To them, as to the *Metro Manila Register* (which had made of him and Harvey Keitel comic fraternal twins), he was American through and through. He played up to this image whenever it suited him and found that he got what he wanted quickly, a kind of deference suitable to a minor deity or celebrity. It did not occur to him to wonder at the paradoxical benefit of Filipino humility during these instances.

Now he tried the same huffy American act on the Frenchwoman. The money was charity, he said.

Charity? asked Virginie with accustomed suspicion. What was the purpose of his organization giving away money to the *sacadas*?

They want to help.

And how would they be helping themselves in the process? What was in it for them?

It was the intention of his organization, the American Society for Foreign Aid, to identify need all around the world and address it. He hadn't counted on how difficult it would be to give money away. However, once he realized that he couldn't do it, or rather that the Frenchwoman wouldn't allow him to do it, without turning not just slightly ridiculous but ridiculous on the order of a French farce (how apropos), he was surprised by how easy it was to be a fool. How easy it was to be led into a territory where the American Society for Foreign Aid was a perfectly feasible place to be from. Among the duties of such an office would be to learn to keep a straight face while telling the most outrageous lies and perhaps to oblige with a pratfall or two to dramatize an abject, winning humility which he didn't possess. He felt he was performing for the entertainment of some deity (perhaps his dead father, whose ghost the caretakers had claimed to have seen) and didn't know whether the woman's suspicion was a function of the Third World craziness or simply that he was being punished for trying to do the right thing.

Addressing it *financially*? Virginie asked with dramatic disregard.

Her facial contortions were aimed at the tactics she considered lamentably, lampoonably standard American: money as the salve for all things.

Meanwhile, Goyanos stood silently by, refusing to comment or look at his friend, who had disregarded his advice to simply tell the truth and was now burying himself in inextricable fraud with each step.

It was important for Caracera, so he had said, that his deed be done anonymously and that it should not be traced back to him and especially not to the family. Giving his name would be tantamount to boasting, he said.

Goyanos had not understood. What was so embarrassing about doing good? It was, he assured Caracera, just as Jesus would have done. Imitation of Christ, remember?

Fuck Jesus Christ, Caracera had huffed, putting an end to the argument.

Let him be, thought Goyanos now. Each lie would lead to another, in increasing magnitude of preposterousness, and when the whole thing collapsed in on him, the impact would be a pleasure to witness.

Virginie asked Caracera what other "places of need" his organization had ministered to.

Rwanda, Caracera replied, giving no confidence.

What did you do there?

Caracera dashed off salient nouns from his newspaper reading: Hutus, Tutsis, intra-ethnic warfare and massacre.

Yes, yes, Virginie cut in. But what did his group *do*?

Refugee housing.

Refugee housing, she repeated.

Along the border.

In exchange for what? Providing the refugees with brand-name products from companies who underwrote his endeavors and who wanted to start Third World market campaigns and consumer demand at ground zero? Or who wanted to be provided touching pictures for their year-end report brochure?

Caracera couldn't believe what he was hearing. Apparently the woman had had a tortuous history with handouts.

And anyway, how was she to know that Caracera's organization had not partnered with the nefarious Philippine government, whose post-Marcos leaders had done nothing to stem the system's cronyism and corruption, the same people who were still seeking to take a cut from the paltry proceeds of the as-good-as-dead sugar industry, and who had been trying to undermine Virginie from the very moment she'd set up shop in Silay? How was she to know that he, James Smith of the US of A, was not another journalist encouraged by the Filipino government to do an exposé of Virginie's "white patronization" of the Negros townsfolk, or, better yet, to trump up evidence of abuse or mismanagement so that Virginie could be cleared out of the way for devious and greedy government officials to do their vampiric tasks?

I'm not affiliated with any of those things.

At any rate, said the Frenchwoman, things were going great and she didn't need the interference—or help, whatever he chose to call it—of another party.

What if I offered to make a contribution to you and your organization to help—

Didn't he hear what she'd just said? She didn't need any *help*. And how did he know that she could be trusted with the money in the first place?

He wished she hadn't asked that question. So your resources are boundless?

They were enough to do the job.

How about if he increased the salaries of her workers?

You mean *bribe* them.

No, help. With each utterance, the word grew in senselessness.

She painted a dark portrait of what the villagers would do with his bonus: The men abandoning families to go to Manila and take up with whores, finally being able to afford the easy life promulgated by the Filipino and American movies they saw. The women refurbishing their humble homes with imported appliances, the money run through at a clip. The children being rewarded for their stopgap schooling and poor ambitions with video games and shiny new TV sets. These people, said Virginie, need the discipline of industry, and to have the connection between money and hard work reinforced.

These people? thought Caracera. Though wasn't that how he himself referred to them?

He was so exhausted. He asked her whether the driver had a mistaken idea of their purpose, mentioning the trip to the Church of the Angry Jesus.

Virginie was apologetic. She explained that Stan did this for each of her visitors despite her having told him not to. She was an atheist, and the driver, a fervent Catholic (rabid, she would even say), knew this. He had felt duty-bound to defuse her perceived ministry (the atheism, not the sugar activism) by warning her guests of Jesus' intolerance as the prelude to each of their visits. Not only had Stan devised this corrective but he'd enlisted the other drivers who worked for the rental company to follow suit. Now they took as their first detour for all Virginie's guests, as well as the other white tourists (figuring they would soon be friends of Virginie), a stop at the Church of the Angry Jesus. No scolding on her part, not even her assurances that there was no such thing as a ministry of atheists—worshiping what? a big nothing?—could convince the drivers to stop, so she might as well get used to their shenanigans. She was sorry that she hadn't warned Caracera beforehand.

Caracera didn't feel like acknowledging his shared beliefs.

The hacienda had three small chandeliers that hung in the middle of the vast *sala*, over which were spread antique sideboards, chairs, coffee tables, armoires and a gorgeous oil-stained upright piano done in mahogany ("*hecho en Barcelona, España*"), which stood next to one of the three big sliding windows. The view was of a dense growth of trees among which were peppered the red-orangeish blossoms of the *gumamela*, with their protruberant central style and anthers looking like lurid toilet brushes.

On tabletops stood various ancient *santos* with their arms either raised in a gesture of welcome or clasped in prayer. Even more impressive were their beseeching, mournful faces with the downturned lips (as if devoutness's strongest requirement were disapproval) that not even the corrosion of time and the usual neglect could soften.

They were directed by a maid to the available bedrooms, all at the back of the second floor. These rooms overlooked the back of several sugarcane fields, a few storage shacks (or were they living and resting quarters?) faintly visible in the distance, their rusted galvanized tin roofs blending in with the dark stalks.

They each chose a room. Marta Goyanos fell asleep instantly, while the two reunited friends were served a *merienda* by the maid, who had to be persuaded to let them eat in the clay-tiled kitchen with the gleaming modern microwave and Gaggenau stove ("Imported," whistled Goyanos).

The house, it turned out, was no simple guest home procured for their visit but was in fact owned, and had been painstakingly restored and reinforced, by Virginie Duhamel of Duhamel, Inc., a business partnership formed with governmental assistance and with monetary investment from several foreign concerns.

They discovered this not altogether reassuring fact at dinner, surprised to see Virginie emerge (as soundlessly as she had apparently come into the house) from a master bedroom, dressed in insubstantial slippers and loose silk pajamas. She walked to the head of the long dining table, taking note of her guests' surprise. How do you like my house? she asked, not accustomed to anything but praise, which she promptly received.

So this was it, thought Caracera. How could she trust him if she herself had built her organization on the principles of self-interest and profit?

Goyanos too was made uncomfortable, though he acknowledged that foreigners always instinctively made him feel prosecutorial.

Where was Marta Goyanos? She had not returned from her postnap walk, though there was probably no cause for worry: how could she score drugs in this backwater?

Her father was calm until Caracera brought up the European teenagers they had driven past that morning.

Stan was dispatched to look for the girl and told not to return until he'd found her.

After dinner they gathered in the sala for coffee and were joined by a young Filipina named Iris Nicolas, who was Virginie's assistant.

Without warning, Caracera got up and disappeared into his bedroom. He returned with the bowling ball bag of money. Goyanos looked at his friend. A strange expression of serenity had come over Caracera's face.

The Frenchwoman, who did not know what was in the bag, tensed her body, sitting back.

Caracera opened the bag and proceeded to take out stack upon stack of bills, placing them on the coffee table. The Frenchwoman asked him what he thought he was doing but he kept on. Soon a pyramid of bills formed—twenty-peso denominations in batches of a hundred, totaling five million pesos or roughly a hundred thousand dollars.

What do you suggest I do with this? he asked Virginie, who didn't know what to say. The look on her assistant Iris Nicolas's face, at once alert and sheepish, suggested she was being made to witness something pornographic.

What will I do with this, seeing that you won't take it?

Put it away. My mind won't be changed that easily. She turned to look at her assistant, who immediately looked away, as if having been caught doing something wrong.

The scene was interrupted by the entrance of Marta Goyanos. The girl, who acted as if she didn't know what she'd done, was accompanied by the driver Stan, who could hardly look at the money. He took his leave nearly at once.

Marta Goyanos also tried to disregard the money, but anger sparked in her, and she had to train her eyes on Caracera. She was sure he was using the bills as a front for disreputable motives.

Goyanos excused himself to take his daughter to her room.

Put your money away, said Virginie.

Iris Nicolas hadn't looked up at all.

There's nothing wrong with my money, assured Caracera.

You fool, she said. Who walks around with a bag full of cash? Do you know where you are?!

I don't understand why anyone won't accept help.

Get out of my house now, she said, standing up. She knocked the pyramid off the table. Stacks scattered across the table and some fell to the floor. It was surprising what an insubstantial noise they made. Get out, she repeated.

Goyanos returned shortly. He knew something had gone wrong and regretted having missed it.

Caracera looked up at his friend, who wordlessly remained at the periphery of the scene.

Suddenly Virginie turned toward a window. She heard the sound first.

Quick, she said, her face drained of blood. Get rid of the money. Her eyes locked with Caracera's, and now he could hear it too. A vehicle, low-humming, pulling up the drive to the front door. Newly pricked, his ears registered other, shocking noises: chiefly crickets, with their mechanistic racket, like a movie soundtrack encouraging mayhem to unfold.

Iris Nicolas took the leather bag and stretched its mouth wide, as if trying to rip it apart, as everyone threw the stacks back in. Caracera and Goyanos exchanged the briefest of looks—in each pair of eyes a ratification of the other's wild disbelief—and yet it was not enough to snap them out of a sensation of acting under some sort of spell, their movements lightning-fast, clearly etched.

Some of the money fell from their nervous grasps but was quickly retrieved, thrown into the bag.

Caracera had no idea how they managed to act so quickly. But by the time the five men, headed by their leader, a young mustached man wearing what could have been a pajama bottom as a pirate's head scarf (Somehow I was expecting worse, thought Caracera), came into the room, the money had been disposed of.

The Frenchwoman had just restored a loose plank of the living room floor and put one foot over it to hear the decisive snap as it was secured, the bag with the money in a hollow under her feet—under all their feet—when the leader approached, striding into the room with a frequent guest's foreknowledge of the lay of the land.

Caracera wasn't sure if the man hadn't caught even the slightest flutter of the Frenchwoman's pants leg, or seen her put one foot oddly in front of the other, like a model, or even if he hadn't heard the giveaway clank of the restored plank. The transition from before to after he himself registered in five quick heartbeats, further accordion-compressed by uncomprehending panic; it seemed as if no sooner had he thrown the last of his stack into the bag than he was listening to the young man ask, Where's the money?

What are you talking about? Virginie asked the man, who circled around each party, frozen in place. The way they looked, they might simply be playing a game.

The man's comrades stood congealed at the top of the steps, blocking access, alternating their weight from one hip to the other.

The leader, who could be no more than thirty, laughed. He had bad teeth. It seemed Virginie's contempt was as much for this as it was a show to stoke up her companions' courage, saying that the men understood power and would get nowhere if they knew the group to be unwilling to relinquish any.

Who's the guy with the money? asked the leader, though he knew, for he stared at Caracera.

What do you want? asked Goyanos.

You're the guy? The leader, confused, moved to Goyanos.

What do you want? Goyanos repeated.

There is no money, said Virginie.

Iris Nicolas was biting her lip so hard it began to bleed. She sucked her lips inward.

One of the men whistled. The note hung low.

Caracera thought of Marta Goyanos in her room, as well as the maid.

The men had arrived, it appeared, carrying nothing except an air of hostile insinuation. No guns, no knives, nothing tucked into the waistbands of their high-water pants, nothing tucked in the space between their mud-caked, thick-soled boots and their bare legs.

You are lying, said the leader to Virginie.

Where's the money then? she challenged.

Where did you hiding it? You. The leader wheeled to face Caracera, staring him eye to eye.

There's no money, Caracera echoed, though he couldn't muster Virginie's conviction.

Did the leader sense this? Where had they come from? Who had squealed about Caracera's presence, his purpose? Had this happened before, accounting for Virginie's aplomb, and the fact of the hidden cavity underfoot, which was like a fairy-tale surprise and which, along with the subsequent surprise of the fairy-tale villains, dressed in ethnic pirate gear like playing dress-up or at Halloween, made Caracera feel like he too was not quite real? Or had Virginie herself arranged this to test him? Or to swindle him? Clearly this beautiful mansion with its museum-quality furnishings had not been gotten by default or simply through good works.

She was the only person other than the leader to attempt movement, bravely. Interceding on Caracera's behalf, she said, The money's gone. It's been given away. She laughed, the laughter saying, Too late for you.

Marta Goyanos stepped into the scene. Her punky demeanor was part and parcel of the ongoing sense of kinked enchantment.

What the fuck, she said.

The leader looked at the girl.

Go back to your room, ordered the girl's father.

Where's the money? the leader asked once more. He was talking to the girl, though as soon as the question was asked, he looked away from her and toward Caracera. Had he gotten hold of a *Metro Manila Register* in which the American James Smith had appeared as the mestizo Roger Caracera, a new, interim General MacArthur, and was he going to reveal the fraud to Virginie, ending the French farce and beginning a Filipino tragedy, capped by inevitable violence?

Marta stood there without saying a word, though she swiveled her head to take in her father, her father's friend, the Frenchwoman and, at the top of the staircase, the four pirates with their awakened interest in the scene, four pairs of eyes fused into a single giant bull's-eye which centered on the heat-giving presence of the young girl.

One of the men said something in Ilonggo, words obviously obscene. His friends laughed.

Benjamin Goyanos, who had been somewhat relieved to see that the men were weaponless, now knew he'd made a premature judgment. They had weapons enough for rape, a crime which the presence of his daughter brought into relief. Before, the thought of either Virginie or her assistant being attacked may or may not have crossed his mind. If it had, it clearly had no weight, as it did now.

The leader grabbed Virginie by the throat.

The other four gasped, started, staying in place.

Virginie wrenched herself free. You came too late, she spat out. Better luck next time. Now are you going to leave?

The leader made a move toward Marta Goyanos.

Caracera saw Benjamin Goyanos flinch.

But before either man, both with mouths open, could give away the game, they heard Marta Goyanos's high-pitched voice: They were counting it just a moment ago.

Virginie was seething.

Iris Nicolas gave an instinctive yelp, as if she'd been pricked by a needle. She looked down at her feet, though it was useless: even the top of her head seemed to be deliquescing.

It's gone, someone came and took it just now, claimed Virginie.

Where is it? the lead pirate asked the young girl.

Ask them, squeaked Marta.

Where is it?

I told you. *They* were counting it.

Marta! her father shouted.

Caracera tried not to look at anyone. All that effort to get here, that planning, acquiring the help of a woman he had, typically, only wavering faith in—and for what?

He heard himself say, tired and without conviction, anticipating failure, It's all gone.

The leader said, We are searching-searching!

How many times have you done that before? Virginie asked.

The leader only swallowed spit. He nodded to his men, who broke through the unseen barrier that had previously kept them from entering.

Have you ever found anything before? Virginie, moving to the leader, challenged.

The men could be seen disappearing into the rooms.

You fucking—!

The leader hadn't moved from where he stood next to Marta Goyanos. So the money's here?

I don't know, she replied. I was—I was asleep.

Sleeping? The leader was tickled by the idea.

A scream was heard in one of the rooms. The maid came out, trailed by one of the henchmen. He wore a yellow T-shirt the letters of which seemed to have been rubbed off on the back of another man's shirt. Did they all sleep together, in confined quarters? Caracera was momentarily distracted from the men's violence to consider that he could, by paying them off, not only end this unfortunate scene but also provide them needed help. They looked like they could use some cash. Look, he thought, they don't even have weapons.

The maid rushed to Virginie, who put an arm around her. Virginie said something in Ilonggo, and the maid calmed down.

You won't find anything! the Frenchwoman screamed, to no avail. Noises of things being strewn about, which seemed to Caracera exaggerated for effect, made the house into a giant box the purpose of which was to send sound out into the night, stilling, for a moment, the crickets, the mosquitoes, the burry croaks and creaks of a thousand unseen things.

I'll give you the money! the Frenchwoman finally relented.

Caracera had to put his hands to his lips to make sure they hadn't moved to utter the words. He felt as if he had spoken them—they were the very same words poised at the brink of his mouth.

Tell your men to stop, said Virginie, with the house-proud's fear of desecration.

You first, replied the leader.

Virginie knelt down.

Caracera burned a hole into where Marta Goyanos stood, but she refused to return his gaze. Her father looked at his feet, stricken with shame.

Virginie began, with exaggerated carefulness, to pick up the plank from the floor.

The leader raised an eyebrow. He shouted something. The men stopped their racket and came out, surrounding the action.

The plank was up. Virginie's hands were rooting inside the cavity. A look came into her face suggesting she'd found what she was looking for.

Caracera didn't realize what he was staring at until he saw the leader rear back, both eyebrows tautened. And even then he was unsure whether he was actually seeing a gun in the Frenchwoman's hand or had been merely hoping for it, so strongly as to have hallucinated it. Only until he heard Virginie say, Get out, I know how to use this, was he finally sure, and, oddly, uncheered.

Virginie switched from pointing at the leader to aiming at his henchmen, who suddenly stopped glowering and, following the conducting motions of the arm holding the gun, swished to one side, away from Virginie's party.

The gun made Caracera feel detached from the scene because it was the confirming facet of the dream he was in—first the hiding space under the floorboards, then the comic villains, and now, of course, a gun—and not even when Virginie shot at the leader, who may or may not have made a sudden move, did he quite snap out of his sense of looking up from the bottom of a body of water.

It turned out that the Frenchwoman had aimed not at the man but in his direction. The bullet was heard to lodge somewhere in the back of the house. What must it have cost the Frenchwoman to shoot at her own beloved possessions? Impressed on her stoic face was a look only Caracera could see: the look of his Aunt Irene, with her custodian's dismay at the prospect of disarray.

The leader, accompanied by his men, departed, doing this leisurely, dramatically. The man did not glower, but was instead smiling as if he had a foreknowledge that things would eventually turn out well for him. This made his spoken threat of return even more unnerving.

Yes, replied the Frenchwoman. And the police will be here waiting for you.

After the men had pulled away, Virginie placed a call to the local police station. We'll pay for a bodyguard, make that two, she barked into the phone.

A half hour later, the cops were on the scene taking notes. The bullet was discovered to have lodged in a leg of the dining room table. This was attributed to the men who had just left, who carried several guns, which Virginie later amended to a single gun. The possession of hers was not disclosed, and those present had been told not to say anything.

The thing that Virginie regretted most, it turned out, was not that she had had to deface her treasured furnishings but that another hiding place would have to be devised, the cavity under the floorboard now useless.

Two policemen stayed behind, one posted at the front door, the other at the back, just below the kitchen window.

Virginie, sleeping with her gun under her pillow, stashed the bag of money underneath the bed. Beside her slept the assistant Iris Nicolas, who had been too scared to venture into the night and back home. At the foot of the bed, on a straw mat, lay the maid.

The next morning, Caracera shook the Frenchwoman's hand and

apologized. Virginie knew no sermon was needed. She couldn't have done a more persuasive job of putting the American off if she paid for things herself.

You've dealt with these people before, Caracera said, a trace of admiration in his voice. Looking at her, he thought, Another woman with frontier toughness, another savior. What was it about the Philippines that continued to compel these people? He thought of his own mother, Teresa, in the Peace Corps provinces of her storied youth, pre-Jesus Caracera, pre-children, before pushing the image out of his head.

There are mercenaries all over the world, Virginie replied simply, hinting that she could catalogue a long history of entanglement if she cared to.

What are you going to do if they come back?

There's always the police. And my gun. Then she waved both the thought and the man who occasioned it away.

Goyanos had brought along a video camera for the trip, and that morning was spent cramming in a profusion of scenes.

They stopped to inspect two impressive haciendas with ghostly auras. This was a good indication that the houses were closed for the season, unguarded. But when Goyanos pointed his camera into their windows, which he had to first slide open with some effort, scenes of eerie abandonment greeted the lens. The ceilings were hung with cobwebs, the floors coated with dust, the rooms devoid of furniture except, oddly, here and there, razzy mattresses that appeared to have islands of dried wetness. Squatters, supposed Goyanos.

On the way to the airport, they picked up Marta. She had insisted on some time alone to try to get over the events of the previous night and had been driven by Stan to the beach, an hour away. They found her sitting by herself, a single, desolate dot turned halfway between the water and a group of wilting teenagers, the Europeans, who were variously sitting up, looking at nothing, or lying on raggedy towels, staring at the sky. At the periphery of this scene were fishermen, skins bronzed, some futzing with their nets, others making repairs to their boats, long, thin canoes outfitted with bamboo outriggers, still others in the distance fishing.

It would be hard to imagine into what shapes they were being transmogrified by the drugs the European kids seemed to have taken.

Why were they here? A detour from, or prior to, the more popular trekking spots of Thailand? Was the Philippines a large virgin rave scene waiting to be uncovered? Were the European kids actors on break from film shoots, new and yet to be reported on? Children of missionaries, like Frannie Prusso's daughter fast-forwarded a few years, turned roving band of vengeance-seeking lapsed Catholics? Did they live off what they could make from petty theft? Where did they sleep? On the beaches, hopping from province to province?

Goyanos mentioned seeing the mattresses inside one of the empty haciendas.

He caught his daughter on tape, a glowering thing dropped from the sky, contaminating the scene, before they flagged her attention. Then they headed to the airport.

Caracera continued to make a point of not looking at the girl. She more than understood, keeping her distance.

Ernesto was there to meet them at the airport in Manila. The father and daughter were bewildered to find their car gone. Had Goyanos misremembered the location? Finally, they accepted that they had become victims of theft. Rings had been stealing from the airport lot, they knew this, though the danger was thought to have long passed, curbed by increased police patrolling.

The cops must be involved, Caracera said, and, in throwing it out so reflexively, felt as if he'd been living here for years, inured to a fact of existence that ought to be properly greeted with outrage or fear.

Caracera had to bear the presence of the young girl a bit longer.

In traffic, her indignation was reignited by the children tapping at their windows, selling cigarettes, garlands of sampaguita blossoms, religious medals and pocket-sized laminated pictures of Jesus and Mary, or simply begging. What, she asked, did you think the money would do? She didn't look at Caracera, and though by using the word "you" could've been talking of both her father and his friend, she knew they would understand whom she was singling out.

Caracera's anger, hours later, had not cooled, and he would make sure, until the girl had been disposed of, to keep his spine punishingly straight.

The friends parted with looks of weary commiseration and met again two days later. They sat outdoors in a café in Remedios Circle, a hip and busy center patronized by the city's rising writers, artists, actors, intellectuals. Thankfully, Goyanos didn't bring his daughter.

Goyanos told his friend that a detective had been hired to track down the lawyers for Caracera's Uncle Eustacio. This was the same man Goyanos used to scope information on his clients' opposition. A discreet man. Highly effective. Justifying his costliness. Though, of course, as his friend had said, money was no object.

Caracera had Goyanos engage a young student in conversation.

Caracera was introduced as someone who wanted to hear the opinions of the "next generation." The student looked at the sunglassed man, trying to place the face but finally unable to.

Would the student be impressed or angered by knowing the man was "from America"? Which (Flip)side would he show Caracera, the one enamored of American pop, or the one critical of American military and business intervention? Caracera held his breath.

The look from the student was neutral. He shook Caracera's hand. He hesitated in his answer. Perhaps he was flattered by being singled out among the crowd.

He said he went to the University of Santo Tomas. He was in his third year of studying literature, emphasis on English literature. He planned to go to the States someday to extend his studies, and so could not have been entirely antipathetic to the idea of America.

About the Philippines he said what Caracera had heard before, though he couldn't exactly pinpoint where. The country's problems were due to its history of being colonized, its character a Frankenstein of contradictory legacies: from the Spaniards, the repulsion of the flesh; from the Americans, the belief in pleasure above all else; and from the Japanese, who were brief conquerors during the Second World War, a frightening mirror image of what, as Asians, they could become if infected with too much ambition—the perverse dead end of the virtues of industry and control.

But that was not how the young man, whose name was Nicanor Roldan, put it.

He put it like this: We were raised in a convent, then released into Hollywood. In between, we were given a sloppy education in business and success.

The first part of that statement—convent-to-Hollywood—was

what was familiar to Caracera, who was dismayed to hear it. Such a magazine-ready formulation, such American glibness.

Besides, had these people never heard of free will? Were the Filipinos forever to be damned by the past, shackled to it, unable to exert any contradicting effort on their own behalf, pushing into the present with the necessary correctives?

And now here was the next generation, and what could they offer? Parroting.

Goyanos was talking to the young student, asking after his education. Goyanos too had gone to UST.

I will leave soon. It was the indisputable, if unexamined, flip side of the famous "I shall return."

I will leave soon. I am leaving. Had Harvey Keitel already left?

RENE CARACERA HAD CONVENED the party for one purpose: her nephew Roger, the willow in the dangerous wind, the only child of Jesus Caracera remaining in the Philippines, had to be straightened out. It was easy, in the neatly aligned world of the family, to spot the askew element. Everyone was here: the uncles and their wives, the cousins, and some of the cousins' friends, successful men and women who, by the handsomeness of their appearance, would be silent rebukes to Roger. But the forty-four-year-old was presenting the new version of himself that Irene had whipped up on a recent shopping expedition he had surprisingly asked her to undertake with him. The black stovepipe-leg pants, tapering from waist to hem, looked flattering on his—so he'd confessed, not without a little pride—newly thin body. So did the long-sleeved shirt, a bright red, a color he claimed to abhor, yet he had bought it and put it on because she had asked him to. By wearing it, those gathered would see that he was ready to turn over a new leaf. No one, Irene believed, would wear red unless they felt ready to withstand the scrutiny it brought. Red was Jesus' blood offered up every Sunday at mass, it was the color of love, it was one-third of the Philippine flag, it was her own favorite color.

This, of course, disregarded the shade's clear association—made most strongly by the movie *Jezebel* starring a defiant Bette Davis wearing a scandalous scarlet ball gown—with mischief and disdain.

Without having been told, the family seemed to understand the evening's purpose, and were working, to Irene Caracera's great pleasure, in a rhythmic concert of effort. Roger seemed always cornered by individuals or parties who promptly engaged him in Q&A's before he was eventually surrendered to other groups who took up, with varying degrees of obviousness, the same tasks. A cousin had brought along an estate planner who asked Roger what he intended to do with his money: this was the big question of the evening. Irene Caracera had come to the conclusion that the money was not, finally, Roger's but the family's and had to be defended against the beneficiary's wayward tendencies.

Whatever infamy he chose for himself—and, more importantly, for the money—in the United States would reflect on him solely, but as long as he was still in Manila, a city filled with enemies eager to undo Irene's hard work by malicious gossip and clever insinuation, any foolish errand Roger tackled would be understood to be endorsed by the family and seen to extend its already long list of follies. The family had long been the subject of bad *tsismis* but that was only to be expected of a clan whose high visibility made it a frequent magnet for resentment and ill will. What mattered most was that none of this bad word of mouth had managed to disgrace them permanently. True, the family was no longer in its prime, but they continued to command respect for managing to persevere, and plaques bearing their name in a number of venerable institutions across the city (hospital wards and concert halls, to cite only a few examples) kept their reputation alive for future generations. Irene Caracera had been elevated by her marriage into the dynasty but now it was the dynasty that was being kept afloat by her diligence as a society matron.

Surrounded by his family, Roger would be made to understand that their love could take the form of infinite tolerance and even amusement, but also, should he continue to repudiate them, for example by going to Negros with his dangerous and shaming plans, they could bring to bear stern, exacting punishment. A few fools had learned this lesson too late. Eustacio Caracera had been banished, and so had

Irene's son. As for Teresa Caracera, she had earmarked herself for a tragic fate from the start. The Caraceras could only slightly exacerbate her congenital talent for dissatisfaction. Truth be told, it pleased Irene Caracera, when talking of what happened to Teresa, hospitalization and all, to insinuate that it was indeed the family, powerful especially when disobeyed, that had brought about such a tragic conclusion to the woman's story. Beware, was the warning proffered by this version.

Irene still hadn't decided whether to let Roger know that she knew of his trip. Because he had not told anyone in the family that he'd sneaked away to Bacolod, he would most likely conclude that the driver Ernesto had snitched on him. Ernesto was too useful for her to give him up just yet.

Nobody in the family but Irene knew, of course. This was among the reasons she had become as good as the head of the Caracera clan. She had what seemed like infinite resources for gathering information—what some women of her circle unflatteringly called her octopus tentacles—and she knew when to withhold it and when to let it loose, harnessing its full potential.

Specially because his trip to Negros had come to nothing, Irene hoped that Roger would no longer need to be confronted and counseled about the money. She hoped the lesson was fully learned: the money had a mind of its own and would create difficulties for its handler should the right outlet for its dispersal not be found. Irene, like any good Catholic in front of plaster statuary, believed in animating spirits; in this instance, the money was filled and made alive by Jesus Caracera, among the best sons of the clan and whose intentions for the money would not now be mangled by the bad seed Roger.

Money was for enjoyment. It was for the purchase of a red shirt to advertise your moral stature—a prime cause for celebration.

It bought weekly routines of pampering from her coterie of young gay men, massages and haircuts and beauty sessions that were consolations for the loss of her youth and beauty and the loss of the emblem that justified and was supposed to make bearable such losses in the first place: her druggie son, whose name she could never speak. Money provided a battery of air-conditioned cars and, to drive them, drivers with licenses for guns, shielding you from the bother, inconvenience and danger of the city's lesser sections. Money was not tantamount to total insulation from the world, however: there were the aforementioned plaques in the hospital wards and concert halls that attested to the family's generosity and awareness of quarters of need.

The Negros sugar workers did not *need*. She chided herself for having made a bad joke which Roger, in his infinite perversity, had sought to turn on her.

The workers were *workers* and what workers did was, of course, work. Their lot was one of hard labor and scant pay. They were at an endeavor's starting point where cost had to be kept low or there would be no money left to see the process through to the end: the refining, the packaging, the distribution, the warehousing, the advertising and, most costly of all under the Marcos regime, the kickbacks. Everyone knew that, even the sugar workers. This was the way of business, nothing personal. And besides, not everyone could be the boss. In this world, there were servers and those whom they served. If everyone was sitting around waiting to be served, who would do the serving? This kind of ruthless, clear-eyed logic cut through the liberal pretensions and foggy romanticism of her nephew Roger, which he'd inherited from his mother, and which, with five hundred thousand dollars, he'd intended to amplify.

What do you propose to do with the money? Again and again, as if to bring him around, this question was asked, and throughout the evening his face was seen to glaze over with a willed cheerfulness, though the tone of his voice, when Irene drew near, was beginning to be curdled.

Don't mind them, she told him, acting the protector. They all want what's best for you, it's just they don't know how else to express themselves.

What had he been telling them? He wasn't sure. He hadn't made up his mind. In fact, he had absolutely no idea.

Why not spend it on himself? they'd asked. But he had, he replied, indicating his shirt, his pants, his shoes and, by arcing his hand, meaning too to include his thin body, which benefited from a membership to his uncle's gym, where film actors worked out to the intense scrutiny of the rest of the members.

Irene replied that clearly they could see that the money was doing him good and wanted to encourage him to keep spending it on himself. He was a forty-four-year-old man, and at the risk of repeating herself, life was only going to get tougher, and wasn't it good that he had a buffer against the creeping discomforts and humiliations of age, which his father intended him to have by leaving him the money? Why else had Jesus decided to give Roger double the amount he left Roberto and Socorro? Wasn't it because the old man knew that the older children had fashioned lives capable of protecting them from fate's capriciousness while the youngest one hadn't? Oh, she didn't mean to make a judgment on his life and the choices he'd made, but perhaps in the quest for a higher ideal (saying which, she gave no faith in her words) he had neglected to look out for practicalities. Certainly his teaching job at Columbia, much as he'd made it out to be fulfilling, wouldn't be enough to see him through retirement?

No, of course not, she laughed, the purpose of tonight's party wasn't to corner and chastise him, like an unruly child. Saying so, she let slip by the expression on her face how important it was to keep the family's good name intact. Tonight had been intended as a check on whatever foolishness he had in mind. The fact that the party had come on the heels of his Negros trip (which, if it had been successful, would've brought them the unending scorn of their summertime neighbors)—well, surely he would know that that was no coincidence.

People want what's best for you, she reiterated. And by ensuring that you do what's best for you, they'll know that you'll be extending the family's good name. Like it or not, she said, you're still a Caracera.

He gave her a look to let her know he doubted her lines. What was best for him?

Well, why else would people be here? Irene asked. His father's death had been a sad cause for gathering, and now they needed the opposite. A celebration.

Celebration of what?

You, Roger. To welcome you. To thank you for deciding to stay here in Manila and not going back so soon, like you initially planned to. This tells us, she continued, that you are willing to give the family a chance. Your past—it's all here. You're willing to consider that none of us are irrelevant to your life.

He was stumped, unable to provide a contradicting reason for his decision to stay. The words and images that came to mind could not be communicated to the woman, who would only dismiss them as characteristic attempts at outrageousness.

A young boy lost by his parents, a missionary couple, in the southern provinces of Mindanao in the late eighties and feared either dead or adopted by Communist mountain rebels had been recently discovered—alive and in the interior jungle. This child, reported nearly every local tabloid on the front pages, had survived by hunting game and drinking from a forest lagoon and, more importantly, by being able to tell apart edible and poisonous plants (helped along by a guidebook from his parents), growing up to be better than average in height and weight. With some difficulty, he had been able to communicate and tell of his adventures, using a few remembered bits of English aided by a lot of pantomime gestures and what could only be described as animal sounds.

The passage of time for the boy was demarcated by the sun's disappearance and appearance, and in between, the hours meant nothing more than an epic span filled with the various sounds of the jungle, a different set of animals for night and day and, all throughout, the sound of the lagoon sluicing on rocks.

In this scenario of unending, unvarying alternation between light and dark, between one set of noise and another, the hours nothing more than a vast, naked exposure to nature's countless fibrillations and caprices, the boy had simply let his mind wander, letting it go soft, while his body hardened with work—gathering food, building one dwelling after another, avoiding detection by predators animal and human. He had no idea how much time had elapsed and he grew to forget who he was and where he'd come from.

The most askew thing in this already fantastical tale—the thing which all the papers seized on with the practiced credulousness and reverence instilled by years of having to report on sightings of the Virgin Mary or God—had to do with how the boy had been able to avoid detection for more than a dozen years.

Over the boy's skin had grown a layer of moss, in essence making him a green thing surrounded by many other green things. The moss had not embedded itself with roots but could be brushed off and the skin underneath cleaned, but a few days later, a new layer would be seen to start sprouting, as if the boy had taken a bath in green water.

This was what Caracera felt had happened to him, which he could not tell Irene. The humidity and the rains could partly explain this feeling. The rest he didn't know how to account for. There seemed over his skin a layer that was mosslike, but unlike the boy's, his was invisible. His movements were slowed, his speech robbed of the more complex vocabulary of his teacher self—moss on his tongue. And enshrouding his brain, a kind of mist or tropical vapor that would occasionally retreat and make clear a few mysteries of the country's sights and customs, but which he would only remember for that brief instant of clarity: a tease.

Did this mean that, like the boy, he too had found himself abandoned to the jungle?

"Jungles of the Philippines": could the words have meant more than he had initially apprehended? Was he being punished for not taking them seriously?

The woman caretaker, who had finally relented and confessed to being haunted by Jesus Caracera, had had to be calmed down and talked out of quitting. Caracera had gone into a there-are-no-such-things-as-ghosts sermon, but knew that there was no arguing against these deeply held beliefs, and knew also that there might not be any such things as ghosts where he lived, but in this place, who was he to say? This was part of the confusion he found himself in, and slowly, if fearfully, he felt his resistance slipping away, or rather being covered over by a different—for lack of a better word—skin, a new way of sensing things.

Into this scenario the money had been plopped as another fantastical element, marking him off from a former identity as a schoolteacher, where he stood in front of young men and women and opined with certainty, clarity, conviction, turning art, in a sense, into carpentry, a series of concrete, achievable steps. What was he going to do with this new, amazing thing that was the complete opposite of writing, received without known cause and to be disseminated, he was beginning to feel, without consequence?

That was it: in this place where the craziest thing was reported on with such fervent belief, making irrelevant any notions such as he'd preached to his students of cause and effect, of character being destiny, the money could be thrown away without making any sound.

This was his vacation from reality. Whatever he did would have no impact. It would have no means by which to chase him back home to the States. Wasn't he perhaps beginning to think just a little like the Australian men, for whom the Philippines was a zone of no responsibility?

What was he going to do with the money, what was he going to do? If he heard the question one more time he would start howling like some irate chimp, beating his chest. He saw the image of the jungle boy come to life and had to keep from laughing.

He saw his Aunt Irene looking at him as if she could read his thoughts, as if she'd ransacked his mind to make away with its most secret and treasured content—his trip to Bacolod. Extending the thought, he wondered if she had engineered its failure. Her powers and control were undoubtedly vast. She had only to snap her fingers, giving the flimsiest excuse, for all these people to gather. Jewelry, upswept and brilliantined hair, perfume, expensive and clearly underused footwear, the lethargic talk of social keeping-up—a veritable symphony of busybody, self-protecting wealth. He turned away.

On one hand, thought Irene, Roger had decided to prolong his stay in the Philippines. On the other, he had gone to Negros to humiliate the family.

On one hand, he was wearing a red shirt. On the other, he felt it necessary to continue a conversational tug-of-war with her, letting her sense that whatever peace he'd made with the family was only momentary, stopgap, and that perhaps he was gathering his energies for one more venture into a vengeful philanthropy.

What would it be? If only Irene knew, she could put a stop to it beforehand. Put the scare into her nephew-in-law. Jesus Caracera had said that he'd wanted his children to reestablish connection with their birthplace, and in his signature diabolical way, Roger was doing just that.

Suddenly the party began to appear to be a massive waste of effort. Perhaps the wives of the Caracera brothers knew the way it would turn out and had come to gloat over her failure. No, it couldn't be. She was tired and prone to pessimism.

They were afraid of her. If she had acted so mercilessly toward her own flesh and blood in order to preserve the new edifice of the family's reputation which she had been solely responsible for, then what could she do to them if they earned her ire?

How could she have known that entry into the Caracera clan would not be the full-stop achievement of her ambitions? At the time she married Amador, the family had once again risen to prominence through its sponsorship of the broadcast of old Filipino classics on television. Everywhere you turned, an ad for Caracera sugar could be seen. A new surge of prosperity promised to sweep the members along. But this, it turned out, was only a false front. How could she have been expected to understand that graft and corruption put a freeze on a majority of the money? How could she have known that Mr. Marcos, whom she had idolized as a child, exacted financial obeisance that would make the family success as good as fictive, and that what portion she would see of it would all be from Amador's personal savings, which, though it had not been paltry, could only be a figure subtracted from and diminished over the years?

How hard she had to work to prevent the dream of her marriage into the Caracera family from deteriorating into a moth-eaten, paltry thing.

There was so much work to do even at her advanced age and it never really got easier. Right down to having to lace a few chosen corners of the house, preferably at the unobtrusive back, near the garage and kitchen, with the sweet ooze of mangoes or pineapples or bananas or apples, and making sure too to leave the cut-open fruits on the ground to attract ants and keep them in the house. This way prosperity was ensured.

Her fear of relinquishing power guaranteed that she never delegated responsibility and took care of everything herself. This party, for instance. Calling up people, garnering promises of attendance, making sure that though nothing outright was said, everyone understood that they were to put the squeeze on her nephew-in-law: this party was "for Roger." Marshaling kitchen forces, hiring additional help, planning the menu with the cooks, checking that the drivers bought enough cases of soft drinks and beer and wine and that there was enough ice and buckets to store them in. All the while giving the appearance that these things had happened by themselves.

How easy it would be to adopt Roger's cavalier attitude, letting the fruits of her hard work all slip away. Her blood pressure would certainly decrease.

For tonight, to be able to put on her red dress, which tapered at the waist, she had to squeeze into a girdle. Long gone were the days when she watched what she ate because she was trying to keep her figure. Health was the primary consideration for everything. For valuable potassium to keep her blood pressure down, there were bananas. Night and day the ubiquitous bananas that turned instantly into mush inside her mouth. She believed these things: partaking of something long enough turned you into a new creature. Being around the Caraceras turned her into a natural-born aristocrat. And the bananas were beginning to turn her chimplike. There was the jut of her upper lip. And above it, in the space between her nose and mouth, could be seen, so she feared, a simian bulge.

She was so tired of having to fight nature. Two liposuction treatments—the second in Denmark, where some medical breakthrough made the patients' recidivism rates much lower—and that was all she was willing to suffer. Now the flesh around the girdle bulged and spilled out but she no longer cared. For the four-hours-plus of the party, she would breathe with constriction—and then it was back to the freedom of letting nature take its awful shape, letting it take its vengeance on her, who had so successfully kept it at bay for nearly a lifetime. Provincial girlhood, unsophisticated tastes, shame-making parents and siblings—all these had been subsumed, transformed, erased by her vaulting ambition and high intellect, which in turn were shaped by her encompassing laziness, her appreciation of money and the comforts it could buy.

She had not been one of those modern career women deluded into beliefs of equality with men. She had never seen work as anything but a heavy cart tied to a yoke around her neck. What she wanted and deserved was to be taken care of.

Meeting Amador at one of her socialite friends' parties had been a stroke of luck. She was pretty enough to be invited to these functions and, once there, comported herself with admirable confidence. This assurance was born of watching her parents and siblings hemming and hawing, acting humble in front of the world. It got them nothing more than contempt and she would not make the same mistake. Conversation with her was always a fascinating, opinionated, sometimes even volatile affair. She held forth on a number of subjects with old-fashioned, that was to say, pro-Marcos ardor, although her youth and background ought to have placed her on the opposition's side. Her friends must've thought that she was rehearsing for the part she would ultimately claim.

Amador was charmed by her and gradually began to be besotted. He was unlike what she'd heard of the Caraceras: steadfast, unspoiled, unpromiscuous. True, he wasn't as handsome as his older brother, the famous Jesus, but Irene knew she was not pretty enough to turn Jesus' head. By then he was already married, and though the wife was a haranguing bitch, Jesus, being a true Catholic, was never going to divorce her, and Irene could only hope to become a lowly mistress, one in a large stable of women Jesus famously kept as rotating standbys and who were no better, despite some of them being famous beauty queens and international personages, than servants.

The years of Irene and Amador's marriage, except for a tempestuous period of facing the public scrutiny brought on by their son's dazzling fall (she could so easily sympathize with Jesus), had been uneventful. Amador, as far as she knew, had not been unfaithful. And neither had she. They had been a good team. What would she do without him? The last years had been a steady stanching of a persistent and, it would seem, imminently victorious enemy. Amador was dying of lung cancer. Nothing was said to the family, although she suspected they knew. The lung operation he went through, though successful, had severely depleted him. Only when smoking was he seen to bound up, gain energy. She let him do this knowing it would shorten his life further. But what choice did she have? She would not let his last years be ones of deprivation and unhappiness. And she would make sure, reviewing his will for the umpteenth time and talking to Miguel Santoses Sr. and Jr., that no money or gifts would be left to their druggie child. She would make sure that Amador, in a fit of dying-induced panic and regret, did not draft a last-minute codicil overriding their agreed-upon shutout of the boy. She would make sure not to make the same tragic mistake as Jesus Caracera who, with $500,000, had kissed his son on the forehead after years of being slapped away by this same child. She would make sure that reaction perfectly matched action.

PART THREE

Pitik Sindit

———————

THE CARETAKER COUPLE WAS gone from the Makati home, having related their tale of yet another haunting, and though this had the benefit of keeping the family away, Caracera himself was unnerved by the ringing emptiness. He found himself left with hundreds of pictures of bygone days in which could be seen his doting, smiling, terrifically good-looking father who was the sole progenitor, who by himself was the governing Trinity, first son (posed next to their grandfather and named Jesus, after all), then father, and now—holy ghost. Mary, mother of God, *the* mother, popular everywhere in the Philippines, was in the house in Makati unwelcome, forever banished.

Caracera released the driver Ernesto, whom he suspected as being a spy for his Aunt Irene, back into the family pool, and with the help of Benjamin Goyanos hired a young man named Christopher Gochengco to ferry him back and forth from the VIP Club—where he spent a majority of his days—to an apartment on the fifteenth floor of a Makati high-rise that he eventually moved into without telling anyone.

To throw off the family, he and Goyanos staged an elaborate scene of farewell at the airport, complete with authentic tickets and packed bags. They were all surprised at this last-minute truncation of his trip but were secretly glad to be rid of him. Something about his manner at the party and before that, at his father's funeral, seemed to indicate that his purpose in staying was to monitor their behavior.

A couple of hours later, he was in a car being driven back into the city.

His new apartment building looked down one side onto the galvanized roofs, rusted blue and green, of a squatter encampment that had bulged out of the husk of an abandoned Spanish colonial building. A fort? A seminary? The walls of the derelict building were scored by illegible graffiti, the scaly dandruff of peeling paint and, here and there, by blackly verdant trails of moss. He was so high up that the clamor of squatter life—the ceaseless gossip, occasional drunken brawls and the sound of water sluicing out of the communal pump—reached him only as the weak staccato of some unclassifiable bird.

He paid for the first and last months' rents, as well as the deposit, in cash, signing the one-year lease under a false name: Gustavo (after the tennis player Kuerten) Punsalan (insignificantly snatched from one of the papers). Seeing him take out the wad of bills, the landlady treated him with a newfound respect as befitting a shady character, one of Manila's wealthy gangsters who controlled rings of prostitution and gambling, shielded from police interference by monthly infusions of payola.

And finally, he called the detective Al Salazar, who came with revelations, and who went into them, it seemed, with a vengeful glee: dirt on the wealthy from a man who kept his own backyard clean.

Pitik Sindit, a he, just as Caracera had suspected, was the name of Eustacio Caracera's beloved. His uncle had intended this man, and not Caracera, to receive his life's savings of sixty thousand dollars. The money had been hijacked by the family and diverted, perhaps following the directives of Jesus Caracera, onto the youngest, irresponsible child Roger Caracera. By this act, Roger Caracera could no longer escape the fact: he was beloved. The one chosen.

And by this act, Pitik Sindit was to remain a secret, written out of the family's history. Eustacio Caracera's life would only be the summation of a voluntary and altogether untragic instinct for solitude; in other words, Eustacio Caracera, if anyone were to ask the family, had been virtually monklike, leading an exemplary, virtuous existence.

What an odd, compelling name. Days Caracera spent saying it over and over, like a mantra, a Buddhist iterative for some wish he was at once fearful and hopeful to see materialize. Only then would he know what he'd been wishing for. He said it while staring at the vast blankness of his white ceiling, in the apartment on the fifteenth floor of the high-rise, where above him, as in his New York apartment, there lived people whose steps he could not, even in the dead of night, make out. But this time, the reason for that pervading silence was clear: money. "Privacy" was among the boasts of this "exclusive" building, listed in a huge sign tacked in the window of the rental office on the ground floor. Another was "centrally located," which, of course, did not count the slums at the back of the building.

To fill up the enveloping "privacy" of his nights, he tossed the words back and forth in his head: Pitik Sindit. And then, for good measure, he said the name out loud. Even screamed it. But there was nobody to hear or, hearing, complain. Or point out the ridiculousness of what he was saying: Pitik Sindit. What kind of a stupid name was that? Even stupider than Donny Osmond. It was a name as falsely folkloric as Donny Osmond was jauntily, heartbreakingly American.

Days later Caracera was trailing this character who, to his shock, had turned out to be not a man, not even a young man, but a boy.

First the pair moved along the garbage-strewn alleys of Bambang, where the boy lived with his mother in a putrid-smelling settlement built on stilts above one of the dead estuaries of the Pasig River. And then, by first taking a jeepney with the boy, and after that jumping onto a second, the action was transposed to the eerily underpopulated streets of Santa Ana. Here Caracera had to stay behind more than his normal twenty paces because of the paucity of any kind of covering bustle. Here the boy eventually disappeared through a front gate from behind which rose a shuttered three-story Spanish colonial abode. Imagine the Pasay residence housing the law office of Santos & Santos, and then add a decade's worth of neglect and defacing—bars of wood nailed crosswise over capiz-shelled windows which had some of their capiz knocked out; and, scrawled by neighborhood urchins, graffiti like the remnant tags of a rape, obscene and cawing—*"Puking ina ninyo!"* All your mothers' cunts!—and you have an idea of the goose bumps that appeared on Caracera's skin watching the boy vanish inside.

The boy had also gone in the day before, and the day before that. And each time Caracera's flesh had prickled at the sight. Always at the same time. Five in the afternoon. He would leave Bambang at 3:20, and by the time he knocked on the useless, heavy door, opened by someone Caracera could never see, because it was pitch-black just immediately inside, as if the house were a divider between day and night, it would always be, per Caracera's Timex, five. On the dot. Punctuality. Caracera could give the boy that at least.

The first time he'd followed the boy, he'd been dressed as himself, Roger Caracera of the aunt-bought expensive long-sleeved shirt and pants, and the comically impractical Ferragamo loafers, now scuffed and muddied. And he had his frosted glasses on. Perhaps it was because, tan or no tan, he still stood out like a sore thumb that the boy had turned to look at him, and then had given him a Mona Lisa smile. Also, and more likely, by transferring to the second jeepney, he had given himself away.

So the next time he'd trailed the boy, he'd put on a disguise: a fake mustache of unnatural blackness, and a straw hat that cast a mottled shadow over his face, making the skin look sickly. Replacing his sunglasses were dime-store reading glasses with thick black frames, giving to Caracera's face a surprising Filipino cast of weary given-upness. He'd worn a tattered, overlarge T-shirt, and beneath it, over his belly, the detective Al Salazar had helped to secure by means of a long strip of gauze tied at the back a pouch made of balled socks that restored Caracera to his pre-Manila body.

That had worked better. Pitik Sindit had not looked at him, much less smiled.

And for the third, and current, try, the disguise was altered by taking off the mustache, and shaving Caracera's head to military severity, revealing an egglike head with, at the tapered top, three unusual bumps, as if resulting from unspecified injury. There were false patches, caterpillarlike, over his original eyebrows, giving him, when he'd checked himself in the mirror, an impish, exhibitionistically up-to-no-good look, à la Groucho Marx. It made Caracera wonder if Salazar understood the intention to be not just to make him unidentifiable as Roger Caracera but, more importantly, to give him no cause to be identified at all. But when he put on the large Jackie Onassis–style glasses Salazar had procured as a last touch, the potent eyebrows were eclipsed, and his eyes, newly doleful and uncharacteristically large, became the focus of his face. Looking in the mirror, Caracera had seen the face of a monk: bald, bland, beatific.

The monk put on a Hawaiian shirt and gray cargo pants, and on his feet were thick sandals whose straps were like intertwined cords of a vine, making him feel effeminate. And suddenly his face with the old-lady glasses was seen to partake of the same quality, and he was no longer a monk but was the legendary architect/homunculus Philip Johnson, or better yet, Truman Capote, and so added to the previous descriptives bald, bland and beatific was a new *b*: *bakla*. If out of his mouth came a svelte reptile's tongue, hissing sibilant *s*'s, no one would be surprised.

So this was the ridiculous character who followed the boy Pitik Sindit on a cooling afternoon, from Bambang, through two jeepney rides, to Santa Ana—an itinerary which had been among the rare few things Caracera had discovered on his own, without the detective Al Salazar's help. Or the help of his friend Benjamin Goyanos. Caracera had paid Salazar extra to make sure that his friend knew nothing about any of this.

And it was this ridiculous character, whom Caracera referred to as Capotecera, a flippant gesture to soothe his nerves, that kept shifting his weight from yes to no and back again on a Santa Ana street corner, standing next to one in a series of abandoned or abandoned-looking buildings, deciding whether or not to confront Pitik Sindit: a situation that, lengthening, began to acquire the uncheering dimension of an existential joke.

While waiting, Capotecera again saw one man, then another, then, depressingly, a group of men, knocking, as Pitik Sindit had done, and then saw the door opened by what could've been the same unseen figure, and lastly saw each man disappear into the darkness of the opened doorway, which was always promptly shut.

This was the thing: all the men looked like Capotes, though he was hard-pressed to identify the details nailing them as such. And if he went in, wouldn't he be a Capote among Capotes, in other words, invisible?

He gathered his courage and walked to the door. Sparrows lifted from the roof, sending a little sawdust to mist the air. He knocked. Three firm, evenly spaced taps on the door with hasty shellac over the wood's weathering. Like the secret knock to an illegal gambling den or an underground speakeasy, though he had an inkling of the specific nature of the place's illicitness. There was a smell of potpourri mixing with the surprising, heady scent of joss sticks, as at a Chinese temple or at the mausoleums of the few Chinese at Kalayaan, their perfumed smoke rising in perfect verticals to heaven.

A small man opened the door. Behind him was a black curtain, which explained the pervading dark of the doorway. Caracera lowered his gaze to meet the man's eyes. The man was Filipino, pudgy, and wearing what looked like a top from a sawed-off cheongsam, purple with faintly discernible, recurring floral whorls. It squeezed his flesh so that there seemed to be breasts above the Buddha curve of his belly. Hello, Joe, *mabuhay*, he said in a practiced low tone that gave the definitive answer to his gender, in case the tits had caused any speculation. Although, at the same time, his pronunciation was definitely that of an over-the-top *bakla*.

Mabuhay, Caracera said back, relieved not to be receiving walking orders.

Oh Joe! said the short man, whom Caracera christened Sancho Panza because of his rice-bowl haircut and excessive cheer. Your accent is so *goooood*! Caracera stepped through the black cloth and Sancho closed the door behind them. You been in Manila a long long time am I right how long?

The place they were in was an unkempt courtyard, with stone tiles buckled as if from the force of several earthquakes. There were trees on which moss, overgrown, hung like botanical pubes, and which helped to further diffuse the weak Santa Ana sun coming in through white plastic corrugated sheets that protected a section of the courtyard from the rains.

A few weeks, replied Caracera.

A few weeks?! What are you Berlitz master of the universe? Your accent is *good-na-good* yes indeedee!

I've been to the city before.

But not here in—and Sancho gestured, as if to demarcate the exact point where reality stopped, and he was breaking into a musical number—House of Beauty and Pain! Thank you thank you, he said to an unseen audience and took a bow. You're a virgin, am I right, Joe?

Yes, I've never been here before.

The sparrows had returned, sitting on the plastic and pecking at unseen vermin, making Caracera's skin tingle. There was a single wheel lying on the ground in the far corner, claimed by choking weeds and baby moss. It looked like it once belonged to one of the horse-drawn *calesas* that still plied their trades in the city's older, slower sections.

Up front was a second door—and leading to it, a rickety-looking staircase, on which paint and incipient moss made shapes that struck him as evil. They were like a thousand miniature eyes, surveilling his bad intent, aware of his pretense.

Immediately, the swampish look of the place, as well as, before it, the joss smell, which was even stronger as soon as he'd stepped through the gate, gave him a premonition of dread. But he was ready. He'd been ready for the last two days, although at the last minute he had decided not to follow the boy into the house—but what would there be left to surprise him? Al Salazar, apprising him of the facts, had been witness to the only show of emotion he would ever provide in public. Caracera knew that Pitik Sindit, leaving his mother for five hours and forty minutes each day, was making his way in a world that no boy should have to know so early in life.

Sancho took Caracera by the elbows, then, surprised by the owner's "smooth skin *talaga!*," began to stroke the surrounding patches on Caracera's arms and then hands.

Tell me, Joe, are you a Palmolive baby like myself?

Irish Spring, replied Caracera.

Reciting the soap's advertising tag, Sancho screamed: *"Fresh, yes, but I like it too!"*

They both laughed.

Up fifteen creaking steps to that second door, the ground-floor space perhaps a shed, perhaps Sancho's private residence, where guests had to truly be friends to enter.

The door had a brass knocker. Up close, Caracera saw the knocker was a big erect penis surmounted by a pair of balls.

How charming, he said, deep into the pretense of being someone else, and perhaps a little grateful. One thing was for sure, Capotecera was hobbled by no gremlin but was instead free—free to be foolish, to dare, invading this odd, decrepit temple.

A gift from one of our friends in Germany. He said he found it in Bali. Everyone loves it! said Sancho. Go ahead, knock, Joe.

Capotecera tapped the penis. Smaller balls inside the pair of balls, knocking against each other and the hollow interior, made a chiming noise.

You like? asked Sancho.

"Fresh, yes, but I like it too!"

Sancho gave him an appreciative, mock-scolding slap on the chest. Oh, don't make me laugh, Joe. *That* is the surest way to my heart!

There was a sudden knock on the front gate behind them. Sancho brushed Capotecera's upper arms and said, Go in, go in, you're all alone now, Joe, but not for long. Oh I hate for virgins to go in without chaperone! He pronounced the last word with a *chuh* as in church, then walked away to welcome the latest guest.

Capotecera pushed the door, which turned on creaky hinges and was attached to a spring at the top, making the door swing back as soon as he'd stepped through.

Hello? he spoke, taking a few tentative steps into the dusky interior and waiting for his eyes to adjust. The floorboards were grimy and there was a mirror that reflected poor light which tried to pour in from the boarded-up capiz windows. There were a few whitish patches on the floor where ancient furniture once stood to block the sun. And where some of the boards ended in the corners the wood was fibrous to suggest chewing by rodents or other animals. The ceiling was high and dark, stripped of its former decorations.

To his left was a narrow walkway which led to another staircase, and above it could be heard the creaking of floorboards, which for a moment put the thought of ghosts into his head; in places like this their existence was inarguable. But the creaking grew varied and a little musical, and he decided it came from the guests he'd been preceded by. He climbed up slowly. On the banisters, streaks in the thick dust and isolated handprints could be made out: human signatures, and recent, which calmed him. The murmuring of the assembled men came to a halt as he entered the tiny third-floor area.

Hello, he said.

A few of the other Capotes nodded, but most of the men quickly resumed chatting among themselves. Like him, they were dressed in the costumes of a tropical holiday: shorts and loose, colorful shirts with psychedelic foliage that most had left unbuttoned to reveal healthy, nearly unanimously hairless and thankfully unbejeweled chests.

The rest of the third floor, presumably sizable sections, was cordoned from view by thick black curtains that hung from the low ceiling to amazingly clean floors. The curtains looked freshly laundered or new, smelling strongly of the potpourri that had first accosted Capotecera's nostrils. They were of shiny black satin, double-hemmed at the bottom for weight, and did not give much when Capotecera brushed against them. In these derelict, improvised quarters, they provided a strong, out-of-place touch of formality and design, like a beautiful gift wrap on an empty box.

The Capotes sat in wrought-cane-backed chairs arranged in six neat rows of six seats per row. Behind them, in one corner of the room, was a small pot of ash where indeed three joss sticks jutted out, trailing their perfectly vertical smoke. There were no windows in this section of the third floor, which he assumed used to be the attic/servants' quarters. Illumination came instead from three lightbulbs stuck on top of what looked like skeletal, improvised hat stands, painted a cheerful red.

A clap, and then Sancho entered, ushering the last Capote into the quarters. Only fifteen of thirty-six chairs were taken. Capotecera took his seat at the back, next to the joss sticks, becoming number sixteen. Everyone came to attention, adjusting themselves, quieting, some even clapping, which Sancho acknowledged with a grabbing of the area of his chest where his heart was supposed to be. He directed the last Capote into a seat in front, and bowed.

Thank you Joes and Josettes, said Sancho. He stood as a proprietress, proud and a little condescending. He was pleased, but in a put-on way that suggested automatic behavior occasioned by a long, recurring run. *Mabuhey*, he said, mimicking some of their touristy mispronunciations.

The gathering laughed.

Well, first, as some of you may already know, I will pass around the contribution basket. And he produced from behind one of the curtains just that—a largeish woven basket empty of what could've been its usual contents of market produce: fish, fruit, vegetables.

Down the line it was passed, and soon the cavity was filled with a growing bundle of Filipino money, even greenbacks and other foreign currencies. Until at last it reached Capotecera, who put in a hundred pesos, and back up it journeyed until it was in the appreciative, tingling hands of Sancho Panza, in cheongsam top and—now that Capotecera had a fuller view—black, hip-hugging capri pants and the local clogs, called *bakyas*. Each time Sancho sashayed to one side of the narrow aisle up front and then back the other way, to emphasize his overdramatic appreciation of the bounty, the *bakyas* obliged with a dramatic syncopated clop-clop of weary in-chargeness. Thank you, thank you, he said, in the breathless tone of somebody at the final lineup of a beauty pageant, waving at nonexistent photographers and wellwishers.

Capotecera laughed, along with everyone else.

My heart thanks you, said Sancho. And now— Sancho stopped, waiting to be encouraged.

Pitik Sindit, mouthed Caracera silently.

You go, girl! said a white Capote made whiter by the unfortunate blackism.

And now, ladies and ladies, I give you—

Hold on, madame, said someone up front.

Capotecera looked: the fingers of the raised hand had several rings that even in the dim light glinted. Hadn't tourists to this country been properly warned against such flagrant displays of wealth?

Oh, that's right, sorry my ladies. From behind the same curtain from which the basket had come, he took out a stack, then another, then another, of plastic containers.

Seventeen containers for seventeen men, the remainder put back by Sancho behind the curtain.

Okay? Happy? Sancho took in the pleased looks on his subjects' faces. Now—clap, clap went his hands and clop-clop-clop his clogs, as if he couldn't brook another delay—I present to you, ladies and ladies, what you've all been coming for, the one, the only—BLUEBOY!

The shiny black curtain was slowly drawn to one side by Sancho. As he pulled, he continued to look at the men in the teasing, mock-serious way they, being delinquent boys, deserved.

Capotecera was aware of holding his breath. He'd been to the Blue Jay, a club with the same atmosphere of congregrant debauchery, of sin sanctified by spectatorship, where young women in bikinis danced in front of beer-sodden tourists, although the Capotes were certainly better behaved than the Blue Jay crowd, comporting themselves, as their name betokened, like ladies at a garden party. And there was also this to say for them, for what it was worth: they were only Mild-Bellied Fucks.

The curtain was nearly all drawn now.

Sancho went around unplugging the lightbulb stands in the corners. Each contribution to the darkness made center stage look a little bit more legible, so that the fog that seemed to stand as a second curtain just behind the satin sheet was seen to be composed of filaments which together formed a mosquito net. And behind it, slowly, yes? Was that a figure? A column that would soon be used as a prop? There went the last lightbulb. And there—the curtain was pulled completely to one side. Still there was nothing to be made out. The men, straining to see, sat forward. The idea of an imminent show was being held past the point of bearing. Someone laughed, as if recognizing that everyone's anticipation, prolonged and tapered to a point of torture, had been devised as part of the show.

Others laughed to ratify the first laugh. Because of this the first-timers—men who had been the most nervous of the bunch—could be seen to relax. They acknowledged each other with shakes of the head, as if to say, They had us there for a while.

Capotecera felt the sudden obstruction of the lidless plastic container on his lap as he too, continuing to see nothing, pushed forward just a little bit more. The container moved the empty chair in front a few centimeters.

Where was Sancho?

Capotecera was all alone at the back. Straining forward, he saw the men in front—the practiced members leading the novices—unzip and unbutton their flies.

Okay, he thought. I'm prepared for this. But immediately he declined to look.

The men took their hands away from their dicks long enough to applaud as Sancho appeared for a brief moment behind the mosquito scrim, caught screwing in a new lightbulb to replace one that had apparently burned out and caused an unforeseen delay in the festivities. Soon he flitted away and taking his place, entering from behind a piece of Sheetrock at the far end that served as the backstage wall, was the young Pitik Sindit, or Blueboy—perhaps so called because of the tiny blue swimsuit he had on.

Another round of applause.

Pitik walked demurely to the lip of his terrain. Caracera knew that he had, by depriving the boy of his rightful inheritance, condemned him to appear in this place. The boy was barefoot, and the bulge of his swimsuit did not seem grotesque in shape or size. He stopped very close to the bulb, so that one side of his body had an electric outline that gave him the look of a mechanical sign—until he began to dance.

After several seconds of silent gyrating, ABBA's "Knowing You, Knowing Me" abruptly came on. Capotecera was no connoisseur but it seemed to him that the boy's moves were substandard, not even meeting the minimum requirement for graceless seduction.

But that did not stop the men, whose hands were jerking in varying, personalized rhythms, while with the other, free hands, they held the containers under them.

After one ABBA song came another, "Waterloo." Capotecera could not turn away. The boy continued "dancing." The lack of expertise was no deterrent for the men, who continued making their chairs move so that underneath the chords of the pop song could be heard scrapings against the floor; in some instances these were perfectly synched with the music, but even when they departed from keeping time, the scratches were oddly becalming, betokening the careful industry of workers: the men were helping to pay back the entertainment they were receiving by helping Sancho improve the appearance of his place of business, sanding, stripping the floor. Perhaps, thought Capotecera, the daily theater was moved from one part of the house to another. And from this shuttered residence the men would move to the next— until all Santa Ana was a revamped community, shining with the applications of a tourist population put to work while reaping the benefits of the local hospitality.

The boy was now taking off his swimsuit. Down slid the flimsy fabric, and the boy stepped out of it, leaving it on the floor, where it snapped into a ball. His penis remained unerect, being cursorily worked over by one hand, then the other. It was as if the boy were afraid to wake a sleeping animal or as if he'd been pulling at it a long time and it was now too sore. Capotecera let his vision go soft and it looked like the boy was trying to warm or otherwise rehabilitate an injured birdling between his legs.

All the while, the boy did not smile, as was customary with workers whose primary goal was to elicit pleasure from their customers, as, for example, the girl dancers at the Blue Jay Club. It occurred to Capotecera to wonder: how many shows did Pitik Sindit give each day, squeezed into the two and a half hours before he returned to his mother in Bambang? How many a week? How many in his short lifetime? And how many of these men were return customers, for whom the boy had long since dropped his ingenue facade, that smile that would simultaneously heighten and contradict the prurience of his act? The irony was that, though the boy was afflicted with a lifer's exhaustion, he looked unfailingly like an acolyte—trying out moves memorized from a guidebook: hand here, switch positions, repeat; change move, change side, repeat.

The bit with the hands akimbo over, the boy turned around. His ass was the new and—to judge by the men's redoubled efforts—long-awaited attraction.

Someone was heard moaning. Seconds later, the moan tapered to its conclusion, and the container was presumably full.

Al Salazar, the detective, entered the Makati high-rise.

Pitik Sindit was slowly bending down until all that was undeniably there was his ass being held up by legs whose backsides were even thinner than their skeletal fronts.

Another groan could be heard. The smell in the air was thickening. The loamy, fruitful scent given off by lawns and trees on warm, muggy nights. Caracera turned his head to the corner where the joss sticks continued fuming. The middle stick was burning down to the wooden nub.

There was a hiccup in the tape and then another song came on. Not ABBA. Whatever it was was new to Caracera.

Pitik Sindit's picture was placed by the detective on the glass coffee table that was the central feature of the Makati apartment's living room—a large sheet of glass supported by two thick hands cupped in prayer, carved out of a dark wood. (The place had come furnished.)

Caracera waited.

This is Pitik Sindit, Al Salazar announced.

Pitik Sindit was, as far as Al Salazar could glean, sixteen. There were conflicting reports from the school he spottily attended and from the various neighbors and urchin friends whom Salazar had had to pay for the information. The figures he received had ranged from thirteen to eighteen. Sixteen seemed a good median. And the boy looked, in the detective's eyes, reasonably sixteen.

The boy attended classes, as mentioned, sporadically, and only as a gesture to please his mother, who, on the other hand, was not unaware of the work the boy did. Salazar quickly specified the nature of such "work," lest Caracera would think the boy, who was the only human link Caracera's Uncle Eustacio had had since his banishment from the family, was his uncle's child. You would think that if it weren't for the nature of the boy's work.

But Caracera was slow to the task. Painfully slow, thought the detective.

Caracera exclaimed that he'd thought all along that his uncle was a homosexual—clearly now, on the evidence of his having had a child—

The detective interrupted quickly. Caracera's uncle was homosexual. Reports had it so. And the boy was nothing if not proof.

There was some more shilly-shallying, Caracera too dense or perhaps too scared to understand the detective's findings. Could Salazar be mistaken? Caracera asked more than once.

There was a slight chance of his having misinterpreted the facts, or even of his having gathered false facts, replied the detective, though he didn't really believe it. The only thing to do would be to ask the boy Pitik Sindit himself. That Caracera could do anytime he wanted. The detective had the boy's address in an area of the city called Bambang.

Still, Caracera was seen fighting the detective's information. If the boy was sixteen now, and Caracera had received his uncle's money, which was rightfully, painfully the boy's, four years ago, then the boy had been twelve when Uncle Eustacio had died. Subtract four years to get back to the time when the boy and Eustacio had first met—the boy had been eight!

Being a homosexual was one thing, but a pederast . . . The vastness of the misery was like staggering from a blow, the surprise of which came from its having been dealt by a supposed friend, an ally against the awful Caraceras. Now it looked like the family might've been in the right, taking care to keep the lid on such a scandalous and tragic event, initiated by their greatest, ablest wrongdoer—a feat, considering the lineage.

But to look, days and endless monologue-wracked nights later, at this boy, the object of what Caracera had imagined to be a tragic process of coercion, Caracera was dumbstruck at the newfound possibility that it was his uncle who'd been corrupted and seduced. The boy, it was clear, was aware of his expert hold on the audience. He'd been stroking his cheeks for what seemed like an eternity. The music had changed and still he was waxing both buttocks with his palms, turning this way for one end of the audience, that way for the other, this way that way, again and again. What could he find to think about all the time that his head was between his legs, near the ground? Caracera could easily guess. The men had been rapt, and now, of course, the undevelopedness of the boy's body and especially the tentativeness and ineptness of his routine could be understood not to be the obstacles overcome but in fact the very direct routes to the men's desires.

The smell in the air was of bodies compressed in a compartment for days on end. Something overripe, rotten.

The boy was pulling the flesh of both cheeks wide so that his hole was expanding, opening out. It looked like a piece of wood cleaved into to reveal at its center the skin of a fruit. More moans. Gratified sounds like putting a bed behind one's back after a hard day, a homecoming, a rest. The containers sitting on the men's laps were filling up. A few, however, continued beating themselves off.

Here was Sancho, reappearing. He politely went down the first row, taking each man's container from him. The men surrendered them with satisfied smiles, as if, along with the money, each container were a contribution.

There was a door, seen for the first time, at the side of the mosquito wire that Sancho opened and stepped through. Five semen-filled containers balanced on a tray. Sancho rested it on the column which had been nothing more than a shape carving into the general dimness of the scene. Now it had meaning.

Pitik did not budge. He remained upsy-daisied, both hands pulling wide his hole. The music, a veritable fiesta serenade, continued thumping and clanging.

Caracera looked at the men. Some were smiling faintly. And all had a glassy look of being mesmerized.

Sancho took the first container. Positioned it above Pitik's buttocks. Give the word, said Sancho.

Yes, please, someone in the audience uttered.

Sancho poured the semen down the boy's buttocks. He did this again and again until the five containers were empty. Then he returned and collected another row's worth, repeating his actions until the contents of all the men's containers had taken their turn coursing down the boy's backside.

Any of the men not yet climaxing had been finished off watching the contents of the containers glide down the boy.

When Caracera surrendered his, he did not dare look Sancho in the eye, and being a good hostess, the *bakla* had made no comment, either verbally or through any facial expression. He had simply put the empty container underneath a filled one and had gone up to finish the ceremony. Nobody had turned around to look at him, making Caracera realize the vanity of his self-consciousness, always believing himself to be the central, jutting facet of every scene.

Applause greeted the end of the show. Sancho pulled the curtain shut. Pitik had not taken a bow. Had not even turned upright, facing his audience once more. At some point the music had stopped. Now the silence was taken up by Sancho thanking his customers, the men getting up, shuffling to the front, where each tried to put in a quick word with Sancho before they took their leave. All expressed their gratitude and pleasure, in whispers Caracera failed to see as anything but conspiratorial. His Uncle Eustacio, known to Pitik Sindit, must've been known to Sancho as well. A few friends departed in groups, conversing solemnly, as if to honor the gift they had received, or maybe doing nothing more than making dinner plans.

Joe, Sancho said to Caracera, poised at the top of the stairs.

Caracera was silent. His disgust had been on the verge of expressing itself earlier, as laughter, of all things. He could not have described the sight of the boy's backside, wet with semen.

As soon as Caracera had understood what was going to happen, seeing Sancho hold the first container aloft, he had looked away.

The boy's body, it had occurred to him, had been used as a trash can, a dumping site, and he'd wanted to laugh as much for the boy's wordless, expressionless gameness as for the congregants' seriousness, convened, it would seem, for church. He'd wanted to laugh at the entrepreneurial bravura of a *bakla* paraphrasing churchly rites—the contribution basket, the call-and-response, the "wine" spilling from the chalice into an open and ready "mouth"—for his profit and the entertainment of worldwide men. Men who jetted here like the Australian tourists. Landing in a playground where nobody knew them, where they could not be known except as facsimiles of one another, blurring into the faceless international patronage this country must be used to by now.

Joe, Sancho said, touching him, using the same hand that Caracera believed to have tipped the containers over the boy. Is anything wrong?

Oh. Oh no. I was—

Not in the mood? Sancho said, stroking his arm sympathetically.

My first time, you understand.

Come back again then. Free of charge. Because if you're not satisfied. . . Sancho paused. I'm not satisfied. Sancho winked at him.

Thank you.

Call me Madame Sonia.

Thank you, Madame Sonia.

Do you know who I'm named after? By this time they were the only ones left in the house, and Caracera found himself being directed, on the second floor, where he had entered, toward the back, to a vast empty room where the windows, also capiz, were opened to reveal, beyond the iron grillwork, the sight of the brown, barely flowing Pasig River.

Have you seen the river? asked Madame Sonia.

Caracera looked. No, honestly he couldn't have said he'd seen it. He'd known it was there. Had been warned off it—by whom, he couldn't remember. The symbol of all that was wrong with the Philippines, a natural resource turned by the citizenry into a dumping ground. All the detritus of Manila life—corpses and condoms—floated by, serving as active reminders.

Now, in the current, he could make out clusters of water lilies, their unseen roots so thick and tangled that it anchored them to the trash-congealed sediment of the river, rising. There were dead dogs, dead birds flowing slowly past. Perhaps his nose had already been stunned by the semen, because he couldn't smell anything.

Guess who I'm named after, said Madame Sonia.

Caracera said he didn't know.

Guess.

Sonia . . . ?

Braga! The actress from Brazil? Not the girl from Ipanema, of course! No. I am no girl. I am a full-fledged wo-man! They called me Sonia because of my "dusky beauty" *daw*. But I know I'm only cute. Not beautiful. So nobody can fool me. Like you, Mr. Joe. You can't fool me. Why are you here?

Excuse me?

You heard me.

I heard about this place.

From who?

A friend?

What's this friend's name?

You don't know him.

If I don't know him, said Madame Sonia, then how does he know me?

You're famous, Caracera stuttered.

You're not here to steal secrets are you?

Secrets?

Madame Sonia had an exasperated look. I'm not stupid, Joe. Nobody else in Manila has my House of Beauty and Pain. Are you competing-competing with me?

No madame.

Why didn't you make come-come?

Excuse me?

I'm asking the questions here, not you, she snapped. Why didn't you, upstairs? Everybody but you did?

I couldn't.

You didn't come-come because either you are straight or you are in love.

It was silly, thought Caracera. The *bakla* was a foot shorter than he, weightless-seeming despite her weight. He could tip her over, or bang some sense into her against the grillwork. How could anyone make a living from the boisterous promulgation of eight-year-old flesh as an erotic ideal, unremarkable and, even better, unpunishable?

If you're straight, said Madame Sonia, then that means you are spying-spying. If you are in love, watch out! Which are you?

I'm not straight, he said to Madame Sonia.

I didn't think so. You don't look straight.

And I'm not in love.

You better not be, because Blueboy is my property! If you think you can love-love him away from me . . . ! He will end up in that river, just like all the trash in Manila, if he tries to go away! Madame Sonia chinned the Pasig.

I'm not in love.

Everyone falls in love with Blueboy.

Caracera doubted that, before remembering his Uncle Eustacio. I'm not everybody, he replied.

Soon she was stroking his arms once more, escorting him out of the property. Come again, Joe, she said, her voice raspy from the quarrel. You forgive me, right?

N YOUNGER DAYS of proud blasphemy, Caracera had delighted in screaming to any family member within shouting
distance and who was gullible enough to provide expected
and, to Caracera, highly needed outrage that the Bible was not, in fact,
the word of God, but rather the longest and most boring and certainly
the most heavy-handed gossip column in the history of existence. In
other words, everything in it was trumped up to provide titillation and
fear, according to the whims and appetites of that particular era and
the talent for trumpery of the particular compiler. So to Caracera's way
of thinking, the word "biblical" was not, and had never been, a positive
adjective. And the Philippines, in this extended viewing, was proving
to be resolutely biblical.

The Bible was the last recorded instance of God's loquaciousness—
talking to some stupid peasant tending sheep or some stupid virgin
collecting water in the town well, it seemed, every other week. Apparently, many such "pure-hearted" people could still be found because
every handful of months, at least as reported in the newspapers and
newscasts in Manila, God was appearing to yet another Filipino. And

what did God have to say during these brief transmissions? Apparently, nothing personal. No special message to the person to whom He had deigned to appear. For example, the cobbler in Baguio who had been thinking of abandoning his work because of the rapidly falling tourist trade. God did not tell him to stick to his work because by the exercise of such skill he was in fact honoring God—in other words, something suitably lessony, or comforting, goods He'd been known to deliver. Instead, God told the man the same thing He'd been telling the others in the same Luzon-Visayas region (but not, tellingly, the Muslim Mindanaos) that seemed to demarcate his Philippine visiting area: He told them that He hated the behavior of "modern" people and that if they did not correct these wanton ways, the world would soon come to an end. The Virgin Mary too put in her two cents, and paid her visits mostly to women who were quickly made hysterical and who, even in repeated tellings, could not relay the incident except in the teary, nervous-breakdown style of such movie stalwarts as the actresses Nora Aunor and Vilma Santos. Between them, in movie after lugubrious movie, where acting skill was determined by how easily and how frequently the actor broke down in tears, these stars helped to perpetuate the Catholic idea that this earth was nothing but a paradise of suffering. In the same way that MacArthur was an echo of Christ, the actresses Aunor and Santos, and behind them, the younger generation of weepy, glamorous starlets, were echoes of the Virgin Mary. And together they said the same thing as God in His various visits: repent, for the time is near; and life, being nothing but a vale of tears, is a foretaste of God's eternal disfavor.

Asked to describe God, all the witnesses could come up with was a big ball of light, too strong to be looked at head-on, and accompanied by a booming voice that announced: I am God. *Dios ako.* Or in whatever provincial dialect He needed in order to be understood. And in the wake of His visitation, the witnesses all described the same state of catatonia and paralysis, as if being aware of having stepped on a land mine and fearful to move or otherwise disturb the stillness.

Religion thrived here because, despite everything, it *felt* personalized, intended as God's word specifically to them, the Filipinos.

He asked his friend Benjamin Goyanos if Goyanos believed these spectral hauntings, and by using the word had tacitly been asking his friend to verify or refute the alleged visitation by his father. Of course he believed, replied Goyanos.

Then did Goyanos expect God to appear before him someday?

Not until the end of the world, when He'd be appearing before everyone.

Didn't he find it to be a kind of judgment from God saying, in effect, that he wasn't worth appearing before?

Well, I don't really have the requirements. The people who see Him, if you look back, usually have certain shared qualities.

You mean they're stupid.

They're . . . Goyanos couldn't finish the sentence.

So Caracera finished it for him: Pure of heart.

Yes.

In other words, stupid. Impressionable. Perfect segue to delusional. Do you think the caretakers were telling the truth about my father?

I don't know.

Do you believe the dead can come back?

Goyanos knew what was being asked of him but felt he could not help. They say it's possible, he replied.

But you've never seen it?

No, I haven't.

As for the specter of Goyanos's daughter's heroin past, it had reared its head in a more benign form: pot smoking. That had helped to dull the anger that was still on the verge of crawling out of the girl's skin at any time. What exactly was the source of this anger, which, looked at closely, became more and more mystifying to Caracera? The girl had been given every advantage of privilege, and had not, as far as he knew, been subjected to Caracera's and her father's generation's regimen of reinforcing lessons with beatings and whippings. In fact, Marta Goyanos was treated with a gingerly bemusement and an absentmindedness as if she were the elder in the family, around whom a cordon of privacy had deserved to be strung. The late-in-the-day vigilance bestowed on her after a heroin overdose could perhaps be understood as self-generated, attention sought out in the only way she knew how.

The girl, under the influence of pot, conducted lengthy conversations with her father about his life, about her mother's life, made curious and sympathetic for the first time since her childhood. And Goyanos would only condone pot smoking if father and daughter could enjoy the experience together. Goyanos's work, which required him to sometimes defend indefensible clients (government officials tried for graft, for example) with whom he was presumed to share, by ties of class, unspoken sympathies, needed, more and more, the alleviation provided by such methods. More and more too, he needed the puncturing disrespect of his friend Roger Caracera. By being an American through and through, in other words, with a lacerating (but not entirely consistent) honesty, Caracera was not beholden to their class or country, making him the Mach version of the man that Goyanos could only look at in wonder and aspiration and envy.

His friend's haircut was the latest surprise from a man who was perpetually surprising him, and who acted as if to oblige a publicly agreed-upon version of him frozen since boyhood: the passionate truant, the committed oddball, the charismatic heretic. In other words, there was more than a healthy streak of performance, of persistent boyhood creation in his friend's persona. This heresy was the sparky center that Goyanos admired more than anything—light-giving, clarifying, spacious not in the sense of generosity, but in that it seemed to allow a vast, active rebuttal to the world (and the boundless energy required to keep up such an antagonism) that would probably not have been possible unless Caracera had left for the United States, the land of tumultuous, perhaps not in the long run sustaining, free-thinking. It was what he, Benjamin Goyanos, whose heart and mind had long been claimed by the punitive instruction at St. Jude Catholic School, the good boy who had graduated into becoming a good man, husband and father of equal burdensomeness but which he'd vaulted over, per his schooling, admirably, wanted to become, if kept only on a plane of wishfulness. A vacation from the goodness which seemed to have been his response to living in a country of such constant, unanswerable, durable yearning. But just that—a vacation, nothing permanent.

Even a haircut, if it involved Roger Caracera, had the power to surprise, to shock, to prod from Goyanos a renewed appreciation of the value of disobedience.

Yet a haircut may simply be a haircut. The heat, though abating, had finally elicited a tribute from his friend. That was all. Simplicity in motivation and attribute was never easy to tack on to Roger Caracera, who was likely to talk for hours, debating the pros and cons, before revisiting the VIP Club, or before going to one of the movies that provided air-conditioned respite from the weather. The movies, in particular, which Caracera had already known to be horrible, could not even be enjoyed for their horribleness, the weeping in them turned into a comedy of willful, and entirely misplaced, masochism. They had to be sat through like attending a sermon, which event then needed to be recapitulated and encapsulated into a mini-essay on Caracera's favorite, personal harangue: the heart of Filipino sadness, as if the country were sitting on a platform barricaded from the world, impenetrable and unaffected by interaction with the rest of humanity; in other words, set off as an exhibit, Caracera the docent. Who, in the end, was Caracera trying to convince but himself? If he was wrong about the Philippines, or rather, if he failed to properly account for his unease in this country and allowed himself to be taken over, might he not soon be going to church with the fervor of a born-again, of a prodigal son made good not just in the sense of being subsumed into Catholicisim, but the even more horrifying sense of being clasped to the bosom of the Caracera clan?

When his daughter had asked about Caracera, Goyanos had been obliged to acknowledge the tenuousness, the oddness of their friendship, picked up and strengthened after so many empty years and after a childhood acquaintanceship that hadn't been particularly eventful or deep. He had admitted that it was like gaining a brother in midlife, toward whom he felt drawn by unidentifiable, subterranean ties but which seemed on the verge of evanescing when the two actually sat across from one another, looking the other in the face.

Caracera, he even joked in one of their pot-smoking sessions, was the devil made flesh, created to test the elasticity, the strength of Goyanos's faith in God.

Marta was smart enough not to say anything, for she believed, in some part of her that could never be anything but suspicious of the royal ease of people like Caracera, that Caracera was indeed demonic in some way. She was scared for her father, whom she believed Caracera was about to draw into some inescapable, doomy transaction.

The three bumps on Caracera's newly shaved head were like places where horns or antennae had been lopped off, but which did not prevent their work from being carried out.

She thought this, and knew that others besides her must think so as well. Her father, a fence-sitter, would not say anything about the bumps on his friend's newly shaved head. When she was brought along to Kalayaan to witness the unveiling of the marble slab at Jesus Caracera's grave, she saw that Caracera's relatives, by their stunning silence and avoidance, believed the haircut to be symptomatic of a larger divestment on the man's part: something that had previously held him to ties of normal behavior had been lopped off along with his locks. And they, just like the girl, were made afraid, and manifested this fear as polite denial. They did not look at him, or rather, looked at him only when he had his head turned to the side, as he looked at nothing but was ostensibly honoring the space left by the family patriarch, now formalized into a stone tablet that said:

JESUS CONSUELO RODRIGUEZ CARACERA
1927–2000
HIS SOUL IN REPOSE WITH THE FATHER

Why, his family wondered, had Roger come back so suddenly and unannounced from the States? He'd grown to miss the Philippines and also had wanted to be here for this ceremony at Kalayaan, he'd told them. Perhaps this was why they'd become afraid of him, knowing that he had his own motives but unable to guess what they were.

For his part, Caracera could not resist this close-hand scrutiny of the guilty. A boy whore had been twice cheated by them: first, deprived of innocence by a pederast, and then deprived of rightful compensation by the pederast's protectors. He, Roger Caracera, stood among them as an unwitting collaborator, taking over the boy's inheritance of sixty thousand dollars.

If they thought that he was just like them, he would show them. He would be delighted to. Going to Negros was only a first step. He realized that now. Astute as he was, he did not miss the nervousness he aroused among them. If he was being honest, would he admit to the basic thrust of his hoped-for philanthropy: not that it should bring him the pleasure of watching lives improve, but instead another kind of pleasure, a lower yet more lasting pleasure: that of watching his family suffer?

Still, he was stymied by the thought of approaching Pitik Sindit, much less talking to the boy. Yes, the boy disgusted him. He could not deny it.

He was the un-Hamlet of Manila. A man whose dead father had appeared to others but not to him. No guidance for Caracera's actions was forthcoming. He would have to carry them out by himself.

After the unveiling of the stone, Caracera went back to his apartment, inviting both Goyanos and his daughter, whose interest was piqued at the same time that a red flag was being raised. The only one of the Caraceras invited back to Roger's apartment was the young girl Cielito, daughter of Celeste and Eulalio. Out of an inexplicable feeling of comradeship with the young girl, Caracera had let her in on the sham of his departure from the country. Ostensibly, Cielito would be at Roger's apartment to keep Marta company while the man and Marta's father conducted business.

Cielito, younger than Marta by two years, was well behaved, soft-spoken, circumspect to a fault, not the kind of girl Marta had ever been or could ever be—not that Marta had ever wanted to be that kind of girl; in fact, Cielito was the kind of girl Marta would've spat on only very recently. But through a benevolent pot haze, Marta was able to look at Cielito as one would a beautiful but helpless animal, whose primary function in life was to be sequestered, exhibited, taken care of.

At Roger's Makati apartment, Marta spoke to the younger girl. They were dressed in the same outfit: a sleeveless black blouse finished off with a long, just-below-the-knee black skirt, making of them (despite their occupying opposite ends of the spectrum of Filipina girlhood: the rebel and the virgin) odd, though not unsimpatico, twins.

Marta solicited the girl's opinions about many things, but most of all about her cousin Roger Caracera, information the girl was more than glad to unburden herself of. It seemed she had been waiting for someone to unlock all that she had to tell. The girl seemed to be in love with her cousin. She had been put in charge, though secretly, of shepherding some of her cousin's boxes and packages which he'd had shipped from the States, helping to transport them from the post office to this new high-rise, and later helping to catalogue them and then decide their fates.

In particular, she spoke of a cache of her cousin's writings that he began when he was about her age and carried on for a few hopeful decades into his mid-thirties, by which time his failure to make a livelihood from it had forced his hand. She hoped to encourage him to reexamine these works. His plays, specially, were wonderful, full of acrid, biting dialogue. Sometimes she entertained the possibility of saying the same things to her parents or her wayward brother, the spoiled princeling Eugene Caracera. One play in particular was the masterpiece her cousin was convinced had eluded him in his decades' endeavor.

Poor girl, thought Marta, nodding the whole time. She turned to look at Roger Caracera, the object of such mystifying adoration. The devil, she thought.

The girl's heart would be broken by Roger Caracera and then become hardened. Had Marta plunged into drugs as a preemptive strike against the same pathetic fate for herself: love? The more she heard Cielito talk, the more she came to the realization of herself as a not-woman, without the capacity to be overtaken, without the graces of such belief.

Do you love your cousin? she asked the girl bluntly, hoping to embarrass her, to shock her into a disavowal.

Cielito looked away.

He's too old for you, said Marta, although as soon as she'd said it, she realized how stupid it sounded. Had such logic ever worked in the history of warning lovers off one another? She knew that she would only push them together.

But Cielito Caracera, the supposedly wide-eyed innocent, shocked Marta Goyanos, replying, I'm not in love. And even if I were, I'm not worried. I don't think he's human.

What do you mean? Marta asked. She imagined awful revelations.

I don't think he's capable of love. Saying which, Cielito looked at her cousin talking and frowning on the balcony, several yards from where the two girls sat, and put a smile on her face, half proud, half pitying, but one hundred percent distant, as if she were regarding an abstraction more than a living thing.

ARACERA TOO HAD RESORTED to smoking weed. This way, he calmed down, and did not, specially when alone, talk too much.

His hair was quickly growing back. Did this have something to do with smoking pot? He'd been disturbed by the bumps on his skull and was glad to have them finally covered over. He'd developed a new habit once his hair was shorn. Every few minutes he was obliged to run one palm over his scalp, hearing the steel-brush give of the bristles and as if to make sure that the bumps on his head were still there. The tic reminded all who witnessed it of a dog being given a reassuring pat by its master.

This was the gesture repeated over and over on the drive one afternoon to St. Jude Catholic School, his alma mater, where the doctrines of Catholicism and its attendant proprieties and warnings were first imparted to him and where, in his imagination, he, along with his siblings, had been deposited by their father in the same manner that pieces of steak were fed into a grinder, by which process the children's *Caraceraness* would be broken down and reshaped into instinctive right-doing. In other words, the hope was that they would neglect the tutorial provided at home by the acrimonious behavior of their father and mother, and pay attention instead to the dry ramblings of spinsterish tutors and fat priests whose words would be like scouring pads clearing a receptive recess in their impressionable brains. *Love thy father and mother. Thou shalt not covet thy neighbor's wife. Thou shalt not take the name of the Lord in vain. Fear hell. Aim for heaven. Do unto others as you would have done unto you. I am the Lord your God, thou shalt have no other gods before me. Sex is evil, corrupting, ruinous. Money is the root of all evil.* Which of these, exactly, had he ever heeded?

Years later he was headed back to this steel box, this grinder, accompanied by Benjamin Goyanos. The school, along with a church, was situated next to the Philippine White House, Malacañang, where the Marcoses once lived.

He remembered having to go past police checkpoints set up along Mendiola in the seventies when Martial Law had been declared by Ferdinand Marcos. The family car was searched by guards who immediately turned any item taken out of the Mercedes trunk into contraband, which of course they were obliged to confiscate.

Every Thursday, a novena was held at the church affiliated with the school and this was a day off for the students, but not for Caracera, who had to accompany his aunts and uncles, and, in the rare instance when the man was present, his father, to Mass, having to first go through the same ordeal of having their car stopped, and then stepping out as the interior was scoured, as well as opening the trunk for inspection. The outstanding memory of such episodes was the look of grievance on his Aunt Celeste's face as, getting out of the car, she turned her back on the scene, refusing to look until the "humiliation" was over. Not until he'd seen her had Caracera understood that his family had once been on a privileged plane, rules of constriction applying to the populace considerably loosened for them.

But as they drove up these many decades later, the access to the school was not blocked by a guard station. Caracera, having hoped for the useful delay of a remembered routine, brushed his scalp several times more. Goyanos saw his nervousness. Was he now having second thoughts?

The two friends were met by one of the assistant principals, whose name was Mrs. Diaz, and who paid particular attention to Mr. Roger Caracera, not because he was known by her to be an alumni or known by her from one of his appearances in the pages of Manila's periodicals or even because she recognized the name as belonging to a distinguished family of legendary industry. But because Mr. Caracera had made himself out to Mrs. Diaz to be a returning parent from America who had a son he wished to enroll in school and who was coming to inspect St. Jude as a potential candidate, having been attracted by its formidable academic reputation.

The students in classrooms that had glass jalousie windows on the corridor side and twin panes that could be pushed outward on the street side looked up as he, Goyanos and Mrs. Diaz passed by. Most of the girls and boys in their uniforms and regulation haircuts looked immediately away, aware that the assistant principal might make a note of their inattentiveness, but there were a handful who continued to stare insolently, especially at the men whose partly casual/partly business attire gave rise to a beguiling mystery. Was the school being inspected by outside authorities, perhaps even by authorities from other schools? Were the men the fathers of students yet to be enrolled at their school? Who was the man with the glasses and the remarkably short hair and why did he not look at them, and why was the assistant principal, an otherwise aloof presence, flashing an uncharacteristically womanly smile at him?

The trio ended their tour on one of the steel bridges that spanned the administrative and classroom buildings. Caracera surveyed the school's buffed cement grounds at an askew, cross-hatched, Russian-constructivist angle. The children in one classroom could be heard chanting catechism, copying their teacher. Factory of souls, he thought.

A factory built by money.

His money, in moments of rare lucidity, was seen to be soaked in the alcohol which his father had needed to consume to be able to organize this money's hoarding, overseeing, along with the lawyers Santos, the investments by which the dwindling family fortune could be buoyed, extended for another generation or two. This was the same alcohol which had enlarged the man's liver over the years and caused his stomach to protrude. Though long regarded as the symbol of prosperous middle age, this Buddha belly had in fact been the swelling of collected poison, like a boil which, unlanced, had slowly leaked its briny effluvia of waste and bile inward, seeping its death year after slow, toxic year, requiring three, four decades to finally overtake the whole of the man's capacious, strapping body. From being a firsthand witness to the cost of such accumulation, such futile, unremunerative work, Caracera had grown up with the idea that he himself could live with far less.

The diffusion of his inheritance would make sure that Caracera's philosophy of life would once again triumph over his father's, his father's family's. But in order to accomplish this, he needed pot much in the same way his father, beginning the process on the other end, had had to rely on alcohol.

What do you think? Goyanos asked Caracera, who stared glumly.

He didn't know what to say. Mrs. Diaz was disappointed.

It hasn't changed much from when I came here, Goyanos volunteered.

You've visited us before? Mrs. Diaz asked.

I used to be a student here, Goyanos replied.

No joking? Were you one of the troublesome ones? Mrs. Diaz asked entirely facetiously.

Are you joking? Caracera asked. Benjamin Goyanos troublesome?

And Goyanos flinched inward, taking the statement as an indictment.

A moment later, it was Caracera's turn to absorb an insult, as, passing by a classroom on the way out, he was accosted by a teacher who took momentary leave of her pupils. Are you one of my students? she asked. If you are, it certainly doesn't look like I did my job very well. No one could tell whether she was joking or simply rude.

The ancient woman had a beautiful face whose autocratic nose and mouth were left untouched by the depredations of time. As, apparently, was her memory. Her gray hair was tied into a bun, and ample flesh on both hips was squeezed by her blue-green teacher's skirt.

The assistant principal Mrs. Diaz looked at Caracera. She was about to say that the old teacher was mistaken, but held herself, wondering if the visitor who had not repaid her curiosity might be about to do so now.

I'm Mrs. Cruces, said the old woman. Are you . . .

Roger Caracera.

Goyanos looked at Mrs. Cruces. He too had had the old lady for—social studies, he believed. And her regime had been one of Dickensian punitiveness. Typical that she would not remember him, Benjamin Goyanos of the gliding goodness, but would remember the student she claimed to have despised for being "spoiled" and "reprobate."

Roger Caracera, mouthed Mrs. Cruces. My, my, don't you look good.

It was characteristic of the woman that her comment could not be readily interpreted for earnest awe or its ironic counterpart, but either way, Caracera felt as if he'd been seen through, the same way he'd been seen through as a child.

I'm sorry, Mrs. Cruces, was all he could think to say.

Sorry for what? asked Mrs. Cruces, who managed an ingratiating laugh. You were just like all the rest who came before you and all the rest who came after. Good-looking, rich, a little too sure of yourself.

But look at me now: Caracera completed the sentence in silence.

You didn't tell us you are an alumni, said Mrs. Diaz, pouting.

I'm sorry, said Caracera, I didn't think it mattered.

Do you have children? Mrs. Cruces asked.

He nearly uttered the truth before remembering the lie he'd told Mrs. Diaz. A son, he said to Mrs. Cruces.

Mrs. Cruces's students regarded the strangers, being sponges for their teacher's rare goodwill, with shy resentment. Some were whispering with one another.

Quiet! Mrs. Cruces huffed, making the whisperers, as well as Caracera and Goyanos, jerk up. How old is your son? Mrs. Cruces asked Caracera.

Sixteen, he said, thinking strangely of the VIP Club tennis player Donny Osmond Magulay, who was as ugly as Caracera, at the same age, had been a beauty.

So now you understand the trial you yourself put us through, don't you? Mrs. Cruces asked, and laughed.

Hi, Mrs. Cruces, I'm Benjamin Goyanos. Do you remember me?

Benjamin . . .

Goyanos.

Of course, said Mrs. Cruces with warm insincerity. Of course I do. How are you, Benjamin?

I'm well, Goyanos replied, though after that there didn't seem much else to say.

Before leaving, the two friends visited the church. Though not open for services, its front door was unlocked.

Hello? Goyanos called out. The sound echoed against the high ceilings. At the back of the pews was a font of holy water recently filled to the brim and into which Goyanos sank his fingers. Then he touched the wet tips of his fingers to his face and chest, making the sign of the cross.

Caracera looked. The marble tabletop behind which the priest conducted Mass was covered with a piece of starched white cloth. Perhaps there was to be a service later that night. Behind the table, built into the marble back wall, was the tabernacle, which was currently empty but which would be filled with the chalices holding the wine and Holy Host just before the services began, by an altar boy.

He had been an altar boy for two semesters before being demoted for uncleanliness and inattentiveness.

He had been given the task, during those two semesters, of holding a circular metal plate under each recipient's chin during Communion to catch bits of the Holy Host that might flake off. The thing had a name. What was it?

Suddenly their idyll was interrupted by an old man, presumably the caretaker. At first the man was taken aback by their presence, but then, taking courage from the docile manner of Benjamin Goyanos, whose voice rose girlishly to apologize for their intrusion, the man began to huff and shoo them out. You shouldn't be here you shouldn't be here, he kept repeating, before he closed the door on them.

Do you regret coming? Goyanos asked his friend once they were back in the car.

I had to do it, he replied simply.

In the rearview mirror he spotted a familiar car. Was that the family? He hoped so. He wanted them to see what he was doing. He thought of his mother, or rather he thought of his mother's memory, as if she were already dead. What would she make of his actions? Would she be proud? No, not likely. She would withhold it, as she'd withheld everything else.

CHAPTER 4

ATHER SHAKESPEARE DE LEON, a burly, bearded Jesuit, had an unconcealed stink of alcohol on his breath at eleven in the morning. He ran a halfway home for street urchins in ramshackle, working-class Tondo. It was at the intersection of several roads where *kanto* (streetcorner) toughs also planted themselves to push drugs or pickpocket or sell stolen goods, showcasing to Father de Leon's wards the simultaneous glamour of easy money and the dead-end cost of hardscrabble living. It was a constant contest between Father de Leon's admonitions and biblical brimstone borrowings and the corner boys' good-timey dereliction for the young wards' allegiances, and because of the stress of seeing a portion of his boys go over to the other side every so often, Father de Leon could be forgiven for tippling from a bottle so early in the day. Not that he did so in Caracera's presence. But in his office, before showing his visitor the premises, the priest had conclusively and carefully locked a cabinet that Caracera, hearing a giveaway clinking from inside, was sure contained a bottle, maybe two, that was among the priest's most treasured possessions.

The boys numbered in the forties at the time of Caracera's visit, though their total could sometimes go as high as twice that. The Father had acquired them through the far-reaching fame of his ministry, though in the early days he and two lay assistants had had to beg them to come with him.

They were a rambunctious, rowdy, irrepressible bunch, much to the Father's everlasting dismay. They were throwing crumpled balls of paper and wadded-up pieces of chewing gum at each other when the two men entered one of the classrooms, which was outfitted with long, low benches for seats and rickety tables that were shared by three boys at once. The desks seemed to have been nailed together from pieces of salvaged wood and whitewashed.

Seeing the men, the boys came to an abrupt but barely successful silence. They giggled intermittently through clenched lips. Say good morning to our guest, said the Father, tiredly, indifferently, as if already resigned to the loss of a number of these souls to the *kanto* boys' membership drive, waged right under the Father and his assistants' noses, out the windows, across the street, every day.

Magandang umaga po sa inyo, said the boys solemnly. Nearly none of the boys looked at Caracera as they greeted him.

Caracera nodded. They giggled under their breaths.

Play time, explained the priest. He also explained that the teacher was out for the day, otherwise they would be learning their lessons. Why aren't you outside? asked the priest. It's a nice day. By "outside" it was understood that the boys were to go to the back of the compound, a playground equipped with a few basketballs and hoops and which was surrounded on three sides by chain link and high walls so that none of the *kanto* boys' activities could be observed.

The boys followed the lead of one of the oldest, to whom Father de Leon gave an encouraging push.

They're at a difficult age, explained the priest as he watched them staggering slowly out, although the look on his face said that he believed they would be at a difficult age all their lives—and for some of them, that span might be regrettably short. Or was that blessedly short?

They ranged in age from six to thirteen, and had either run away from home or been abandoned. Either way, irresponsible and morally lax parents were to blame, the children's wildness quickly encouraged by finding peers. They looked as thin as the urchins along the side of the road in Bacolod, with the same bedraggled hair and faces, though nobody wore tattered or torn clothes. The worst that could be said for their dress was that they were unfashionable and ill-fitting and sometimes overpatched with incongruous fabrics. Caracera learned that they were taught to darn their own clothes and for the patches had to choose from a supply of old bolts either donated or found in the trash.

Also, their thinness reminded him of Pitik Sindit.

Every single one of the boys, explained the Father, was working to earn wages with which to buy small pleasures, such as candies and comic books (though these had to be preapproved by the Father), and soon the young ones would join their older "brothers" in vocational school, to learn skills with which to achieve self-sufficiency in adulthood. "Respectable" self-sufficiency: that was the goal of the ministry.

The priest "loaned out" the boys for sweeping the grounds of St. Jude Church (whose members donated a yearly sum for the upkeep of Father de Leon's ministry) and the making of handicraft goods at several "factories" in and around Manila, for which the boys kept a portion of their earnings, again with which to buy candies and comics. These seemed to be the extent of what Father de Leon imagined young boys to need beyond God. The rest of the earnings went back into a "pool" at the ministry to help with food and the upkeep of the place, such as fixing the beds which broke down occasionally because the boys, despite being told not to, jumped on them again and again. Almost everything that broke down or malfunctioned could be traced to the carelessness of the boys, whom the Father figured were displaying the rebelliousness common to boyhood (which, in the ministry, was given no vent, was in fact being suppressed in exchange for shelter and protection).

Shakespeare de Leon conducted the tour without any hint of trying to sweeten his descriptions, at least none that Caracera could detect and, when asked about how he distinguished between finances meant for the boys and finances which he put toward the purchase of his own needs, admitted that he didn't keep strict personal records but that anyone wishing to investigate, such as the parish priest at St. Jude, who was in essence his superior, was welcome in his office and bedroom at the ministry, for these were the places that held all his possessions in the world. And as for clothes and items for personal grooming, he had only his priest's uniform and his priest's "loss of vanity" between him and the world. Saying this, he patted his stomach with a disgusted given-upness, as if he wished no longer to be housed inside a body, which inconvenienced him no end, needing, for one thing, to be periodically refreshed by alcohol.

Caracera didn't have his friend Benjamin Goyanos's prosecutorial habits and couldn't bring up the subject of the priest's breath, asking how much he drank and how much of the mission's money he spent doing so.

Caracera did not ask to sample any of the catechisms the boys were indoctrinated with. He was an enemy of the very religion the Father propounded, a religion that found easy and numerous converts in the boys (though enough of them were eventually lost to the *kanto* boys to keep up a competitive tally), but he pushed his enmity just enough out of mind so that nothing interfered with his work. Besides, in what corner of this godforsaken place could he sniff out anyone who wasn't even remotely touched by the superstitions of Spanish Catholicism? For that, he would have to go far south, to the Muslim Mindanaos, and that was a trip he'd been here long enough to know not to take.

Caracera had not come introduced as a potential donor but rather as a "writer" by Benjamin Goyanos, who had known of the ministry through his membership at St. Jude. Perhaps this accounted for Father de Leon's candidness, the way he freely betrayed his tiredness, and hinted at the losing battle he was waging for his wards' souls.

Shakespeare de Leon: his name was given to him by parents who were not educated folk wishing to bestow a knowing, poetic touch on a son, but rather because they had enlarged on the word's euphoniousness to will it to mean something "first class," "imported." But Father de Leon, growing up, had felt it his duty to investigate, and so had become an ardent, industrious student of his namesake's work. He'd thought the language opaque at first, with twisty locutions and riddling metaphors, but slowly, arduously, after many rereadings, the stories had clarified, the characters and their motives had become starred with thrilling meaning and the whole world, under Mr. Shakespeare's tutelage, had turned spiderweblike in its mesmeric symmetry, held together by threads of silken language and, at its center, by the controlling efforts of a single, voracious protagonist: Lear, Lady Macbeth, Hamlet's father.

He'd realized, soon enough, that in real life the controlling protagonist was God, and so had decided to devote his life to the Holy Father, becoming one of His minions.

By his current tiredness, at forty-seven, he was not discouraged, as discouraged-sounding as he knew he might be. It was only a period of eclipse for him, much like for one of Shakespeare's beleaguered kings, a lapse from which he hoped to emerge, sooner or later, triumphant, refreshed. Saying which, he laughed.

Even in his low moments, he was held aloft by the knowledge of the hell he was saving his boys from. He mentioned criminalhood and destitution. For him criminalhood meant murder and robbery and kidnapping. And Caracera wondered whether the man failed to cite prostitution because he was trying to be polite or was in fact naive or unaware, or thought of it as being the province of young girls.

Father de Leon, I would like to make a contribution to your ministry, said Caracera after the tour was concluded.

The priest gave a shocked look. He said he had no idea, and Caracera believed him.

Only a few days ago, he had been in a parallel world where the young boys (and girls) parroting passages from the Bible (Genesis and Psalms were his own boyhood favorites) had been well fed, handsomely uniformed, with untroubled and slightly bored expressions that acknowledged the superfluousness of having to court God's patronage for futures that were already assured.

Caracera signed over a check made out for half a million pesos. And asked the priest for an itemized accounting, within a year, of where the money had gone—not that the entire sum needed to be spent by then. Benjamin Goyanos had advised him to request such an item to discourage abuse, or, heaven forbid, embezzlement. Still, nothing was foolproof, and this was understood to be among the difficulties of Caracera's task: to make an unwitting test of the recipients' characters by putting in their paths quantities of money they must certainly be unused to, seeing if they weren't tempted to reroute the sums from causes or recipients they were the custodians of to their very own accounts. Hunger, and therefore corruptibility, was endemic to all levels, and all walks, of Manila life.

The fact of the speedy dispatch of the money to Father Shakespeare spoke of a *fait accompli*—the visit had only been intended to verify the basic premises of Caracera's charity: the man Shakespeare de Leon, not being an unctuous, oily sycophant, could be trusted, and his mission, sound in principle, did not seem to depart in any major way in its practice.

Father, said Caracera before leaving, my name is Roger Caracera.

He uttered it as a last safeguard, hating it but knowing no other name would do. Goyanos had tried to convince him that his family name still held a power over people, and might make them think twice before misappropriating his donations.

Oh, I see, said the priest, recognition burgeoning, as his friend Goyanos had predicted, into awe.

At the last moment, Caracera, who had been going back and forth on the matter, held his tongue about the Father's drinking. There was a paradox in his donating money to one of the guardians of a religion he claimed to be unable to abide; further, there was a potential pitfall presented by the man's drinking. Yet it was only when Caracera understood that he would be unable to find anyone entirely immaculate to "deserve" his father's money that he surrendered his fears.

Meanwhile, the bags of letters forwarded by the newspapers seeking donations from the new "sugar daddy" (this according to Dolores Macapagal-Arroyo of the *Metro Manila Register*) continued to sit in Caracera's high-rise apartment, unopened.

The rough canvas bags, yellow-white and scuffed by having been dragged across the ground, were secured at their mouths by thin hemp cords, and resting against a mirrored wall near the front door, where they multiplied from three to six, looked like forlornly bulging props left behind by a derelict Santa Claus.

To want to do good was one thing, but to be expected to do it was another thing altogether.

With his cousin Cielito's help, he finally decided to tackle his responsibilities.

Caracera hefted the first bag to the middle of the living room, untied the cord, and tipped the bag over. The contents spilled out in a spray. His emotions wavered between self-importance and impotence. He gathered up a fistful of letters and playfully let them fall back down, as if at the beach sifting sand. He did this over and over. Already he could hear the teeny-tiny beseeching voices barely muffled by the envelopes. He could imagine how, once opened, they would try to emboss their earnestness, their pleas for special attention on the various surfaces of his world: the chairs, the tables, walls, ceiling, the sliding glass door and beyond it the view of Manila sky—all covered over by scrawls asking for special dispensation of comfort.

Cielito, seeing the look on her cousin's face, didn't say anything.

He was beat and looked alarmingly unkempt. She had no idea of his trip to Negros, or of his donation to Shakespeare de Leon's ministry, and thought he might look haggard as a preemptive measure against the sheer volume of need that she knew he would never be able to answer.

By the second batch of letters, it was clear to Caracera and Cielito that the requests were alike, no one more special than the other and, what was more important, no one seeming trustworthy. All of them shared the hysterical tone of contestants trying to edge each other out by inflating the drama of their stories. The letters were a veritable listing of Job-like afflictions that had the ring of hyperbole about them, although in this country who was to say that they couldn't be true? They nearly always sought to flatter Caracera by invoking the name of God, who must surely have sent him to rescue them.

Still, Caracera continued to open envelope after envelope, and continued to listen as Cielito, piqued by a particular letter, read certain passages out loud to point out their similarity to those that had already been disregarded, or highlight some factual errors or inconsistencies that gave a clue to the devious intentions of the correspondents.

Not until they had gone through the first bundle—what seemed like at least a thousand letters—did Caracera finally admit to being defeated. Cielito argued, knowing that the contest had been unfair and impossible from the start, that her cousin could not be expected to rescue everyone, and even if a letter had managed to survive their screening process, who was to say that the act of rewarding that special case would not inspire, weedlike and in such crippling multitudes, more letter writers, so that the apartment would be finally overtaken by bags and her cousin had to move elsewhere?

What would he do with the bags? she asked.

He mentioned a furnace in the building's basement, which must surely have been part of the draw for the people who lived there. He made a joke of the wealthy residents who must have had troves of documents and other incriminating papers they needed destroyed, amassed as part of the routines of wealth-building. This building thinks of everything, he said.

The joke covered over a sadness in him, and she tried to reassure him: You did good. You didn't even have to open the letters and you did. You gave them a chance.

I know, replied Caracera, with the same deep-rooted, ineradicable sadness. Why, Cielito wondered, did he stay in the Philippines when it was so clearly having an unfavorable effect on him?

She asked about America, and though he said he didn't want to talk about it, he gave her the impression that he couldn't go back until he had found something he was looking for in this country. What that was seemed a mystery even to him.

The next day he brought the bags down to the furnace, careful to choose a quiet time when he wouldn't run into anyone. He took three trips in the elevator, lugging them down one at a time. The furnace provided the heat for the hot water in the building and had a tiny door through which the letters could be stuffed in only a few at a time, though immediately the fire claimed them with a great relish and was ready for the next batch.

It took nearly two hours to finish his task, by which point the last thing on his mind was to go out into the heat—even if waning—of the city. But that was exactly what he did, having a week ago made an appointment to see the Italian-American missionary Frannie Prusso and wanting to get it over and done with.

Frannie Prusso did not recognize him because of his short hair. Oh my God, she said, after he introduced himself. You look so . . . different.

He must've flashed a look because immediately she felt the need to clarify, It looks good. It suits you.

He thanked her for agreeing to take him on a tour of her day.

Their first stop was a slum in a section just outside the city called Balut, to which they were driven in a secondhand and donated Pajero by a hired driver, who usually accompanied Frannie Prusso to and from her rounds, but did not himself get out of the car to walk the slums' narrow and sometimes dangerous alleys. Usually she was partnered with a young *medico* gotten through one of the training hospitals she had been canny enough to establish a relationship with. She acquired the interns in exchange for the religious comfort she provided at the bedsides of some of the hospital's terminal cases, whom she visited once a week. She was a gifted reader from the Bible, as well as a cheering storyteller. For the genuine caring she exhibited, sometimes being known to even shed a tear or two, she had become a popular and much-requested visitor.

Today was not among the days when the interns were free to accompany her, and so this served as a "scouting" trip to identify medical needs and demands, for which she would later return with the necessary personnel.

The narrow entrance to the Balut slum was in an alley between two medium-sized middle-class homes.

The shacks were magpie constructions from salvaged trash, a nail-scarred plank here, a rusted galvanized tin roof there, and they stood next to one another haphazardly. Some residences were subdivided two, three years into their life because the original family had to rent out to another, so that sometimes upward of a dozen people shared a shack that was meant for only half or a third of that number, the multitudes separated from one another by unstable alloys of plywood and tin or by flimsy curtains. Misunderstandings and fights were frequent in these kinds of households, and these conflicts sometimes led to homicide.

This was, relative to other slums, a fairly clean one. There was access to several gutters nearby into which the residents could pour the water from the washing of food, clothes, dishes, and pour too the previous day's collected urine and feces. For toilets this particular slum improvised large ten-gallon cans or jugs (formerly containing cooking oil or soy sauce) on top of which were carved holes large enough to sit on. In most of the other slums, especially those over estuaries of the Pasig, the residents simply did their business over the water. Because the waters were stagnant, the waste stayed put and the residents were thus condemning themselves to "eating where they shat."

Because of the novelty of their portable toilets, most of the residents of the Balut slum were free of parasites, which was a common ailment besetting the people Frannie Prusso visited.

The Balut slum dwellers looked at their visitors with mouths agape, though no one inquired why the visitors were there. The residents were docile in the manner of people used to being dictated to by their surroundings; by their employers (should they be lucky enough to have jobs); by the police, who were often drafted to officiate between warring neighbors or warring members of the same family, though these cops were really responding to the middle-class neighbors calling in to complain of the noise; and by people such as Frannie Prusso, for whom they served as captive audiences, showing the greatest pliancy to her requests—such as that they read the pamphlets which she'd brought with her, printed in Tagalog, about God and His ministry, and be prepared to answer questions upon her return. She was like a traveling schoolmarm, thought Caracera.

One moment the mothers were handling the pamphlets with great eagerness, then suddenly their faces sank when it became clear that no money was being handed out, no aid being offered other than the divine variety, which, they immediately made Frannie Prusso understand, was too far into the future to do them any good. In the meantime, what were they to do, starve to death while waiting? There was free medical help, said Frannie Prusso, which they shrugged off. What good would it do to have their lives prolonged? They communicated this not exactly cheerfully, but certainly without the moroseness that such sentiments warranted. It was the same resignation that had made them lift not a finger to improve the address they festered in.

Some of the women, scandalized by the absence of what they had believed was an implied offer of material goods, handed back the pamphlets and, laughing, spat out, *Wala kaming DDT!* We don't have DDT! The acronym was their way of punning on "Ph.D.," saying that they hadn't been to school, couldn't even read and the joke would be on Frannie Prusso leaving behind literature that would most certainly end up being used as toilet paper.

Frannie Prusso plowed on, her grim face always locked on an unseen target in front of her. From these brief episodes, Caracera began to have a deeper understanding of why she'd spoken the way she had at the VIP Club, and from that grew a kind of sympathy, although she still carried around an undeniable, unrepentant air of superiority as if it were a shield to ward off the infectiousness of the slum dwellers.

There you go, she said, concluding their tour of the Balut slum. That's typical of the people I try to help.

I thought this country was Catholic, he confessed. I didn't think they would be so resistant.

Catholic in name is one thing. Catholic in deed, another.

These people don't go to church? He was surprised. A lot of the shacks, primitive in almost every way, had at least the obligatory decoration of an altar filled with pictures and/or statues of Catholic saints, chief among them Mary, mother of God, and on most of the walls was a plastic crucifix, rosaries draped around some.

Those crucifixes, explained Frannie Prusso, were mostly superstitious touches, meant to ward off vampires and other such creations of the overactive Filipino mind.

And besides, there had been so many reports of the approaching end of the world that by now the fear that once held the Filipino people, mostly the poor, to the faith had slackened. Never use an ultimatum, said Frannie Prusso, unless you're prepared to deliver.

Frannie Prusso's next destination made Caracera do a double-take. They were going to Bambang. This was the same slum where the boy Pitik Sindit lived, where he left his mother every day to go to school or to work in the anonymous, abandoned atmosphere of Santa Ana.

In Bambang, said the missionary, the residents were more pliant. It was a typical slum in that the dwellers were riddled with illnesses that would make them grateful for Frannie Prusso's visit, more amenable to the idea that God was a benefactor, providing an immediate turn-around for the negatives in their lives.

Is it a large slum? asked Caracera.

Larger than Balut. Why?

Caracera shook his head. Perhaps it was large enough that they wouldn't run into the boy.

Caracera soon knew what Frannie Prusso had meant when she'd described the first slum they'd visited as "above and superior to" most.

The Bambang squatter area, in comparison, was built on stilts, under which sat the slow-to-stagnant waters of a Pasig canal, too dark to reflect the sky or any of the shacks above it. In its soup of accumulated garbage, which included tin cans and shards of glass and also feces, of both the human and dog variety, things could be seen wriggling, and the whole offering attracted hordes of flies busily scribbling in the air.

Caracera walked with exceeding slowness, careful not to slip through the flimsy wooden slats. There was a smell being pushed under his nose. The odor was multilayered and it was hard to determine the individual components, except every now and then, passing by a particular shack, or a more infested part of the waters below, a sugary facet would be detected, the way vinegar sometimes got. Once, Caracera almost threw up. He was aware of holding his nose higher than usual, and though this made him miss seeing most of the shacks they were passing by, he was just as glad to miss them, in case from one of them should rear the face of the boy Pitik Sindit, or in case he might come face-to-face with the source of the sugary-shit smell. He could feel the flies coming in to land at the back of his neck, where sweat must've formed a trove of slime. In front of him was a vague shape that he knew was the missionary woman.

There—he nearly slipped and was forced to lower his eyes.

The missionary woman turned around.

Are we there yet? asked Caracera with a faint laugh.

Frannie Prusso produced something from a small bag attached by Velcro to her belt. It was a paper filter for the nose. I'm sorry, she said. I forgot to give you one of these.

Am I taking it away from her? he thought, but didn't ask. He put it on.

Directly to your left. And don't mind the dogs.

Sure enough, as they rounded one corner, dogs could be heard making a racket. They turned another corner and there were the creatures facing them—mangy mutts, one of whose ribs were prominent under the shrunken skin. Frannie got out something else from her bag. It was an uncooked hot dog, which she removed from its plastic wrapper and snapped in two. She threw a piece to each dog, and both dogs immediately scarfed them up. When they finished, they came to heel at her feet to receive their pats. Good dogs, she said.

They can't afford to feed themselves, but these people have dogs, he thought.

As if reading his mind, she said to him, They're Nanang Tata's guard dogs. We leave a lot of the medical supplies with her, and this way people are discouraged from trying to steal them. I'm sure they would fetch somebody a week's wages on the black market.

Caracera wasn't sure whether she was referring to the dogs or to the medical supplies.

She added, This way also, because they serve a purpose, the dogs don't get eaten. It takes getting used to, the idea that dogs are food in this part of the world. But that's only true of these people. I mean, the poor ones, or the ones from the provinces. What are you going to do? she asked, showing the first sign of generosity and understanding. If food is scarce, you'll eat anything you can get your hands on.

Have you had any? He surprised himself with the indelicacy of such a question.

She shook her head.

Nanang Tata was an old, toothless woman the walls of whose shack were covered in yellowing newspapers, some of which bore the salacious pictures of starlets in wet T-shirts or other articles of skimpy clothing. There was a low chest sitting on the floor, pushed against the wall that separated the room where the woman lived from the kitchen. This chest, presumed Caracera, was where the medical supplies were kept. On top of it was a neatly folded stack of clothes and beside it on the floor was Nanang Tata's *banig*, which she unrolled to sleep on. These were her only possessions in the world. Nailed to the wall facing the metal chest was a plastic-laminated picture of the Virgin Mary, with melancholy, lowered eyes, two fingers on her right hand raised in mid-benediction. Around the picture Nanang Tata had draped a pink plastic rosary. On the floor directly underneath the picture was a small weed with yellow flowers inside a tin can filled with water.

Frannie Prusso and Nanang Tata exchanged warm hugs. The old woman's speech was riddled with mystifying sounds due to her lack of teeth, but Frannie Prusso seemed to understand everything she said.

The missionary woman checked on the supplies—bottles of rubbing alcohol, containers of Band-Aids, spools of gauze, aspirin, penicillin, and a container of some thick green liquid that was supposed to evacuate parasites from the body—which had not dwindled considerably since Frannie's last visit. It was to Nanang Tata that the slum dwellers reported any ailments, and it was to her Frannie had given the responsibility of dispensing the supplies to help her neighbors. For any illnesses that the supplies couldn't remedy, Nanang Tata kept a record that was reported on during Frannie's visit. But for those that required immediate attention, Nanang Tata had the number of the hospital that Frannie was affiliated with, and a small purseful of change to make emergency calls. The old woman was trusted to know which condition would qualify as an emergency, not exhausting the hospital staff's energy and limited patience.

It was also at the old woman's shack that Frannie visited with the slum dwellers. Barely a minute after Frannie and Caracera had arrived, a line had begun to form outside Nanang Tata's. Someone had spread the news as soon as they had appeared.

Most of the supplicants were women—young girls, really—the same as at Balut, but this time, their docility did not give way to peevish disappointment. Each one Caracera met with a wondering gaze, asking himself whether he was looking at Pitik Sindit's mother—to even the young girls he applied this question, for who was to say when they'd started having children?

After brief consultations, during which they set up subsequent appointments with the *medico*, the women departed with small bags full of candies for their children. Most of these girls were pregnant, and Caracera assumed by the gifts that these were not first pregnancies for them. Nothing was said to the girls about contraceptives or about the difficult circumstances they were delivering their children into. Caracera asked Frannie Prusso why she wasn't responding to the obvious. Didn't a direct correlation exist between the women's pregnancies and their poverty?

Frannie replied, I'm forbidden to do anything like that. The church doesn't believe in contraception. She said this in a sheepish tone, as if she too saw the practical wisdom in Caracera's suggestion, and yet was prohibited from bringing it up, much less seeing it implemented. And yet, for all her embarrassment, the inaction her words amounted to seemed to Caracera downright criminal.

The pair retraced their steps in an hour, dispatching efficiently with the women's complaints, most of which were minor and needed no more remedy than being listened to, and this time Caracera looked in on the shacks that he was passing by, the open mouths of the doorways giving on to cavities filled here and there by pieces of furniture whose first lives were as other implements—fruit crates, overturned pails, loose planks balanced on top of cement blocks, car tires used as seats. Sometimes a shack would be seen to have, standing in its middle, an inexplicable and surreal sight: one shack had two car batteries keeping each other company to one side of the walls; another had a new plastic trash can, the kind whose top could be lifted by a foot pedal, shining in the middle of the home, the residents' faces glowing from the sheer newness of the object; yet another had a small pile of keys with no locks in sight to which they might belong.

There were holes in the roofs and walls of these residences through which the afternoon's still-bright sunshine entered, casting silvery slivers and slash marks on surfaces, sometimes even bathing the residents in an angelic sheen. Though what happened, thought Caracera, when it rained?

He was left with a lingering impression of what Blueboy was trying to gyrate his skinny ass out of. What, essentially, his Uncle Eustacio had tried to lift the boy and his mother from.

Eustacio, the family queer, had a good heart. This was intuited by his nephew, then dropped upon the discovery of the inappropriate age of his beloved. Now, upon firsthand knowledge of Eustacio's act of sponsorship, of benevolence, Caracera was again sure of it.

Caracera asked Frannie Prusso if she would accept, along with a donation, a restriction that forbade her from using the monies to deter young women from getting birth control. Bodies piling on top of more bodies in this infernal city. Surely, her visits to the slums had illustrated for her the outcome of the outmodedness, the sheer irresponsibility of her church's teachings.

She gave her answer calmly. She was neither excited by the mention of money, nor showed anger at the suggestion of her faith's irrelevance. She was a follower of the Catholic church, she said, and therefore a follower of every single edict passed down by the church. She did not have the luxury of picking and choosing which of these commandments suited her tastes.

What if there was a commandment that asked you to kill people—would you?

But there is no such commandment, she replied. In fact, the commandment asks the opposite of us. Thou shalt not kill.

But didn't she know that, by causing these children to be born into a life so lacking in basic necessities, she was in fact assigning them long, slow, undignified deaths?

But by tolerating birth control, she said, you are asking me to tolerate the killing of unborn children.

But they are not children. He realized that this was what his mother must've sounded like at the height of her Peace Corps involvement: slightly hysterical with the conviction of her rightness, angered by her inability to put across this rightness; and angered even more by the tenacity with which her opponents clung to their erroneous ways and, rejecting what she had to offer, made a fetish and a trophy of their backwardness.

He wrote her a check for a hundred thousand pesos, much less than he'd written for Father Shakespeare. For the first time a burden seemed to lift from her chest, and her breathing became less audible, less labored. If Caracera felt like being truly generous, he would even have said that she looked a different woman altogether, she could even be said to be pretty. But when she started to thank him, out came the flattery and unctuousness that Caracera had been grateful not to have been subjected to. She began speaking of "God's appreciation and His habit of rewarding the generosity of the righteous."

Did she really use the word "righteous"? He stopped her before she could say any more and told her that she was free to spend the money however she saw fit.

I'll be sure that your Aunt Celeste hears all about this, she said.

He told her that the contribution was being made completely anonymously.

It was something he didn't think he'd needed to tell Father Shakespeare. But apparently, by emphasizing his name to the Father, he'd given the man the wrong impression. Several days later, he found himself once more the subject of a newspaper article. By now he ought to be rolling with the rhythm of the farce of his unwitting celebrity. Yet, once again, he was floored as he found himself floating around on public benches, atop garbage cans, littering the gutters. The same picture of him doing an uncanny impersonation of Harvey Keitel masquerading as General MacArthur illustrated the caption: "Positively Shakespearean: Roger Caracera donates to Father Shakespeare de Leon's Tondo ministry."

He called the priest and released a series of invectives. How dare the priest misconstrue an act of pure charity for a naked bid of self-aggrandizement! Was that what the man thought of Caracera's gift? A publicity stunt? Was that what his study of Shakespeare had wrought—a worldview that tried to seek out villainy even where it did not exist? The Father went completely silent on the other end. Caracera threatened to withdraw his contribution if the priest spoke to the press once again. Profuse apologies followed. And the next day came a messenger with a peace offering. This was also a "show of thanks from the boys whose souls you have helped save from ruin": three baskets that were among the native handicrafts the boys made to earn their keep at the ministry.

They were a welcome touch in the otherwise anonymous apartment. He aligned the baskets in a neat row on top of an empty bookshelf.

Staring at the baskets, he was brought back to the abandoned-looking house in Santa Ana. Caracera saw Madame Sonia holding a basket filled with currency. Remembered how she shook it and ran her fingers greedily through the bills, expressing delight with the men's generosity by flashing a repulsive, sneering smile. These were the same baskets, with the same handles, the same glossy shellacking over the fibers' weave. How could he have forgotten?

Immediately he knocked them down from atop the bookcase.

PART FOUR

Two Sons

———————————

CHAPTER I

IN SCHOOL, he was the only child with days-off privileges, and this made him feel as if he were being offered up on a plate for special ridicule—and they did ridicule him, with a passion, or like a vocation, or simply by animal instinct, smelling out his weakness like vultures drawn to carrion. Some of the boys before classes or during recess called him names having to do with reasons they'd made up for his absence for two days each week: *sakit ng puso* (hurt of heart) and *sakit ng ulo* (hurt of head)—words to suggest that not only was he exaggerating his sensitivity, but they could see through the masquerade clearly, even if the teachers couldn't. They put their hands to their foreheads and their chests in a pantomime of feminine bereavement, like penitent churchwomen whom they had seen, having internalized this country's sinfulness, to clutch at their weakened bodies. That was as much of an inkling as they had about his being *bakla*, for when he was not at Santa Ana he made sure to play down any effeminate tendency that might expose him to greater ridicule. At least this way they believed the affliction to be within the bounds of his body, not his heart or sex, and their derision was undercut by pity— even if they wouldn't admit to any such feeling.

When younger he used to see such taunts as tests of his Christian charity and conviction, much like Job. Not that his life had been comparable to the early, cushy stages of Job's—and not that in the end the punishments were retracted by an apologetic God, as they had been for that biblical hero, explained away as crucibles in which faith, not having buckled, was fire-strengthened and reinforced. The thing about the Bible he resented most was that no amount of bad luck he or his mother received (a dead father, his mother's recurring bouts of TB, neighbors who sniffed at the strain of Indian blood they claimed to see so strongly in his complexion, making them spit out poisonously, "Bumbay," every time he drew near, the malicious ribbing at school) could ever compete with the list said to have afflicted Job, or with the plagues visited on Pharaoh's Egypt, to name only two examples. For him there remained no choice but to consider his complaints minor, trumped, and to take them with the same silence and stoicism that was the benchmark of virtue set by those stories, and at once the symbol of complicity with God and triumph over Him.

His only friend had been a girl, Consuelo, who, like him, was fifteen, but last year Consuelo's family moved away to Pasong Tamo so Consuelo's father could be nearer to his new place of work. Now there was nobody to talk to, so during recess he stayed inside the school's one room, while the other children convened in boisterous gangs by the cinder-block wall. Next door was the Church of the Sto. Niño, the infant Jesus whose cloak was a starched A-line studded with the sequins of His celestial bounty and who wore a bulbous crown on his toddler's head. The face, as befitting one whose experience of the hardships of the world would not come until he'd reached manhood decades later, consisted of two tiny, expressionless dots, an almost imperceptible bump for a nose, and for a mouth, the most precious of upturned brackets—perhaps smiling, perhaps gloating. There, by the low wall spiked at its top with shards of broken bottles, his schoolmates played games, told dirty stories and boasted about what they would do once they reached eighteen and gained their freedom, some even boasting about what they were already doing under the noses of watchful parents, whose tiredness caused them to slip up. They told stories of sneaking off to the movies after school, using the excuse of "class projects" to explain their tardiness coming home. Stories of slipping into after-hours clubs, having to expertly orchestrate their escape from their rooms beforehand. Smoking, sexing, gambling: these were the adult things they did in those clubs, which they wished to continue doing when they had permanently escaped their parents' clutches. Their tones, in the telling, were already triumphant, disdainful, for hadn't their parents done the same things in their own youths?

There were others who, like him, remained in the room during recess and even during lunch, eating the school's bananas and cellophane-wrapped sandwiches and drinking from their Pepsi bottles at their desks, but none of those who stayed behind talked to each other much, except to share homework solutions or to show off shots from the celebrity magazines so thrillingly new they occasioned a temporary break from the legislated diffidence.

But Pitik Sindit had a secret, and this was the leveling factor (and gave him more solace, more sense of worthwhileness than the Bible did). He sat quietly during classes, hoping none of the teachers would call on him, and quietly endured the knowledge that the others talked about him in the yard, right next to the Sto. Niño, who did nothing, who, famous for interceding on behalf of suffering children everywhere, had not once put the scare into his classmates. But perhaps, no longer being a child, Pitik was no longer under the jurisdiction of the Sto. Niño? Having said goodbye to childhood at the tender age of seven, hadn't he forfeited the right to be under the protection of the Holy Infant with His narrow range of sympathies that extended only to the hapless young?

During catechism class, in particular, Pitik's secret burned, heated up by the restraint required not to throw it out and at the faces of his teacher, his classmates, whose schoolyard boasts could so easily be upstaged by what he had to say. Consuelo had known, although to her he had modified his job description to being the "companion" of men as they drank at a "club," holding these men's hands, listening to their stories, allowing them to kiss him. Pawing—that was as far as things went, as far as Consuelo had been told. The fact that these men were largely foreigners added immeasurably to the glamour of Pitik's position. Telling Consuelo, he had been made to consider that he was in the same circle of shininess as the pop stars and the young actors they saw and admired on the TV game and variety shows. Like them, he was in touch with the world of sophisticated Americans—and Germans and Australians and Japanese. Like them, he performed for a living, collecting applause and money and adoration. Because he himself had been on the other end, watching a live TV game show with Consuelo as the latest stars from WEA and Vicor Records performed, he knew what the men were thinking as he danced in front of them. He was familiar with the phenomenon by which an audience snatched hungrily at every detail of the star, and by the union of these details created a whole new person of unbearable importance. When he was in front of the men, he was nobody but Blueboy, and Blueboy did not go to classes, much less suffer the indignity of having his actions copied and, in the copying, having the cover turned up on the ludicrousness, the mundaneness, the powerlessness of his person. Blueboy did not eat or sleep or go to the bathroom, was not subject to anything but a timetable: first, knocking on Madame Sonia's door; then, being ready, after the curtain was drawn, to spring out of the hoisted-up drywall, like a creature who materialized from the shell of the ancient house, like the very transfiguration of the house itself, secret and sequestered; then, to dance and position his body for the maximum enjoyment of strangers who paid tribute by turning the air a chemical scent that, to his mind, was the very scent of a foreign country—they brought these smells all the way from the other end of the world; then, to have the scent translated into the oozing touch of liquid on his skin; then, to wash this liquid off, forgoing the pretense of its being some silky emollient and seeing it instead as syrup, pesky when dry, and a telltale sign of shameful bingeing; then, lastly, to collect the bills offered by Madame Sonia, who, having only herself to support, was always generous with the cut. This last was his favorite. All the preceding cuts of his time had been leading to this final, transforming segment, the crowning hour, when the two sat across the floor from each other at the bottom level of the house, where Sonia lived, and she handed Pitik the share of the afternoon's business, always translated into the peso equivalent, of course. Then, going home, he gave up most of the money to his mother, who made sure a portion was given over to the priests and seers who promised that his dead father would be happy in heaven, that he hadn't been crowded out by others whose relatives kept up the afterlife payola.

The little he saved was for . . . what reason? He had no social life to speak of, except what he did twice each work week, and over the weekend.

Blueboy was the name of a magazine from the United States, favored by Madame Sonia. The handful of copies Madame possessed featured clean-cut collegiate white boys in poses of willing lewdness, their nakedness enhanced by an article of clothing hanging low around the inessential parts, like ankles and knees. Their hair, often blond, was gelled and wave-separated, or feathery, or long and straight, being a counterpoint of softness to just-burgeoning boy-man muscles starting to manifest in the chest and the shoulders and arms and upper legs; one would imagine these things to give far differently under the fingers than the nearly girlish prettiness of the hair, and their contrast suggested what sexiness was all about. Another contrast: the hard looks of malice and knowing on the boys' faces undercut by the softness, the curledness, the curvedness of their features—that extra fat at the cheeks which no amount of working out could diminish, carve into, suggesting both lack of experience and the eagerness to be freed from such burden.

Madame Sonia had come up with the name and he had agreed, proud to be thought worthy of being grouped with the white boys who were, to him, far superior, being able to push far above the temperature of desire he could realistically set in the world.

But that had quickly been proven wrong. He was the star. He was the good dancer who made the men lose control. He was Blueboy. Madame Sonia's pet.

Madame, just like his mother, encouraged him to keep up with his studies. He lied to her, just like he lied to his mother, making Pitik Sindit sound like a well-adjusted boy with many friends—far different from the creature who was relentlessly teased, cast out, the unfortunate scapegoat of his peers' adolescent talent for persecution. No matter, he thought. It was his destiny to be alone, cast out. His treatment by his schoolmates only confirmed his specialness.

Madame instructed him on how to keep the two planes of his life separate: imagine the door of the Santa Ana house to be a door to his own mind, his own insides. Stepping through to enter, he was going into the deepest recesses of his being, where his hidden desires of money and fame fused with the hidden desires of men. Stepping back out, he was entering the larger world of signs and objects, all of which required silence regarding his desires to keep these facades up and straight. In other words, there was a power in him that it was his duty not to unleash upon the world, lest he destroy it. Next to what he contained, the world was weak, knock-downable.

Often, thinking of the coiled, highly nihilistic strength of his "insides," Madame Sonia its trainer, he let his eyes sweep across the classroom to take in his teacher and classmates: *I am letting you live.* Of course, he only half believed his possession of such power. But still, that gray half of not-quite-belief was slowly being overtaken, every day being supplanted by the confidence born of his Santa Ana life.

By not disagreeing with the catechism, not divulging the existence of Blueboy, who didn't exist because he was not permitted by Pitik Sindit to exist until the knock, the door opening, one foot through the black curtain, then the other foot, until both feet were on the buckled tiles of the courtyard and the lock of the front gate snapped shut behind him; by not telling the girls in class, specially, that the gothic locks placed on their adolescent bodies by God, once unclasped by their own "sinful" actions, would not send an alarm to ring irreversible ruin (wasn't he proof otherwise?); by not opening his mouth and by cleaning his skin, evincing no residue of being spilled on, marked by men's desires, he was becoming more and more powerful, more and more convinced of a future scenario of victory. From this withholding which was beginning to make of his flesh a metallike substance, a cabinet of secrets, not chest but "chest," he would triumph over his stupid classmates.

Nodding at his teacher's stories of the creation of the world, the banishment from paradise of Adam and Eve for having disobeyed God and eaten from the tree of "knowledge," he put an attentive expression on his face, pretending to side with God's unreasonableness, all the while thinking: Why shouldn't people have knowledge? Wouldn't they be in the dark otherwise, no better than animals—is that what He wanted them to remain? And why, if knowledge was so bad, were they in class soaking the stuff up? Looking at him, the teacher must think she was creating one more object to be put in its proper place in this world of objects whose inner lives conformed to their shells, who retained whatever was introduced to them, unmodified by experience, unable, in the end, to have any experience other than what was stamped on them by education—certainly the most formative experience they were going to have their entire life, sealed for them in the high tones and moral goodness of English, a language that in his classmates' minds (and his as well) was the language of Jesus himself.

It wasn't the idea that he danced, or that he danced for men, or that the men did things while he danced, transforming the meaning of his act and giving him an influence he didn't possess in any other sphere of life, that was the warming center of his revenge fantasies—no.

Rather: as in a fairy tale where evil people had only a momentary reign over the heroine before she delivered, by escaping, the final, satisfying comeuppance, he too would show up the teacher, his classmates, his stupid neighbors who were mock-squeamish at the sight of him and his mother. He too would take flight in a carriage, in this instance, a Philippine Air Lines plane that would deliver him abroad to live with a foreigner. This prince would be a white man, one of Pitik's fans so besotted with the boy that he had to have Pitik by his side. Pitik would become a lasting, living souvenir of the man's trip to the Philippines. Everyone in his old life would finally see him, Pitik, magically princesslike. Or rather, they would discover that he had been royalty from the very beginning. He would be granted an ascension (much like the Mother Mary, ha-ha) into heaven—living in a house, dressed in clothes and being driven in cars and eating food that, being American, would have a natural cellophane of superiority over them; objects that were the living embodiment of English, which acquisition meant that native-born handicaps like poverty and brown skin were being improved upon, overcome. He would be elevated to a status that none of his schoolmates and neighbors could ever come close to in this life except by dreaming.

Eight years going and he already had a long list of admirers, a few of them more than willing to take him out of his situation to be absorbed into theirs. But he would not allow himself to be taken away until he felt himself to be deserving, until he was beautiful not just in the eyes of the men but, most importantly, in his own eyes. That was what he was saving his money for. Because to be beautiful—every day he felt himself inching closer—he had to have things like creams and gels and shampoos. His skin had to be softer, whiter, his hair less kinky.

But an even more crucial reason for waiting was the promise he'd made to Madame Sonia that he wouldn't leave until he was eighteen, by which point he would be too old to suit her clients. By the application of his creams and by trying to avoid or minimize hard labor, like lifting the five-gallon containers to and from the communal pump for his and his mother's daily water (which they paid a laborer to do), he had managed to keep his boyish (girlish) figure, retarding the onset of roughness and musculature.

Madame had seen him being talked up on a street corner by a German tourist when the boy was seven. Cameras had been slung like garlands around the man's neck and in his sunglasses twin Pitiks were made to confront their sudden prettiness. Madame had intervened, "saving" the boy. By talking with the boy, Madame had ascertained his advanced grasp of the way the world worked. He'd claimed to have known what the German had wanted of him. He'd thought "kissing," being "touched." Madame had elaborated. She'd said that talking was all well and good, but that actually doing it, or having it done to you, going through it, was another thing entirely. There was the physical pain, for one thing. The first time—would it be his first time? He'd lied, said he'd done it before. Madame had humored him but had continued to explain. The first time, as you would know, said Madame, and Pitik wasn't sure whether she'd winked or not, the first time is painful. But when you get used to it, you'll get to like it. As I have, said Madame. She'd explained about the necessity for lubrication to ease the discomfort. And at— How old was he? Seven, he'd replied, as if he'd failed a test. And at seven, the discomfort would be even greater. Because his "equipment," continuing to grow, hadn't yet reached the size where it could fully accommodate the German's "equipment." But then he already knew that, having experienced it, didn't he?

Madame had guided him through his first time. Had held his hand while a client Madame had procured fitted the man's "equipment" into Pitik's "equipment." Then Madame had nursed him for several days afterward. There had been a doctor brought in, a friend of Madame's who'd applied some ointment to advance the healing process. And

Madame had taken a cut of the client's payment, which Pitik, after all that she had done for him, did not begrudge her.

Afterward, Madame had encouraged confessing the act to his mother. He'd tried to run away. He was so frightened that he thought he would die, literally. But she had, demonstrating the ease of someone who had long inverted the natural flow of apology so that it was the world which had to make its amends to her, talked calmly to his mother, explaining that the woman should have nothing to be ashamed about. His mother had at first cried. But her tears had quickly been dried, and she had, surprising him, given him a kiss. She'd even thanked Madame for "discovering" her boy, by such an act saving the both of them, who'd been left to the whims of Manila life by the death from TB of a husband weakened by unforgiving work in construction sites all around the city. Who knows what would've happened to them if Madame hadn't come along?

Mostly, he danced. Every once in a while, to assuage the desire of a particular fan, Madame would pluck him from his performance routine to have an assignation. It was only because Madame controlled with the strictest vigilance the schedule for and frequency of such get-togethers that Pitik was allowed to be with these men. As a show of gratitude, and perhaps also a little out of fear, Pitik had never dared violate Madame's orders that any meetings with the Joes should first be cleared with her. Although he believed the cuts Madame took to be generally fair, he knew that every once in a while she was prone to siphon more than her alloted share. Such instances could be traced to specific losses she incurred gambling on horses and on jai alai. But Madame did not lie to him about life, about the world's meanings and machinations, unlike his teacher and her teachings, and for that he would forever be grateful.

Not that he, Pitik, being able to see through the inconsistencies and elisions of his school catechisms, had forsaken God wholesale. He still believed in God. He believed that somebody oversaw his actions, and though he also believed that these actions were more frowned upon than applauded, he thought that they were, at bottom, only misdemeanors compared to the abilities of the rest of the world. He knew that his activities were "bad," and yet could badness be performed, be let out into this world, and have absolutely no negative repercussions at all? In his case, he firmly believed that doing bad produced no bad whatsoever. By such "badness," after all, his mother was made happy. And so were the men who came to see him, from whom he leeched their very "badness" in the form of the liquid that would be poured on him at the end of the show, half an hour after he'd begun. His function was to bleed such toxins from the men's bodies, in the aftermath of which they were clearly seen to experience a great relief.

He believed in God because his mother and his other mother, Madame, also believed. And their faiths he saw to be capacious enough to embrace the idea of a punitive Father and the contradictory idea that their actions, though punishable (said so in the Bible), were to be commended, because of the degree to which they prevented other, greater crimes.

The distinction between his faith and the faith instilled in the rest of his schoolmates was that he could so easily overcome its burden of guilt. By looking at Madame, who presented no sad side of her personality to him, as if she had planed her soul free of any kinks born of the conflict between faith and action, he knew one very clear, admirable way of behaving in the world.

In the end, he believed in God because in the movies that he saw and loved, God, even when making no appearance, was so strongly felt.

How could he explain it?

He couldn't. Except to point out a shot in his favorite movie, *Namamatay Kahit Pagibig* (*Even Love Dies*), starring his mother's and his favorite, the superstar Nora Aunor, who, even though aging, was sprightly, specially in the way she broke into tears at each new misfortune. In this movie, Nora suffered through the usual combinations: pining after an unworthy man; then being suckered into marriage with him (he was more interested in the inheritance left her by a deceased spinster aunt than in her); almost immediately he treats her cruelly; then the cruelty reaches a peak when he cheats with one of Nora's best friends; after which, still believing in the power of love, she takes him back. But only after the man, attempting to kill her, is arrested and sent to jail does she break free from the binds of love's illusion and, doing so, goes insane.

This shot that he loved so much and which, to him, was a strange testament to God's existence and His power, was the last shot of the movie, and which had been replayed constantly on television during the film awards season to highlight Ms. Aunor's acting skills as she transforms from despairing to quietly insane. It was the movie's artiest shot, lasting all of three minutes, and in one continuous, uncut length.

We follow Nora out into the streets, on her face a stunned expression of having been told that she had never been loved, and we continue to follow her, registering the contrast of the street bustle with her tiny body radiating a growing panic, until, near the end, we move high up into the sky, making of Nora a dot and the street a widened panorama of toylike lean-tos sprouting next to one another, and wending their way around them, bodies upon sloppy bodies of such ordinariness it is a shock to realize that they are on film. Camera perched from on high, everyone looks like they are being looked down on by God, specially Nora Aunor, whom He, by finally allowing her to escape from the frame, frees from the responsibility of goodness. She goes insane, no longer required to hold the ideal of love aloft in this world.

Pitik believed this without being able to articulate either his reasoning or the depth of his emotion: He was Nora, and Nora was he. Both walking, on an arduous journey through Manila life. But soon, if he was patient enough, and if he continued to log mile upon mile, taking his suffering without complaint, he would be rewarded by the terrestrial view yielding to the celestial—God would be made to notice and, noticing, reward him, the striver. He, Pitik/Nora, would be released from having to keep company with the city's multitudes, be allowed to disappear into the edges of the frame, to wind up in a new land that would not be demarcated by such ruin and poverty. It was a movie he'd seen a dozen times, and only for the satisfaction and solace offered by that last shot—a shot accomplished by angels. And each time he'd cried.

That was why he believed, continued believing, in God.

In three years he would be eighteen—the clock counting down a period of grace for him. He would need to be in America by then, and there be freed, like Nora, from God's surveillance. But instead of letting go, like Nora, of the ideal of love, he would cling to it even more.

He would cherish until death the man who would take him away from everything, even from his mother whom he loved. Even from Madame whom he loved. Even from God, whose approval Pitik earned at great effort, much as he would have to earn the love of his father if the man were still alive—whose love would have to overcome, valiantly and ultimately impossibly, the liability of a *bakla* son.

Perhaps Pitik's love for God had its root in that very simple cause—God was the father life had deprived him of. And when that need was eventually filled by any of the various men who would be Pitik's new "father," taking him to his new life in America, Pitik would no longer have any need for God.

The two strongest candidates for this new God were a man named Feingold, who had told Madame of his great love for Pitik, but whose love Madame hadn't yet sanctioned, and a new man whose name Pitik didn't know but who had followed him to Santa Ana three days last week, each time wearing a disguise by which he'd meant, Pitik knew, to obscure his great love for the boy. In Pitik's thoughts, he gave this man the name of Cary Grant. Cary Grant was his mother's favorite movie star, whom the man resembled in some odd way, specially if you looked at him sideways, as Pitik had, trying not to appear to be looking.

Cary Grant, Pitik said some nights before he went to sleep, come and take me away. Every day he put on his gels and creams, and every day he was more prepared for Cary Grant's reappearance—even if, in the end, it would mean that he would have to violate Madame Sonia's orders, in the same way that his schoolmates were making of their parents' injunctions little tests and dares to prove themselves: sexing, gambling, drugging every night as their parents slept. For Pitik, it was loving, the greatest transgression of all, the most lancing, for which he was willing to sacrifice his popularity, his livelihood. He was ready to be overwhelmed, longing for it. Love, love, love. In this way, he was truly his age. He was a fifteen-year-old boy, blue with pining.

CHAPTER 2

H E WATCHED AS Pitik Sindit again disappeared into the front gate of the Santa Ana house; as, shortly after that, men began to emerge from either one end of the quiet street or the other, their feet purposeful and quick, but their eyes dulled and cast low, until, following Pitik in, he imagined their whole persons to lift as at the hungry's sudden sighting of food; and then waited, hours later, as these same men, coming back out into the darkness—indeed, looking, as he'd imagined, "lifted"—heralded the reappearance of the boy.

And so there he was, scrubbed and showered. Into his pockets was stuffed the cut of what looked like the day's paltry business. An ordinary-faced boy whose androgyny was a result of his startling skinniness and the way his body hung, suggesting curved vertebrae, or no vertebrae at all. It was a look that, nearing his home in Bambang, he was always seen to surrender, as if illustrating prehistoric man's journey from slouching beast to upright sophisticate, giving the lie to his Wilting Lily act, or was it the other way around, his look of Bambang sturdiness the pretense he had to indulge for his mother's sake, wanting to become the pillar of strength for her?

Caracera felt like a criminal, skulking to accomplish his duties. But in a sense wasn't he a criminal? Transgressing against family rule and risking injury to their pride by admitting in public their responsibility for this boy, among the Caracera-trammeled. Why, then, wasn't he happier? Hadn't he wanted to find irrefutable evidence of his forebear's wracked, puny souls, confirming the heroism of his estrangement? With this boy in his hand, the family could no longer shirk knowledge or blame.

To carry out the task before him he had gotten off pot. He'd wanted to be awake, aware. Now he was too awake. Looking around, he realized they were alone. Still he couldn't escape feeling afraid. There had been more than a convincing hint of threat from Irene's party—a coven, he thought of those gathered. For goodness' sake, he was succumbing to the melodramatic impulse so prevalent in the city—in its tabloids, its movies, its religion. Why did he have to be sober for this assignment? He was an amateur whom pot rendered capable, fearless—under its guidance, the bequest from his father had dwindled convincingly, usefully, peacefully. He would return to take up his teaching life at Columbia and, looking at him, his students would have no clue in what way he'd been enriched and decimated. He would return as the zero-sum old-fogey he'd always been in their eyes. It would be his secret to cherish, this adventure. His secret accomplishment. No, not accomplishment. Perhaps, looking back, years later, he could allow himself that vanity, that satisfaction, that satiation. But to think of himself as anything but a failure would be to violate the pact that he'd made with himself, if that made any sense. In failure was comfort and, having seen his family again, he knew that in failure he had become his own person.

He reminded himself that by usurping—knowingly or unknowingly didn't matter—the sixty thousand dollars meant for Pitik, he was just as responsible for the boy as the family.

He tapped the new driver Christopher Gochengco's headrest, and they followed the boy through two alleys, before finally pulling abreast, not surprising the boy, who knew he was being followed from the moment the car had started up but who had the presence of mind, developed since the age of seven, not to turn around, giving the game away.

The boy saw that it was Cary Grant and gave a big smile. He didn't care that they were only two blocks from Madame Sonia's and could so easily be spotted by either the matriarch or one of her dozens of fans, the white men who applauded and masturbated at the sight of his toothpick body.

But the boy's smile was short-lived. A panicked line took its place when he heard Cary Grant call him: Pitik?

Only his mother called him Pitik. To Madame Sonia and the men, his name was Blueboy. At school, a place that intended to elevate him from the penurious circumstances of his birth, which included the unfortunate apellation given him by his mother, he was called Peter. It was understood that his adult life would be a journeying up toward that name: Peter as in mythical Peter Pan, sprightly and beloved; or the suave, debonair Peter O'Toole, of *Lawrence of Arabia*, or . . . There was one other in his teacher's enumeration, forgotten. Oh, yes, Peter Frampton, the sexy-haired seventies pop singer, an idol from his teacher's youth, and whose songs were still in heavy rotation on Manila radio stations owing to the soft-rock leanings of a generation of Filipino music programmers (and advertisers). "Oldies but goodies," in the nightly parlance of the velvet-voiced disc jockeys, which he listened to when he couldn't sleep, and which, along with imported eighties programs like *The A-Team, Dynasty* and *Dukes of Hazzard*, helped to shape the images of his dreamtime refuge, the not-Manila where he would eventually go to live—as a full-fledged American whose process of naturalization could be traced, years back, to his rebaptism with that short, bulletlike name that had the coarse double meaning, perfect for his chosen livelihood: Peter peter peter; *Peeh*-ter, or Pee-*ter!*; or per the Brits (or the Japs), *Pee*-tah.

But this Cary Grant, calling him Pitik, revealed access to information that was entirely personal, which he could not have gotten unless he'd been snooping around. Suddenly the man's face and haircut, and the way he moved, lumpen and creaky of joint, all fused into the impression of a stolidly heterosexual man, not a man who could love Pitik back. Only now, up close, did it become clear to the boy: Cary Grant was straight. So what did he want with Pitik if he wasn't in love with the boy, wasn't capable of it? So the boy ran. And Caracera, getting out of the car, ran after him, both of them followed by Gochengco propelling the car ahead, the passenger-side door open.

Stop, said Caracera. I'm not going to hurt you.

The boy didn't stop.

Do you understand English? Caracera asked, holding the boy by the neck of his shirt.

The boy nodded.

Okay. Caracera let go. Took a breath. Gochengco and the car were beside them. Get in, Caracera said to Pitik.

The boy didn't move.

Get in. I'm not going to hurt you.

The boy looked at no-longer-Cary-Grant. He felt like crying. What you wanting to me? he asked the man in a voice that he tried to make seductive but which cracked midway through. His jaw began to tremble.

I'm not going to do anything, don't cry. We'll just talk. My name is Roger Caracera.

The boy didn't give any sign of recognizing the name.

Get in.

You is knowing Madame Sonia? asked Pitik.

The man was silent. Yes, he replied after a while.

You *are* a customer of Madame Sonia? he corrected himself.

The man didn't answer.

I saw you, the boy said accusingly.

I was there once, yes.

So you are maybe gay-gay? The boy's voice went up, with a sudden flash of hopefulness.

No, replied the clearly repulsed man.

They drove to the VIP Club. The boy refused to have anything to drink, staring at his feet.

I'm not going to hurt you, Caracera repeated, and again the boy gave an appearance of not believing.

Are you sure you don't want anything to drink? For clarification, Caracera added, I'm paying.

The boy shook his head.

Caracera wondered whether his uncle had ever brought the boy here. I have just one thing to do, to check up on, and then we can go.

Where are we going-going? asked the boy, and tears fell from his eyes.

Please don't cry. I'm not going to harm you. Have I hurt you so far? My mother is missing-missing me.

I'll take you back to her after we're through. We're going to get you, get us, something to eat. Are you hungry?

The boy shrugged.

But before we go, I just have to do one thing. He looked up to see the boy Donny Osmond Magulay on the court, playing.

Donny had on the same pair of worn-out sneakers, and was playing with another boy who was also employed as a hitting partner for the women. The two boys looked to be the same age, though of unequal skills. Again, as with the fretful young wife, Donny was the better by a wide margin. His friend knew it too, playing with abashed and self-dramatizing churlishness.

Caracera walked to the side of the court. He motioned.

Donny played so intently, as if wishing to obliterate from his consciousness all traces of his surroundings, that it was the other player, his friend, who had to flag his attention, stopping the point.

The boy, whose features had gone slack, ugly as soon as he'd stopped playing, came over to Caracera. Hello, sir, he said. Thank you, sir.

Caracera asked why the boy wasn't wearing the shoes he had had Christopher Gochengco purchase for him. Didn't they fit?

The boy looked down at the ground.

Caracera said that he shouldn't be afraid. Caracera would have them exchanged for a pair that fit. But Caracera was mystified, he thought he had had his driver make sure what size shoes the boy wore before buying anything.

Still the boy was silent.

Is there anything wrong? Caracera asked.

The boy shook his head.

Then why wasn't he wearing the shoes? Didn't he like them? According to Gochengco, they were the top of the line among tennis shoes. What brand were they?

New Balance. The boy pronounced each word carefully.

Well, what was wrong?

The boy finally revealed that he hadn't wanted to crease and dirty the shoes.

But they're meant to be used, Caracera told him.

Donny Osmond registered the insult of being told something obvious. Trying to keep from rolling his eyes, per natural reflex, he studied the ground again, inadvertently looking at his pathetic shoes. He saw what he had to do to get the man off his case.

Five minutes later, he was playing with the new shoes. A little too cautiously, as if they were impeding his movement, which worried Caracera. But then Caracera realized that the shoes, being new, needed breaking in. And the sooner the young boy got used to them, the better. He could've assured the boy of more shoes in his future to take the boy's mind off this hobbling dutifulness, but Caracera didn't feel he should attach himself in such a manner: as a guarantor, a protector, misleading the kid into believing that a period of hardship was completely over for him.

Although such a thought, considering the boy's flintiness, could only be entertained on one side.

He returned to Pitik's crestfallen face. Was that jealousy?

They drove to a restaurant along Roxas, where Caracera was sure they would not provide such a startling sight, being one more foreign man/brown boy couple whose quick friendships had been struck at the nearby seawall looking out at Manila Bay, or at the benches along the periphery of Rizal Park, a few blocks away.

He watched as the boy took the bread that had been provided while they waited for their meals. I have money for you, said Caracera.

The boy stopped chewing and looked up. Unfortunately the bread, in various stages of mastication, could be seen through his open mouth.

Caracera had been able to pry a picture loose from one of the family albums stored in the attic of the Makati house, a group shot of his uncles and father taken at some party during the men's youth. He needed the help of the caretaker Segismundo to identify Eustacio. This was the picture that he took out of his pocket and put on the table between him and the boy. He pointed out the man supposed to be Eustacio. Do you know him? he asked Pitik.

Pitik screwed up his features. Then he looked up at Caracera, shaking his head. He swallowed the bread.

Look closer. And this was when he was younger. Very much younger. So try to imagine him with . . . white hair, something like that.

Pitik shook his head.

His name is Eustacio.

Dumb.

You've met him.

Where? the boy asked.

At Madame Sonia's?

The boy tipped his head in order to think. I meeting a lot of people at Madame Sonia.

You didn't just meet him. You and he were—

They were interrupted by the waiter with their food, fried chicken for the boy, and a sour *sinigang* soup with shrimp and fish in a clay pot for Caracera. But Caracera didn't touch his order. He let the boy finish his chicken, not having to wait long.

He asked the boy if he ever did anything with the men who paid to watch him dance.

The boy took a long time to answer. It seemed to Caracera that his motive was neither embarrassment nor deliberation, but rather coyness, turning Caracera's question into an attempt to procure him.

Caracera brought his fist down on the table, making the plates, as well as the young boy, jump. Part of his anger undoubtedly had to do with the sacrifice of forgoing pot. I'm not joking, he said, turning his voice as grave as he could. Have you ever done anything besides dance for the men? Do you understand my question?

The boy nodded, his face reddening.

Have you?

The boy nodded.

Did this man pay you to do things besides watch you dance?

He is not familiar-at-all to me, said the boy.

He left you money, said Caracera. How can you expect me to believe he was a total stranger to you? How many men have you been with? Caracera asked.

The boy shook his head.

Give me an estimate.

The boy shook his head.

Fifty? A hundred?

I am only fifteen! said the boy.

Listen, you fuck. Don't play innocent with me. I've seen you. You know I've seen you. So why are we doing this dance where you try to make yourself innocent and expect me to believe you?

The boy was silent.

Caracera motioned for the check and quickly paid, laying down a mess of bills that, contrary to what he expected, did not attract much attention from the boy.

What are we going to do? Caracera asked out loud.

The boy was quiet.

How was the chicken?

Good, Pitik Sindit answered meekly.

Aren't you curious to know how much you're getting?

What do I having to do for the money?

Nothing. It's yours. He left it to you. You still don't recognize him?

The boy looked once more at the snapshot and once more shook his head.

Eustacio Caracera—that's his name. Do all the men you go with use their names?

Pitik shook his head.

So what do you call them when they don't?

I calling-calling them the same thing as Madame Sonia. Joe.

This guy was no Joe. He was Filipino.

Oh, then for sure I do not knowing him. I do not going with just-Filipinos.

What do you mean?

The boy acted hurt. I only going with foreigners. I am special-special. You asking Madame. That is why my name is Blueboy. Because blue is coloring of passport abroad, specially American.

He was no ordinary Filipino. He was rich. Caracera, pronounced Roger.

Like the sugar? the boy asked.

Like the sugar.

Even this did not seem to have an effect on the boy.

He's going to be pissed off in his grave. He certainly loved you enough to leave you sixty thousand dollars.

The boy looked up. Was this a joke, a trick? Dollars? he asked, to be sure.

Sixty thousand.

You are American?

Yes, replied Caracera, knowing that the boy probably meant to ask if he was a *white* American, but he didn't bother to clarify. Actually he left you the money in pesos. Three million. He pronounced the figure slowly.

A word the man had used along with "dollars" finally clicked inside the boy's head—or had he imagined the word "grave" in their conversation? This man—the boy hesitated—this man, pointing at the snapshot, he is dead?

Yes, Caracera replied. He was taken aback: three million pesos dangled in front of a boy who lived in a slum and who had to feign conviviality, to say the least, with a bunch of Stateside rejects who had to fly half a world away in order to get off—and the boy was more curious about the giver than the gift?

I guess it's an everyday thing for you to have guys die and leave you money, huh? he asked, contempt unchecked. To him, the boy had never looked much like any object of desire.

The boy understood the insult, giving the man the evil eye.

I want to talk to your mother.

Pitik Sindit opened his mouth, but said nothing.

Listen, I already know where you live, so either I visit her with you or without you.

Do not telling her anything.

You still won't admit you know this man?

I am telling the truth! Please!

Okay. Caracera tried stalling, thinking of some way to force the boy to confess. Then, looking at the picture, he realized that there would be no way of identifying, from such a long-ago image, the older version of the man the boy knew.

The money is being given to you on one condition, lied Caracera.

The boy was silent.

The condition is that you should stop doing what you're doing. Even as he heard himself uttering the words, Caracera was at the same time thinking, what did it really matter whether the boy continued or stopped? His was a vocation that seemed like a natural fit. Even now, as they were sitting across from each other, Caracera could detect flirtatious little filigrees thrown by the boy into the conversation, into the way he sat, twisting one foot over the ankle of the other, making sure Caracera should take note of the arrangement, and specially into the way he looked at Caracera, with chin lowered so that his eyes had to be slightly upraised. It was instinctual on the boy's part, a little funny, and succeeded only in churning up a gut revulsion in Caracera. That was what the boy was: a whore, an opportunist through and through. And nothing could change him. And wasn't it hypocritical of Caracera to want the boy changed, when he himself had devoted his adolescence to the anti-Catholic cultivation of sex as a life mission?

Cannot be, said the boy, staring down at his empty plate. He shook his head, and kept shaking his head, as if trying to erase the appearance of the man sitting across from him.

You'll have more than enough to live on for years and years. You and your mother. I'm talking to you—look at me! Another fist on the table. This time, a few people turned their heads. What must they think of the boy and man sitting together, behaving acrimoniously? A realization of his pesky fame, that the people staring might recognize him, made him even more irritable. But no, his new haircut had more than rendered the MacArthuresque shot at the funeral procession obsolete.

The boy looked up. He did not notice the people looking at them. All he was aware of was the anger of the man sitting across from him. It didn't occur to him that the man had anything to be angry about— it was he, Pitik, who had been duped. Cary Grant was not in love with him. Hadn't even wanted to harm him, by such an act proving that his desire for the boy was too strong. No, the boy was nothing more than an errand to this man, something which he'd been dispatched by a dead man to tie up. Three million pesos—he was unmoved by the amount for the simple reason that the man who would take him away from everything (who would no longer be Cary Grant, but the remaining candidate, none other than Feingold, another man from America) would be able to provide him material comfort whose monetary equivalent would put three million pesos to shame.

But with three million, wouldn't he finally be able to go to America, taking with him his mother, who would have the gift of a few easy years before her death? And wouldn't it be much more enjoyable to be in America without the curtailment of freedoms that having a boyfriend represented? No. He wanted to be loved. He wanted America as part of a package that would include, first and foremost, a beloved, a lover who, understanding what he deserved, gave it to him, gave him America, thereby broadcasting his specialness to the world: he had been singled out of an entire nation of hopefuls.

He tried to brush the thought of money out of his head. He would not be swayed by it. The man's anger would be matched by his own. Who did he think he was? And who was this stupid Eu-Eustacho? The name made him picture a man with a thick black mustache—no, he certainly didn't remember any man like that. And a Filipino—ugh!

I don't know him! I am telling the truth! Okay? He stared Cary Grant down—come to think of it, Cary Grant didn't look that much like Cary Grant at all. It was only when you looked at him sideways, and not too carefully, that he appeared movie-star-like. Head on, he was a little sad-looking, and pudgy too, nothing like the debonair Englishman. He was, considered coldly, only slightly more good-looking than Feingold, who was not very good-looking at all. In fact, Feingold wasn't Pitik's type—neither handsome nor worldly-seeming. He was only saved by his genuine and overpowering love for the boy.

Pitik looked at the man and narrowed his eyes, suggesting that if at one time he had been mesmerized by the man's presence, he was now no longer under such a disadvantage.

I'm sorry, said the man, surprising the boy. I shouldn't have expected you to recognize him from this stupid picture. Saying which, he pocketed the photograph.

The waiter brought back change. The boy observed that Caracera didn't even bother looking at the money, and left the not-insubstantial stack of bills on the plate. This was the exact same way Feingold had behaved every time Feingold and he had gone out for meals.

This rekindled the boy's great love of Americans, his admiration.

He was astounded by their indifference to money, the casualness with which they dealt with things like a good and hearty meal, taking them to be facts of ordinary life, no more than their due, no sooner gotten over with than having to deal with the next. In his mind, they sat at the end of a conveyor belt which kept pushing along into their ready and open mouths various articles of food, though mostly he saw pieces of cake, of all kinds and colors, sitting on dainty white china. Feingold loved his cakes—and no wonder, the man's figure needed to be supported by a steady diet of sweets and fats.

He got a warm rush of affection that made him have to look away, as the man guided him, in the style of a policeman trying to make sure a felon would not escape, by holding tightly at an elbow, back to his car.

The man still had not introduced himself, and began talking in a dictatorial style that was at once part of what the boy loved about Americans and, paradoxically, an example of all that he had tried to break free from: a life beholden to precepts dictated by cantankerous, killjoy elders.

The man repeated that the boy should quit his job upon receipt of the money. And of course, he said, the boy would go to school.

I *am* going to school.

Judging by your English, you need a better school.

Fuck you, said the boy. How's my English now? he thought but didn't say.

The man chose to ignore the comment. And the boy and his mother would move to a better home. I've been to Bambang, said the man, shaking his head.

A sudden anger inflamed Pitik. Not only, he realized, was he not even remotely an object of desire to this man whom he had foolishly built up into a dashing figure of romance, but it was clear that he was no more than a case for whom the suitable emotion was disdainful charity. His life needed to be remade because it offended the man's sense of what was proper in the world.

Fuck, he thought, using a word that he had never had much occasion to say. Now, in the span of five minutes, he had already used it twice. And it did not make him feel sophisticated or worldly, as he'd felt when he'd secretly used it before, imagining himself to live in the same land from which the Peter Frampton songs and his beloved TV shows issued. Instead it only made him feel sad, a little lost. On his lips it felt fraudulent. He wanted to be in love, he wanted to greet his lover with proper words of affection and endearment, not curse him, causing him to flee.

The Mercedes attracted a horde of young children. They opened

their palms and hounded Caracera, but, seeing one of their own follow immediately, coming out of the dark interior after the man, they
stopped, backed off. Caracera told Gochengco to wait blocks away.

Pitik made a turn in the slum's alleys that Caracera hadn't taken
with Frannie Prusso. They entered a hut that was secluded from its
neighbors by being built onto a strip of planking so narrow it had
room for only a single home.

The woman who looked at Caracera as he crouched through the
low entrance was short, her thinning hair streaked with dull gray. Her
forehead was the most distinct feature of her wizened, browned face:
Caracera couldn't remember if he had ever seen a more lined forehead
in his life. Thinking him a guest of her son, who was the decision
maker in the household and whose caprices she bowed to, she nodded,
smiled weakly, a little fearfully perhaps, and indicated a spot on the
floor for him to sit. Caracera smiled back but remained standing. By
now the woman had expected to get a word from her son, some ex-
planation or introduction, especially if this was one of his johns for
whom she was expected to make tea or coffee. Not only did Pitik not
do any such thing, he stormed off into his quarters, disappearing behind a floral-print curtain, and soon was heard plopping his body on
the floor.

I'm sorry, began Caracera.

He switched to a halting Taglish (Tagalog and English) to explain
his purpose.

He thought it best to cut right to the heart of the matter, not even
pretending to honor her role as a mother, or, more properly, a good
mother, by sidestepping the touchy subject of her son's livelihood. He
told her about his uncle, his uncle's will. He told her that the man had
probably met her son at Madame Sonia's. By not backtracking to
explain who Madame Sonia was, the clear implication was that the
mother must know and had been condoning her son's relationships
with men. He knew, as he was speaking, that the boy was listening in,
possibly seething.

Then he told the woman the exact figure of his uncle's inheritance.

The woman staggered and had to be helped to sit on a stool that
was an old rusted tin of some sort. Still, the boy did not come
out. One wall was decorated by a plasticized sheet with pictures of

various fruits trapped inside a grid of diamonds—the same kind commonly wrapping tabletops in cheap restaurants and that must've been discarded in some renovation. Caracera thought he could detect ineradicable stains here and there. Pitik's mother rested her cheek on a pineapple. With one hand she fanned herself.

Call your son to come out, he asked her.

She did. She had to do it over and over before the boy, pouting, staggered out.

The mother and son had a brisk conversation. The boy answered desultorily, still sticking to his claim that he did not know this man who had left him all that money. Hearing such an admission made the mother clearly nervous. She stole worried glances at Caracera. Would the money be rescinded? Could Caracera have the wrong boy after all?

How, she asked, did he know that it was to her son that the money had been left?

Well, his name was Pitik Sindit, wasn't it?

The woman, glad to have even ventured her one risky question, had no others. She began to cry. Then, catching Caracera by surprise, she leapt at his shoes and put both arms around his ankles. Her prostrated body convulsed in up, down and sideways motions, while out of her twitching face poured not just the tears and snot of unself-conscious and ugly-making servility but also the spit of copious gratitude, word upon word of thanks to Caracera, his uncle and to God, a trinity whose rescue had been years in the making and long awaited, and which, coming to her now before her death, proved that heaven was no posthumous reward but could be enjoyed while still on this bitter earth. Her tributes were at once put-on and heartfelt and made their recipient feel queasy. Tell her, he told the boy, to please stop.

But Pitik didn't need to be told. He yanked his mother from her humiliating position and communicated in no uncertain words that there was no way he or she would take the money. This stunned Caracera. He had not been prepared for the boy to refuse. How could anyone refuse? Even he, Roger Caracera, though avowedly against all that the money stood for, hadn't had the temerity to do such a thing.

The mother asked Pitik what he meant.

How did they know that the man before them didn't want something nefarious for which the money would be payment in advance?

If he wanted something nefarious, then why couldn't he just take it from them without paying?

They went back and forth for a while, not afraid that Caracera could understand every word. Until, finally, the boy came up with a question that rendered his mother completely silent. He asked, What about Madame Sonia? He explained that the money was being given on condition that he quit. Caracera, being looked to by the woman, confirmed it.

But didn't the boy want to quit? Hadn't he always complained of how tired work made him, and of how around his classmates he felt funny, as if a visible curse had been put on him by what he had to do for a living?

He didn't remember saying the last part to his mother and looked at her dumbstruck. How could she have known?

Pitik? asked the woman.

He said, in as calm a voice as he could find, that Madame Sonia would tolerate no disloyalty. He reminded his mother that they owed their lives to Madame Sonia.

I'll pay her off, said the strange man, who seemed to have an answer for everything.

Why do you want me to quit? asked the boy.

It's not me. It's the man who's giving you the money, Caracera said.

Why does he want me to quit? asked the boy.

Is he a priest? asked the mother.

No, replied Caracera. He was in love with your son.

He just has a beautiful heart, said the mother, providing a capping moral and nodding at its wisdom.

Love—there it was, finally, the word the boy had wanted to hear. But it did not come from the man he'd wanted it to come from. Instead, it was coming from a dead lover—if he could even remember who this man was. But he did not want a dead lover. He wanted proof of someone's love for him in proximity, touchable. He wanted Cary Grant. He looked at the man. He'd been wrong after all. Cary Grant had been rendered only temporarily ugly by the meanness of his expression, hoping to put the scare into the boy. Now, seeing the man with a placid expression, Pitik knew that he was exactly Pitik's type: dark-haired, older, distant and with a sexy streak of sternness on his face even when relaxed. There was a certain sense he gave of being, even though well provided for, a sad sack, perhaps a failure, a man with diminished expectations from life: this was key because then the standard Pitik would have to meet would not be impossibly high.

Madame Sonia, was all he could think to say once again. He felt defeated. He couldn't look at the man. He specially couldn't look at his mother, the edges of whose mouth were still shining with spit. Her cravenness would've been his own a few years back. He would've leapt at the chance to have even a fraction of the money being offered. But he had since grown up, and his ambitions had considerably widened. And more importantly, he was convinced that his ambitions could and would easily be met. He had every right to ask as much from life, having grown used to the idea of his desirability, his preciousness from Madame Sonia's clientele. Nobody would understand how, next to the idea of being beloved, and beloved by an American, and furthermore, by a Handsome American, the money was like a decoy, a thing of value that, looked at closely, disclosed its tawdriness.

He wanted Cary Grant to offer the money in exchange for him. He wanted it as a measure of Cary Grant's love, nothing less. The fact that he couldn't remember this Eustacho was a clear sign that the man was among those clients whose faces he'd turned into a blank screen onto which he'd superimposed the imagined face of his beloved, by such a method making the bad days bearable. His brain was all-powerful. With it, he was able to transcend the life he lived. With it, his body could be at Bambang or at Santa Ana, and his soul and heart swaddled in the comforts of his imagined America. With it, he could be dancing in front of dreary, anonymous men, his head bent groundward causing his face to turn red at the onrush of blood, and at the same time be deep in a narcotizing dream of being wooed, chastely and with offerings of flowers or lines of inchoate poetry, by a handsome man of distinctively foreign and superior features.

The fact that he had introduced himself to this Eustacho as Pitik Sindit was a sign that he could not have cared less what the man thought of him. A slovenly slipup to indicate the slovenliness of his feelings for the customer, and from this, it was clear that Eustacho was definitively a Filipino, to Pitik entirely without interest. Otherwise wouldn't the man know him by Blueboy?

I'll be back tomorrow, Caracera said.

Madame Sonia, the boy repeated.

I told you, said Caracera. I'll take care of her.

The boy looked at his mother. He loved her and she disgusted him. He could tell that she would be willing to see him forfeit his dreams just so she could cavort with the money. At the same time he could gauge in her eyes, in her open, silent mouth the same desire which he himself had of wanting to show up their neighbors.

In the end, he let the man leave without saying anything. What could he say? Certainly not the truth, confessing his one-sided love. It would mortify him.

Only after the man left and their shack was restored to an indicting dimness, its gingham walls and newly cleaned floors closing back in on him, did he drop his head, surrendering his sham posture of control. He didn't want to look at his mother, choosing instead to be met by his feet. On his left foot, the underside of his big toe was heavily callused, owing to his being out of balance and having to rest his weight, specially when dancing, on his left side.

He went inside his room. He did not pull the lightbulb to turn it on. His mother did not dare follow him in. He was the tyrant in the household and though it pained him to reduce his mother to a peon, even she had to recognize that his work, saving them from penury, exacted its payment by turning him into a monster.

He lay down on his unrolled mat, stared at the dark ceiling. Suddenly he brightened. Face-to-face with the man, he hadn't been able to keep his head up or convincingly hold his end of the conversation, he was all gangly spurts and ejaculated nonsense or evasion. But as soon as the man disappeared, returning to his original status as object of pure contemplation, so too did Pitik resume his dream role as a silken, resourceful Juliet. Facing an obstacle, he knew what he must do. He would get Cary Grant yet. And make the man think that the process had been entirely natural, preordained. The point of dreams, after all, was to pretend not to have forced the hand of serendipity and by doing so reveal a blueprint of manipulation and tacky will. He would, from all outward appearances, continue to be Filipino, be seen to believe in fatefulness, in other words, continue to be acted upon, while inside, concealed by the clever performance, would beat an

American heart, the heart of a go-getter, earning his reward—the man's love—by exercise of planning, of hard work. Like any regular American he had identified a desire and would now go after it.

Suddenly he remembered that the man had introduced himself after all. Perhaps Pitik had simply refused to surrender the name he had given the man and had pretended not to hear.

Roger? Was that the first name? How completely blah.

Caracera. As in the sugar. *You're so sweet*, he imagined the man saying as a prelude to their on-screen kiss, the cameras moving in to swallow them.

Cary-cera Grant. Ha-ha.

Roger Cary Grant-a-cera.

Caracera? That wasn't an American name. And the man knew Tagalog.

Well, so what, that didn't prove anything. So many Americans, aiming for charm, tried to learn the language. And there had certainly been the trace of an American accent in the man's Tagalog.

Roger Caracera, Eustacho Caracera.

Perhaps Roger was from the American branch of the family, completely unconnected to Eustacho, or perhaps, at worst, he was only half Filipino, half ruined?

Three million, his mother whispered, peeking her head inside his room. And then she began crying all over again. He went to comfort her, though he found that the hand that ran itself over her hair, and its companion which settled on her back and began to knead away, were both hardened, requiring a great effort not to be transformed into fists.

CHAPTER 3

GOCHENGCO CONTINUED TO drive Caracera, and most days, wanting to kill time and thought, Caracera was shepherded to the VIP Club. There they did not seem to know what had happened with the boy Pitik Sindit, who was a direct inheritance from his Uncle Eustacio, they did not seem to know about his Uncle Eustacio and they continued to treat him with respect, as well as the abiding awe an appearance in the newspapers merited. He was aware of being pointed out to visitors and other members who, with varying degrees of stealth, would emerge in his peripheral vision, studying, fighting the urge to speak to him, storing for anecdotal use giveaway kinks in his appearance and behavior, which, try as hard as he could to smooth before appearing in public, he was sure remained, marking him out as the opposite of his real self: a man full of stories and verve.

Inevitably, the family was alerted and Irene Caracera, bringing an investment counselor recommended by a wealthy Filipino friend living in St. Louis, was soon sitting next to Caracera along the side of one of the courts.

How long do you plan to stay this second time?

I don't know.

She was glad he was trying to fulfill obligations set forth in his father's will, except by this logic shouldn't he be living in the Makati house?

Now that the caretakers have found new jobs, it's too empty.

Jesus Caracera didn't by any chance appear before him as well, did he?

No. Of course not.

Where are you staying now?

Not far from the Makati house, actually. He gave the name of his building. This was easier than having to argue or hide.

She asked him about plans for his money. She said she hated to sound like the people at the party of a few weeks ago but . . .

The investment counselor asked what investment options he'd considered for "growing" his inheritance.

I'm not interested in growing, he replied. Again this was much easier than hiding or feigning agreement.

What does that mean? asked Irene.

Maybe you should think about it, said the counselor.

I've been thinking of giving it away.

You don't mean all of it?

All of it.

It's a little too late in your life for this kind of joke, Roger.

Who's joking?

At least, said the counselor, retain a fraction for yourself. For protection. Roger asked him what protection. The counselor listed a number of emergency scenarios: accident or hospitalization, unemployment, sudden unforeseen homelessness. Irene told him to stop, this was all very morbid.

Why are you still angry at us? Irene asked him.

I'm not angry.

Then why give the money away?

Is there something you wish to tell me?

What do you mean? she asked, genuinely baffled.

Nothing at all?

She looked at his self-satisfied face. Are you insane? she asked.

He flinched, remembering his mother. Was this the occasion to mention the boy whore Pitik Sindit? He replied that being a forty-four-year-old man, hadn't he earned the right to be left alone?

I always encourage a measure of adventuresomeness in my clients when seeking investments, said the counselor, but you, sir, could do with a lot less adventure.

Adventure, huffed Irene, intending it as an indictment.

The young boy Donny Osmond Magulay was the frequent center of Caracera's attention during the VIP visits. The boy knew that Caracera had asked the staff, particularly the supervisor, about him, and had been told that the boy, along with some of his colleagues, was seeking sponsorship for an upcoming citywide tournament that pitted talented youngsters against one another. Though this was largely an intramural competition between designated (mostly private) schools, players of the right age (under eighteen) who managed to get the backing of a reputable party could enter. The sponsor, in a letter, needed to assert full financial responsibility for the boy. This would include an entrance fee of one thousand pesos, a coach's fee (every participant needed one and could choose from among a list provided by the tournament, or could use school or private coaches), and practice fees for courts as needed, as the tournament progressed.

The winning player would be awarded four hundred thousand pesos and a full scholarship to the Nick Bollettieri Tennis Academy in Bradenton, Florida, famous worldwide for having turned out such champions as Andre Agassi and Jennifer Capriati.

The boy was confident that Caracera's sponsorship was only a step away, his for the asking. The man had kept turning up as Donny practiced with the clients, or as he played with his friends. Didn't this show that Roger Caracera was a fan? And being a *rich* fan, wouldn't he see sponsorship as a natural progression, a more active form of applause? The boy's victories, accomplished alternately with actorly bravura and sly casualness, were like backers' auditions. This was why he'd refrained from asking Caracera outright. Also, there was the precedent set when the man had given him, without prompting, his New Balances, now worn to the point of comfort.

Back home waited a mother, who sold fish and vegetables in the markets of Divisoria and who took on sewing and mending work for Chinese families in the neighborhood, and a sister, age fourteen, who was being groomed for life with the nuns. This vocation had been offered in exchange for her safe birth, a bloody and protracted event which had seemed, until the last minute, to be headed for yet another stillbirth that was the family's punishment for the father's waywardness. And when she had emerged from the ten-hour procedure miraculously alive, her toes uncurling and feet kicking petulantly, it was thought that the marriage was now on safe ground, the union sealed by the portent of her survival. For this her future had been bartered and she would become a bride to nobody but Christ.

But the marriage lasted only another two years before the husband left to live with another woman.

And seeing that their mother's barter had been conditional upon the marriage's success, there seemed no reason why his sister, Rose Red Magulay, should still be held to her end. But the mother would not break a promise to God, and so Rose Red continued to be trained, by being sent to the nuns to brush up on catechisms every Saturday, for a life as a virginal Christ bride. But she underwent the training halfheartedly and only to deflect attention from her true vocation, which had been, from the first moment her consciousness had registered the effect she had upon the neighborhood men and boys and from the next moment in which this effect produced the most intense and fulfilling pleasure in her, to become the coveted prize of a boy or man who, either because of good looks or wealth or skill in sports or hopefully all three, was himself highly coveted.

Though this setup was undoubtedly headed for tragedy, for the moment it had only a comic dimension to the boy, which was not to say that he condoned his sister's deceit—but neither did he approve of his mother's foolish God-drive, especially when God had so clearly failed her, foremost by giving her a dud husband (whose bad genes had been unfortunately passed on to the boy, via his teeth and his skinniness, but not to his sister). The father gone, the sister mortgaged to God and therefore the fulfiller of their mother's grandiose moral ambitions, it was left to him to satisfy their mother's other ambitions, which had to do with the practical, the monetary world. It was up to him to move them out of their single room in Binondo, to allow his mother to retire from menial work so that she could indulge in bingo and do volunteer work for the church, up to him to underwrite the ceremony at which his sister would formally take on the vows: her habit, a floral tribute, a contribution to the church at which she would be welcomed into the God-harem.

This was the environment that greeted him every night after work, in other words, the constriction against which his playing could better be understood. At the VIP, he was free for the moment from the pressing concerns of his family life and played accordingly, with pleasure and pride, in the full throttle of youth, cherishing the brisk aloneness at his end of the court, the only part of the world that mattered—except in fleeting instances, when the game took on the inescapable dimension of a yoke behind which he was pulling the weight of his history and family, and then he played as if the person at the other end were the future: he played in a frenzy of a desire to annihilate, effecting full submission. Thankfully, this would lead to heavy sweating, which would, in turn, lead back to his awareness of the game being only a game, full of physical effort that needed all the concentration he could give to it.

This sense of grievance was his justification for secretly withholding a portion of his income from his mother, which he was supposed to surrender every two weeks so that she could buy groceries, pay the rent and offer up contributions during Mass each Sunday. He saw the money, which he put into a savings account, as rightfully his, with which he earned the needed reward of being able to go to clubs and cafés and the movies each weekened with his workmates. But he was unable or unwilling to make the gamble on his own future with it: to withdraw a portion (granted, roughly three-quarters) as an investment that might possibly yield a trip to Bradenton, Florida, and more importantly a trip *away from* his mother and his sister, the impending conflict of both of whom he did not want to be around to see. He didn't want, by putting his own money on the line, to have play transformed so prematurely into work, talent made joyless by being turned into a line or a lure for money.

Another day of waiting for the man Roger Caracera to make his move and finally the boy, breaking character, went over to ask the man himself. He was unaccustomed to being the suitor, and his tone of voice continued, though he intended the opposite, to wobble perilously close to a well-oiled petulance. It was almost as if he believed he would be rejected and so tried to convince himself that he didn't really want what he was asking for.

But the man said yes. Of course he would say yes. And Donny Osmond smiled, and his smile, once again, was the smile of a confident and devious young man, who believed that things were due him.

The next day the man arrived with his letter of sponsorship, plus a check for the entrance fee.

The day after that, following a night of thinking it over, the man asked the boy if he could be the boy's coach. The boy had not foreseen this intrusion and, in reply, opened his mouth and said nothing. Granted, none of the names provided by the tournament had registered with him and he'd been forced to conclude that one was just as good, or rather as bad, as the next. He had no intention of letting their coaching override his instincts about the game anyway. He would take whatever nugget they tossed but fully expected to have to wade through a barrage of outmoded or clueless edicts to get at these rare nuggets. He had long been a student of the game, his studies perhaps predating some of these coaches' beginnings. He had learned the most important lessons at the feet of the best, whose stratagems he could view over and over again on tape: Borg, McEnroe, Connors, Lendl, Edberg, Becker, Courier, Chang and Sampras Sampras Sampras. (Loving Pete, he could not allow Andre Agassi, Pete's chief rival for greatness in this generation, into the instructors' pantheon.) He had a library of thirty-five tapes, all of them well-worn, and stretches in some of which were fraying from having been rewound so often. In these points, the ball was slowed down to better comprehend its clever dispersal until the shocking, gorgeous dismissal, the audience at once on their feet to crown the effort. He understood, during these clinics, that no opponent would let the ball die without a fight and that to effect this death, you had to be cunning (wrongfooting the opponent; drawing a mistake by changing the pace or the spin), powerful (equating the serve with firing a gun, the ball either zipping beyond return or kicking up or going straight into the opponent's body) and not averse to gambling (low-percentage shots that had to be conjured out of nowhere).

This had been the method by which his game was built: cobbling together from a list of greatest hits: Pete's overhead smash, Edberg's net play, Lendl's tenacity, Becker's dangerous dives, Chang's scurrying,

Courier's baseline power, Connors's devious and boisterous showmanship, hooking into the spectators for a charge . . . In this way, he was a
typical resident of his country: one more in a nation of copycats. And
though he recognized this (the legacy of his public school education
being the knowledge of indebtedness to foreign forces), he was not
overly alarmed, did not consider it a disadvantage. It was simply the
way of the student, learning by repetition, dating all the way back to
antiquity. What separated him from his country—although he did not
pause long enough to take this into consideration—was the fearless arrogance of feeling that history, yellowing right there on his three
shelves put atop his bed, was nothing more than a warm-up act before
his entrance on the scene. He did not feel burdened by the tapes he
viewed over and over, felt he would soon be the subject of one of these
tapes himself. If copycatting was the straightest line to achieving this
glory, so be it. Let it be a necessary evil. Originality in tennis was not
the point. Winning was.

What he was aware of was this: there had never been a Filipino
player on the world stage who reached the second week of a major, or
who'd managed the quarters or semis of any of the other tournaments.
At least none who did so with the consistency of a true contender.
Currently there was not a Filipino player, male or female, in the top
two hundred, maybe even the top five hundred in the world. He was
determined not only to remedy the lack, but to make of the numerical
ranking before his name a single, awe-begetting digit. And by this accomplishment, he wished to raise the question in his countrymen's
minds: why was tennis not more popular in the Philippines?

The tournament, in his opinion, wanted coaches to show that the
skills of the youngsters were embryonic. They had no confidence in
the talent they would draw, the Philippines being largely basketball
country, and wanted it known that what the audience would see would
be improved in time by the coaches at the tournament and, for the
winner, a first-rate education in the USA. He welcomed the training in
America that was being offered as the prize but did not consider it essential to his development.

Thinking of this, he also thought that the tournament was his for
the taking. The coaching would be something he would outwardly
abide. But his instinct, as usual, was aligned along his talents for mutiny,

secrecy, which, being some of the same talents that made him a good competitor, were to be cultivated.

The man looked like a pushover and could easily be disobeyed, without repercussion. Donny Osmond finally pushed out the word Yes from his open mouth. Caracera would be his coach. They shook on it.

CHAPTER 4

I T WAS A MONDAY, the official day off for Madame Sonia's House of Beauty and Pain, or rather, a day off for the former commodity, as Blueboy was giving no performances, but not the latter, which was everywhere present on Pitik Sindit's face as he sat between the two antagonists: Cary Grant, a.k.a. Roger Caracera, who wore an expression of seemingly imperturbable confidence, and Madame Sonia, whose face could not be read for any mood or feeling, even by someone who knew it as well as Pitik did. This certainly betokened imminent danger, which Pitik did not want to be around to experience, as he had a feeling that he too, along with Cary Grant, would be its focus.

It was he who had brought Cary Grant to Santa Ana; he who had knocked on the front door and then stepped aside to reveal behind him Cary's figure, dressed in newly pressed shirt and pants and whose eyes were armored by frosted glasses (how they completed him!); he who had bowed his head and given the floor to Cary Grant to state "their"(!) purposes to Madame Sonia; he who, by going nearly mute, had as much as indicated to Madame Sonia his compliance with Cary Grant's scheme; he who, in other words, was the prime betrayer, whose treachery had found a convenient accomplice in the man. He had been unable to look at Madame directly to answer her questions, and could only mumble inconclusive but clearly apologetic and therefore guilty replies: I don't know, I'm not sure, and shrug upon shrug that Madame had to greet with sportsmanlike equanimity in front of the American.

Is this your idea? she'd asked.

I don't know.

Is this your idea or not?

I'm not sure.

Do you want to leave me, Pitik?

Shrug.

Is that a yes?

Shrug.

In Madame Sonia's "living room." The proprietress seated on one end of a futon sprawled with countless cushions, the mattress covered over by a blue-and-white-checked blanket, fringed at both ends and spotted with islands of discoloration. On the other end of the futon was Cary Grant. There were no chairs except in the kitchen, which was filthy and therefore off-limits. The pair had caught Madame Sonia by surprise, and Pitik especially had been shocked by how slovenly Madame turned out to be, although there was contrasting evidence of Madame's characteristic fastidiousness, a recent touch of home improvement: the *calesa* wheel which had forever lain in the courtyard under the shade of the scary trees had been taken indoors, cleaned and was now hanging horizontally in one corner of the ceiling above the bed, transformed into a kind of native chandelier by being strung with Christmas lights, but which unfortunately looked like something dislodged by an earthquake and about to fall at any moment.

To Caracera, the revelation of the proprietress's uncleanliness was no surprise. A moral pig wallowing in a sty, he thought, pleased at gaining the upper hand almost immediately. There were resealed cartons of food and opened packages of cookies shoved underneath the bed but whose odor continued to permeate the airless front room. Besides batik-style curtains that, blocking out already dim light, helped to give Caracera the impression of being in a cave, the room was also equipped with pots of ivy and other plants that were greenly glossy. In this environment, the proprietor, just like her plants, was an obdurate fact of nature—disregarding inadequate nourishment to triumph vengefully.

Madame Sonia had not recognized Caracera. And even after Caracera had described their last (and only) encounter, it had taken her a while to understand who the man in front of her was. She had no choice but to invite the pair into the house, not wanting to give the neighbors any more reason to complain. The neighborhood wives, in particular, had let it be known that they were wise to the purposes of the white men who trekked through the nearby streets, and some of the women's husbands had even intimated that arson might be a fitting end to the condemned property that Sonia was no better than a squatter in and which she had surely inherited from its previous owner through some underhanded transaction. Now, with her in it, the property was doubly condemned and needed to be "taken care of." And so she had responded in the only way the men and women could understand, by bribing them, making them understand that there was prosperity to be had by silently suffering the white men's patronage of the neighborhood. But Monday had long been understood by the snooping neighbors to be a break in the regular traffic pattern. Though there had been nothing said about keeping the day particularly sacred, a secular church day for the neighborhood, so to speak, that was the way things had turned out, and Sonia was not about to endanger the neighborhood truce by confronting Caracera, who was clearly a disgruntled john, on her front steps.

Sonia had quickly dragged the pair inside. The man had introduced himself and after a few moments a memory had come back to Sonia of a dowdy, clearly effeminate man and how, because he had not been brought to orgasm by Blueboy's show, there had been an altercation between him and Sonia. The man in front of her was supposed to be the same person? Somewhere a lie had been told. Then? At their first meeting? Or now?

She listened to the man's claims, his plans, his proposition. She took note of the implied disrespect in the man's confidence, as if Blueboy's release were a foregone conclusion. And yet, by not getting up, by remaining seated, her short frame made shorter, wasn't she sending a message of accommodation to her visitor?

She asked the boy a series of questions and had to stifle her grow-

ing anger at the boy's charade of ignorance. She would take care of the
boy when they were alone.

You are lying-lying, she said to the man Caracera.

I'm not.

You say you are not in love with Blueboy?

That's the truth.

That's what you told me the last time.

And it's what I'm telling you again. Because *it's the truth*.

So then you are starting-starting a business and taking away my
number one property!

No. I told you—

What is your reasoning for taking away Blueboy? The proprietress
put on an exaggerated look of befuddlement and placed arms akimbo
on her waist.

It's not me. It's the man who left him—he nodded at the boy—the
money.

Where is this man?

I told you he's—

Dead, yes, said Madame Sonia. How convenient. She turned to
Blueboy, whose head had not been raised the whole time. Do you hear
that? she asked the boy. He's not in love with you. Is that what you
want? Blueboy! I am talking-talking to you.

The boy looked up, remaining silent.

He is not in love with you, repeated Madame Sonia. She looked at
Caracera. Say it to the boy again.

He knows that the money is not from me.

The boy and I have making-making an agreement, said Sonia. This
time she finally stood up, moving to the windows and gathering the
curtains to let in some light. She turned around, sat down on the window ledge. I taking care of the boy and before I letting him go I make
a promise to give him to a man who loves him. I *release* him—she
looked at Caracera—that's your word, right? My promise is that I *release* the boy to another caretaker, who is loving-loving Blueboy. Isn't
that right? she asked the boy.

The boy nodded.

I can't hear you.

Yes, Madame.

In other words, said Caracera, looking at the proprietress coldly, you'd sell him to the highest bidder. What's the difference? I'm offering you a lot of money right now.

After you giving him the money what are you going to do?

I don't understand. To do what?

You are leaving him alone?

Doesn't he have a mother?

She is super-useless, said Madame Sonia. She crossed one leg over the other.

The boy looked down once again, having no will to defend his own mother.

He can take care of himself.

So you won't help?

If he needs me to. The reluctant tone of Caracera's reply was hard to miss. The boy, humbled by his irrelevance, dug his sneakers farther into the furred old carpet.

How?

By sending him to school. Giving whatever guidance he needs.

Guidance, said Madame Sonia in an elongated, lampooning manner, turning the word lascivious.

Listen, said Caracera, himself standing up. I don't even have to be here. I could go to the police station. Give them a report. Instead I'm offering you money. Because I understand how important the boy is to you. At heart you're a businessman and—

Stop talking to me like that!

So you're not a businessman?

The proprietress glared. She turned the hem of her shirt inside out to encase her fist, thrusting the shirt forward. She stood up. No, she told Caracera flat-out. I am not giving-giving Blueboy away. Specially not to you. Good afternoon. You, she said to Pitik, stay.

You don't seem to understand, said Caracera. This was where he was aided by his conviction of Filipino humility: Madame Sonia, despite a bravura performance, would be subdued, made to see the foolishness of her stand. You are going to let the boy go and for that either you receive some compensation or you get time in jail. That's the only choice involved.

You thinking the police do not know about me already? huffed

Madame Sonia. You don't think I haven't taken care of them already? I am not just a business*woman*, I am a *great* businesswoman! She dragged the boy up and pulled him close.

Come here, Pitik, said Caracera.

Madame Sonia held tight to the boy.

Come here!

Sonia could feel the boy hesitating, pulling his feet back from their initial impulse.

Tell her what you told me, Caracera ordered the boy. Tell her that you want to come with me.

Madame Sonia looked at the boy. Is that true?

Pitik was stricken.

Blueboy! huffed Sonia.

Caracera urged the boy, You don't have to be afraid. Come on. Tell her.

Blueboy, are you wanting to leave me?

I'm sorry, Madame, said the boy, who began to cry.

Why do you wanting to leave? Am I being evil-evil to you?

The boy shook his head.

Am I not giving you enough pay?

The pay is very good, Madame, squeaked the boy.

Are you getting tired of the dancing-dancing? These questions were clearly meant for Caracera's enlightenment.

The boy was silent.

Yes, he is, uttered Caracera.

You are putting-putting the words in his mouth!

Tell her, Pitik.

The boy didn't speak.

Tell her!

I don't know, he said to Madame Sonia.

You don't know because he is forcing you. Right?

I don't know, said the boy.

But you liking the dancing-dancing, don't you, Blueboy?

Pitik nodded.

And your fans liking it very much. What are they going to do when you leaving them all alone?

You can find another boy, said Caracera.

Where?

Wherever you found this one.

"This one": hearing, Pitik's fears of irrelevance were reconfirmed and he renewed his tears. He put his head into Madame Sonia's ample breasts and shook. Madame took this as a sign and flashed a victorious smile for Caracera's benefit. She stroked the boy's head and said, Blueboy is not so easy to make-replacement. Do not leaving me, please, she said to the boy.

One million pesos, Caracera said, doubling his offer.

No, Madame Sonia replied.

The boy raised his head. He ran a forearm over his runny nose. His eyes, dull and seeming not to see what was in front of him, were trained on the American. Both men looked to him with fearful curiosity. But still he did not speak.

Blueboy? asked Madame Sonia, whom the boy knew, despite her love for him, to be putting on an exaggerated show of concern.

A mental fog of confused and confusing love, the possibility that it might exist after all, coming from the American, had paralyzed the boy momentarily. Hadn't the American, in the car on the way to Madame Sonia's, been adamant about how he would not be made to go higher than his offer of half a million pesos, no matter what ideas the proprietress might have about either her bargaining skills or Caracera's gullibility? Hadn't the American poisonously suggested that his offer was already far in excess of what the boy was actually worth and that, whatever inflationary tactics Madame Sonia decided to use, the balance of power would not shift in her favor, that she would sooner or later have to acknowledge that the sum being offered was a generous padding onto the figure she stood to lose upon losing Pitik? Suddenly, in front of Pitik, the American had gone back on his word and upped the figure to a million pesos!

Pitik? asked the American.

One million? Pitik asked the American.

The American looked at Madame Sonia. You know that's more than you stand to earn with the boy in the remaining three years he has left with you.

You are not the right man, said Madame Sonia.

I am not the right man? What does that mean?!

Madame, piped the boy. The word was barely audible but from the way the men turned their heads you would think the boy had set off an explosion.

What is it? Sonia asked him.

I want to stop, said the boy. And when the proprietress, shocked, released her grip, the boy took advantage and moved away, standing apart from both men.

There was an uneasy silence.

Finally, Sonia spoke. Why?

I am getting tired, the boy replied.

You are not telling me the truth, said Sonia.

I am. I want to do something else.

What are you going to do?

The boy wrapped his arms around himself, revealing nothing, not even by his face, which he made to regard the dirty patch of floor beyond the furred rug.

Do you know what he is going to do with you? asked Sonia.

The boy didn't answer.

What is he going to do, Blueboy? Answer me!

I'm not going *to do* anything! I'm giving him his freedom. My God, how long have you been making the boy work for you? Doesn't he deserve a new life?

You! Sonia pointed a finger at Caracera. I did not do any forcing-forcing on him! You understand! Don't talk to me like you thinking I am Filipino and you are American and I am not so smart as you, Joe.

My name is—

I don't care! You are not getting the boy. Sonia hurried into the kitchen and returned holding a knife. Caracera and Pitik backed away.

Madame, said the boy. Please please *lang. Huwag kayong magalit sa akin!* Please *lang! Ayoko nang magsayaw. Pagod na ako.*

The American was transfixed by the object in the proprietress's hand and put all the stress of his body on his right leg, which was slightly bent, as if in preparation for a bolt forward.

What am I going to do if Blueboy leaves me? Sonia asked the American.

Spend your one million, Caracera replied.

Joking-joking! screamed Sonia. I am a joke to you? The proprietress, dressed in overlarge shirt and barely-there cotton shorts, showcasing her sausage legs, turned over her left arm and with her right began to slowly slash away, making what seemed like shallow cuts, but which soon began to brim over with blood. This is what you are doing to me, Sonia said calmly.

Madame! screamed the boy, who was held back by fear.

Afraid, then spooked, Caracera was now oddly becalmed. The proprietress, despite drawing actual and copious blood, would not endanger herself, Caracera felt, and was doing this largely as a demonstration. Then Caracera was overtaken by envy. The person before him was exhibiting a quality that Caracera could only get close to from the outside, as a witness. The short proprietress was filled with a passion that expressed itself in utter perversity, lack of restraint, tackiness, and was more alive than Caracera knew how to be. The melodrama, the masochism—they all fit into the mold of Filipina womanhood Sonia was at once a tribute to and travesty of. Caracera rushed forward and seized the knife from Sonia, who collapsed sitting on the floor.

The boy, without being told, went into the bathroom and came out with wet towels, which Sonia took from him and placed on her arms, stanching blood.

He went to the kitchen and brought back a mop and bucket, making reddish swirls on the floor that grew fainter with each pass.

After he put away the mop and bucket, he came to sit beside Sonia, who draped an arm over him.

Do you want to leave? asked Sonia.

The boy said nothing.

What does he want, do you know? asked Sonia.

The boy shook his head.

Why him? asked Sonia.

The boy shrugged.

Why not Mr. Feingold? He loves you.

I know, Madame.

But you don't love him, said Madame Sonia with understanding. Do you love this one? Madame Sonia chinned the American.

Pitik didn't reply.

But he doesn't love you, Blueboy. He is saying-saying he is not in love.

Don't be ridiculous, said Caracera. There is nothing between the boy and me.

Oh, that is not good, said Madame Sonia to the boy. That is sadness for super-sure. Oh, but you are young. Maybe you will learn that it is better to be loved than to love. It is very safer. Why do you choosing-choosing to make yourself be unhappy?

Pitik didn't think he was choosing unhappiness and kept quiet.

Why, Blueboy?

Finally the proprietress looked up at Caracera, resigned. By this tiniest of expressions the boy knew that a conclusion had been reached. Sonia had run out of the energy to resist a million pesos, to resist the easy new life the figure promised. Because of this, he clasped Madame's hand with sudden forcefulness. The proprietress looked at the boy and asked, Who is this dead man?

He knew Pitik—Blueboy, replied Caracera. Years ago. I guess he was in love with Blueboy. And when he died he left his estate to the boy. And yet, Caracera was beginning to develop a suspicion that his uncle hadn't been in love with the boy after all. The two must've had a relationship, that much he felt certain of. And yet, the event had been either glancing or nondescript, as the boy couldn't even, under the shock of being apprised of three million pesos falling into his lap, be moved to recall it. More and more, Caracera was beginning to believe that his uncle's choice was shaped by the enormity of his disgust with the family: even someone as inconsequential as a boy prostitute was far better than any of the Caraceras, holding a more meaningful place in Eustacio's short, embittered life than anyone bound to him by blood.

You are so loved, Blueboy, said Madame Sonia, who began to cry, and whose tears, just like her act of butchery, had a streak of performance that, like an insane person's, was riveting.

Would a check be okay? asked Caracera.

After the longest time, Sonia replied, Cash. Everything is in cash.

Caracera made arrangements to return the following day with the money.

I always knowing this day is coming to me, said Sonia.

The boy was grasped by the proprietress, who held on for the longest time.

I'll come visit you, Madame.

Do you promise? asked Sonia, who knew the boy was only saying the words she wanted to hear.

Yes, Madame.

I do not want you to be unhappy.

I am not.

We have to go, said the American.

But before the American and the boy disappeared, Madame Sonia made sure to have the final word. You cannot changing him, she said to the American. You think I'm making him dancing? You are wrong. He loves to dancing. He loves to hear the applause-applause. He is going to miss it. She looked at Blueboy. You are going to miss it, she said. And then what will you be making-doing? Missing dancing, and with a man who is not in love with you. You can come back here, she offered. If you leave him you can come home. Blueboy?

CHAPTER 5

A MILLION PESOS. The bank's officials had grown used to the quixotic and overlarge requests of Mr. Roger Caracera and did not bother to ask anything other than if everything was fine with him and his family, to which he replied in the affirmative. His reply inspired no confidence, was affirmative by only the narrowest of margins. There were many theories about the man's profligacy, chief among which involved drugs and female escorts, for which the reports of his largesse in the newspapers were nothing more than convenient covers, paid advertisements intended to obscure his true nature. You could see the decadence in the sunken features of his face and the newly gauntish frame he carried.

First he had been fit, in the style of an athlete, but with a moderate amount of padding for a man his age. And then he had been seen to have gained weight, which was doubly normal, considering that he had been grieving over the recent death of his father, and resubjected to the fatty cuisine of his homeland: *adobo* for lunch, *pancit* for *merienda*, *bibingka* for dessert . . . But now, surprisingly, the weight had been more than successfully shed. Indiscriminate drug use, a wanton sex life:

the high-amorality workout, siphoning mass and heft from beneath the skin, until the skeletal reminder of Death was brought near the surface to serve as the trophy of getting away from God.

The man at the center of these wild hypotheses would have been gratified to learn of his plummeting reputation. What he did for Donny Osmond Magulay and Pitik Sindit, who represented forks in the same road of lower-class encumbrance (but which, running into Roger Caracera, would be zippered into the same happy upward trajectory), was done so that he could quell the nagging certainty of his utter uselessness. He was the Abolisher of Discomfort, the Aider of Dreams. Ambition, much as he would like to think himself free of its taint, was not dead in him after all. He was still under the spell of wanting to leave some kind of signature behind. His actions had a bedrock of selfishness, and the last thing he wanted was to have them trumped up into works of civic magnanimity. It would have been to him the most delicious of ironies if he'd known that instead of being considered a man of civic do-goodism, he was being talked about as that man's dark, shadowy twin.

His Uncle Eustacio was a complete mystery. The closest he would ever come to gaining some insight into the man was by looking at his beloved, much in the same way that a surprising facet of his dead father's character had been revealed by the vivacious, hotheaded beauty who'd stormed his wake. She was a woman so temperamentally opposed to his mother, so alive in all the conventional ways, that Caracera had been moved to admiration and approval.

He took the boy Pitik Sindit and his mother to see his friend Benjamin Goyanos, who had arranged for a meeting with an accountant. For starters, the man would explain how a savings account worked and how storing one's money in a bank was not tantamount to signing over one's assets to a bunch of scammers, as the mother assiduously believed and stutteringly communicated.

The mother and son had no cards of identification, and so a trip to city hall was quickly set up. A baptismal certificate was unearthed from an old Fita biscuit tin which held sentimental knickknacks from the mother's girlhood. The piece of paper was accepted, if grudgingly, as proof of the old woman's existence. With it, she walked away with a new piece of city-issued identification that showed, in the lower right-hand corner, a photograph of an unsmiling, worried, if not downright suspicious woman with no idea of the heavy burden attached to what she thought would be a life-enhancing, weight-reducing gift.

Pitik Sindit had a birth certificate, which his mother kept more for sentimental than practical reasons. He too was given a brand-new ID card, which he knew was supposed to make him feel connected to the place in which he lived. It was also understood that the city's governing body or bodies would be casting an invading eye out for him to make sure that he no longer had anything to do with his former criminal life. He felt like a dog from the streets being adopted and given a new hindering collar. His picture, however, betrayed nothing about what he felt. Instead, there was a smile that owed as much to the boy's vanity as it did to his continuing fantasy—to him entirely legitimate—of an approaching affair with Roger Caracera, whom he was forced to call Mr. Caracera.

When it came time to discuss leaving the Bambang slum, the mother and son grew depressed, though the message was conveyed by their downcast looks more than by anything they said. They found themselves, in Roger Caracera's presence, even more inarticulate and shy, confident that there would always be a gap in understanding between the man, brought up in and conditioned by circumstances of refinement, and them, who were so used to ways of living—scavenging, hoarding, stealing—that until contact with the man they had not been forced to consider as subhuman.

The logic of their resistance was simple: even if the slums were dreary and spirit-killing, not to mention a hazard to their health (most likely the incubator of the mother's TB, which she occasionally relapsed into), it was still home to them. Expressed like that, of course, Roger Caracera would understand. But they were so stymied by the conviction of the man's bad judgment that they could utter nothing in their defense.

Still, Mr. Caracera told them that he understood their predicament.

The next day, however, he returned with a proposition: how would they like to live with him, in his apartment in Makati, for a week, just to get used to the idea of being surrounded by things which they could now, with three million pesos, afford? (The man believed that luxury would spoil them into wanting more of the same, making them see the true meagerness of the lives they were to return to.)

Already the Sindits' neighbors had gotten wind of the family's predicament and were casting suspicious glances every time the mother or son walked past the various areas, such as the general goods store and the communal pump, where the gossips gathered. For the moment, as mother and son walked by, the whispers lowered to a hush, but there was no doubt in the Sindits' minds that when their backs were turned, the talk would bear down on them like a predator with its eye on soft flesh. There was also no doubt in the mother's mind that these words, gathering strength, would eventually encourage an initial sally against her and her son. And so the process of changing their minds had already begun, and the mother and son were glad to accept Roger Caracera's kind offer.

This way too, in Pitik's thinking, he could get closer, at first physically, and then, whatever followed the cracking of the hard nut that was the man's physical self, to Cary Grant: What did he like to do? What foods did he favor? How was he in the hygiene department? Who were his friends, and would they, introduced to the boy, approve of him? And most importantly, would these friends, weather-vane-like, point the boy to the true sexual orientation of Cary Grant? In other words, would there be, thrillingly, a group of *bakla* friends to make of Cary a self-abnegating and latent homosexual, obvious to everyone but himself? Pitik's mind was transcendent. In it, he pictured Cary overcoming a first impression of blockheaded heterosexuality, he willed it. And besides, weren't professedly straight men among those who had been Pitik's admirers when he was Blueboy?

It turned out that the apartment in the Makati high-rise, where nobody greeted Pitik or his mother in the lobby or at the elevators (which wasn't so bad, considering how nobody greeted Roger Caracera either), was just like its owner: frigid, clean, with luxurious carpeting to muffle the sounds and other giveway traits that might emanate from the man. His closet was stocked with only a few articles of clothing, which he did not give any appearance of being too fussy over. The man's items for personal grooming amounted to nothing more than cheap soap, cheap shampoo, a razor, cheap toothpaste and a tooth-brush whose bristles were like steel wool and which the boy imagined to be the dental equivalent of a flagellant's spiked whip, drawing blood each night. This could be construed as proof of the man's conflicted inner life, punitively homosexual.

Among the hippest things belonging to the man was a canvas Adidas bag that sat in the shadows on the floor of the cavernous closet. Asking after it, the boy was surprised and touched by the man's easy generosity. You can have it, Roger Caracera said to Pitik. Pitik also divested Caracera of his Walkman, with its medley taped from newish American and British CDs. Now that the man was no longer running, the Walkman had become superfluous, an embarrassing reminder of one more project taken up and then abandoned midstream.

Pitik and his mother were given their own rooms. Each had a window looking down on Manila stretching to the end of the horizon in an awe-inspiring grid that seemed like an illustration of what math and science were capable of when pushed onto a larger scale. Here and there was the rubble of either con- or destruction, either of which would take years, a whole lifetime, to conclude, having to contend with the workers' lassitude and the vicissitudes of corporate and governmental bureaucracies. Above the grid was the smog of industry and of the city's growing car population, which gave the impression to Pitik of a city slowly choking on its own poisons. This was not the celestial view that he dreamed of acquiring one day, for the sight brought him more than ever to an earthbound reality: when not in the apartment, he was down *there*, it was his city, he was among its millions of wayfarers and strivers, and he too was being slowly poisoned, reduced each new day to a grayer, more stooped version of the boy he was the day before. This same fate applied to Madame Sonia, to his schoolmates, his teacher. And he realized that, even if God was looking out from the same high perch, He would not be able to see much: no Madame Sonia, no school, no Pitik Sindit; their struggles hidden by a fog that was like a mythical emanation of His very indifference.

Why does your mother never come out of her room? asked Caracera one day.

She is very much liking the room.

Doesn't she want to go out?

Where?

To see the city.

But we living-living here.

You cannot keep acting as if you don't have the money. You do. It's in a bank account. It's not lost. It's there whenever you want it. Doesn't she want to spend some of it?

Spending on what?

Don't you want new clothes?

Are you going to taking me to ShoeMart?

Fine. We'll go. But not until the weekend. Tomorrow we're going to take you to a new school.

You do not like me? asked the boy. Immediately he regretted jumping the gun.

You're good, you're a good kid, said Caracera.

It had already been arranged: Roger Caracera's imaginary son—materializing to surprise even the man himself—was about to make an appearance at St. Jude Catholic School, introduced to the assistant principal Mrs. Diaz; he would be demoted from the grade level he was in at his former school to pick up essential things that he'd skipped over or which had never been part of his curriculum. He would be the oldest boy in his class by a margin of two, perhaps three years, and this shameful setting apart from the other students was prepared for by Caracera in two ways. First, Caracera bought him a new school uniform (a short-sleeved white shirt with sharp collars—the school pin worn on the right collar—and a line of pearlized buttons down the front, matched with just-above-the-knees dark blue shorts with pockets on each side, and another atop the left buttock), which Caracera said made the boy exceedingly handsome, although as a boy Caracera himself had remembered hating it, thinking it uncomfortable, stupid. Second, Caracera inflated the formidableness of the institution the boy was about to enter, telling him that the lower grade level the boy was to find himself in was really the equivalent of where he had been at his other school.

It was important that should anyone ask, the boy was to say that he was Roger Caracera's son.

But my last name, said the boy, is not the same last name as you having. In his heart, "son" was as bad a demotion as, if not worse than, being pushed back two grades. I do not wanting to be your son: he held back from saying this to the man.

You're adopted.

Are you adopting-adopting me?

Come on, Peter. You of all boys should know the difference between what a thing is and what you tell people it is.

This was heartening: "son" was only for show! While the reality was something else entirely, something more valuable. I do not understanding, he pretended, wanting to hear the man's justification. Why shouldn't I telling people you are helping me to go to school?

For the same reason you didn't tell people you danced.

Because it is full of shame-shame? Fear caught in his throat.

People are bound to misinterpret. It's simpler that we're related.

Just like Donny Osmond is your son also?

This took Caracera by surprise. Sure, he said.

No, he didn't want to be on the same level as Donny Osmond. The boy thought but didn't say: How can you have two sons, one is ugly, which is him, and the other one is pretty, which is me?

It baffled him that Roger Caracera was behaving as if the only reward his generous actions would incur were punishment, humiliation.

Pitik was learning lessons that were completely different from those he'd learned from Madame Sonia. In both instances, lies and secrecy were the best methods for dealing with the world. But with Madame Sonia, a lie was a symbol of triumph, the world's censure cleverly circumnavigated; while with Roger Caracera, it was a fearful hedge meant to protect oneself against the public's omnipresent, watchful and certain wrath.

The boy came back from his first day in school—slipped into midstream, as the other students had been at their studies for a month—silent and depressed. When his mood darkened over the following days, Caracera decided to expedite their shopping trip to the ShoeMart MegaMall.

They took along the boy's mother, but first stopped at the bank (which was not the same bank used by Caracera), where she presented her passbook and made a first withdrawal: ten thousand pesos. With it, she bought extravagant and unnecessary items: clothes; a formal portrait of mother and son in front of a backdrop of blue curtains; a gift of a snowglobe containing a miniature of the Statue of Liberty to thank Roger Caracera for his generosity; and for the boy, a new radio with a built-in CD player to replace his old one and, to go with it, a starter's batch of new CDs. It seemed to the mother that they were shopping to please Roger Caracera more than themselves, although soon enough, watching the expression on her son's face, she got into the spirit of things.

Appearing before a large public with mother and son, Caracera was setting into motion a whole machinery of Manilan checks and balances, a Rube Goldberg contraption which end point must surely be banishment from the family—another wayward son going too far and just like his predecessors to be gifted with excommunication. Word had been circulating for a while about the predilections of the mysterious American celebrity, and for the first time, caught by acquaintances of the family, there was physical corroboration: here sidling next to the man in broad daylight was the boy prostitute, a creature for whom Roger Caracera, as his uncle before him had been rumored to, was willing to give up his good name.

An unacknowledged fear grew among the uncles and aunts when talk got back of Caracera's appearances—a fear that the family was being haunted a second time around.

The eldest brother, Jesus, not the first to die, had been the first to appear. The youngest brother, dead so many years now, and whom everyone was confident had been properly disposed of, was now following in Jesus Caracera's wake. Eustacio Caracera had come back in the form of his nephew, Roger, the unearther, the burrower, the fomenter of new (old) troubles. Eustacio's dangerous actions, successfully submerged by Irene Caracera leading a quorum of family decision makers a lifetime ago, were being brought out into the light by Roger Caracera, who was striking out in what was beginning to be regarded, unavoidably, as a campaign of destructiveness which aimed to take down not just himself but the whole of his father's family. His animosity against them was clear and irrefutable. Before, his delinquency had been seen to be rooted in his privileged youth: the spoiled princeling who always took the easy road. But now the princeling had aged into a man with a kinglike megalomania.

On the one hand, the donation to the priest Shakespeare de Leon had brought attention that was favorable, flattering. But on the other, gossip in Negros told of a family spokesperson who had visited, intending to apologize for things that needed no apology.

Further, Roger Caracera was making a public spectacle of one of their own's mental illness and moral weakness, adopting it for his own. On top of this he'd tried to pass off the *puto* as his son, enrolling him in the hallowed halls of St. Jude Catholic School, as if the boy fully deserved to be given the burnishing touch of respectability imparted by such institutions, as if such institutions had not been created with the very intention of keeping out boys like Pitik Sindit, keeping in place the divide in Manila society by germinating, through its lessons and catechisms, a new class of proprietors and controllers.

Another visit from Irene Caracera followed. She was the outraged emissary who hoped to try one last act of peace. What are you doing? asked Irene.

The boy was in school. The mother, as usual, was in her room, doing God knows what.

Where are they? asked Irene. I understand they're living with you.

Whatever else happened, Caracera would not allow his aunt to meet the parent and child who were the wards of his dead Uncle Eustacio. Why didn't you tell me about Uncle Eustacio? he asked Irene.

You say his name like you know him. But did you? Certainly not better than we did.

Electroshock (a startling disclosure from the detective Al Salazar). A grave in Malate (in the same cemetery alloted for Teresa Caracera, which Caracera had jokingly referred to as the "Outcast Caracera Family Plot"). Ignoring his will.

That, that . . . boy! He's a professional, said Irene, even though she had never met him. Your poor uncle was a victim, don't you understand that?

A victim of a *boy*? Eustacio knew what he was doing. Did the boy?

This is an old argument, said Irene. The family's discussed this, we came to the right decision years ago. You are not going to reverse our decision. *Hijo*—

Why give Uncle Eustacio's money to me?

It was your father's idea. He heard you were—that you were not doing well. And he was afraid that you would reject any money if it came directly from him.

Money was never my problem, said Caracera.

Lack of money was never your problem, it seems. But money *is* your problem. You are not the conscience of the family, *hijo*.

I never said I was.

Why be a hero? And if you're the hero, am I then, is the rest of the family then the villain?

Let me do what needs to be done.

Who needs it to be done?

Me. All right? *I* need it to be done.

Why?

Silence.

Are you in love with the boy?

Is that what people are saying?

Can you say it's not true?

Did you come here, Tita Irene, to warn me? So all right. I've been warned. You've done your job.

There are consequences, Roger.

What? Electroshock? Excommunication? A grave in Malate? A boy with a better life because he has a little of what we have more than enough to spare?

Go back to the States.

Not until I'm done.

Done what? Destroying the family? How many other people do you think have tried before you? Even your mother. Up to a point the only way we could understand her behavior was to see that she wanted to bring shame on the family. Do you think she succeeded?

Are you threatening to lock me up?

What's wrong with you, Roger? I did not come today as an enemy.

So please leave me alone. Please.

You look sick.

I'd be better if you leave me be.

Maybe that's why your father's come back. He wants you to know he's not happy with what you're doing.

He's not appeared to me.

He will.

I don't believe he will. I don't believe in ghosts.

Let me talk to the boy.

He's not here.

Is he in school?

Don't do anything to him. Just leave him be.

You make me sound heartless. Of course I'm not going to do anything. But he can't live with you. If you're not in love—if you *say* you're not in love, then you shouldn't keep putting yourself in a situation to give rise to such malicious gossip.

I never said I wasn't in love with him.

Irene was silent, her face remaining composed.

Don't look so serious, said Caracera. It's only a joke.

But was it? More and more he could not avoid the facts: he was a middle-aged man who'd lost all desire for the opposite sex. And he was now, going above and beyond the call of duty, evincing concern for a fifteen-year-old boy who was a hand-over from his own gay uncle. He was gay.

But could you be gay if the sight of your supposed beloved failed to arouse even one bit? Was it not proof of his utter lack of feeling for the boy that, giving in to the boy's request to kiss him good night on the cheek one evening, as a capitulation not just to the boy but to his own growing suspicion of his gayness, he had felt first nothing, and then underneath that nothing, underneath the very skin the boy's lips had touched, he had felt—disgust? A conviction of uncleanliness? Hatefulness?

But gayness explained his actions more compellingly than any of the other reasons provided. It shrank his motives to the basest and in that way linked him conclusively to his family.

Don't joke about things like that, Irene said coolly. Even to a joke there are consequences.

They are not living with me. They're only staying with me for a few more days. Until they can find a new home.

Why do they need to stay with you?

They don't *need* to. I invited them.

After she left, Caracera knocked on the mother's bedroom door.

She opened it and stepped aside for the man to enter. She had heard but not understood everything, though it was clear from a word here, a word there and from the general tone of voice that the visitor's purpose was bad, and it was equally clear that the visitor would have the power to make their host's life difficult—and all because he had been kind enough to provide them his hospitality (no, she would not go so far as to say friendship). She was afraid to hazard a guess as to the man's relationship with her son, and though she had pressed Pitik for particulars, he had remained tight-lipped—yet on his face there had been a telltale, characteristic mischievousness that suggested secrets which, by being undivulged, were made more enticing. Secrets of the flesh, implicating the man.

And yet this man, Mr. Caracera—whose name was a vivid reminder of her girlhood, calling to mind boxes and sacks of sugar stamped with a tricolor cursive (the middle white outlined first by red and then by blue, recalling both the Philippine and American flags) and, flying at the right-hand corner, a dove whose whiteness was meant to suggest the purity and the crystalline taste of the product contained within— was different from all the other men who had preceded him in the carousel of Pitik's affections. Mr. Caracera seemed unreal, surrounded by an aura of, appropriately enough, pure whiteness. His goodness threw no shadows, concealed no base motives to render him human. She waited for her ignorance regarding Mr. Caracera to evaporate, leaving in its place the man in his full measure.

And yet he had continued to reveal nothing.

She chided herself for her lack of faith. But surely so late in her life a miracle was not about to reverse her hard-won knowledge of the world? Surely he would turn out to be like the other men Pitik had brought home for a visit to the Bambang slum or who the boy had described in stories that emphasized his secret value, like a diamond obscured in coal, all but unrecognized except by these foreign experts, while minimizing or obliterating altogether any mention of the process by which such value was established? The fact of these men's foreignness gave their appraisals a stamp of easy expertise, to which surrender was the only appropriate response.

No, no. Her faithlessness was reprehensible. Goodness was as much a feature of this landscape as lust and covetousness, only it had been obscured—like a diamond by coal, yes. Looking at the city from her window, she could not believe that this was the same city she had lived in for thirty-plus years. If such a view was possible, surely other changes might yet be imminent in her old life?

The man was now trying to assure her that she didn't need to worry about anything. Of course she'd told him that she hadn't heard any of his conversation with his guest.

When the boy came home, she told him that she'd finally reached a decision and they were moving out of the Bambang slum. At last she'd yielded to the man's goodness. It was her lack of faith that had been hindering this goodness. By overhauling their sorry lives, the man had wanted to put distance between the boy and his youthful entanglements: ShoeMart, St. Jude, a sparkling new residence would help bulldoze all that had gone before . . . If their lives continued to be miserable, then she had only herself to blame. The proper thing to do was to accept the man's help. They were not to return to Bambang, not even to retrieve any of the sparse belongings they had thought they were only leaving behind momentarily. All the essential things had been brought over to the Makati high-rise anyway: their pieces of identification; the boy's few scrapbooks, inside which were collages of his favorite pop stars and the printed lyrics, culled from the *Song Hits* magazines, to his favorite pop ditties, as well as page after page of images of Nora Aunor, in various melodramatic scenes from her thousands of movies; all the clothes they owned which were considered "presentable," and in which they could not possibly cause any damage to the reputation of their host.

Tomorrow they were scheduled to go looking at various apartments lined up by Mr. Caracera's friend, the same one who had helped explain how a savings account worked. Mr. Caracera would be accompanying them.

Couldn't they move into the Makati high-rise? Pitik asked Caracera.

He didn't want to be separated from the man so soon. Still, he had not discovered the secret key with which to unlock the man's mind, much less his heart.

There were no empty units, was the reply.

But the boy knew this was a lie. Available, said the sign that he encountered walking in and out of the building every day, in the rental office's streetside window. It was the same word the man had denied applied to him, though again the boy knew better.

The Makati high-rise, though Pitik and his mother had lived there with a sense of being stifled by decorum, had been the site of a brief heavenly interlude that, the boy now saw clearly, was going to be all too brief, cruelly foreshortened. It would've been better if they'd never been made to leave their home in Bambang! At least then there would not now be this painful expulsion from paradise—being next to the man, studying him, making him see that he, Pitik, meant no harm, bore no malice, that his affection was not the practiced concern of someone of his profession, but rather was the first and entirely genuine crush of an adolescent boy finally demarcating a space within himself for normal, unmercenary human emotion. He'd listened attentively to the man's sermons during dinner, had volunteered answers which he believed to be the "correct" ones, even if some of them went against his true instincts, as for example the belief that education was crucial to success in life. The words had been hollow, it was the desire to see Roger Caracera happy that had shaped the boy's declaration.

From Pitik's history with foreigners, he had come to know this crucial fact about them: they did not land in the Philippines by accident; there was something in this country which held them. Sometimes, they called this pull "love." In the case of the men Pitik had come across, *Pitik* was this factor.

For Roger Caracera, this "love" was thrown over a wider net—over the Philippines itself, which he was reacquainting himself with, like meeting himself as a child, when he'd last lived here. That was if "love" was the right word, encompassing as it would have to the bitterness and revulsion much in evidence in the man's dinnertime lectures. "Passion"—the man's passion for the Philippines, then.

The trick for Pitik was to provide a lens that shrank this generic wash of passion until Pitik became its sole focus. Or, if the man was not to be waylaid from his abstract ruminations, to get him to see every Filipino as a Pitik: the whole country a paradise of Pitiks, though Pitik remained the chief, the highest-ranking original.

The boy put up a heroic effort to disqualify every apartment that they were taken to see—citing nothing more substantial than that he didn't "liking" each—but in the end they were moved into a building a stone's throw from their former home—which had probably already been taken over by some enterprising neighbor.

CHAPTER 6

DONNY OSMOND MAGULAY had waited so late to ask for sponsorship that he beat the deadline by only a day, and the tournament start date by a week. His prep time was spent listening to the man lecture him on the need for a wider variety of shots in his repertoire. He humored the man by practicing what were supposed to make him a more formidable player: the topspin lob, the drop shot, the underspin, the slice—strokes that required a finesse which he didn't feel comfortable with and really didn't feel, when push came to shove, that he needed. The practice partner, being paid to be so, was his friend and workmate Raul Zamora, who himself had wanted to enter but had not been able to find a sponsor. Perhaps next year, was the unspoken consolation offered by his employment, at which time, having practiced with the clearly superior Donny Osmond, he might be brought up to the next level of competency. At any rate, he would be earning extra money, which could go into next year's tournament fees.

The man was largely placid, easy to please, and though being fastidious and able to tell that Donny's exertions were halfhearted, might've been allowing for a distinction between the boy's performances in and out of competition. Their conversations were rarely touched by the personal—certainly Donny would not ask any intimate questions of the man, being both incurious, on the one hand, and moved by rare gratitude into shy circumspection, on the other. Still, he had the man figured out completely. A loner, a wealthy bachelor on vacation from the States? Couldn't he be one of those gay tourists who came to this country looking for boys like the one he'd brought to the VIP one afternoon, who was skinny and clearly effeminate? And was he thinking of coercing Donny Osmond into joining them? The boy tried to preempt any transaction which might end in physical contact. He did this by falsifying the degree of his shy circumspection so that the man understood that he was unsettled by being touched and would rather receive approval verbally. This way, the boy's skittishness became a tribute occasioned by the man's presence as opposed to, in reality, an insult.

Days of serene repetition. But one day, just when the boy was relishing his full triumph over the man, a triumph he considered a portent for his chances at the tournament, as the two got into a rare argument about the boy's fondness for showboating, in particular, his leaping overhead smash for which Pete Sampras held the copyright, the man evidenced a disorienting streak of malice. He told the boy that Pete Sampras *sucked*. The way he'd spat out the word you knew he'd clearly meant it. How in the world could anyone say that of a man about whom the indisputable wisdom was that he was the greatest player in the game's history?

To add insult to injury, the next day the man arrived bearing a tape he'd had FedExed from America, procured specially for the purpose of putting the boy in his place. It was a tape of a match that Donny, having heard about, had chosen not to see. The vintage was recent—three weeks ago in Montreal (or Toronto?), at the 2000 Canadian Open: Pete Sampras losing the finals to the Russian upstart Marat Safin. The man forced him to watch it, in one of the VIP member lounges equipped with a TV.

And there, during one point, was Pete Sampras overhead-smashing the ball into the net, the audience groaning.

The man argued that the ball could just as easily be put away without having to resort to such a risky and effortful move. As to the risk—

there was no question that the boy's overhead was nowhere near as breathtaking, as second-nature as Pete's. And the leaping up to get to the ball was a waste of energy, and if he did it often enough it might take a toll during the later stretches of a match. As yet, the boy had been good enough to win his VIP matches in straight sets, but what if he were to encounter someone who stretched him to three?

But how could the overhead become second nature unless he practiced it and used it as often as he could?

The man would rather the boy become a smarter than a showier player.

The boy argued no more, and decided to wait until the tournament to sneak back his old, to him more profitable, ways.

Days passed, the tournament began and Caracera began to feel doubly alive: the disturbance on his family's end was momentarily stoppered, and via the game, the only one he condoned, he found a direct access to the buoyancy of his dream self.

The boy, true to his promise to himself, snuck in the overhead smash in his very first match. Not just one, not just two, but three in the first set, which he won by 6–2, and another two in the second, in fact, the match-ending shot, for a margin of victory of 6–1. What could Caracera say? The boy, winning so decisively, had bested his argument.

Nobody had been alarmed by the boy's victory, the victory of the only entrant who was not among the top private school players. It was conceded that his first-round opponent, lucky to have even won three games, was a neophyte. He had been pushed to follow in the footsteps of his elder brother, who'd won a tennis scholarship to Stanford, where he was now on the school team. Clearly, lightning would not strike twice in the same family.

Most of the other players had taken up tennis harboring more or less the same ambitions: if not to be accepted into places like Stanford on the strength of their tennis play, then to make of tennis one element in a highly attractive, more "American" portfolio to assure these colleges of the boys' easy adaptability—a transition into membership abroad which they had already begun to undertake.

In other words, nobody except the boy had thought to harbor

dreams of professional play, much less eventual domination on the world stage. He played his ambitions close to his vest, and not even Caracera had an inkling.

By the time Donny Osmond won his second match, defeating a boy by the name of Ignacio Cordero, who was acknowledged to be among the top two or three players—and defeating him by a score of 6–2, 6–2, no less—a buzz began to be heard around the courts in the Two Seasons Club in Greenbelt, and even the smallest detail about the boy was taken up and studied. In the process, each facet was coated with an alienating sense of wonder and annoyance. Who was this hubristic kid with the bad haircut, the bladelike skinniness and the laughably derelict New Balances? And more importantly, was this kid's name for real? The parents and relatives of some of the boys, who formed the core audience for the matches, had to be told who the boy's namesake Donny Osmond was. Hearing, they expressed pity and disbelief and swore at the earliest opportunity to get a front-row seat for the boy's next match.

The staff, taking the boy seriously for the first time, were moved to trace his sponsorship to Roger Caracera, the mysterious man who, along with being returning royalty, a fresh millionaire and patron of Shakespeare de Leon's school for wayward boys, was newly, and effectively, an amateur coach. Had he come back from the States to take on, Hindu deitylike, one face after another, one more mysterious visitor presenting all the faces they couldn't back home, withholding the essential one?

The third-round match, which occurred on a Thursday afternoon at the Two Seasons, was so popular that it was switched from the smaller, indoor Court 2 to the Central Court, located at the far end of the property. Court 2, with bleachers set up on all four sides, seated roughly two hundred people, while the Central Court, which was also used for the InterCollegiate Varsity Tournaments (nearly always a showdown between the University of Santo Tomas and Ateneo de Manila University), had built-in seating for up to three hundred spectators. The court overlooked the back lawn of a gigantic private estate where, at match time, the only sounds competing with the ball's wallop and the occasional coos and *errrrrs* from the audience was the metronomic whir of the lawn sprinklers, whose emissions reached courtside as miniature rainbows visible over the horizon. As a concession to the monsoons, the plastic seats were of the kind that snapped back when nobody occupied them. They were royal blue with numbers on metal plates screwed on the armrests which were repeated on the upper right-hand corners of the backrest. Many spectators brought cushions to sit on and against, and a fan was always welcome, for the matches were usually held in the siesta-inducing heat of the midafternoons, when visibility was at its best, before the estate trees cast defacing shadows over the court.

The third match, due to the late venue scramble, was pushed back to five, and by the time the young players appeared on court, the penitentiary shadows of the trees were already inching onto the court.

Donny Osmond's opponent was known to be a middling boy, and therefore the audience already shared among them, as could be heard from their lethargic talk, a sense of leisurely inconsequence—as of watching a game on tape, in which the victor had been decided. No question Donny Osmond, having defeated one of the top players, would make mincemeat out of tonight's far less talented opponent, who himself had defeated even less talented players to advance. Spectatorship was transposed from an active to a passive key: each detail, not the denouement, was the object of study.

So necks were craned to take in the paltry, stooping person of the boy—Oooh the shorts the shoes the toothpick extremities, murmurs began almost immediately—as both players entered. The bad teeth (for the boy, even in repose, had a hard time keeping his top lip joined to his bottom). The scaly patches of skin at the knees. The haircut, spiky but unstylish. The cheeks puffed not from being well fed but from a constant lack of occupation—sure to lead to delinquency. All of these details were salient indices of slack parenting. The audience began at once to take pity on him, laughing at themselves for having elevated him to the position of a crasher at the gate. The watchers could not square this schlump with the figure of overnight legend around whom so much speculative resentment swirled. But there he was, nothing more than a dork in need of mothering. Excitement, which had been relaxed, was rekindled at the thought of watching his slack features pulled sharply together by his talent in motion, his swiftness, his showmanship, his strokes with no touch of the teenager about them.

The transformation was looked forward to with the trepidation and voluptuousness of something occult. Supposedly, the boy was self-taught, with skills the expatriate Caracera son had only helped to put a spit-shine on.

Donny Osmond felt the heat of their looks, burning holes into his exterior, as if the audience were trying by such a method to leach him of power. At the coin toss, deciding which player was to receive and which to serve first. There, shaking hands with the far more handsome, better groomed opponent, who was outfitted with shiny new sneakers, so large and cumbersome they looked as if they'd been intended for walking on the moon. While Donny Osmond's were streaked with dirt along the cushioned sole near his toes and heels, and the laces, tied too tightly because the boy loved to feel the material of the shoes snug against his feet, were already fraying at the ends.

The match did not keep up with expectations. By the third game, with Donny Osmond serving, it became clear that either the publicity was interfering with the boy's performance, or the two-hour delay before the match had unnerved him, or perhaps the opponent had been better than anybody had been led to believe. This boy, named Sirco Quiñones, playing for Don Bosco, ended the third game by breaking Donny Osmond's serve. Four games later, he was up by 5–2, and, with Donny Osmond again serving, had drawn to 30-all, two points away from taking the first set. By the next point, drawing yet one more error from Donny Osmond, who couldn't seem to find his range and continued to spray balls wide, earning groans of commiseration and angry disbelief, Quiñones had gotten himself to break and set point.

Was this when Donny Osmond's talked-about killer instinct would emerge, pulling him off the precipice of his own frantic unpreparedness?

No. The next point was won by Quiñones, in a daring volley at the net, leaving Donny Osmond slack-jawed at the baseline, his arms too conditioned by their lack of effectiveness to even attempt a get. The set went to Quiñones.

During the break, Caracera went and knelt at the side of the boy's chair. They were shielded from the sun by an umbrella on a pole. Caracera didn't know what to say. The boy, in turn, was too shamed to look at Caracera. Skill had never deserted him so drastically, and all he could think about was God and His sudden disfavor, even though he was not normally inclined to think about God or religion. Only in instances like this did it occur to him that his talent welled from some hidden spring which nothing, not even the American compound of desire and hard work duly and daily fused, could account for, and that there might be something in the legacy of his mother's faith after all. By this way of accounting, his talent was either a bequest from God or the devil, given for great good or its black twin. So he did not know, in fact, if it was God who had done the deserting, maybe it was the devil, and therefore he did not know which party to appeal to to intercede. In his peripheral vision, the boy could see a banner being held up by the Don Bosco classmates of Quiñones, and their cheer pushed down his already low spirits:

> Kickem
> Lickem
> We know how to pickem! Gooooooo . . . Q!

Just try, Caracera finally forced himself to say. Even when you're down, even when your shots aren't making it in, just hang in there because you never know what might happen, at any moment momentum can shift. This is good practice, he admonished, feeling his words flail against the steely shield of the boy's chipped pride. I suppose you've never been in a situation when you've been down before, right?

No response.

Listen, Caracera said, almost hissing. His anger finally made the boy turn his head, though the boy continued to pout.

I know you're good, said Caracera. You know you're good. They, he said, chinning the audience, may know you're good, they may have heard you're good and that's why they've come to see. They may now think otherwise because you've lost the first set, but ultimately—

The boy looked away.

Don't you fucking turn your head away.

The boy obliged him with a glare. This was why Caracera was here. The boy was a freak twice over and it exerted a magnetic pull on him. First was the anomaly of the boy's absolute lack of humility, which made him treat patronage and tutorial as nothing less than his due.

And second was the riveting fact of his tennis proficiency, cultivated on his own, perhaps even in secret from family and friends. He was a full-grown tennis creature sprouted from a country and, more breathtakingly, from a class that emphasized other, more fruitful endeavors.

The fact of his discovery attested to the pell-mell, absurd, bountiful, magical nature of the Philippines.

Are you angry at me?

The boy was silent.

Are you angry at me?

Finally he spoke: No.

Who're you angry at then?

I'm not angry.

You're not? Well you could've fooled me. Who're you angry at?

Me. Okay? Are you satisfied?

It doesn't matter what they think. He noticed the audience was staring passionately at them, as if witness to a classic scene: was a change in the boy's performance soon due?

Time, said the umpire into his microphone, making the audience sit up.

You've never been down, now you know what it's like. Try something else. If what you're doing isn't working, try other things. Like what we practiced. Maybe he's on to your power game. Surprise him.

Sir, you have to leave, the umpire, covering the microphone with one hand, said to Caracera.

Caracera gritted his teeth and said quickly, Think to yourself: Pete's been down too. Did he give up? Think: what would Pete do?

This last question was heard by the audience, for whom it attained the cryptic significance of a fortune cookie fortune, and they waited.

The second set began as poorly as the first had ended for Donny Osmond. Quiñones held serve, winning at love. The Don Bosco crowd cheered. But strangely, the audience, taking Donny Osmond's imminent defeat for a given, began to send him parentlike looks of concern and support.

Donny Osmond deserted his bravura skitterings and kept close to the baseline, where he continued to hammer his shots deep and vengefully, as if wanting to injure his opponent with the ball. He was beginning to get a feel for his range. His shots started to land consistently on the lines or just in front, where in the first set they were missing by a wide margin. The audience gasped at each shot, and when the boy scored a point, they applauded heartily. Soon the mistakes were flowing the other way: Donny Osmond, by the depth of his shots, was drawing errors from Quiñones. Donny pushed him farther away from the baseline to the back of the court, where in front of the audience hung a placard saying, METRO MANILA MERCEDES-BENZ, OFFICIAL SPONSOR OF THE TWO SEASONS TENNIS CHAMPIONSHIP, bookended by the Mercedes insignia like starred cartoon eyes. To Donny Osmond, it seemed as if he were being winked at with approval.

Tied at 1–1, with Quiñones serving, Donny Osmond began to try out his coach's advice. He had won the previous game by effortful work and thought an experiment that took some pressure off his hitting arm might be called for. Though uncomfortable with finesse, he began slicing the ball, making it bounce low and forcing his opponent to hit up. This made the ball easy to volley away, and he did, once, then twice, then again. Soon he was up 5–1. The set ended with Donny Osmond reversing the humiliation he'd received at the close of the first set, replaying the exact same point by which he'd lost that set. He clearly intended by the repetition an up-yours gesture. Pinning the boy to the baseline and forcing a weak reply with the depth and vigor of his stroke, Donny Osmond rushed the net to make the ball die just beyond the other side. And seeing this, Caracera understood why Pete Sampras was the boy's favorite. Like Pete, the boy used arrogance for fuel. He was fired by the conviction of a divine right to victory. The umpire announced, Game and second set, Magulay. But even before then, the crowd was on its feet, thrilled at the prospect of a third set, and exhorting their new, unforeseen favorite: the upstart turned underdog turned rejuvenated would-be champion.

Hearing the umpire's declaration, Donny Osmond smiled and gave himself a small but emphatic fist pump of approval. He even tried to stare down Quiñones, who wouldn't look his way.

The close of the second set confirmed Caracera's potency as a coach. The audience was impressed. The staff, alerted, came out, gathering at the side of the court. They heard the whispers, saw some people pointing to Caracera conferring with his player. Someone was dispatched to get the official photographer of the tournament. From a distance, the photographer began to shoot Caracera smiling at the boy, nodding his head and speaking in tones clearly approving, confident. The boy was smiling, in his eyes a feral glint. His arms were holding up his head, his chin resting on the mini-podium of his entwined hands. He was nodding back at his coach. If the photographer had arrived earlier, the two would have been seen to be fenced off from one another, barely tolerating the other's presence. The boy's look would be desultory, the man's seething.

Third set. A bell could almost be heard to have been rung, as at a boxing match. Quiñones was not about to fold easily. Every player has a shining moment and perhaps this would be his. Up until now he had been a no-account, but this would be the test dividing his life into a before and after, his future about to be decided. The games kept evening out, 1–1, then 2–2, then 3–3, each player guarding his serve.

Donny Osmond tried everything. Perhaps Quiñones's coach had whispered some essential corrective, because the boy had an answer to Donny Osmond's slices, his changes of pace, his underspin, everything Caracera had emboldened him to try and which had won him the second set. Even when he switched to his regular MO and began to hit out, shots hard and deep, the boy seemed ever ready with comparable replies.

4–4.

Quiñones serving. If he won, following the trend, he would be up 5–4. And the pressure would settle on Donny Osmond to hold. Knowing this, Donny Osmond hunkered down, fully intending to break Quiñones's serve and give himself a chance to serve out the set and the match. He kept at each point, showing, to Caracera, a beautiful patience. Stroke for stroke, he matched his opponent, not going for a winner outright. He wanted to frustrate his opponent into a mistake committed from weariness or a desire for a shortcut. And Quiñones did, three times in a row in what amounted to nothing more than three consecutive strokes of bad luck. Two net cords that sailed over into Quiñones's side, and one bad bounce when the ball hit a line and, defying its regular trajectory, skedaddled just beneath Quiñones's racket. Each time the audience's groans grew progressively louder.

The three bad points drew a fourth from Quiñones, visibly shaken:

he committed a double fault serving and thus surrendered the game to Donny Osmond.

Donny Osmond, showing the same feral glint of concentration captured by the tournament photographer, served two aces to go up 30–0 in the decisive game.

The next point was a close one, in which Quiñones, going for all or nothing, hit a shot adjudged, after a suspenseful three-second delay, to be out. Arguing ensued, but in the end the point was awarded to Donny Osmond: 40–0.

The next and final point was capped not with ingenious play, or even by a clinching ace, but because by that juncture the fight had gone out of Quiñones. Returning serve, he hit a weak reply that Donny Osmond overemphatically put away with, yes, an overhead smash.

The crowd stood up to cheer. A hero was born. But Donny Osmond, at the net, gripped his opponent's casual handshake with an uncharacteristic warmth, and then exited without taking in the audience's tribute, his head bowed. He knew he had won by great good luck, and he was determined never to have to be at the mercy of such caprice again.

As if he didn't already know, Caracera cautioned him not to get too cocky.

The following day, Caracera's fame was rekindled. This time his photo appeared in the sports section. The write-up described him as a "passionate and effective" coach to a "potential superstar of the tennis world." This ensured that a day later, the fourth-round match of Donny Osmond Magulay against the San Beda star Richard Lacsamana was sold out. Everyone was there, except Caracera, who took his leave with profuse apologies that his protégé only pretended to accept grudgingly.

In the coach's absence, the boy would be able to play the game his way, would not have to be compelled to replicate the coach's tactics, which, in truth, he was still uncomfortable with, which he'd only taken as a last-ditch measure, having run out of options.

CHAPTER 7

'T HE SEVEN-STORY APARTMENT BUILDING on Magdalena Street was called the Petal Towers. It was a blockish
structure that had gone up in the late 1960s, and had a gray
exterior which showcased a few seismic cracks. It was surrounded on
each side by a two-story house in which business (a hardware store on
the left, a tropical fish seller on the right) was conducted on the street
level while the proprietors lived on the top floor. A few blocks down
was the Metropolitan Hospital, and across from it, St. Joseph's Church.

There were four residences of equal size (that is to say, three bedrooms) on each floor, and each floor was accessible by an elevator on
the left side of the building and a stairway on the right. Their apartment cost seven hundred thousand pesos—a figure that discombobulated Pitik's mother, who, for their shopping trip at the ShoeMart
MegaMall, had only withdrawn ten thousand pesos as a show of fear-
lessness to Mr. Caracera and which dispersal had pained her at every
step of the way.

Their apartment, just like all the others in the building, was fitted
with two doors: on the outside, a metal-frame door with prison-thick
bars and a heavy-duty bolt, and a wooden door on the inside, painted

a robin's-egg blue, that had three locks over the squeaky knob. The twin doors, with their cumbersome and slightly macabre locks, were the clearest indication that the mother and son had vaulted several rungs to find themselves squarely ensconced in the middle classes, filled with the trademark fear of the middle classes, who were moved to protect themselves against rampant hooliganism and thievery, against destructive ill will and devouring ill luck, at the very perimeters of their property.

As a precautionary measure the mother and son were given a sermon by Mr. Caracera's friend about how to behave with their neighbors: they were not to be too deferential ("Remember: you are just like them now"), and should, if asked, say that they had moved to the Petal Towers from Makati following the death of the family patriarch, who had been in the "trading" business. They were not to volunteer any information about themselves, except to shut up overly inquisitive residents, and divulging which, were not to exceed the simple outlines provided them; and further, they were not to encourage participation in their lives by the neighbors or participate in the lives of those around them: no acceptance of dinner invitations, no outings, no contributions to collections being taken up. The message to be imparted was one of coldness, even arrogance, and therefore segregation. In other words, a crucial aspect of their Bambang life would be preserved: there would be no escape into an easy and anonymous fellowship with the rest of humanity. How much longer, wondered the mother, would they continue to pay for the premature death of a weak man that was the sealing statement of their barely begun lives?

The floor of Apartment 3B was made of wood tiles, with images of cubes on them. Attaching to each other, they became Escherlike staircases simultaneously rising and descending diagonally, into infinity, and going nowhere. To the boy this was mesmeric, not a little frightening, though at the same time was a vast improvement over the yellowing plasticized sheet spread over the wooden slats of his former home. He wondered whether the tiles were a distinctive feature of their apartment or could be found replicated up and down the building.

The kitchen was a makeshift area near a window that looked out into the shaftway of the building. Of the three bedrooms, two had small balconies that faced the back of another, similarly modest building, and were perched just above the plastic-corrugated-sheet roofs of what they were informed were greenhouses that belonged to the neighboring building. The concept of a greenhouse had to be explained to the boy, and hearing, he marveled at the idea of an entire room used just to shelter plants.

Two used beds had been donated by Mr. Caracera's friend, and though they were not as luxurious as those found in the Makati highrise, they provided the mother and son with what they considered the best sleep of their lives. The Makati high-rise beds, softer and more plush, were hardened by the awareness that Roger Caracera was next door, and that any noise or utterance mother and son made would be immediately audible to him.

Pitik and his mother were amazed at the size of their new home. The mother walked in and out of the rooms all day long, pacing the floor with slow, deliberate steps. Sometimes it took her nearly an hour to go through every inch of the apartment. Reaching the corners, she would touch the off-white walls, test their sturdiness, see if the ceiling moved and, if the wall happened to adjoin another apartment, see whether vibrations could be felt from next door, or if her own motions would be greeted by voices of complaint or a knock on the wall or on her door. But she never pushed hard enough for this to happen.

Another clear sign of their new, alienating station was the quiet that suffused not just their apartment, not just their building, but the very air outside their windows and on the balconies, specially during the noontime hours, which had been reassuringly cacophonous at the Bambang slums. Only once in the early afternoons since the mother and son moved in had there been any disturbance: a scratchy foreign song—English? Italian?—from what the boy later deduced was an opera, floating singly and uncontested in the air just above their balconies. Was it from the building they faced? Or some upper apartment of the Petal Towers? It sounded melancholy but pristine, and, hearing, the mother had shuddered as if she were being issued a warning: this music, which communicated pain being muffled by civility, human emotion neutered by commitment to beauty and appearances, gave her, as had nothing else previously, a clear idea of the facade she too was required to keep up as a resident of the Petal Towers. Those seismic cracks outside the building were beginning to look like the collective psychic strain of everyone who lived there, forced to adhere to a code of perfection that she knew she would never manage.

Five days into their residency at the Petal Towers, Caracera came to visit, informed of the boy's tremendous unhappiness by the mother. Though she too was unhappy—her sleep cut into by the oppressive certainty that not only did she not belong at the Petal Towers, but she didn't *deserve* to belong—she never would have called their patron simply because of her own suffering. The boy eclipsed her unhappiness with his, forcing her hand.

She told Caracera that Pitik had come home crying every afternoon, and had to be pressed to reveal that he was being made fun of at school. At St. Jude he was targeted by bullies during lunch break and after classes. Also he had been cornered before classes until he'd put a stop to that by hanging out on the streets until just before the bell rang. The mother had been unable to find out why Pitik was being singled out, and Caracera, though he himself had no luck in getting the boy to say anything, had an idea. Though Pitik was taller than the tallest boy in his class by a good head and a half, he was incredibly skinny, and his effeminacy was probably made worse by the inwardness and shyness of finding himself among peers Caracera, in his portraiture of St. Jude, had unwittingly set up to be superior.

You are just as good as any of them, Caracera said.

The boy, lying in bed, refused to look at him. I don't wanting to go.

Yes, thought Caracera, that was another thing: Pitik's horrendous English was one more entry point into a highly weak defense system.

He spoke to the teachers at St. Jude Catholic School and was informed that far from being the victim of bullies, Pitik was often surrounded by admirers, drawn to him for a special quality the teachers termed "charisma." There was an air of sophistication about the boy that communicated knowledge of the world, in marked contrast to his schoolmates, the majority of whom, being cherished offspring of well-to-do or ambitious households, found themselves sheltered from it, overprotected and stifled.

What exactly this "knowledge of the world" consisted of, Caracera was relieved to hear, had gone unspecified by Pitik.

Despite his English, which admittedly drew a few titters from his schoolmates, the boy was clearly very smart. In Religion class, for example, called to speak about a biblical character from the Old Testament, the boy had chosen Jonah—the man swallowed by the whale—and had been able to expertly expound on the story's meaning: he'd spoken about the persistence of faith in a world that would seek to extinguish it. Even the Religion teacher, Miss Acevedo, had been moved to tears.

This was all too good to be true. Perhaps the teachers were only telling Caracera what they thought he'd wanted to hear? He went to Mrs. Diaz, the assistant principal, and revealed that Peter Sindit was not really his son. He had only lied to facilitate the boy's transition into a new life. In actuality, Caracera said, he was the child of his Uncle Eustacio, long dead, and had been conceived out of wedlock, thus being out of the family loop until recently. Now, knowing the boy's demotion in importance and familial affection, would the teachers tell the truth?

But no, the assistant principal, having conferred once more with the teachers, came back with the same mystifying tale of Pitik's popularity.

The teachers tell me that you are not being teased, Caracera said, paying a second visit to the apartment that had been left distressingly bare. Where did they sit? Where did they have dinner? Would he have to do everything for them—pointing out that they had merely substituted one residence for another and were going about their lives as if nothing had changed?

The boy was again lying in bed, and again refused to look at Caracera.

You can't stop going to school. It'll make you a better person. Saying which, he wondered how many lies he would be obliged to tell the boy.

I don't liking it.

Your English has got to improve. You know that, don't you?

In America, said Pitik.

What about America?

In America I needing good English. Here, what is the point?

You want to go to America?

The boy looked at him. How dense could the man be? Pitik felt like a kept boy whose keeper was a ghost. But he didn't say anything. No mention of the new malevolent significance taken on by the Escher staircases on the floor tiles. Like those tiles, the new life Pitik and his mother were guided to in the Petal Towers led nowhere: mother and son seemed to go up and down at the same time; in other words, they were being held in place.

They'd come no farther from their old life than the distance between spit and pavement. From their balconies the sooty, rusted backside of the Bambang slums could be spotted. They held their bodies tense in expectation of the day that they would run into their former neighbors on the streets. Their new life kept at bay the true voyage, the true rescue: the apartment was limbo to a heaven that would continue to elude them; in other words, there would be no America. The Petal Towers was the unsatisfying end point that their sponsor and savior Roger Caracera had decided for them. And to top it off, no celestial view was possible: they were no higher than the third floor.

Do you want me to sponsor you to go to the States? asked Caracera. It'll take a long time.

You are coming with me?

I'm not going with you *anywhere*. Brutal frankness, thought Caracera, was the best policy with the boy.

You hating me! Do not buying-buying me from Madame Sonia if you hating me!

It was clear from the way the man backed off from the bed and the way he turned around at the doorway to look back at Pitik that he was leaving for good. This forced Pitik to hazard a guess. I would liking to hear about tennis, he said, and immediately regretted it. The blatantness—he deserved to be laughed at by the man!

Caracera had mentioned tennis a few times over dinner. He regretted not learning when young, when he had had the chance. And then too Pitik remembered, at the VIP Club, the solicitousness shown the boy Donny Osmond. Because the boy was so ugly, this must owe to Roger Caracera's appreciation for a talent he wished for himself.

But it seemed to work. The man had stopped at the doorway. He made a face of discomfort, of thoughtfulness. You want to learn? he asked.

Can you teaching-teaching me?

I don't know how to play. Another lie. What Caracera meant was: he didn't know how to play well enough to teach.

The boy thought but didn't ask, If I learning how to play tennis, will he loving me also?

Slowly the man began to let his guard down. He even came back into the room. He found a spot on the floor and sat down. The boy was sitting up and returned the man's gaze. His interest was at once genuine and exaggerated.

First Caracera explained himself by talking of other sports: basketball, the preeminent sport in Manila; and then baseball and football, American obsessions. He even brought Europe into the picture, by mentioning soccer, known there as football, though this was entirely different from the American variety. Canada was also ticked off, via hockey. (The man's worldliness thrilled the boy.) These were sports that required groups of players. And so, encountering them as a spectator, the thrill was in the thrill of bodies moving in concert and opposition, scrambling. The man spoke of zigzag lines and confusion, of an unclear visual field. He mentioned the words "skirmish," "squabble," "sloppiness."

It was characteristic of him, he explained, being a man given to solitude, that all these should be seen in a negative light; there was an unavoidable sense in these games that effort, by being quartered, and eighthed, and sixteenthed, wasn't as taxing as it needed to be, and therefore not as worthy of admiration.

He said that he believed in the fight of solitude against solitude, in which effort was shouldered by a single individual competing for primacy over another—without aid, without having to siphon off a companion's strength. As in life, he said, so too in the events he admired, into which he would occasionally project himself, seeking escape from the disappointing plane on which he found himself: a failed writer, though a good teacher. Tennis had never been among the things he'd meant to take up, it was mostly its poetic vindication of life lived as a single unit that he loved. Though in his twenties, and living in San Francisco, there had been a short period when he'd received lessons. But by then, of course, it was already too late. His arms, legs and shoulders could no longer be bent and twisted to the game's ends. And so he remained someone who continued living in his head. It was in this head that tennis, over the years, began to take on a significance disproportionate to its actual practicableness, its application in his life. He admitted that among the reasons—if not the main reason—that he had "found" tennis so late in life was because he'd recognized it to be what someone of his class, his breeding should be engaged in. The middle- to upper-middle-class air of the sport had made him defer his involvement until it was too late. Caracera was given courage by the idea that the boy might not understand what he was talking about, so that in essence, he, Roger Caracera, was only talking to himself, confessing. Meeting Donny Osmond Magulay had been a moment of lift, when his dream self and his physical self could happily, momentarily coincide.

Solitude against solitude: those were the words the man used, and though Pitik thought they sounded pretty, he knew that everything that came out of the man's mouth had been rehearsed to buttress the one point on which he could not afford to be seen to budge: he was resisting the boy, afraid. Fear to Pitik was a clue. But still he couldn't say anything.

How could he? Never before had he been placed in a position of weakness, in which the declaration of love was to come from his side. Up until now, he had been the cavalier adjudicator of, and dispenser of happiness to, others. His professions of love—though rote, and understood, he believed, by the men receiving them to be such—had the power to lift them out of whatever misery had brought them to Madame Sonia in the first place. His job, though it made him the well into which so much self-serving adoration was poured, also had a benevolent component. His was the charity benefiting the aged, those no longer desirable, giving them contact with the young skin that was the stock feature of their erotic imaginations. As they got older, proximity to such skin became less and less frequent.

With Cary Grant, however, he had an idea that the man's sadness and lowness of feeling were handsome coats self-tailored as declarations and badges of perverse pride, inside which the man was warm and protected. None of Pitik's gifts, developed since the age of seven to a blithe sheen, would seem to fit the occasion. They could not take the man out of a misery he gave all indications of cultivating, enjoying;

by such defeatist self-imposition distinguishing himself from a family who, like their money, brought shame. In this, he was beginning to recall, however faintly, the man who had supposedly dispatched Roger Caracera to the boy: Eustacho Caracera.

There had been a man like that in Pitik's past, kingly and yet beset by unspoken complaint. The boy remembered the way of the man more than the man himself, more than his looks or the way he had made Blueboy feel. Oddly, this sense of indulgent loserliness had not been found sexy in the other, now-dead man, but was entirely irresistible in the person of Roger Caracera.

Damn it that that ugly Donny Osmond possessed the only gift—specialized and peculiar—able to take Roger Caracera out of his programmed funk. What was so great about hitting a fuzzy ball from one end to another of a court which looked distressingly like a blackboard? Clearly it was subterfuge, concealing the man's infuriating infatuation. That Pitik should lose the contest of love to a *pangit* like Donny Osmond! *Putang ina talaga!*

On Caracera's face could be seen both surprise and gratefulness. He wondered if Pitik was looking for a new vocation to replace the one that was no longer allowed him. Tennis, why not? He was still young enough, pliant.

But the next afternoon, the boy did not come home from school. And the morning after that, he remained missing.

This was when Roger Caracera excused himself from the fourth round of the Two Seasons Tennis Tournament.

CHAPTER 8

EINGOLD WAS the prime heir to a Southern California dairy empire whose annual revenues topped the tens of millions, though you could hardly tell this state of affairs from what he wore: a Hawaiian shirt of typical garishness stained in the underarm by b.o. and sweat, and in the front and back also by sweat and what looked to be greasy food stains, and large, ragged-at-the-hem, pale green army shorts. His sandals were old and had seen many miles, the leather soles warped at the toes. He had been on "extended leave" from a low-end managerial position at the dairy firm in Altadena. For the sixteen months he'd racked up in Southeast Asia (spending twelve of those in his "beloved" Manila), all he had to show were impressively bronzed skin and an expanding trunk of a body ringed by a series of ever-widening but still too-tight shorts.

Caracera knew him to be a pederast because he had freely declared himself to be so, in a public place, no less, a café in the busy section of Remedios Circle. Although, of course, he didn't use the word "pederast." Instead, he called himself a "lover of children." "Lover of boys," he elaborated. If all around Caracera the flesh (though largely female) was so eager to be commodified, so eager to be thought worthy of the visiting tourist population, then this—hearing the country talked about in such flagrantly consumeristic ways—could be logically seen as a just conclusion.

Next to Feingold was the runaway Pitik Sindit, who had been brought over by the man from a private home he had been renting for the last six months in Fort Bonifacio, a glossy, thriving section of the city filled with newly built skyscrapers.

The three of them, seated around a table on the street outside the Cactus Café, were conspicuous and funny-looking. Caracera saw them as they would be seen by an outside eye, mercilessly taxonomied: a whore with two middle-aged johns. How despicable, that by sitting here he could be considered this man Feingold's twin. In Manila, his usual habit of seeking a correspondence between himself and some person who was preferably lowly, as for example a derelict on the street, dressed in rags, in other words, empathy, had been momentarily suspended. The people he saw in the city seemed rooted in conditions of willing smallness and devoutness he had long since surpassed. Yet every once in a while a membrane would lift and he would see above some harried jeepney driver's body his own face; his face floating above the bodies too of happy schoolchildren, released en masse from the iron gates of their schools; of church matrons, with their voluptuous Christian suffering and voluptuous disregard of the world around them, beautiful veils with eyelets of roses or crosses draped over their averted faces; of the priest Shakespeare de Leon, whose earthly reward was not the warmth of his benevolent custodianship but rather the warmth of drink, hidden from sight.

When faced with Feingold, however, this membrane of arrogance remained, became shrunken, in fact, wrapped even tighter around Caracera's body.

Yet he felt compelled to stay put, further denigrating his already low reputation. The student who, when last encountered (at this very same café, with his friend Benjamin Goyanos), had been explaining the Philippines to Caracera, the American visitor, was looking at the shameless triumvirate. What was his name—Nicanor . . . Roldan, was it? Melodious, old-timey. The name of a poet. Nicanor Roldan. Shooting him daggers, having finally understood what Caracera's "interest" in the Philippines amounted to: the skinny kid being fatted with ice cream by Caracera and his "partner" in crime. The two were bringing their Stateside largesse to bear on the brown toothpick who was wearing a ridiculous canary-yellow Lacoste shirt and pastel pants (with the hems cuffed and folded to showcase bare ankles) and (really, this was too much) red espadrilles: a failed makeover befitting the charade of privilege the boy was no more than a temporary receptacle for.

By sitting next to the oily American, with his head of beautiful black curls, and sitting across from the smiling boy, who was encouraging the appearance of a contest between the two men for his favors; by keeping quiet as the oily American spooned ice cream into the young boy's mouth; by not putting a stop to the actions, Roger Caracera was imparting cool approval to anyone who bothered to look. And who, passing by the busy intersection, could not help but look at this blatant incursion into their respectable, artsy-fartsy midst of the whore trade? The courage and affront of these three were eye-popping.

Feingold called Pitik by his trade name, Blueboy, and in return was called Mr. Feingold, no first name.

You're so pretty with your mouth like that, cooed Mr. Feingold, who daubed a paper napkin at the corner of the boy's lips, where the ice cream had left glossy patches.

The boy opened his mouth, releasing the spoon, which Mr. Feingold took and rested above the pedestal of the soda fountain glass, just below its stem.

And what do you do in Manila? Feingold asked, looking at Caracera for the briefest moment before returning his attention once more to the boy, who was putting on a sickening performance of utter contentment.

I grew up here, said Caracera, containing his anger.

Lucky you.

Feingold had been enjoined to appear with the boy through the intercession of Madame Sonia, who had known all along where Pitik was—and who, Caracera had no doubt, had encouraged and engineered the flight.

This time persuading the Santa Ana proprietress to cooperate required no money changing hands. Caracera had been shocked, calmed by his own capableness—the return of the hot blood that had last coursed through the veins of his San Francisco youth, decades and

decades past. He'd overturned various pieces of furniture in the proprietress's dark front room: the futon bed, which had been shockingly insubstantial in his hands; the crates bearing various potted greens,
which, besides the odd *calesa* wheel chandelier, had seemed the only
caring touches in the place; the stool, and, resting on it, the black plastic phone. The noise had been to Caracera like merriment. All at once
all the rage and disdain that he'd had to put a lid on had come tumbling out, and the gremlin, shocked by the revolt of what had seemed,
up to that breaking point, an inward, reserved, compressed man, scampered off. The freedom was adrenalizing. The proprietress's arrogance
forced Caracera to repeat his question one more time: Where is Pitik?
Where are you hiding him? Receiving no answer, he flew to where
Madame Sonia stood crossing both arms defensively over her chest,
and had started beating on her, drawing whimpers.

The name Feingold had finally been blurted out, while Sonia was
frantically inspecting her arms, shoulders, chest for the patches of discoloration already apparent.

Had Sonia sold the boy to Feingold, in essence making a double
profit from Pitik?

No, she had hastened to assure the angry man, who looked ready
for more violence. It was entirely the boy's idea to go to someone who
loved him, as she believed Roger Caracera didn't. Why did you taking him away if you cannot be giving-giving what he wants? asked
Madame Sonia.

What does he want?

Loving. He is wanting to be loved. How blind-blind can you be,
Joe?

I've given him the money.

Money is not love!

That's all he's getting from me.

I should not have letting him go.

Where would he be in three years, after you've used him up?

With somebody who is loving-loving him.

Caracera took a final look at Sonia's living quarters. Here was another new millionaire who, by continuing to live as slovenly and
starkly as she did, gave off vibes of disbelief and fear, as if the money
that had come so effortlessly and without preamble into her lap would

just as quickly be taken away, and therefore needed to be safeguarded by stealth.

Pitik Sindit, sitting across the small café table, did not look at Caracera. Frankly, Pitik was disappointed. It was perverse, but true: his plan had been entirely too successful. Not only had he forced Roger Caracera to come to him once more, but he could see from Caracera's expression the seething jealousy the man felt when confronted with proof of the boy's prolific desirability. It was because of this that he couldn't stop grinning. Still, he would've preferred if the man had come later, after he'd gotten tired of Mr. Feingold's attentions.

What do you do in Manila? Caracera asked Feingold.

I do business in these parts, sometimes. Mainly I'm retired.

What exact business are you involved in?

Am I under police investigation? He gave a loud, unnatural guffaw, making his face turn red.

The sight exhausted Caracera, and he turned his attention to the boy. Why aren't you in school? Caracera spat out.

The boy doesn't want to be in school. They make fun of him.

That's a lie.

Isn't that what you told me, Blueboy?

Pitik nodded.

He's lying.

I am not! said the boy. Still, he refused to look at his accuser.

Coercion is never a good policy with the headstrong, Mr. Caracera—may I call you Roger?

Caracera kept silent.

I know you're interested in the boy too, Mr. Caracera, but I tell you that not only do I have first rights over him, the boy tells me that he doesn't want to be with you.

First rights? Why do you have any rights at all?

I met him first. Madame Sonia promised I was first in line.

My interest in the boy is different from yours. Let's get that clear.

You don't want to help? You don't want to make his life better? That's the extent of my interest.

There's a law against people like you.

Not in these parts, thank God. Feingold laughed, running a handkerchief through his forehead.

But of course there were laws—even if foreigners, in particular, found them encouragingly relaxed. I could call the police.

No, said the boy, taking Caracera seriously for the first time.

Why don't you? encouraged Feingold. You have my address. Have them pay me a visit.

The self-satisfied tone hinted at payola, connections. Still, Caracera was willing to wager that the man was bluffing.

In this part of the world what Blueboy and I represent is entirely natural, Feingold declared.

That's wishful thinking on your part.

No? Walk down most streets, offered Feingold. It won't be uncommon to find a young boy and an older gentleman.

Those are *business* transactions. Was that what you meant when you said you were a businessman?

Business is only one component of a many-sided relationship. The boys have something missing in their lives that we provide. Same with us: we need something that the boys can give. It's mutual. Business does not preclude love, Mr. Caracera.

Clearly the man had a deep fund of self-justification that would not be exhausted soon. If this *love* is so natural, asked Caracera, how come you need to go skulking to the other side of the world for it?

Because, thought Caracera, you are ugly. Not only do you have to pay to have somebody come near that body, you have to travel all the way to the Third World, where your ugliness can be leavened by the paleness of your skin—which, preceded by history in these parts, is misconstrued as a potent definition of attractiveness.

In a few respects, America is not the First World, Feingold answered. It has its backward aspects too.

Laws against what you do, for example.

You're not getting me to say anything I haven't already said. Yes, I'm a pederast. There—the word Caracera had been thinking all along, and yet he felt no satisfaction. Feingold's was an exasperated tone of voice. I use the word for the dictionary meaning. Minus the moral judgment implicit in the way others use it. Like I said, I would rather be called a lover of boys. Which is exactly what I am. No more, no less. He turned to look at Pitik, who, despite trying to ignore the fight, had been drawn in. Aren't I a lover of boys, Blueboy? Don't I love you?

The boy smiled.

You are so beautiful! Every time you smile it's like the sun coming out of the clouds! You know that, don't you? The man caressed the side of Pitik's face, making him tip his head and smile further, more shyly. That smile kills me every time. And that skin.

Caracera felt a nausea made worse by the cheesy, obvious dumb show being conducted for his benefit. How many boys have you been with, Mr. Feingold? He bit down on the word "Mister."

A handful. Feingold laughed.

What are you going to do when he gets tired of you? Caracera asked the boy.

I've been with a few boys, but among all of them I chose Blueboy. He's the best. He's the one I love. I do love him. And what are you to him that I should be answering all these questions?

The boy looked eagerly for the answer.

Caracera was dumbstruck. But of course he would have to justify his presence in the boy's life sooner or later, other than that he was the emissary of a man controlling the strings from beyond the grave. That had never been much of an excuse and had only been waiting for a man like Feingold, who, justifying his self-description as a "business-man," would see through the profitlessness in Roger Caracera's relationship with the boy.

He was not, like Frannie Prusso, a missionary. By helping boys like Pitik, she was seeking to perpetuate, to extend the domain of her belief. He was not like Father Shakespeare de Leon, for whom the same description held. What other motives could there be?

Come home to your mother, Caracera said to the boy. She misses you.

Yes, that was it: it was for the mother that Caracera had been moved to act. The boy could not have chosen a worse time to disappear. Once more the fervid imaginations of the citizenry, uncontent with sporadic sightings of the Virgin Mary, had to create yet another emergency: tabloids and the television told stories of an *aswang* in their midst. The creature manifested itself as either a sharp-toothed crone or an unnaturally pale young man with a skin-poking, hungry tongue. Dead bodies "salvaged" from the estuaries of the Pasig were attributed to it, and young people especially (with their youthful, "rejuvenating" blood) had been warned to lock themselves in after midnight. Holy water blessed by a priest and stored in a plastic capsule worn on a necklace had become a much-sought-after remedy. So too had crucifixes, not simply crosses: the body of Christ was what was needed to repel the ghoul.

Caracera had quickly assured the mother that there could only be one *aswang* responsible, Madame Sonia, and that he would bring her boy back immediately. And Madame Sonia had led him to Feingold, who now spoke: She knows Blueboy's fine. We called her. Just this morning. And she knows me. We've met before. She knows I'm good for my word. And we'll visit. We haven't yet but we will. Right, Blueboy?

The boy smiled. There was another performance of spooning ice cream and then wiping off his mouth, which the boy instigated by tapping the man on the arm and then winking at the glass of melted dessert.

You haven't answered my question, Mr. Caracera. What are you to Blueboy?

Caracera sat stone-faced.

Are you his father? Feingold said this with a high degree of mockery, trying to spur on a game between himself and Pitik, but the boy would not smile, would not participate, at once riveted and fearful. Are you his brother? continued Feingold. His priest? His . . . lover? His pimp? Have you taken over from Madame Sonia? Do I owe you money now?

Caracera's jaws were tight, defined.

I can assure you, Mr. Caracera, that the boy and I get along beautifully. We'll continue to get along beautifully until he gets tired of me. Because he has my assurance that I won't get tired of him.

Do you want to be with him? Caracera kept his gaze on the boy.

I do, Pitik answered defiantly.

You love him?

Tell him, Blueboy. The man stroked the boy's hands, clasped together on top of the garden-style table.

He loves me, replied Pitik.

Yes, yes, I do, you know I do. Disgusting baby talk, as the man pinched Pitik in the nose, shaking it back and forth teasingly.

And you love him? asked Caracera.

The boy looked away. He loves me, he repeated.

Why are you trying to make something ugly that is not ugly except if you look at it through a prejudiced viewpoint? asked Feingold.

Do you loving me? Pitik asked Caracera, though he looked away immediately.

It's *love*, Blueboy, corrected Feingold. Not loving. Do you *love* me?

Do you love me? repeated Pitik meekly, and once again turned away from the man he wanted the answer from.

The short English grammar lesson was incongruously touching to Caracera. Not in that way, Peter, was all he could reply, knowing it would not be good enough for the boy. You know that. I've said that to you before. I'm not . . . He hesitated. I don't like boys.

You like girls, said Feingold to himself, sneering.

You like girls? asked Pitik, seeking assurance of his dashed hopes.

I don't like anyone.

How about Donny Osmond?

I don't like him.

Lying! You are helping him! Madame Sonia showed me the newspapers!

Helping, yes. That's all there is to it.

You are *helping* me also? asked the boy, mocking.

I promised my uncle I would help.

Like a job! He turned away definitively from Caracera. Let's go, he said to Feingold.

Goodbye, said the man, taking the boy by the hand as they simultaneously rose.

Please don't go, said Caracera, recognizing at once the forlorn, besotted aspect of his voice, which must surely be matched by some facial contortion. It caused him to look down, look away.

The boy waited.

Caracera could not look up. Was he in love? Now? Could dormancy have twisted whatever passion remained in him into this new, unexpected, unwanted shape? *He was gay. He wasn't. He could be gay. He couldn't, not truly.*

The boy waited.

Finally, Caracera looked up. Are you going back to school? he asked.

The boy didn't answer but was clearly displeased that this was the question he had been entreatied to stay to hear.

Are you going to visit your mother?

We already told you we would, answered Feingold. Listen. I'd offer you my friendship but it seems you've already made up your mind. About me. And the boy.

He's a boy. So you recognize that. He knew that he was grasping at straws, repeating accusations that had had no effect the first time around.

I recognize that we're in love.

He didn't know why Madame Sonia should suddenly be a suitable touchstone, but a paraphrase of her concluding words came tumbling out of his mouth. He said to Pitik, Listen. Look at me. If you get tired of him, or if you don't want to stay with him, for any reason, you know you can come to me. Don't you? You know where I live. Or you can go back to your mother. She misses you. She worries. You owe her—well, maybe you don't *owe* her that. But it would be nice. To reassure her. And me too. Again you don't owe me anything. But it would be nice. To know you're fine.

He's fine with me, said Feingold, dragging along the boy, who was suddenly seen to be unhappy. Perhaps the boy's pants were uncomfortable, for his walk looked obstructed, hemorrhoidal. This caused the pair to slow down, so that Caracera had the benefit of watching them take a long time to walk away.

The man, big as a house, with the skinny boy next to him, their hands disentangling—as the boy adjusted his shirt, his pants, as he did something to his face. Caracera knew that the boy wanted to turn back to look at him but was unwilling to risk it, risk exposing the sign on his face which he'd tried to wipe away with those hands. Perhaps he was trying to erase the nervousness of realizing that he'd made the wrong decision, and was about to mortgage his youth for nothing better than spite.

Could love, Caracera wondered, be molded from a base of pity? That was what he felt most strongly looking at the boy, at the mismatch between who the boy was and what he was wearing, and most importantly the mismatch—which drew other stares as well—between the giant man and Pitik. The contrast spoke not of a custodial, protec-

tive union but rather of the relationship between master and slave, between hunter and dog or, less kindly, between hunter and prey. This
was what everyone who looked on gave all appearances of thinking, in
a concert of disgust much like that which Caracera had felt on the
plane with the Australian johns, an echoing-out of said repulsion,
wavelike, toward where the man and boy had last stepped, lapping at
their backs but not quite reaching them. It wasn't only because the
people in the café had seen how the pair had behaved while seated at
the table earlier, with a flaunting, flouting affection. The more damn-
ing factor, it seemed, was that the American was clearly so American:
prosperous, oblivious, a giant not only physically but in spirit, with his
booming announcer's voice and his suave boulevardier's stride; and the
Filipino next to him, so junior, unformed, unprotected, so eager to be
swept up.

In this, it was clear that the heart of the Filipino view of American-
hood was a palpable, thriving distrust. It was a distrust he, Caracera,
had momentarily forfeited by not joining the pair.

But what would they have thought if they'd known the things
Caracera had done for the boy? There was no doubt that the distrust
would flare up with him at the center of its sights.

The evidence was against him: He'd bought the boy's freedom for
a million pesos. He'd given the boy and his mother three million pesos
with which to turn over their lives. Had helped them with banking
matters, with matters of getting right with the authorities. Had helped
them locate an apartment—in Binondo, one of the hearts of middle-
class Manila.

Now, why would a man, an American, do all these things for a boy,
a Filipino whose trade was whoredom and whose one exchangeable
commodity was therefore himself?

It always came back to the one thing.

Love? A laugh. He felt no stirring inside that cavity where the emotion was said to pulse, over which the gremlin had its seat. Not a rise
in temperature watching the boy walking away—the boy was still
walking away, plainly visible. God, how slow could anyone go?

Perhaps the boy wanted to be prevented from disappearing.

Caracera made it just in time to see the pair enter Feingold's car. He
dashed quickly to tap the window on Feingold's side.

Feingold lowered his window, said something to the driver, who put on the brakes. What do you want? All the friendliness of his earlier persona had been stripped away, and in its place was a transfixing contempt.

I paid a million pesos for him, Caracera replied, with a tip of his head in the boy's direction.

You want me to pay you back?

Get out of the car! he barked at the boy, who seemed to be at once afraid and happy, but who immediately put on a theatrical, steely insubordination, refusing to look at Caracera.

I'll pay you back, you don't have to worry, reassured the fat American. With that, he gave the signal for the driver.

Traffic was so thick it took only a few steps for Caracera to catch up. I don't want the money! he shouted.

What do you want, then? The boy already made his feelings clear! Tell him, Feingold beseeched Pitik.

I don't want you, said the boy, as if reading off a card.

Good, Blueboy, that is the right way. Not wanting, but want. Feingold patted the boy's knee.

I own you! said Caracera. He had been so convinced that the boy's perversity would respond to the cruelty and brusqueness of being treated as a piece of property (for the boy clearly had not been touched by concern)—but now that the words were out of his mouth . . . he felt stranded.

He could simply lie. Tell the boy that he loved him. It was the one thing the boy wanted to hear. The one thing which he, Caracera, by arriving on the scene as a prospective john, had unwittingly set up an expectation for.

Just tell the boy what he wants to hear, he told himself. Three simple words, easy. It wasn't as if he hadn't lied to the boy before: *Education is important. Sex, the work you do, is corrupting. Pay attention to what the world says and stay away from its anger.* The boy would believe him and leave Feingold. But what would happen afterward? Would he have to monitor the boy's every move? Imprison him? Forbid him the right to make decisions about his life? Or would Caracera have to be compelled to follow through: *I love you?* Another kiss? This time on the lips? More than that? Would the boy be content to settle for a chaste love, like the love of father and son, or brother and brother? For he finally had to face the facts: there was no way he could get naked and lie against this boy, or any other boy.

People were looking at him, in that brazen way that they'd felt they had the right to since the very first day of his arrival. Some were pointing. Whispers: The American, with its ringing indictment. It was the Australian johns and the Frannie Prussos all over again.

This city—sitting under the sign of the savior.

The boy said nothing, steadfastly maintaining his avoidance. The car moved a few feet.

The image of him replacing Feingold, spoon-feeding the boy melted ice cream . . . Caracera shuddered. The image of the boy with Feingold, being undressed, pawed over, ministrations of mouth and hand and dick . . . He shuddered.

The car moved another few feet. And this time, Caracera was the one who walked away.

CHAPTER 9

WHEN CARACERA LEFT the boy, he had an almost physical sense of his old, cold self regaining tenancy.

The feeling did not abate, was in fact heightened by his resumption of life as a tennis coach. His favorite sport, which relied on the strivings of an individual fighting against another individual.

The fourth round had been won by Donny Osmond, occasioning another day's worth of coverage in the sports section, this time in two new papers. Caracera's picture as he conferred with his player was reprinted in both articles. Strangely, his head was seen to favor the ground, bowing low, just as in the picture of him at his father's funeral procession. One caption read: "Millionaire Caracera talks seriously with wunderkind tennis player Donny (Osmond) Magulay, an employee at the VIP Club, at the Two Seasons Tennis Championship. Tickets still available."

Hopefully word would reach the family about Pitik Sindit and they would leave Caracera alone.

Donny won the quarterfinals as well, easily. The score was 6–3, 6–2.

His semifinal game quickly became the most anticipated lineup, the unschooled savant about to meet his match in the highest-ranking player.

The Saturday afternoon in which the semis were being played was typically hot, the visibility perfect. Not a cloud to hide the sun. The audience came outfitted in caps and sunglasses. Caracera was lost in the rows of spectators. He wore a nondescript blue baseball cap, his face cupped by shadows extending from the brim.

Donny Osmond's head was left unprotected from the sun, and the striking light revealed patches of browned scalp between his thick hair, which was beaded with sweat or gel.

His opponent, whose father was a tennis pro entered into the 1974 U.S. Open as a wild card, getting to the second round, had been last year's runner-up. Rafael Pimentel was a serious boy who excelled in school. He applied the same concentration he brought to his studies to his tennis game. He was the very definition of the triumph of will over natural talent. By it he'd bested players far more easeful with the racket, whose serves and strokes were more free-flowing, and in the exertion of which their bodies were not bent or wrested so grievously, creating unnatural lines. He came to the semis with a bandage over his midsection, to protect a back that had been put through more than its quota of paces, and a wrap over his left knee, which continued to hurt every time he served.

The first game went to Donny Osmond, holding his serve at love.

Some in the audience were familiar with Donny Osmond's game but not Pimentel's, some were familiar with Pimentel's but not Donny Osmond's, and only a handful, mostly the umpire and the staff and the coaches who had done their scouting of the opposing player, had seen both kids in action. All, however, had heard the extravagant claims made for each, and waited to see if Rafael Pimentel had come prepared to hold up his end. He too served and won at love. His style, noticed Caracera, was more Pete Sampras's than Donny's was, winning points by quick serve-and-volley.

How did Caracera know that his player would follow immediately by mirroring Pimentel, trying to wrest the mantle of Sampras play-alike from his opponent, and by doing so, mocking? Donny won three points in a row serving and volleying. The hard serve forced Pimentel to move out of position, and then the weak reply was volleyed into the open court. The audience's applause was polite, uninvolved, undecided.

Game points one, two and three were quickly lost by Donny Osmond. On his serve, he found himself suddenly from 40–0 to deuce. It seemed Pimentel, grooving on the serve-and-volley tactic had found his range and began to send returns at Donny's feet, each time forcing an error, twice into the net, once out of bounds.

The next point was an ace, making Caracera breathe with relief.

The point after that, a double fault, and they were back to deuce.

Two points later, after a passing shot from Donny was run down by Pimentel, Donny's serve had been broken. From that point on, Pimentel never let up. He was the one who forced the action, though you could tell that each shot sent deep into the corners was done with a lot of wasted effort. Between points, recovering, he took his time. Still, the longer Pimentel played, the more the court became like a blackboard. At all times he was thinking, making up for his frequent awkward stances by devising schemes with which to rattle Donny or to draw from the boy a weak reply or to force him into an untenable position, and he knew when to keep the ball in play, not attempting too much, and when to go for his shots. Patience and studiousness. All Donny Osmond could do was react, running, and even though the effort cost him but little in physical expenditure—he was ready to resume play immediately, striving doggedly to redeem the last losing point—Caracera could tell that the gears in his brainworks were slowly coming loose. Desperation and blind flailing. Each beautiful shot he sent across the net would come back, never as beautifully or well struck, of course, but Pimentel's ball, with its clear take-that signal, would sooner or later frustrate Donny. In reply, his ball would fly not just out of Pimentel's reach but out of the court's parameters. Each groan from the audience only made the next point worse. Points kept being lost the same way and soon the pile-up was against Donny: a 6–2 first set victory for Pimentel, who retired to his umbrella-shaded seat and put his head into a wet towel, breathing raggedly.

The audience studied the sight of Donny in his chair, being spoken to by his coach. Could it be that, as with his match against Sirco Quiñones in the third round, he was a late starter when confronted with a particularly intransigent rival? Or was this as far as the boy's talent would take him—straight into the wall of a more classically trained, more experienced competitor? The sight of the boy's face, dumbstruck and scowling, gave them no confidence, so the speculation began to be passed around that last year's runner-up, Rafael Pimentel, would reprise his role—in two quick sets. Certainly they were disappointed. They had come expecting a toe-to-toe race and here was a player ready to fold. They looked at Pimentel's father, already accepting the hearty congratulations of a few friends and beaming with paternal magnanimousness.

Talking to the boy, Caracera himself was flushing, his investment in the boy's playing never more fully underlined than today. He was sweating for reasons that had nothing to do with the heat. He gritted his teeth, dug his eyes into the ground, attempting to see things as his player was seeing them: looking across the net at the barrel of a gun, above him no sky, only an echo chamber that magnified the sound of the ball's return, which was running away from him as fast as it could. And he felt as if the same sad story of fetch was being replayed in the spectators' sunglasses every time he looked up.

Donny Osmond could not get his head around the fact that it was he who used to be the player issuing the orders for the ball to heed.

Caracera heard the far-off shuttering of a camera lens. Another classic scene being recorded?: *The calm before the turnaround. Caracera talks with his prized player, encouraging him to victory.*

But his jaws were clenched. The kid Pimentel, he knew, was not Sirco Quiñones, who had let bad luck defeat him. Pimentel would not let luck into the equation. Industry was the hedge against such luck and Pimentel was the young master of industry. Donny, on the other hand, was wildly talented, in this instance the accent clearly on the first word.

He said to Donny, Make him run. Let him do the retrieving.

Don't you think I'm trying?

Then try something else. Do what we did when you played Quiñones. Surprise him. Vary your shots.

I did.

Do it more.

What if it doesn't work?

It won't work if you already have that attitude.

Donny was silent.

Caracera continued, Do you notice one thing about him?

Donny was silent.

Look at him right now.

Donny refused to turn his head, by such method acknowledging his inferiority.

He's breathing hard. What does that tell you?

Donny was silent.

Make him run. Get it? He'll break down. I guarantee you that.

I'm trying to make him run. I don't know what's happening.

Slow down the point. Think out there. Don't just rely on your talent, good as it is. Do you want to win?

Donny was silent. The question was too stupid to answer.

Do you want to win?

What do you think I am? Of course.

Then never give up. If one method fails, try another. If that fails, try both. At the same time.

Time, said the umpire.

Make him work, repeated Caracera in parting. If this was what coaching was, throwing around the obvious, trying to exhort a block of stone not to be a stone, then they could have it! Returning to his seat, he was aware of people looking at him, and this only increased his sense of fraudulence.

Donny Osmond won the first game of the second set, which he served, not by his usual flashy shots, directing the ball toward impossible corners, but by unremarkable play. There was a hedging in his shots to ensure that they didn't go long, as they had in the first set. By this method, his shots landed well within the court, but possessed none of the sting by which he normally unbalanced his opponents. But oddly, this played to his advantage.

Either the first set had so exhausted Rafael Pimentel, his vision gone bleary and his energy drawn to dregs, or the break had interfered with his momentum and his timing was off.

Or could it be that Donny Osmond had unwittingly stumbled onto an effective change-up? And not by using the Caracera-encouraged arsenal of slices and dices, but, oddly and with no other intention than to hang in, by playing with careful mediocrity? By not being Donny Osmond, Donny Osmond had managed to do what he couldn't during the entirety of the first set: throw his opponent for a loop. Thinking of this, a picture began to form in Caracera's head: Rafael Pimentel, armed with insider information on Donny Osmond's playing style per his coach's vetting, had come fully prepared, having practiced, in his regular studentlike manner, a counterplan—first, taking away Donny's beloved serve-and-volley tactic, and then, more importantly, frustrating him into the indefensible position.

Suddenly, confronted with midcourt shots that should have been easily muscled away for winners or to move Donny Osmond out of position, Rafael Pimentel began to overhit, sending the ball past the lines. He and his coach hadn't practiced for this eventuality and his sense of timing and range became erratic. Caracera had a vision of a handsome hat knocked off to reveal a threadbare scalp, vulnerable to a sudden change in the temperature, and he sat forward, riveted.

Still, in the next game, Pimentel stuck to his guns, serving and volleying, and he won.

1–1.

It was in the first set, at this exact juncture, that Donny Osmond had lost his serve, signing over the set to Rafael Pimentel. Now, looking across the net to try to fix on any of Pimentel's physical advantages to stoke his anger, Donny could find nothing. Pimentel was not his handsomest opponent. That was the second-round opponent, the brother of the Stanford player. Pimentel was not, from what he'd heard, his wealthiest opponent. It must've been Sirco Quiñones in the third round, with the new, moonwalking sneakers, seeing which, Donny Osmond had been determined to mock their heaviness, their shiny expensiveness. That match, in Donny Osmond's mind, was fought against those sneakers, their cost, their ineffectiveness, and against the feet they'd so dandled and petted. Donny Osmond relished the memory of them squeaking around, always a second or two too late. Jealousy was the method by which he'd won that round.

But Pimentel was the highest ranked. This was what Donny had fixated on during the first set. He wanted to make a mockery of that ranking in front of this posh, Mercedes-driving crowd in this Mercedes-sponsored championship, reminding them that a number preceded one, and that number was zero. He was this zero, the open mouth of victorious laughter, the swallower of all opponents. But it hadn't worked, or rather, he himself was reminded of the value of the number he'd chosen for himself: zero. 6–2. He'd lost the first set. It wasn't the first time he'd lost. That historic humiliation had happened two rounds back, but he'd survived, and in surviving had, or at least he'd told himself he had, grown stronger. But there was a marked difference, he feared, between his earlier loss and this. He didn't know how to, and didn't think he could, outwit Rafael Pimentel. He conceded the contest of brains to this opponent, but was observant enough to know, just like his coach, that Pimentel's effortful playing style would sooner or later cost him—if not in this match then in his later life. Injuries were being built on the foundation of other, older injuries. The way the guy twisted his upper body to hit a backhand made even Donny Osmond, seeing from the corner of his eye and across the net, wince. But what good would it do Donny Osmond if the harm to his opponent came after the match? *He had to hurt Rafael Pimentel now*: this thought suddenly became paramount.

Or . . . or what? Because if Pimentel hadn't been hurt by now, the chances of Donny Osmond being able to hurt him were slim to none. By this point in the tournament couldn't the guy be running on Tylenol? Whatever pain was wracking that body had to fight its way past the velvet cloak of medication, Donny was sure.

Still, there must be something for Donny to do. He had only to find that single thread, picking at which, he would cause the whole tapestry to unravel . . .

Even if Donny held serve, he would have to break Pimentel's serve sooner or later. And he'd had no opportunity all throughout the first set, not even close, drawing to deuce only once. The guy's serve-and-volley technique was better than Donny Osmond's. All right, thought Donny, another concession: Pimentel's serve-and-volley would make Donny's idol Pete Sampras proud.

Perhaps, having been trumped at the serve-and-volley, long one of the patented techniques by which he beat his opponents, Donny Osmond could return the favor and trump Rafael Pimentel at Pimentel's trademark scheme: the thinking game.

Donny Osmond, foolhardy and vain, and who wouldn't desist from a strategy that he knew his opponent was the better at, decided in the end to serve-and-volley. This technique had won him the first three points of the first set's third game, and then after that Pimentel had gotten wise, and it had all been downhill for Donny.

Still, though foolish, Donny was not entirely without fear. He held his breath each time the serve was struck, as he waited for Rafael Pimentel's reply. But yet again, he won the first three points, and was up 40–0. Would Pimentel once more find his range and turn Donny's 40–0 score meaningless? Donny Osmond wouldn't let him. For the fourth point, he didn't serve-and-volley. He tried an ace . . . which was called out. The audience groaned.

Donny composed himself, aware of his coach's stare, intense and telegraphing some counsel from the stands. For a moment he even thought he saw his mother and sister sitting in the last row, silhouetted against the white light. But that couldn't be. They had no curiosity about this part of his life, seeing it only as the means to their own ends: his mother, the money; his sister, the freedom from their mother's policing and from life as a spinster for God. He bounced the ball more than his regular number of bounces, six instead of three. As he threw the ball into the air, he was aware of Pimentel's body across the net with the concentric rings of a target over it. His second serve headed for Rafael Pimentel's body, kicking high. Pimentel, moving out of the ball's way, gave a grimace and hit the ball into the net. Donny Osmond noticed the grimace at the same time that he gave himself a fist pump, hearing the umpire: Game, Magulay; Magulay is up two games to one, second set.

The crowd breathed a sigh of relief. Had Donny Osmond finally come to play, and would he draw even, forcing a third set? They were fully prepared, electricity at the back of their legs, to give the players a standing ovation should a third and decisive set become a reality. Once more the spectators were heard to buzz, some even wringing their hands, not sure who to cheer for. The staff of the Two Seasons were yet to be convinced of Donny Osmond's worthiness and reserved their goodwill and thoughts for last year's runner-up, Rafael Pimentel. Besides, Donny Osmond and his coach were representatives from the other camp, the VIP Club, long since superseded by their very own, more luxe, more contemporary establishment.

Donny Osmond had noticed the grimace, and had, in the next two points on Pimentel's serve, been able to trace this pain to his opponent's bandaged knee, which seemed to give a little wobble when he served and again right after, as his body readied itself for the first stroke. So this was what he decided to do: again he sliced the ball low, forcing his opponent to have to bend. Each time he sent the ball lower and each time Pimentel bent his knees just as low, adjusting perfectly and without a grimace on his face. Eventually, Donny Osmond's low strokes began to go into the net. This way, Pimentel pulled even, 2–2.

Then 3–3. The audience made intolerably anxious. Fans waved energetically from the need to vent nervousness, not to be cooled. *Swish swish swish*: Donny Osmond thought he heard the propellers of a distant plane about to take off.

Enough little signs, such as Pimentel's grimace, which continued when he served, were spotted to make Donny Osmond feel encouraged. There is an opening, I only have to keep at it. Such a voice had never been heard in his brain before. He recognized the voice as Caracera's, and knew that it would forever play in a loop in his head from now on, in instances such as the one in which he currently found himself. This was a discovery to him: that there were things he had yet to learn in playing and that he was more than willing to be a pliant student, so long as the effectiveness of such an apprenticeship could be proven to him, success not too long forthcoming.

Now 4–4. Each player having his little moment, capped by ringing applause, of deceiving the other or of conjuring, from out of meager resources and forced into a split second decision, a passing shot that the opponent could only stare at hopelessly. Once, from the Siberia of an alley, Donny Osmond hit a down-the-line shot that even Pimentel, ever ready for any Olympian probability, did not see coming—in fact, did not see at all. He wondered where the ball had gone, and the next second was listening to the umpire say, Game, Magulay.

The next game was crucial. If Donny Osmond was successful, holding his serve, he would go up 5–4, only one game away from claiming the second set and one game away from leveling the match. What would he do? Caracera couldn't bear to look, having no faith in his player's mental fortitude. He lowered his gaze, taking in his tassled Ferragamo loafers. His footwear, he noticed, found perfect matches in those of his row. A lot of other patent-leather loafers, and also boating shoes, women's low heels, all perfectly polished. The few sneakers were neat and new, prominently insigniaed with overturned death scythes: Nikes.

In the all-important ninth game, Donny Osmond again hit weakly during rallies, and again he forced the same discombobulated returns from Pimentel. This way he got up 30–0.

Then he switched to his old playing style. Pimentel, because he'd practiced for them, was more able to handle the difficult shots and sent them back offensively. In the middle of the point, however, Donny hit a drop shot. What genius! The crowd had only to look at Pimentel's face to understand.

Getting to the drop shot, Pimentel had been required to speed up and then stop on a dime, and this proved too much for his highly vulnerable knee, already taxed by his forceful serves and by the low bends Donny had drawn. Not only was the pain apparent on his face but his earlier expression of steely concentration became an exploded crystal that revealed its component parts to be fear, futility and a glimpse of possible defeat.

In such pain, Pimentel managed only a weak return. In reply, Donny hit a lob—the first time he'd done so—which sailed over Pimentel's head and landed near the baseline. The crowd cheered.

All this time Caracera had been looking at his tapping feet, determined to avoid the spectacle of what he was sure would be his player succumbing to the pressure. He was nearly certain that Pimentel, good chess player that the boy was, would not let the opportunity of taking it to Donny escape him. Pimentel would put his foot in the door of Donny's game, kicking it open. Hearing the audience gasping at Pimentel's injurious move, Caracera had believed them to be commiserating with Donny Osmond for having hit a crucially long shot. And by the time Caracera looked up, hearing the umpire recite the score (40–0: Caracera's boy had won the point!), the boys were already getting ready to play the next point.

Donnie won it too: 5–4. Pimentel was hobbling, and he would serve.

Now Pimentel was approaching the umpire. Caracera felt an odd prickling sensation, as if his stomach were lined with fur.

The umpire spoke into the microphone: Time-out injury called by Mr. Pimentel. Fifteen minutes.

Pimentel's coach approached to consult with his player.

Donny Osmond returned to his seat but did not look up at his coach.

A sports trainer was sent for. He began to talk to Pimentel. In a minute he was taking off Pimentel's bandage, gingerly pressing the affected area. Each time Pimentel grimaced, nodded. Then the trainer began applying some salve to the knee. Pimentel was clearly in pain now, dropping his head backward and forcing all his features into the middle of his face.

Caracera couldn't hear but it was easy enough to guess what the coach was asking: Do you want to keep playing?

Pimentel kept nodding. Did Donny see this? A ball boy rushed to the coach with a bottle of Tylenol. Pimentel swallowed three pills, taking a swig from his bottle of water.

The trainer put a fresh bandage on. Pimentel stood up experimentally, shifting his weight from one leg to another. His expression was stoic. He closed his eyes, as if praying, and took a deep breath. After a few minutes, he was on his side of the court, serving. The audience hushed, tilting dangerously forward. And Pimentel rewarded them with a miracle: serving four aces in a row. Pimentel knew his best chance lay in keeping the points short and sweet. So now the set was tied 5–5.

In the next game, Donny Osmond, ever the opportunist, won his serve at love. He forced Pimentel to run on each point, and Pimentel, unable to do more than skip, simply conceded, his eyes yearning after the ball.

Would Pimentel, serving again, pull out another rabbit: another four straight aces? It turned out he didn't need to. Donny Osmond, knowing the momentousness of the game, and suddenly and prematurely visited by visions of glory—a third set in which the hobbled player allowed desperation to steer him—became alternately distracted and overeager, returning shots either into the net or long. Caracera hit his knee in disgust, knowing it was because he had looked up that his player had been jinxed.

Six games all, tie break, said the umpire.

The audience yelped. They stood on their feet. Clearly they were now cheering for Rafael Pimentel, the injured hero. They wanted him to win. They knew that he could not afford to be dragged into a third set. And more importantly, they knew Donny Osmond's game plan, which was outright villainous, and didn't appreciate it. They wanted Pimentel's sore knee to get enough time to heal for the next and final round. They wanted Pimentel to take the clinching match and the trophy, the money and the scholarship. They were applauding as much to channel energy his way as to announce the thrill of having come to a decision: now they were united in their desire for the same ending to this up-down-and-now-up-again story.

Caracera couldn't bear to watch, yet knew that desertion would be evident to his player. He was the lone symbol of goodwill in this suddenly treacherous crowd, the sea turned rough, bearing on the young boy with overwhelming, capsizing force.

Pimentel to serve the first point.

Donny knew his opponent would try for the ace and was ready—but which shot would it be, down the line or wide? Faking, he favored the wide serve, ready to cheat toward the center if needed. The shot came through without as much force as Pimentel's previous aces. The injured knee was clearly getting to the serve now. Donny saw the ball coming as if in slow motion. He yanked his backhand and made perfect contact with the ball, which zipped right at Pimentel's feet.

Somehow, with miraculous speed and agility, Pimentel forced his legs to retreat a few steps. Then he hit the ball with great force and in an angle away from Donny's side of the court. The ball flew past Donny. The audience cheered thunderously.

Donny, angered with himself, hit his racket on the court. Boos attended his behavior, construed immediately as spoiled.

Racket violation warning, Mr. Magulay, said the umpire.

Donny approached the umpire's chair. He was red in the face. Caracera could guess what his player was saying, spittle flying fast and furious from Donny's jutting, challenging mouth.

Profanity warning, Mr. Magulay, announced the umpire to the crowd.

The crowd booed.

Donny threw his racket to the ground, denting the frame.

More boos.

Racket violation, Mr. Magulay, said the umpire, who automatically gave a point to Donny's opponent. Mr. Pimentel leads the tie break two–zero.

Rafael Pimentel, to his credit, turned his back on the spectacle and went to a corner of the court.

There was a momentary delay while a new racket was procured from somewhere in the bowels of the club. A Two Seasons employee ran on court and handed Donny a new racket, pulling the plastic wrap from around the frame. Donny hit the strings once, tentatively, then again, harder against his palm, again, yet again, trying to get an idea of how tightly the racket was strung. He realized only now how stupid he'd been, not only forfeiting a point, but forcing himself to play with a racket not strung to the specifications of his game.

All the while Pimentel had been taking advantage of the rest, using the time to massage his knee. Now he walked slowly to the baseline.

Donny served, and sure enough, with the new racket, the ball missed the service box.

Second serve, said the umpire.

He double-faulted.

Three–zero, Pimentel, said the umpire.

Tears were stinging Donny's eyes. Though they usefully blurred out the crowd, whose malign concentration he could feel like a sticky layer of gasoline in the air, he could hardly see his opponent on the other end of the court. He returned serve and the ball did not even go past the net.

Four–zero, Pimentel.

Donny made a gesture for his opponent to wait. He moved to pick up his ruined racket. Caracera, looking up to see what the silence betokened, saw and nearly broke into tears. Too bad, he thought, the boy had to learn the hard way the consequences of his arrogance. Donny's arrogance would not move him as easily in the world as he thought it would. He needed other talents in reserve. The crowd waited for him to return to the court, distrustful now of his every move, even seething.

The umpire, seeing the conked racket in Donny's hand, did not argue.

Pimentel served, Donny returned, but so furiously as to turn tennis into baseball: he scored a home run and the ball flew above the spectators' heads and out into the green yonder of the neighboring estate, forever lost.

The umpire did not want to risk another argument, though he felt that Donny had intentionally hit the ball long. All he said was: Five–zero, Pimentel.

The goal in Donny's mind shrank to a pinprick of light: it was no longer that he wanted to win, in fact he *didn't* want to win, he didn't have what it would take, he admitted it. Never mind that he'd come this far, and never mind that his mother and sister would forever be soldered like embarrassing giveaway chimes to his side. Never mind too—though this was the hardest to ignore—that the man Roger Caracera, his coach and sponsor, who, by being willing to embarrass himself and cheer like a drunk for Donny, had had the power to lift his heart, would, by his disapproval, have the power to move him negatively, lastingly. Now all he wanted—if it could be managed, *please please please*—was not to be defeated at zero. Just a point, maybe two, and then he would gladly, or rather passively, retire. He would assent to the gods' favoring of Rafael Pimentel. They had first tested his worthiness by causing his knee to give out and seeing how he'd managed to pull himself together, all the time remaining calm and concentrated, had pushed him to where he stood, underneath the portal of light and blessings which they were widening by the minute. Against that you could not argue, could not fight. Divine power consolidating with tenacity was the foe facing Donny across the net. With only precocious talent to answer for him, Donnie might as well have a frying pan in his hand with which to hit the ball.

But he was a boy who, once a goal had been identified, was accustomed to bringing this goal into the harbor of action, of tracing an arc from abstract thought to material completion. And he did, winning the next point, following which, as was the custom in a tie break after six points had been played, the players changed ends. Donny Osmond did not let the walk to the other end of the court weaken his purpose. He won the next point. That both points had been played with an irregular racket frame did not escape notice, and the audience gave him warm, if guarded, applause.

Five–two, Pimentel.

Caracera looked up.

Five–three, Pimentel. It was Pimentel's turn to get angry at himself, but unlike Donny, the anger rose to the surface of his face, where it evaporated.

Pimentel served and volleyed. Caracera didn't know why this should catch Donny by surprise, but it did. The boy caught the ball too late, hitting it with the dented frame. Miraculously, the ball sailed into the other end, before being slapped away by Pimentel.

Six–three Pimentel.

On Donny's serve came the first match point for Pimentel. But Donny dispatched Pimentel's return with steely resolve, hitting behind his opponent, who was heading to the other side of the court.

Six–four, Pimentel.

Caracera couldn't look. Would his player draw even?

The next serve was yet another match point. Donny managed an ace. Applause, led by Caracera, who stood up and hooted unabashedly.

There he was again. Donny couldn't look. He felt like clutching his chest but stared at his feet instead, then pretended to find something compelling in the strings of his twisted racket.

Six–five, Pimentel.

Now the crowd was twisted in knots. They were afraid for Pimentel, who was serving. Pimentel took his time. His third, and for now, final, match point. He bounced the ball a routine four times. Then stepped back, not feeling quite ready. He gestured with his hand to apologize to his opponent. And then, wouldn't you know, Pimentel did a devious thing. There was the devil in him after all, not just in the boy across from him. Donny had taken advantage of his injury, and now Pimentel would get payback. Having given his opponent a signal to wait, Pimentel rushed his serve. The serve hit the box before Donny was ready, and suddenly the boy found himself flailing after the ball, trying to make contact. He succeeded but did not hit it with the needed strength. The ball bounced to Pimentel's end, and Pimentel muscled it away for a winner, *the* winner.

A lone, loud boo was heard amid the cheering.

Then the booer rushed on court, heading for the umpire, who was in the midst of announcing to the partisan gathering, Game, set, and match: Mr. Raf— Caracera tapped at the umpire's feet. The man looked down, irritated. Caracera's player, more than willing to concede defeat, stood still, transfixed to his losing spot, unable to look at his opponent, who at first had been moving to the net to receive his congratulatory handshake but was now aiming to hear what the complaining was all about—as if he didn't know.

Pimentel's coach, not wanting to be left behind, got in on the act. He approached Caracera and the umpire, just at the moment when the umpire was denying Caracera's request for a replay of the last point. Though the umpire knew the underhandedness of Pimentel's tactic, by this point his sympathy for Donny Osmond had more than run dry. Besides, who was Roger Caracera kidding? He had only to look at his player's destroyed racket to know that there was no way his player could triumph, maybe a point here, a point there, but ultimately even with Pimentel's bum knee the match was Pimentel's to decide. No, Mr. Caracera, the umpire said with finality, before returning to the microphone: Game, set and match, Mr. Rafael Pimentel. Quickly, he stepped down from his chair.

Donny Osmond moved to his seat. He didn't shake the hand being offered to him. Pimentel shrugged and hobbled to where his coach awaited. The boy seemed to delight in exaggerating each tentative step, and for a moment Donny wondered if the injury time out had not been some ruse intended to tamper with Donny's momentum, buying Pimentel more time to strategize. He considered the possibility that he had just been brain-fucked.

Boos were begun because of Donny's unsportsmanlike conduct in not taking the hand of his opponent. Derisive whistles on top of that. And then a few people stomped their feet. Others were encouraged to take up the racket, aiming to drive Caracera and Magulay off the court in disgrace. But Caracera lingered at the umpire's side, peppering his accusations with swearing. You'll hear about this, Caracera threatened, putting his face right next to the umpire's. This is corruption! Have you been bought by their side? Who paid you? Do you hear me?

The umpire kept mum, refusing to look at his accuser. Finally, he snuck into the corridor that would take him to a room where he'd kept his belongings. A Two Seasons employee flanked one side and with an outstretched arm kept Caracera from entering.

Meanwhile, Donny Osmond, whose slow boil found no antidote in the sight of Rafael Pimentel surrounded by a horde of eager children clamoring for autographs, entertained the idea of doing something to justify the catcalls that were being prolonged by a few diehard Pimentel fans. They stood in the stands trying to stare him down.

Just one more, he said to himself. Just one more boo and then— He received it.

Caracera was rehearsing words of adequate sympathy which he truly didn't feel. He believed at bottom that, aside from the last, corrupt point, his player had defeated himself. First, he saw a scribble of activity in his peripheral vision, like a conflagration casting off orangeish sparks. And then he heard the gasps of some fans. Only then did he realize that the chair he was heading toward had been vacated, and that the person who had been sitting there the last time he'd checked was at the side of the court, his white shirt improbably orangeish with—was that blood? Donny was tangling with Rafael Pimentel at the same time that Pimentel's coach was brusquely but ineffectively trying to tear him loose. The fans were gathered, spaced at intervals like numerals on a clock face, grouped around the ongoing fight. He dashed to intervene, all his consolatory offerings disappearing behind his running figure like ribbons torn to shreds.

The next day, though there had been no photographer present to capture the historic moment, much ink was devoted to Donny Osmond Magulay's behavior in the papers, chief among them the *Metro Manila Register*, which had this to report: "A lifetime ban on entering the Mercedes Championships, as well as entering the premises of the super chichi Two Seasons Club in Greenbelt, was imposed on the player Donny Osmond Magulay, who yesterday, with his unrefined, peasantlike actions, proved that he knows absolutely nothing about 'Lollipops and Roses' (wink-wink)." Also, the semifinalist check of fifty thousand pesos was withheld from him.

Caracera too was banned from ever setting foot at the Two Seasons, a sentence the club had proclaimed very light considering how he'd profanely attacked a respected tournament official and, by such a bad example, inspired his protégé to a fit of violent jealousy, engaging the innocent winner, Rafael Pimentel, as well as his coach, in a skirmish. It was lucky, the club PR official said to the papers, that both the umpire and Mr. Pimentel's father, for the sake of putting an end to the affair immediately, had declined to press charges.

Caracera, for his part, refused to be goaded into a back-and-forth via the press, and simply smiled like a practiced politician from his outdoors perch at the VIP Club, where Donny Osmond continued to work, defiantly employed as a rebuttal to the Two Seasons. Sometimes the boy even felt he was being pointed out to curious members and visitors as a star attraction, and considered whether or not he could get away with asking for a salary hike. Certainly the number of members who asked specifically for him to practice with had increased, and he found himself with less time for solitary reflection, much less to spend with his friend Raul Zamora, who took Donny's scarceness for an inevitable forking in their relationship: the star's steep ascension needed the marveling, the testifying of an earthbound witness.

Caracera and Donny didn't talk all that much anymore. The man came to drink, to be alone, before his driver fetched and ferried him back home. From five days a week, his visits were reduced to three, then two. Donny regretted his behavior at that final, losing match and knew that the blame lay entirely with him. He was grateful that there was not enough time in his life to replay the events of that day in his head, and when he went home he was grateful that his busy work schedule drew from him nothing but a dead, dreamless sleep. But the guilt of loss, of disappointing both Roger Caracera and himself and, though not as important, of disappointing his friend Raul Zamora, who had been living vicariously through Donny, lingered.

The sun's heat that day was forever welded to God's trumping of his plans. God knew the designs of desertion Donny had drawn up for his poor, undeserving mother and his sister, and had rightly dashed them. But that wasn't what he felt most guilty about. No, what shamed him most was a scene that had happened right after the match, in Roger Caracera's car, being driven home.

He had cried, his chest shaken by successive and ever more powerful waves of feeling. All the high drama of that day, welling up, had had no place to go. He had confessed all the hobbling, humbling particulars of his life: his pathetic mother, who wore her "widowed" status as a Christian mark of approval; his slutty sister, who he was sure was no longer a virgin, making a mockery of his mother's communion with God; and himself, the most shameful member of the trinity, who had intended, by winning the Two Seasons Championship, to abandon them both to life's tricks. He had said that at least by losing he would have no money with which to accomplish his awful plan. He would be forever stuck to them, he'd said, looking at Caracera. Even when tearful, he was not averse to slipping in the emotional blackmail that was part and parcel of how he dealt with the world.

But Caracera had appeared unmoved. Not only that, a look of repulsion had flitted over his face, turning that upward-turned nose higher, the top lip a squiggle to reveal shiny, unshaken, perfectly composed teeth, top row clasped to bottom, unopened, releasing no sympathy. At that moment, Donny had known that the man could not be gay. No gay man, in his opinion, would be so unfeeling, so immune to blackmail seeing the boy's lashes wet and stuck to each other, his eyes red and his nose sticky with mucus. (He knew how he looked because he caught himself in the reflection on the car windows, and also in the rearview mirror, checking to see what the driver Gochengco could make out.)

Roger Caracera was a bastard for whom detachment was the mode of choice. Roger Caracera had the characteristics of an abandoner, and was therefore straight, just like Donny's first and most lasting apotheosis of straightness: his father, who had left his mother, his sister and himself.

Still, it was his fault. He had been cool, by such means attracting Roger Caracera, and having lost his cool, it would make sense that he should lose Caracera's support.

But this conclusion was proven, a week later, to be premature.

Goaded finally into responding to the expert taunting of the press, Roger Caracera (as an "anonymous sponsor moved by the young boy's plight") announced that he would match the tournament winnings for the ousted Donny Osmond, who had been deprived of his rightful chance to compete for the championship. Like Rafael Pimentel, who won the championship, Donny would receive four hundred thousand pesos with which to live and travel, as well as a scholarship to the Nick Bollettieri Tennis Academy in Bradenton, Florida. There he would once and for all prove to his schoolmate, Rafael Pimentel, that he, Donny Osmond, was the superior player.

There was eventually a ceremony in which an actor from one of the nightly soaps presented to Donny Osmond the check, as well as a plane ticket (good for travel to Sarasota, Florida, any day within the next nine months) and a certified letter of enrollment to the academy.

Caracera knew full well that his gift would allow Donny to make good on his original scheme of abandonment, leaving his mother and sister without a trace, leaving them wedded to one another in enmity: the mother having to release the daughter from the grip of her promise to God so that the daughter could make a living for them, as most likely, what? A prostitute? A maid? A wife? Not a single scenario was encouraging.

So be it, thought Caracera. He himself had abandoned his family, and hadn't everyone in the end learned to adjust to his absence, some, like his Aunt Irene, even thriving because of it?

Around this time the young boy Pitik Sindit left the American Feingold to return to the man he couldn't seem to shake free of. Caracera received him with a heavy heart.

CHAPTER 10

HEY WERE DRIVEN to the cemetery by Gochengco. The place was in a desolate section of Malate. They cruised past once-festive restaurants and beer gardens which used to be at the center of the tourist trade. The nights were formerly emblazoned with multicolored bulbs like Christmas all year round and were raucous with the sounds of drunken Americans and Japanese and Germans vying for the prettiest of the "hostesses"—bar girls with provincial accents and city-hardened malice. They passed the squatters, who strung their wash out in full view of the streets, and whose children looked up from roughhousing or torturing the neighborhood dogs to regard the family car with bobble-headed incomprehension. They passed gated construction sites beyond which rose tall piles of rusted junk and smoke from hidden vents.

The cemetery had no name, no caretaker on the premises, no lock on the rusted iron gate. They pushed it open and walked toward a tightly packed middle section. The lot was half the size of a city block and seemed, despite its bad location, to be somehow exclusive. The members interred were in a twilit world that straddled classes—the grave markers ranging from wood to marble; allegiances—a few pagan inscriptions ("Rock 'n Roll Forever") to balance out the infinite homages to "Our Lord and Savior"; and ages.

Near the periphery of the pushed-together graves was a marker for Eustacio Caracera, a slab not of marble, like for his elder brother at Kalayaan, but of granite. The dates: 1932 to 1995.

Sixty-three. A young man. Had the family pushed beyond electroshock therapy in search of a cure, in effect killing him?

Caracera indicated a tiny corridor between Eustacio Caracera's grave and the next marker, for a man or woman whose name he didn't recognize: Soxy Sandoval. A thirty-four-year-old. One more tragically premature casualty of a family wanting to keep up the high-maintenance fiction of their cleanliness, their respectability?

That, he said to Pitik, is where my mother's supposed to be buried.

Pitik nodded.

My mother's in Mandaluyong.

Pitik didn't know where to look.

Caracera gave the boy some time to absorb the sight of the grave marker and to grasp its surrounding sadness before finally asking, You still don't remember him?

I know what you are doing, accused Pitik.

Caracera didn't reply, mentioning instead that he was thinking to ask the family lawyers to secure a space in this very cemetery for himself. He didn't say that it had started out as a perverse joke from Miguel Santos—"one outcast to join two others"—it only mattered that in thinking about it, he had come to realize its circular, poetic aspect. After all, his father had never let on that he'd wanted to be buried in the Philippines, and yet to the Philippines he'd returned—though perhaps not exactly at rest, if the caretakers were to be believed.

Whether or not he would be buried in the Philippines, a place in which he still felt, at best, an interloper, he ultimately wasn't sure—but at least now, as it had not been before, the possibility had been entered, a seed, a scratch.

During their entire visit, no one had shown up. The braver of the squatter kids, thrilled by the appearance of the silver family Mercedes, had followed as far as the previous block. Once they'd guessed the vehicle's purpose, however, they'd immediately dispersed.

This was the cemetery where the dead were known to rise at midnight and wander the premises, Gochengco told them.

Let's going now, said the boy.

After a silence, Caracera asked, How about me? Do you think I'll haunt the area too?

Don't joking about that! said the boy.

The driver Gochengco, not getting the joke, sought to pacify Caracera by explaining, They say it is depending, sir, on if you are making peace or making war before you are dying.

Making peace or making war, said Caracera.

Pitik Sindit didn't know if the man was taken by the driver's phrasing or if he was making fun of his English. At any rate, the driver took it for the latter and reddened.

Caracera continued to fix his eyes on the boy, who withstood the silent reproach for what seemed an eternity before he screamed, I don't remember him! I don't want to remember him!

Night came and so did the rains, which let loose with such fury that the streets began to flood in less than an hour, but still Gochengco pulled up outside the Makati high-rise, to take Caracera and the boy carousing.

Manila's nighttime signs had the glow of ocean coral, mysteriously beckoning. So many headlights, like tireless schools swimming past his eyes. Churning across the brackish deluge that poured out of the gutters to overflow onto the sidewalks, wheels made twin streaks of foam like the wake of boats. There were street people who stared dumbly back at Caracera, their eyes sparking from the glare of the nighttime lights and looking for all the world—to continue the marine analogy that came effortlessly to Caracera's mind, which included an image of him as a sailor going through a nighttime river, banks of virgin forests on both sides—like vulnerable fish parked between the flimsy recesses of their thatched-together dwellings, waiting out the rains until they could swim away to their usual hubbub.

The Blue Jay Club was filled to the gills with foreigners, all without exception Fat-Assed Fucks. The rains had apparently been no deterrent. A strange smell hung over the air inside. Puffs of sickly sweet smoke, intended to camouflage some stink. Hotted-up men were clustered around the edge of the stage. Dancers wearing bikinis and on whose flanks were pasted, as if they were beauty contestants, little prize ribbons with numbers on them, gyrated to the whomp-whomp of the dull music. The air smelled of smoke, spilled beer, cigarettes, women's hairspray and something that he couldn't identify and which came closest in his mind to the floral putrefaction of his father's funeral procession. Gochengco identified the smell as Lysol. Of course.

They were seated by a hostess who encouraged Caracera to touch her wherever he wanted, at one point gyrating her ass on his lap as he tried his best to smile and appear game. She was wearing a sequined top and a short black Lycra skirt with dangerously high slits up both sides. There were men all around them who didn't notice. All energy and attention were directed to the group of—Caracera counted—sixteen women on stage. Rotating balls of colored lights tried to render them seductively inhuman, all waxen, smooth, firm flesh, their faces the faces of dolls or mannequins. They were programmed only to smile and recite lines in broken English whose purpose was to maximize the sex appeal of their backwardness, squeezing the noose of covetousness even tighter around the men's necks.

Gochengco, the young driver, had even more of a tourist's manner than Caracera. He looked around, his mouth open and eyes flitting like insects unsure where to land, everything vested with the potential to snap him up. A rictus split open the lower part of his face, and it became different things depending on where the light was coming from and what color the light was. Grin/grimace. Grin/grimace. Pleasure and pain took turns on his face, and the sight seemed to confirm the tale he'd offered Caracera about being alternately flagellated, like most everyone in this country, by religion and by his body's needs. Still, with the aquarium atmosphere, as much shadowed as lit, it was hard to tell what the driver was thinking. Caracera caught a glimpse of a stoned stranger in one of the several walls made up of mirrored strips, and the man looked back at Caracera with a piggish stupefaction that was so familiar, so distinctly kin, that Caracera knew at once that the man must be American. And yet, a fraction of a second later, with the lights putting a veil over one part of the man's face, the man was Filipino. American/Filipino. Foreigner/native. Foe/foe. And then Gochengco was talking to the man, whispering something into the man's ear. Except Gochengco was talking to Caracera. And Caracera realized that he had been looking at a slivered version of himself all along. The smell in the air turned sharp and metallic, a scent of disgust.

Yes, Caracera replied. I want to be here. I want to stay.

Pitik was seething. Sure, the man no longer insisted that Pitik be at school, but that did not stop him from arranging tutorials in how the world worked. In this instance, visiting the Blue Jay Club, a den of disgusting heterosexuality, the lesson was in Cary Grant's incorrigible straightness, just as at the no-name cemetery the object was for the boy to confront his own heartlessness in not being able to accept the love that had made possible his three-million-peso inheritance. Caracera would have the boy believe that the source of that money was trying to communicate with him from beyond the grave.

He would show Cary Grant. He would be game, unflinching. Cary Grant would never be allowed to see and, seeing, rejoice in his disgust at the untalented, fattish bikini-clad dancers. The other lesson he was supposed to absorb from this laughable field trip was the ludicrousness of his own former profession—as if he, having alienated himself from Madame Sonia, could ever go back. The proprietress had probably found a new dancer by now. Had Pitik been made to relinquish his stage name, someone else freshly crowned Blueboy, as if there were no original before him?

Caracera and the driver drank their beers. For the boy there was iced Pepsi in a glass. Afterward, Caracera ordered another round for them. There was a two-drink minimum, said a sign. Their waitress, a sad-looking woman wearing a slutty costume of bikini top and denim mini, echoed the sign. Caracera assured her that they would more than comply.

The drinks soon allowed him to put great energy into his pretense at appreciation. Looking at the women, he licked his lips. The hostess, seeing, clapped her hands, although ostensibly she was doing this in accompaniment to the music and to the bold gyrations of one of the dancers, who had broken rank and taken center stage, putting herself ahead of the others. Caracera saw that the men around the stage were pointing to certain women and whispering into the ears of an ugly woman who, looked at closely, turned into a drag queen. The drag queen would then yank the corresponding girl to meet her chooser, then the two would disappear, as pairs before them previously had, through streamer curtains, into the darkness of—it wasn't hard to imagine—an awaiting cubicle or room.

Hours later, drunk out of his skull, Caracera was shepherded by the young boy and the driver into the car and back home.

The man had wanted to appear disgusting to the boy, to puncture the veil of romance layered over him. The boy, looking at the drunken, babbling, skinny and at the same time potbellied man, was indeed repulsed, seeing no difference between this American and the other whom he'd just abandoned. Like Feingold, Caracera behaved with a sense of limitless entitlement, whose flip side was this sweaty, knocked-unconscious, fool-making satiation.

Yes, disgusted he was—but out of love? Cary Grant would not have it so easy.

This romance was abetted, deepened, unknowingly, by Cielito Caracera. A few days later, she offered her departing cousin Roger a "gift." From among the boxes Caracera had had removed from his New York apartment, intending either the Makati high-rise or the Caracera residence to be their final dumping ground, Cielito had unearthed a play called *In the Shadows of Giants*. She had read through the manuscript with mounting excitement and had convinced a theater group to take it on.

There were two things to recommend it. First it was considered "modern." In it, people behaved acrimoniously toward one another, and this was considered not only "cool," but would provide ample opportunities for the group's actors to showcase histrionic talents. And second, it was in English. The fact that it had been written in that language gave it, in this country, an immediate gloss of being above the ordinary, special, and so the choice was sealed.

Cielito Caracera did not tell her cousin Roger anything. He was made to appear under false pretenses at the theater. This had been converted from the assembly hall of the school the girl attended—Immaculate Heart in San Lorenzo.

Seeing the name of the play and beneath it his name, Roger Caracera knew that it was too late to do anything but follow the usher to the seat assigned him, right dead center. He smiled sheepishly the whole way. Without his frosted glasses, he felt he had to improvise another defense: a shield of even white teeth to prevent his tongue from clucking out its usual toxic observations. *Look at those curtains!* Hung vertically on either side of the stage so that they cascaded loose at the bottom were crepe-paper streamers, yellow and purple and green—the chief clue to the age of the perpetrators, which simultaneously alarmed and touched Caracera. Or perhaps they had been left over from some school assembly and which the theater group had been too busy to remove or were prevented from removing by the school authorities.

What a brave man Roger Caracera was! This was no self-assessment, but rather the shared thought lancing the minds of the gathering, as they looked on surreptitiously, pretending to take in something else in the same line of sight that conveniently included the American. In this instance, Caracera's usual suspicions were justified: he was the central, jutting facet of *this* scene.

Every single uncle and their wives were there, as well as a smattering of cousins. Manila's avid theatergoers were decked out in glittery muumuulike costumes for the women and natty suit-and-tie ensembles or *barong Tagalogs* for the men; plus the khaki- and cotton shirt–clad critics. No one was aware that Roger Caracera had been kept in the dark about his own play.

What, then, did Roger Caracera's "bravery" amount to?

Seated next to him was Peter Sindit, and next to the boy, his mother. Her heavily lined forehead looked even more furrowed as she realized that she was among the evening's star attractions. Only weeks ago, she had been squatting over the side of the wooden planks next to her Bambang home, dumping feces into the waters below, thinking no more of her actions than she had for the last three, four decades of her life. Now she felt newly shamed, surrounded by people who, if they knew, would turn their faces away—instead of doing as they did now, burning holes into where they sat, next to Roger Caracera. He was the deserved star of the evening, being the "intellectual" author of tonight's performance. She knew that these unfriendly gazes were being encouraged by her son, who played to the crowd's interest by leaning in to whisper unnecessary comments ("It's so hot," etc.) into Caracera's ear. He knew full well that the glinting-eyed audience would take these for sweet nothings. In case they didn't get the message, he let his fingers brush against the man's shirt, pretending to clear lint, or against his pants, reassuring the man that tonight would more than go well for him.

In the Shadows of Giants, a tragic drama. About a father who crushes the lives of his three offspring by his dictatorial rules and pronouncements. Until the youngest—a son—in a long, enraged monologue near the end, makes him understand that his tyranny is to come to an end.

This son revokes his rights to the family money and therefore to any kind of life that his father had mapped out for him: success in any of the family-sanctioned businesses such as law or medicine. He would not become a game piece in his father's campaign to front the family name with a formidable public image.

Eugene Caracera, Cielito's older brother and another of the family beauties, played the part of the youngest son with earnest conviction, which only helped underline, to Caracera, the contrivance of the tinny dialogue—at once overwrought and underfleshed. The father was being set up to be knocked down, and the music of the family's frequent onstage fights was nothing more than amateurish point-counterpoint, like a child banging a two-tone song on the piano: one note high, the other low; one pronouncement wrong (and arrogantly so: the father), and the other moral and right. A bad, predictable tennis match.

YOUNGEST SON: You will never be able to understand what living your life in the highest key is like—and not the key to which you have selfishly and slavishly devoted yourself to all these wasted years, Dad! Never!

FATHER: And what key is that—irresponsibility? The refusal to grow up?

YOUNGEST SON: I *am* grown up! More than you'll ever be! More than you realize. Or maybe you refuse to realize it. I know you look at me and you're disappointed. I'm disappointed too. Or at least I was. That I couldn't be more like you. That I would always fall short of where you wanted me to be. Until I realized just where it was you wanted me to be. You wanted me to be you. To make the same sacrifice of my happiness, my youth, to follow you like you yourself followed your father. In pursuit of what? Money. And money to build what? A wall, a fortress to keep the prying, criticizing eyes of the neighbors from looking in. Fear, Dad. That's what you've spent your life being a slave to. What would the family say of me? What would the neighborhood say of the family? You know what? They can say all they want to. They will never have a hold on my life the way they had on you and on this family—this cursed family! This family that is like indolence and fear laid on top of a cushion of money! I will not have any part of your money! I will be free!

FATHER: Free to be what? A bum?

YOUNGEST SON: I will be an artist! A writer! And do you know what I'll need first and foremost to be able to do my job well?

(Besides talent, mused Caracera, which he, confronted by his hand-iwork, knew himself definitively, even invigoratingly, to lack.)

YOUNGEST SON: I'll need the truth. I'll need to start cultivating a habit of it, the complete opposite of what this family has been doing for the last hundreds of years! And I'll write—I will, Dad, I'll write everything that you won't want me to. Everything that you're ashamed about and don't want the rest of the world to find out—I'll write about your hatred of your wife, my mother, because like me she refused to be cleaned up and presented to the world as a cooperative prop. I'll write about your hollow Catholicism—attending church and fucking women outside the bonds of holy matrimony. I'll call it that—"holy matrimony," the way you do, and then undermine the name by showing how flippantly you disregarded it yourself! I'll write about the family money. Ill-gotten gains! I'll call it that too. I'll tell about the abuse of the factory workers which was a great cost-cutting measure to ensure a lower overhead and thus greater profits—greater, yes, at the cost of the family soul! I'll write and I'll write and I won't stop until you're dead or I'm dead, until one of us is dead and the other will wish he were there too! I'm free! I'll be free! That's the key that I'll be living in. I'll be here [gestures with hand at shoulder level] and you'll be down here [gestures lower] and I'll have surpassed you but

not in the way you've envisioned or hoped for, not in the way that en-
sures the family business grows when I inherit it—no, not like that.
I'll have surpassed you as a human being and you can't stand it. You
can't stand the very idea of it. So go ahead. Tell me what I already
know—the family money is not mine. I know it's not because I didn't
put my signature on the line that requires me to be complicit in the
ruin of your own life and the potential ruin of mine. I'm your son,
Dad, but I'm not your son. I'm your enemy. Because people like you
need to be stopped or else the whole world goes along with them,
down the fucking drain. Down to hell. You've ruined the lives of two
of your children. You think their success is a signal of their happiness?
They're afraid. Just like you. Afraid of the poverty that might be the
price to be paid for disagreeing with you. You, with your narrow definition of usefulness in this world. They're useful, yes. They're useful
to you. So you can show that your old age has come to fruition.
They're useful as appendages, in other words. They've never had a
moment's thought to themselves, always told instead what to think,
how to behave. They hate me too. The way you do. The way you've
instructed them, without having to say anything. And they'll be rich.
The way you're rich. And my—my repudiation— Isn't it ironic, Dad,
that these expensive words were bought by the education you've provided me but which you never believed would lead to the place where
I am now? My repudiation, Dad, will guarantee that I'm poor but next
to you, next to my brother and sister, my poverty will be—it will be
mine, it will have my name, and, thinking of you, thinking of my sister and brother, I'll polish it every day, as the trophy that it is, and I'll
make sure it shines and shines and shines and outlives you all and
makes a mockery of all that you stand for and all that your money
builds in this lifetime to be knocked down by what I myself will leave
behind—even if, in the end, what I leave behind, is nothing but sheer,
abundant, vibrant, everlasting hate!

For a moment, Caracera had a feeling that Jesus Caracera would be
moved to appear. Finally. But nothing happened.
 The utter awfulness of the evening was apparent to nobody but
him. Looking around, he saw the contradicting, riveted witness, and, at
the end, heard their triumphant, stinging applause.

Intending one kind of rejuvenation for her cousin, Cielito Caracera had given him another. The "gift" which Cielito Caracera had given her cousin Roger was the unwitting gift of a razed horizon line: in his future, decisively, was no more writing. Or, more accurately, no more secret harboring of the hope that his youthful writing could be resuscitated. Once and for all, *In the Shadows of Giants* as proof and warning, the writer Roger Caracera was to be a rightly posthumous figure. Wasn't that why it had been important for him to keep his job at Columbia? Because he'd moved from hero to teacher, from the actor to the observer, who looked for proxies for his correctly deferred ambitions? He'd found his true talents after all. Perhaps happiness only consisted of recognizing that the achievement had come sideways and not, as he'd been trained to expect, from the front; that the writering had not yielded and so he'd stumbled onto a lower plane, a lesser plane as an instructor, and had lived his life adjudging from that sequence of compromise, and so had missed out on the realization that he was a man *in* place, not out, for the first time in his life.

Disregarding the scandalous fact of his very public pederasty, the crowd whistled and applauded, encouraging him to take a bow.

The "gift" of Cielito Caracera was to make Caracera recognize that sitting beside him was the most concrete and gratifying realization of any "writering" talent he could ever hope to have: the disadvantaged boy Peter Sindit lifted out of a tragic plot and settled into a romance creatively engineered "by" Roger Caracera.

My talent, he thought, is not for tragedy, after all. Something more along the lines of light comedy. He looked at the boy, who was caught in the net of the evening's distorting crush, as, apparently, was his mother. No, he corrected himself, more like dark comedy. Farce. For the boy was a crimp on the simple plot he'd concocted: first allocation, then location. Deciding to give back his uncle's money, then finding the boy.

Now the boy had taken over as the force behind their relationship, effecting his own kind of rosy-toned, vigorously misguided romance, which he wanted to make an odyssey: not-quite-begun and far-from-ended.

The critics chimed in with approving notices for *In the Shadows of*

Giants in the next few days, concurring with the opening-night crowd's assessment. "Powerful" was a frequent adjective.

But proud as the family was made by this reception, they had come to an unhappy decision about what was to be done with Roger Caracera masquerading as the reincarnation of Eustacio Caracera. Or, more precisely, they had come to a decision about the boy Pitik Sindit. They sent the driver Ernesto to warn Caracera. This was what, in the end, Irene Caracera's hard work and policing amounted to: violence, if necessary.

Your life is in danger, ser, said Ernesto, whom Caracera took seriously. He asked the driver to send a reply to the family: The boy must not be harmed. And more importantly, the boy would no longer be part of Roger Caracera's life. Apologies for Caracera's unthinking behavior were sent back. Tell them, said Caracera, that now that I'm leaving there will be no more of the boy in their lives. Caracera realized the mistake he made in trying to be generous with the boy, to the point of treating him as an equal.

The man Feingold came to the Makati high-rise pleading for the boy, his "true love," back. He appeared in the guise of a courtier, his eyes wet with incipient tears, and his lips always slightly parted, sighing in advance over the failure of his mission. In his hands were gifts Caracera had unavoidably come to regard as heartfelt: valentine chocolates in a gold foil, flowers, gossip magazines with the superstar Nora Aunor on the covers: sly temptations for Pitik Sindit. He came to see Caracera and the boy three times, and each time Caracera was treated to the same professions: His life in Altadena, California, had been abandoned as any man would abandon a desert. His family did not know that he was gay. His presence at the dairy firm had been a token gesture of respect for his father, whose death Feingold had been awaiting before he could finally pursue his dream and flee for more tolerant locales, such as Thailand and the Philippines. His secret had been well kept, at the cost, he would even say, of his entire youth, and now for the sacrifice of his relinquished good looks, he would have the reward of a happy late middle age, capped by a loving, lasting relationship with Blueboy. He took out a few photographs of himself from his wallet: a graduating senior in college; a skinny, furtive-eyed, suit-wearing twenty-something on a first date with a woman; and posed next to his father, the unremarkable-looking exactor of such filial sacrifice.

Caracera's initial moral outrage at Feingold's "tendencies," at Feingold's exploitation not only of a boy, but of a Third World boy—so prone to mistake being taken advantage of for protection, or perhaps indifferent to the difference—was being considerably relaxed. Feingold's emotionalism, his easy tears and willingness to humiliate himself by naked pleading, by his whiny rendition of the same song in front of Blueboy—Please please don't I love you don't you know that please please—could be seen, and without much stretching of the truth, as a badge of shaming love.

Feingold was sent back empty-handed each time. And though Caracera thought the boy would soften eventually, the opposite was true: the boy became more visibly unmoved. I am not going back to him, he said to Caracera.

Feingold was prepared to make a sacrifice of his one good feature as a testament to his heartache. He plastered his beautiful hair limp and flat against his skull. Begging for Pitik, he had shown qualities of eager debasement that seemed as good a hallmark of love as any. His pederasty was being reformed into something more forgivable, a saturnine avuncularity. He had moved from the shadowy arena of sex and into the spotlight, reducing and clarifying, of love. True love, as he'd vouchsafed.

Still, Pitik would not listen to his own mother, whom Caracera had encouraged to speak about Feingold's worthiness as guardian, as lover.

How could a man who would rhapsodize about the Philippines at the drop of a hat be made to forsake it and go back to a place he had frequently and unequivocally termed a "desert"? No, Feingold would never bring him to live in the States, it was an outright lie his mother might fall for, but not Pitik.

But, said Caracera, he himself would not bring the boy with him to the States.

Why would Caracera help the boy Donny Osmond and not Pitik?

Donny Osmond, replied Caracera, was not going to be abroad permanently. And besides— Here he bit down on his words, stopping.

Besides what?

Caracera shook his head.

Besides what? What did Donny Osmond have that Pitik didn't, making him worthy of America?

Talent. Finally the man revealed all at once his faces: snob, arbiter, immigration official; being very much a Caracera.

No, he refused to let Caracera go.

But today, claimed Caracera, was the very day of his departure.

No!

The man brought his bags into Apartment 3B. They were supposed to be proof. Pitik scratched at the luggage, intending to open them to reveal the ruse. They were locked. His mother put both hands to her ears, knowing his cries would be heard by their neighbors.

How, Pitik wondered, had this day descended on his head? How confident he'd been that the man could be softened.

Don't! Don't go please! He was screaming. Don't don't don't. Crying now too. A wild animal. His mother's arms were slapped back by his frenzied gesticulations. He would not be satisfied until he made a successful barricade between the man and the front door of their apartment.

No no no!

The mother's arms went to her stomach. She too was given to an animal *err*ring and *arrr*ing, and tears flowed from her eyes to see her boy so committed to making a fool of himself. Wasn't it only yesterday, or so it seemed, that they were sharing in the refracted glow of Caracera's victorious playwriting?

There was no doubt that the neighbors were exercising judicious restraint—in itself a kind of comment, scornful.

Her strongest hope was that the words her son chose to scream out loud would be generic ones, and so far he had obliged—LOVE LOVE LOVE was the piercing, repeated lyric, which she knew could be any number of loves to anyone within hearing distance, but chiefly, she hoped, the love between father and son, or between brother and brother, separating.

But I LOVE you! screamed Pitik.

I'm sorry. I have to go.

You cannot be! I LOVE you!

I don't love you. I've said that to you.

How could the man be so cruel, after having spoiled them with his friendship?

Caracera explained that the family would no longer tolerate Pitik's presence in Caracera's and, by association, the family's life. Couldn't he see that his family was mercenary? How could they have gotten to their high mount without having disposed of enemies along the way? Couldn't Pitik see that he was now an enemy of the Caracera clan? The same way that the boy's lover, Eustacio Caracera, had been? And look what happened to that old man—sent to an early grave by the family's corrective mania. Pitik's life was in danger!

I don't care!

Don't you believe what I'm saying?

If I am in danger truly-truly, then why don't you helping me to leaving for the U.S.?

As soon as I leave, you will be fine, replied Caracera. You have a bright future ahead of you. Without me you'll do fine. You have all that you need.

What? What do I having?

You have your mother.

This made him cry even louder. His eyes seemed to be stretching back into his head.

And you have the money.

I love you I love you I LOVE you. He was kneeling now.

And he had Mr. Feingold, who most definitely loved him, who, having the choice of any number of Filipino boys to throw his money and affections at, had chosen Pitik—wasn't there something romantic in that?

But it is YOU it is only YOU I LOVE NO!

The door was open. Caracera was at the elevators. Out into the common hall Pitik dragged his pleading, his shamelessness. Caracera was a destroyer, not looking back, pressing and pressing at the elevator buttons. How, Pitik kept wondering, had they gotten to this day, all his powers, which he once thought ascendant, confiscated? Wasn't he pretty enough?

A loud, high-pitched shriek. Pitik's arms flung out. Take me with you please! Please!

The mother's confusion was hysterical.

Finally Caracera showed some emotion. His mask of resolve slackened around the mouth and nose. Each exclamation from the boy only strengthened Caracera's resolve. He would not, by staying with Pitik, be responsible for the boy's death. He would not give the family that satisfaction. And ultimately, he had offered help, not love—he could not be held to a promise he had never made. And he had helped, he had done what he'd set out to do. Now let the one helped help himself.

The elevator doors opened. Caracera and his bags disappeared into the car.

I HATE you HATE you YOU YOU YOU don't go please DON'T GO!

The boy hugged the floor, screaming. He would make sure that they were run out of the Petal Towers. He would crumple, with his obnoxious demonstrations, the gift of their new life on Magdalena Street, the gift of his tuition at St. Jude Catholic School (which he'd already forsaken anyway). He would crumple with all his might even the most tangential gift—like a burgeoning (if willed) appreciation of the game of tennis—offered by Roger Caracera. Like that man, he too would be a destroyer. He would not be satisfied until his mother was sacrificed, her happiness short-lived—making clear the role of the man Roger Caracera in their lives, with his unwelcome, unfulfilled promises. His lies. The ease of his comportment and the smoothness of his speeches concealing the edge of a knife. Pitik cried and cried. He was fifteen and felt ancient.

The building's tact lengthened for days afterward, overwhelming the mother and son with gratitude and absolute sadness.

PART FIVE

Inside the Whale

CHAPTER I

CARACERA HAD READ somewhere once, long ago, that an immigrant could be likened to a visitor from Mars, and had quickly condemned the metaphor, though vivid, as facile. But now he wasn't so sure. Back from the Philippines, he saw things with a sense of wonder, and New York City as a series of signs which needed a key he didn't possess.

He used to have this key—or rather some interior wiring in perfect concordance with the immediate frequency. Now his inner eye looked at the wide New York streets and avenues, and saw them as space gone to waste: you could house so many of the indigent and homeless on the concrete dividers and do away with the plants and blooms currently in place. And why hadn't anybody taken advantage of the fact that some of the sidewalks were large enough for whole families to erect apartments on? And why was it that, when stuck in traffic, people no longer came up to his window and tapped, begging? It wasn't that their need didn't exist. Need was everywhere, here as it had been there. But the sound of the need reaching him did not seem direct; rather, it was muted, muffled, having to fight its way through layers of decorum.

His new students at Columbia were similarly mysterious. Achingly young. And the school term being new, they looked eager to be compelled.

He didn't disappoint. There was a new lift to his steps going to work every morning. His body was being overtaken by some spirit that he didn't recognize as his own. It was a happy accident whose cause did not bear too much looking into.

In class, he spoke of his beliefs about what constituted good writing as if hearing them formulated for the first time, making the young girls specially, looking like newborn things with their soft hair and thin skins, lean forward.

His tan, a deep brown-gold, suggested variously to his acquaintances at Columbia the onset of midlife vanity or the touch of newly acquired (perhaps hoarded) money. He had only this tan to show for his seven weeks in that alternate, Martian world.

Benjamin Goyanos sent him a tape of his last day in Negros.

There was the Ford Explorer stopped by the side of the road, next to an unseen field of sugarcanes. His face in profile, shadows of the canes darting on his skin as he walked around. The camera moved to take in the canes themselves, growing thick and so glossily black that in some lights they looked purplish. He had to crane his neck upward to take in their full height. Above the scene, a splendid blue sky. His face moving, reacting to something said off-camera. Probably by Goyanos's daughter, stuck in the vehicle and eager to depart. Only a flicker of disturbance and then the face resumes its look of coolness, of a vast indifference: exactly, thought Caracera, looking at it months later, *exactly* the state he'd hoped to acquire by dispersing half a million dollars. Sugarcanes, Caracera? Looking at the picture, one could hardly grasp their connection. The man had been plopped into the picture, next to the surreal sugarcanes, as a disconcerting prop of unassimilation. Either he was holding himself stiff against being affected or the landscape had soundly rejected him.

The girl Marta came on, caught at the beach. The scenes somehow chronologically jumbled. Only her backside seen. Stiff, unmoving, unmoved. Broken periodically by the subject stealing a surreptitious glance to her left, revealing a profile the video camera rendered a dark wash of barely legible features. What was she looking at? The camera panned. On view were the young Europeans, showing a drunken, shrunken camaraderie, throwing crumpled cigarette packages at one another, kicking sand, mock-fighting for space on their meager towels, shouting indistinct insults that rose in intonation at the ends of sentences, like bird cries.

Enclosed along with the videocassette was a letter updating the young girl's condition. Was it all right, asked Goyanos, for his daughter to visit Caracera's mother at St. Mary the Immaculate? Caracera's family did not see what harm could come of it and had given their approval. Perhaps it was only to make the young girl Cielito Caracera happy that they had consented. She was the one who told of Teresa Caracera's existence, putting the idea into Marta's head. The two girls were developing an odd friendship, though it seemed the Caracera family had nothing to fear, for the direction of influence was moving from the idea-thrilled high schooler to the former heroin addict.

What did Marta Goyanos find to occupy Teresa Caracera once a week at the courtyard of St. Mary the Immaculate? The young girl read from some book, in weekly installments, and though nobody could vouch for the patient's comprehension, she seemed to find the experience peaceful and was seen to smile often in Marta's company.

Other than the tan, he did have one thing, one concrete proof of the reality of his visit. The pin showing the family coat of arms which he'd worn for his father's funeral procession. Worrying it with his fingers, staring at it from time to time: I was in the Philippines and this is what I have to show for it.

Soon, bits of "news" began to pop up about the imminent release of the film *Fiesta of the Damned*, which aimed to get a jump on Francis Ford Coppola's *Apocalypse Now Redux*, so the audience could trace a natural storytelling progression from war as a vivifying experience to war as a pickling jar of madness. Or rather, so the audience for *Fiesta* would not have to be fighting through the scrim set down by *Apocalypse*. So war could be fully appreciated for what it was: a purifying rite of manhood; a vista of tentative eclipse that a lineup of men, emerging, would disperse, making the sunlight burst through.

John Travolta, doing the rounds for other movies, could already be heard to opine rapturously about the prospects for *Fiesta*. His oft-repeated words were "kick-ass."

And soon it was December, and he was headed back to the Philippines, to attend the unveiling of Jesus Caracera's crypt.

CHAPTER 2

FULFILLING THE WISHES of the patriarch, Roberto brought his two children, and Socorro and her husband brought their three youngsters to stay at the Makati residence. Two weeks were to be duly subtracted from the required total of thirty days specified in the will.

All five beautiful children were cooed over by the family and Aunt Irene, especially, made sure that her grandnieces and -nephews were given a crash course in the history of their legendary family as well as the history of the country which was Jesus Caracera's dying legacy to them. A selective itinerary was set up for the children, alternating between sites educational (the walled city Intramuros; various museums; the Marcoses' extravagant Coconut Palace; the Cultural Center of the Philippines) and for entertainment (the VIP Club; ShoeMart Mega-Mall; the Japanese gardens of Luneta Park). Bodyguards and drivers were assigned to ferry the children everywhere and *yayas* or nannies were assigned to the youngest kids and told specially to watch that they didn't spend too much time in the sun.

This left Roberto and Socorro free to attend to the reopening of the Makati home. They arranged for minor renovations such as restoring pictures of the young Teresa Caracera—discovered in a chest in the attic—among the various groupings on the walls and tables once conspicuous for her absence. Socorro also hired an interior decorator recommended by Irene Caracera. He would reconfigure the Makati residence so that all resemblance to the brother and sister's childhood home was forever obliterated.

The uncles and their wives came to monitor the refurbishments and to make sure that the niece and nephew remained in the dark as to their father's reappearance. They paid particular attention to the moods and behaviors of the grandnephews and -nieces because young people were known to be extremely sensitive to the presence of ghosts in their midsts, but the children seemed spooked only by the onslaught of relatives they regarded, perhaps following instruction, as rightly strangers.

Socorro's husband, a white American, was paid extra attention to as well. He was staying in Manila for only three days, and Irene and Celeste Caracera took it upon themselves to ensure that his opinion of his wife's country should not be derogatory. They took him and Socorro to dinner each night at a different expensive restaurant. On the night before his departure, they arranged for a bunch of family members to accompany him and his wife to the Cultural Center to catch a performance by a local symphony, with whom a renowned Filipina pianist who'd won the Van Cliburn two decades previous was performing. Manila, they wanted it known, was a world-class city and would make a great summer vacation destination for the children in the years to come. It was Christmastime and everywhere you looked *parols*—star-shaped paper lanterns recalling the celestial lantern on the night of Jesus' birth—were hanging. Also there were carolers everywhere.

After the concert, a suite of family cars brought the family to the city's tallest hotel, with a bar at the very top that provided a breathtaking view. Too bad, they said to Socorro's husband, that he could not stay longer to take advantage of the warmer climes of Negros Occidental, of Bacolod, where the family had a mansion that was only an hour's drive from the beaches—some of which were even white sand. Perhaps they could all repair there during his next visit. When would that be?

The children, used to being fussed over, were compelled by the glacial behavior of their Uncle Roger; especially the children of Socorro, who were being introduced to him for the first time. They had never heard their mother speak of this man. As far as they were concerned, the word "uncle" meant their mother's elder brother, the father of their older cousins and a man at once gregarious and calming.

At the sight of this new uncle, Socorro's children became like a string of little talking birds—why why why why—or, as their mother put it, "like a broken record—and I don't like it one bit!"

Why is he so strange?

He's not used to you yet, that's all.

Why does he *look* so strange?

He does not. What do you mean by strange?

Even when he's around he acts like he's not here.

Maybe he's thinking.

Do you think too?

Of course.

How come you don't look like that then?

Because we don't think the same thoughts.

Why?

Stop asking these questions.

Why is he related to you?

Because he's my brother.

Why is he your brother?

I said stop asking. He's my brother the way your brother is your brother. Because we have the same father and mother.

And Uncle Roberto is your brother too?

We're all brothers and sister. Grandpa is our father. And this house is where we grew up. Manila—that's where Grandpa came from. Where I went to school and lived when I was your age.

And where's Grandma?

Socorro hesitated before replying, She's dead.

Is he older?

Who? Uncle Roger? Does he look older?

He acts older.

Once you get used to him you won't find him so strange.

He doesn't talk to us.

Give him time.

Doesn't he like us?

He doesn't like children who ask too many questions.

Regarding the people they saw around them, in the streets, or at the museums and restaurants and movie theaters and churches, people they found "funny-looking," the children were not encouraged, as they had been for their Uncle Roger, to modify or even conceal their incomprehension. In fact, they were encouraged, by playing up the natives' strangeness, to find themselves superior in comparison. This way, Aunt Irene explained when asked by Caracera, the children would always be a little afraid and therefore less susceptible to the lures of potential kidnappers.

The mausoleum at Kalayaan, surprising everyone, turned out to be a simple affair. Simple, that is, relative to the pomp that had thus far been expended on Jesus Caracera. On the outside, it resembled nothing so much as a rustic cottage with a peaked roof of red clay tiles and was surrounded by a six-foot-tall fence of vertical iron rods painted a lustrous black, rising to sharp three-inch spires at the top. The gate was filled in, near the foot, by a horizontal band of leafy, rococo design. The mausoleum's doorway was narrow and only one person could pass through at a time. The interior could accommodate no more than eight people, so viewings were organized in shifts of ten minutes. The entire back wall was filled in with a colored glass mosaic depicting a bright white dove with a jeweled eye casting celestial rays of blessing that shot out diagonally to the floor so that the coffin that was trussed up on a slightly raked platform, when viewed head-on, was bracketed by the rays of peaceful benediction cast by God's dove.

The coffin was surrounded by floral tributes the caretaker would have to dispose of in a week—unless the cool that greeted the visitors was not a by-product of the marble interior but rather some refrigeration unit piping in from a disguised vent.

The floor, with its squares of gray-green veined marble, reminded Marta Goyanos of the floors of the detox facility she had been sent to, a place that had struck her as a suitable environment to wake up to after a suicide attempt, where the messiness of human life, held at bay, became a memory, and the touch and ministrations of everyone around her were focused not so much on her body as on the surviving, durable part of her: her soul. It would forever be emblazoned on her mind as a suitable re-creation of purgatory. Just like this crypt, even with its celestial dove shining jeweled light on the scene. Mr. Jesus Caracera was in purgatory, just as she had been. But at least it was an improvement over the hell he'd been consigned to by his son and by her father, Benjamin Goyanos, both of whom had agreed on the dead man's out-and-out perfidy. They made him sound like a king in the process.

The family doyenne, Irene Caracera, could not help but look disappointed. Had she believed that the structure, which had looked dour and unfestooned in the plans, would somehow be transmuted to tacky splendor during the building? No doubt she would not be conducting tours for her friends, showing off. The only consolation from her disappointment seemed to be the presence of her nephew-in-law Roger Caracera, whose hand she clasped firmly, obliging the family to treat him with copycat deference.

A priest, perhaps the same one from Jesus Caracera's burial, was on hand to sprinkle holy water on the premises, uttering largely incomprehensible prayers and blessings as he did so. Nobody dared confront him, not even Caracera, who was convinced he was spouting gibberish. But even were the man intelligible, Caracera would've felt the same way. Irene Caracera explained to listeners that they were "being treated" to some Latin.

The grandchildren were suitably dressed for the occasion, in what Caracera thought were hampering clothes—a starchy dress with a pinafore skirt for Socorro's young girl, and suits and ties with stiff shoes for the young boys. Yet they gave no indication of being impinged on by such costumes. Their good behavior was unsettling, incomprehensibly inhuman to him, and yet he was grateful—that the children of Socorro, in particular, had not inherited their mother's high-strung, officious ways.

The manner of the two older children of Roberto Caracera was exemplarily sober. They were shy in the presence of their uncle, despite having taken their father's story about him at face value. They were told of his "dangerous ways," none of which could be seen in this visit. For the first time, his eyes were not hidden behind glasses. Had he forgotten to bring them on this trip or maybe waylaid them? As a result, the man, averting his glance often, gave the impression of being extremely shy, even humble.

This new creature bore no relation to the one whose picture had appeared in the papers.

Marta Goyanos, befitting the occasion as well as her new life as an acolyte of Cielito Caracera, was dressed in a simple off-white number with a collar that looked cut from a doily. Caracera wasn't sure, much as he had wished her punk appearance and demeanor gone, whether the change was for the better. He missed the sense of prickly fear she aroused in company, being the same fear he sometimes inspired, which job he was glad to have passed on to someone else every so often.

Among the reasons Marta Goyanos had been eager to commune with Teresa Caracera was because Marta herself had been thinking of joining an outfit like the Peace Corps, bringing her to needy countries, or to provinces in the Philippines. She'd been warned that the patient's memory was famously arbitrary, and so far she had not been able to get Teresa to talk at length or with any consistency about her past. Marta's correspondence with Virginie Duhamel, engineered by her father, proved more helpful.

Caracera flitted along the periphery of a succession of groups until he found himself with his friend Goyanos and Goyanos's daughter.

He asked Marta about his mother, feeling obliged. And then asked her what she read to the woman.

Marta gave a hesitant, embarrassed pause. Barbara Pym, she said, mispronouncing the last name: *Pime.*

He suppressed his shock. Why Pym? he asked.

She noticed his correction. She said that the books were passed on to her by Cielito Caracera, which was true. But neglected to add Cielito's apt logic: that the mother, who could reasonably be assumed to want to hear from her children, would get a chance via one son's favorite books. That these were his favorite books had been passed along by Cielito.

Oh, said Caracera.

Meanwhile, what new projects was his young cousin Cielito getting herself involved in?

She would graduate from high school next year, and after that there would be college. Her parents wanted to send her abroad to study, but more, she suspected, to rouse her out of her obsession with good works, which they strongly hoped was a phase of girlish infatuation, and less to extend and amplify the learning she had already accumulated at Immaculate Heart. Marriage to the right boy was the proper outcome envisioned for her. And motherhood, of course. Going abroad, it was hoped she would be made to realize how much a struggle life truly was. Her family's prosperity would, in America, slow to a trickle. And she would wake up to the cold, hard work of having to support herself. Let others fight for their happiness, she would soon have so much to take care of.

They had allowed her, along with Marta, to visit the mental patient Teresa Caracera because they believed that seeing the woman would help Cielito come to understand the final, lasting lesson of goodness in the world. Trying to improve the lives of others, she could only ruin her own.

Eulalio and Celeste Caracera spoke little on the day of the mausoleum's unveiling. When seen next to Cielito, they smiled ear to ear, clutching her in the manner of proud and secretly hopeful parents. None of the malevolent motives attributed to them could be detected from the long, wordless glances they gave their youngest child, whom they seemed to consider as if gazing at photographs of their young selves.

CHAPTER 3

H E   T R A C K E D the woman caretaker to her new job. Could she tell him about his mother?

The look she gave him seemed to be asking why he didn't come sooner. She said that the Mrs. wasn't, strictly speaking, really in Mandaluyong, the city's best-known mental hospital. Rather, she was housed in the basement of a hospital in the Mandaluyong area that had been given over to psychiatric cases, while its upper floors were favored by Manila's wealthiest for treatment (specially for plastic surgery) and recuperation. Mandaluyong Hospital was, after all, a public hospital—by which she meant to echo, in her own way, what she'd doubtless heard countless times from Caracera's father and the rest of the family: "public," abraded by contact with commoners, not fit for a Caracera, not even one who was a Caracera by marriage and had been as good as abandoned. Even while going nuts, his mother would not be separated from the class she had married into.

He asked the woman for directions. He told her that he intended to head off on foot, on his own. She looked at him doubtfully, but withheld any advice or comment. He was to take EDSA, make a left on Boni Avenue, then turn on Connecticut. He would keep going until he found himself in the vicinity of the WackWack Golf and Country Club's famous greens, where former president Marcos entertained such visiting dignitaries as the Sultan of Brunei and Henry Kissinger. He didn't mind that she spoke to him like a tourist. That was how he himself viewed things.

The only appropriate thing to wear seemed to be the black shirt he had worn at his father's burial. He couldn't bring himself to put on the whole outfit, even if the black pants that went with the shirt were the best pair around. Instead, to lighten the graveness of the shirt, he opted for the olive khakis he'd brought from New York. They were a little loose around the waist and needed a belt, one of which he found in a closet in his father's room. In the mirror, he confronted the sight of a young man whose chief attribute seemed to be unsureness, much like one of his own students. Though the belt's accent gave him a fastidious, almost female air, and spoke of its previous owner's confidence regarding his effect upon a casual observer. He felt ludicrous and, thinking of his father and his father's exertions for the opposite sex, briefly sentimental.

The aura of courtship that surrounded his nervous rehearsal seemed completely right for the occasion. He felt himself to be nothing less than a neglectful suitor trying to win back some measure of affection from a jilted sweetheart; which jilting, though it seemed to have always been by mutual consent, was now revealed, on closer inspection, to have been entirely his own doing. How could a mother not want to have been reunited with her own flesh and blood; how could a child believe such a thing, when it was probably closer to the truth to say that she had been prevented by intermediaries from reestablishing contact?

Returning to America had made obvious his cowardice. There was no other word.

Going to Negros, singling out the two boys—it had been one long track of running from the obvious. It was his mother who might most benefit from being looked into.

His outfit, chosen to impress, found immediate discerning admirers two miles from the Caracera residence. The street urchins looked up from a game of banging marbles against sardine cans on the sidewalk opposite their encampments—improvised one-room units whose walls and roofs were cobbled together from cardboard and stray plywood and flattened-out ten-gallon-sized Baguio oil tins and whose doors were nothing more than sheets of clear plastic or discarded shower curtains or canvas rice bags stitched together. They'd in fact been banished to the other side of the street by harried mothers trying to nurse and lull to sleep their infant siblings. They saw the man passing hurriedly by, glommed on to his fastidious outfit, his obscuring (and clearly expensive) frosted glasses, his shiny patent-leather lace-ups (he wouldn't be able to run fast enough away from them), and made an immediate dash for him.

Being experts, they turned out to be exactly right. He was much too slow. They had the quickness of jungle things, two strides and they were at his side. By the time he was aware of them, they were resting their hands on his shirt, tagging, tugging, clutching.

There were fifteen or sixteen of them, encircling him. Whichever way he tried to evade, there was a child, in rags and smelling strongly of—rotten grease? Even when he burst past their cordon, they caught him up again almost immediately, reassembling to pin him in the center.

Some of the brasher ones tried sneaking their hands into his pants pockets, front and back. He slapped them away with more force than he'd meant to. Go away, he told them.

Come on, Joe, they said. Money please Joe please, they echoed. Some money please. Please please *lang ho*.

His discomfort caused some of them to laugh, celebrating the quarry's imminent surrender. They were old hands, having had ample practice in getting straight to a victim's marshmallow center; and though the littler ones were not sure of getting something from the foreigner, they hung on and lent their parries and shrill cries to the concerted effort, hoping later to be let in on a share of the spoils, which depended on how much the man surrendered and on how generous the older kids were feeling.

Please Joe please please *lang*. And in the gaps between these louder words slipped a few others: money; OK?; good; time; sorry; and more pleases like the whirring of a thousand small brushes setting to work on the plaque of his stoic condescension.

They were like brown-skinned piranhas converging for a kill. All jaws and throats and jutting arms. They had the skinny bodies of their ages, but even more so. Dressed in overlarge, tentlike T-shirts on which were printed images and insignias—a sphinxlike Bob Marley smoking a reefer and Faye Dunaway with the supernatural eyes of Laura Mars—they could not have understood, being positively billboards from his own youth. He was being attacked by his past. They crowded in some more, laughing and clamoring. "Star Margarine" in yellow with a green neck. Joe, Joe! "San Miguel Beer": *Panalo ka na!* Money, money, Joe! "Toyota," red letters against white, now yellow-white, like unbrushed teeth. Michael Jackson in a grimace, his mouth a cavity filled in by brown flesh. Holes everywhere, and frayed strands giving the clothes a country-and-western fringe look.

Money! Money! Please Joe! Joe please! Laughter and shrieks.

There were so many of them, he couldn't possibly give to every child. Which ones would he give to? And if he gave to them, would it be understood that he meant for the money to be shared equally among them? Okay, okay, he said, finally stopping. He feigned exasperation so that they would understand that he had nothing beyond what he was about to surrender.

Yay! they cheered, as one.

He knew enough to turn his back on them. They were supplicants one minute, pickpockets the next. Hold on a moment, he barked, making the brasher ones, who'd followed to face him, go back. He took out his wallet. He could feel the eyes burning into his back, making a note of where he kept his money. He took out a few bills. Held on to his wallet by pinning it against his chest with his arms, while he counted. Three ten-peso bills, two twenties, four fives. Ninety pesos. Barely two dollars' worth. He took out two more fives.

He pushed his wallet into his shirt pocket, too high for even the tallest boy to reach. Then began distributing the bills. Although he would've liked to have disbursed the denominations according to some scale of apparent need, the hands jabbing up into the air caused him to lose his cool. Into the nearest quivering palm was thrust each bill—he couldn't even tell if he gave twice to the same boy. As soon as the last bill was gone, he made a quick dash forward.

Two boys continued to follow him. One looked no older than two and was completely naked. His penis was floured with gray sediment, as if he'd been playing in a construction site. He was being dragged along like a broken doll by what looked like an older brother, six, maybe seven.

Caracera turned around only once and therefore missed what he thought was the older one hitting his brother on the head, to make him cry in order to attract Caracera's attention.

What lungs the young one had! His toothless mouth was livid. At that age he already knew, beyond the immediate reflex of pain to which he was responding, that he was supposed to perform for the stranger who stood before them, and he darted frantic eyes. Did he meet his older brother's approval? What would the stranger do next? Would there be candy in his, the boy's, immediate future? Finally the eyes turned up at the sky—a look perhaps cribbed from parents who often did the same, a silent remonstrance against God's punishments: *Bakit kami?* Why us?

Caracera glared at the older boy, who glared back, daring.

Finally, knowing he was no match for them, he took out two more fives from his wallet. The younger one began to calm down. Just two and already an expert. He looked as the stranger approached. Looked as two tiny mirror images of himself grew larger in the stranger's glasses as the stranger bent down to pat his head. The pat was a signal and he obliged. He smiled and even, it seemed to Caracera, widened his eyes. Put his finger to his mouth. Caracera cleared some dirt away from the side of the boy's face. The older boy came near. Joe, he said, palm outstretched.

Is this your brother?

The older boy nodded.

What's his name?

Dodoy. He hit the young boy on the head. Say hello to *Amerikano*.

Don't do that, Caracera admonished.

He's *tanga*.

Don't say that.

The older boy laughed, tickled. You understand Pilipino?

Caracera asked the older boy, What do you eat? The little brother had the protruding stomach of malnutrition, while the older one looked fine, if a bit thin.

Again the older one hit his brother on the head. Say hi.

Stop that!

Hi, piped the little one finally.

Hello.

His name is Dodoy, repeated the older brother.

Hello, Dodoy.

Dodoy recognized his name and smiled.

Caracera put the bills in front of the older brother but snatched them back when the boy made a move for them. Whatever you eat, he said to the boy, make sure you give your brother some. Okay?

The older one nodded.

You can't let him eat nothing.

The older one nodded.

This was out-and-out blackmail. He let the boy know by his look before finally giving him the bills.

Receiving what they had come looking for, the older boy dragged the young one away. They didn't even say thank you. A moment later, Caracera heard the older boy screaming at his back, Cheapee cheapee-ass Joe! Fuck you USA! Fuck you USA!

He turned around and saw the older boy giving him the finger, the younger one laughing, jumping up and down.

Caracera pretended to run after them. They disappeared in a flash.

The exterior of St. Mary the Immaculate in Mandaluyong was off-white, though he couldn't tell whether it had once been white and was aged by smog and rains, or whether a tincture of yellow had always been in the paint to counterpoint the nearby greens of the WackWack Golf and Country Club. There was a statue of the Mother Mary on a pedestal surrounded by an immaculate mini-lawn that looked fake un-til he came closer. To the left and right were bright flowers growing on bushes. They too were real enough up close. Mother Mary was in her usual posture of praying, her blank face yielding to any number of interpretations—she could've even been asking for a new outfit, not wanting to be outdone by the matrons in their Chanels and St. Laurents whom he saw coming out of the sliding doors.

He went in, headed for Information.

The woman at the desk was surprised to hear the name of Mrs. Teresa Caracera. Though she recognized the name, it looked as if she'd never heard it spoken and had expected never to hear it during her stint at St. Mary the Immaculate. I'm her son, Caracera explained, which added to her stupefaction.

Just a minute please, she said. She buzzed and spoke into her desk. Then, turning to him, she said, We'll be with you in a short while. She stole a few glances at him, trying to judge the truthfulness of his claim.

Beyond the desk could be seen a sunny courtyard through a second set of sliding doors. There, beneath a few patches of needed shade provided by bougainvilleas and some other blossomless trees that he couldn't identify, sat patients who looked rested and not, as he'd expected to find, traumatized. They were in wheelchairs and were looking at the sky, at the bougainvillea petals littering the ground, and were listening to nurses without comment or comprehension, looks of Mother Mary–like Zen on their faces: perhaps they were even silently praying.

The tranquil setting was a nice surprise. He felt uncomfortably like an auditor for his family, making sure that they got their money's worth, which by the look of things they did. He was glad in this rare instance to belong to a family who could afford so much. At least his mother was provided by her confinement—a word he began to feel he needed to revise—with a nice cushion against unpleasant realities like the one he had had to confront in the sixty-five-minute walk from Makati to Mandaluyong. Perhaps it was not the word itself that needed revision, but rather the pronoun that preceded it: not *her* confinement, but rather *its* confinement—the world conveniently curtained from view.

Perhaps, like his isolation in that parallel existence in New York, hers could be seen as a canny, self-imposed stratagem, undertaken to save herself from having to engage in the constant, futile battles a world in perpetual need of correction demanded.

He entered the courtyard just as an old man wearing sunglasses was being wheeled out. The man seemed to find something comical in the sight of Caracera and kept pointing to his nurse, who smiled in mysterious agreement. Only after the man had turned out of sight did Caracera realize that he had been pointing at Caracera's glasses, which matched his own. Caracera felt a shiver go up his spine thinking that he had just encountered a premonitory version of himself, before realizing that there were worse places to end up than an exclusive hospital a stone's throw away from a luxe golf club, far from the pressing troubles of real people.

The woman who was his mother did not look like Socorro.

Teresa Caracera? he asked, to be certain.

Yes, sir, the nurse replied for her ward.

Teresa Caracera wore no makeup. Her face, lined as it was across the forehead and around her mouth, was strong, handsome.

Either his mother or her nurse had combed the woman's silver hair rigidly back and tied it into an imperious bun. She wore a white blouse, and over her legs was a check-patterned blanket. Her hands, which lay atop the blanket, were, like her face, lined and sturdy-looking: certainly not the hands of an aristocrat, and which had always, if he remembered correctly, been deemed her worst feature: hands which had gotten that way not from the effort of climbing the social ladder, as Caracera believed was the case for the women who'd married his uncles, but from having toiled in the fields as an agricultural worker for the Peace Corps—which his mother had increasingly viewed with pessimistic disdain and had eventually dubbed the Peace Corpse.

Hello, Caracera said.

The woman smiled. And with it vanished any sense of fragile familiarity Caracera had felt upon seeing her. How had his mother appeared when smiling? He couldn't recall because it had happened so infrequently that it might as well not have happened at all. Perhaps this was a sure sign that she'd really gone mad: here was someone who did not think of a smile as a violation of the look she had trained herself to train on the world, on her children: grim, accusatory, with an advance sense of having been failed.

Behind her, the nurse looked at him and waited for a signal.

He gave it to her with a nod and she left, but not before assuring Teresa Caracera—whom she called exaggeratedly by her first name, for Caracera's benefit—that she would be back in half an hour.

Shall we go in the shade? he finally asked, taking the nurse's position behind Teresa's wheelchair.

I like the sun.

Do you want to sit here?

She pointed. He took her to a spot between two trees, beyond which there was a nice lawn that appeared scorched in places. He wrested a heavy metallic garden chair from its spot near a dry pool encircling a grotto depicting Saint Bernadette kneeling before the Virgin of Lourdes. It brought back the memory of Jennifer Jones in the movie *Song of Bernadette*—which had been part of his curriculum at St. Jude Catholic School. Perhaps the grotto had even been designed from a still from the movie. It would not have surprised him. (Perhaps future generations, when erecting yet one more memorial to General MacArthur, would call upon pictures of Harvey Keitel in *Fiesta of the Damned*.)

She saw him looking at the grotto and again smiled.

He wiped the chair with one hand, then sat down.

They looked at each other for a moment. Then she repeated, in a cheerful voice, I like the sun.

I'm your son, he said.

Silence.

Do you recognize me?

She shook her head no.

Do you remember your family?

She shook her head.

I came from America. Looking at her, he questioned why he was here.

Suddenly he heard a *thwack* and looked to see if she had heard it too. Perhaps a bird had smashed into a tree or a pane of glass? He couldn't see anything on the lawn or the ground around them.

She closed her eyes, drinking in the sunlight with her upturned face.

I'm sorry I haven't come until now. It's just. I've been busy. Saying which, he laughed. He wanted to let her know the joke of his busyness, as well as the joke—in the face of her obliviousness, her questionable comprehension—of his monologue, lengthening. The joke of his need for her audience, hoping against reason.

Your name is Teresa Caracera, he said.

Of course, her expression seemed to say.

My name is Roger. The order of your children are Roberto, Socorro and me. Do you remember me?

She shook her head, smiled.

You gave me my name. (Could it have meant, as he'd always believed, Roger, over and out, as in a call of distress? Could he, her last child, have been her final hope?)

On a corner of the lawn, he spotted what he thought was a waylaid bird's egg, flecked with gray. Then the gray spots slowly turned into indentations and the bird's egg became a golf ball. That was the *thwack* he'd heard.

I'm not lonely, she said.

Excuse me?

I'm not lonely.

I'm glad to hear that. He waited in vain for her to continue.

Finally he said, You lived in Madrid. You came here when you were twenty-three. Here is the Philippines. Manila. But before you came to Manila you were in the provinces. With the Peace Corps.

From the bosom of her Madrid family she had escaped to the peripatetic setups of her Peace Corps assignments. These too had withered from their tropical promise to become yet another bereft landscape. Finally she was pushed into the arms of a rescuer who brought her to live in Manila, transforming her into the jewel-cold insignia of his campaign to resuscitate the family name: seeing her, Jesus Caracera had at once known that her beauty and her lack of animating force were one and the same, known that the frozen aspect of her surroundings was not an accident but rather had taken its cue from her: she had, stretching out her hand and touching, turned it to ice. Had he believed he could thaw her? Or had he wanted her preserved in that state, from which he believed the Caracera family would reap the benefits of being envied by other families: first the spectral wife, then the angel children?

Having been designated the high point of the last few years of Caracera history, all she had to do was tear herself down and with it the hopes, the delusions of the family. She turned into the Hydra-headed gorgon, spitting out poisonous truth. Up until her arrival, they had been able to get away with the lie of the family's continuing prominence. Soon, Teresa Caracera threatened family members with violence and had to be prevented from causing harm to others, as well as to herself. There had been talk of knives in her hands. With those same hands, she had also ripped up her passport, her bank book, her marriage certificate. This orgy of destructiveness was typical of her later years, long after the children had been taken away to live in the States.

So once more she would travel, or rather be sent away. Entombed at St. Mary's.

He informed her that the man who had met her in the provinces had since passed away.

He told of Jesus Caracera in Socorro's home in San Francisco. How he'd gone from one room of the second floor to another. Then, when he'd grown too weak to use the stairs, he had been put in a room at the front of the house that had the further advantage of being shady, because by this time to the dead man's many disabilities had been added a new sensitivity to light.

He described the room to her, its disconcerting dimness. There were thick curtains pulled over the windows, only letting a thin wand of light in, and this light had seemed to Caracera like a surgical finger of blame that his father, by choosing to be sequestered in that room, had been hoping to escape entirely. He told her that it had occurred to him that he was just like this light, an intruder from the outside world disturbing the quiet scene of not-yet-death. He was among the things his father was avoiding. Redolent of the active, roiling, punitive world's scents and its powers of infection (being fresh from New York, after all). Walking in with all this, he had caused his father's immune system to finally buckle under.

He didn't expect her to console him, and she didn't.

There was the dead man in his bed. It was one of those hospital beds that you could adjust to make the patient sit up. There was the dead man sitting, looking at him as he slowly, fearfully made his way to his bedside.

He didn't know what to think. His mind was blank. He was conscious only of the room being no place and any place at the same time, aware that this dreaded reunion was taking place exactly as he'd imagined it once, long ago: inside the abstract realm of imagination, with the antagonist of his life and of several other lives, helpless, deprived of his strongest weaponry of words, so that he, Caracera, was free to decide the outcome of the encounter to his satisfaction, to triumph, in other words. And yet, Caracera had felt untriumphant, reduced to mere tears. The same tears that were on Socorro's and Roberto's faces. The three of them knew the general meaning of the scene—a reunion, a conciliation, a tying up—but he felt that there were deeper secrets that eluded them. They knew that the man was dying and that, by living, by not following him to the grave, they had finally become, too late in their lives, their own selves. They were crying for the tardy knowledge as much as for the man's suffering.

The man had thin greenish tubing up both nostrils, connected to an oxygen tank that had a circular meter with a needle inside it that went up and down with each tiny breath. As Caracera approached he noticed that the needle went up and down with alarming speed, as if the man were afraid Caracera meant him harm. Socorro had rushed to the dying man's side, coddling him. But he had hit—more like patted, actually—her hands away.

The man's arm had been stabbed into to connect him to two IV drips, one to kill pain, the other to deliver food, and there were bruises from other entry points.

He told his mother about the lies he told his father, to comfort him. He told her that though he did indeed teach writing at Columbia University in New York City, he had exaggerated the achievement of his job by inventing successes for his students, which reflected well on him. He told her that he didn't know what had taken hold of him, it had all come out unbidden.

His father, he said, had been unable to reply to any of his assertions, but—maybe he was only imagining it?—the man had seemed to have been grateful and maybe even a little proud.

During his time away from the family, Caracera had become the perfect nobody—not brother, not husband and certainly not son. But his father had the power to give to Caracera's accomplishment a sudden reverse image, a revelatory flip side, so that he was, in fact, "somebody," a success by his attachment to, not his separation from, people. Because wasn't he, by his own admission, connected to his students, acting as the catalyst for their success in the world?

He turned to look at his mother, who had suddenly given a laugh, and that was when he saw she was crying.

This seemed a good sign and he continued, telling her about their shock at his father's death, their panic. He told her about what they did—what he did—when it was obvious that the man had died and could not be brought back. He told her about the undertaker, the cleaning lady who had been charged with returning the room of death to normal, the people who had sent their condolences via telegram, fax and by sending floral tributes, which had turned Socorro's home into a virtual hothouse, stinking of decay. He told of the notes of gratitude that had to be sent to each of those people, numbering in the hundreds. Who knew how far back their friendships or acquaintanceships or partnerships with the family stretched and what, in the end, besides the faded yellow background of failure into which the family had disintegrated, had been the lasting images in these people's minds when the word "Caracera," triggered by the death, initiated memory's scavenging hunts? To what set of adjectives, what stories understood to be emblematic would his father have been attached? He and his mother both, perhaps, knew the answers but hoped that it was only they, exercising the luxury of being family, who judged him as harshly as they did.

He told her nearly everything, except for the fact that it had occurred to him that because his visit and his father's death had been so closely linked in time, he had come to the awareness of himself as being the Angel of Death. That part he was careful to leave out, although he felt that he had as good as suggested it.

You know what? she asked, suddenly sparking.

What?

I had a nice talk with someone just like you. The other day? Two weeks ago? Maybe longer than that. Yes, longer. But maybe I made it up? They tell me I make things up sometimes.

What do you mean someone like me?

I think I made it up.

I'm here. Did you make *me* up?

No, she replied.

But I won't be here always. Soon I'll leave. And I don't want you to think you made me up. He thought of the scouts Marta Goyanos and Cielito Caracera. Girls, right? They come to talk. And read to you. Do you like what they read?

Oh no. This one didn't read.

No?

No she didn't read.

She: he thought of Socorro. Did she say who she was?

She was looking at him very intently, as if she were seeing him for the first time.

What is it?

Your face, she said. It's the strangest . . .

My mother's from Spain. My father's from the Philippines. The combination makes it a little strange.

Spain, she said. Just like me?

Maybe you knew each other.

What's her name?

Teresa, he said. He had both hands inside his pockets.

Just like me, she said.

Do you know her? he asked.

Do I?

The longest moment passed before he said, I guess not.

Suddenly she looked behind him and smiled.

He turned in time to see the nurse approaching them.

Hi, Teresa, said the nurse.

Is it time? he asked the nurse.

Yes, sir, she replied. She stood behind Teresa. Did you have a nice talk? she asked her ward, who smiled back.

Good, replied the nurse.

Can I talk to you for a moment? Caracera asked the nurse. Excuse us, he told his mother.

He stepped away, and the nurse followed.

Did somebody else come and visit her recently? he asked.

You mean the girls, sir?

She said it was somebody else.

She did, sir? I don't know anything about it, sir. Sometimes she imagines things, sir.

Please don't call me sir.

I'm sorry, sir—I'm sorry. Nobody visited.

You're sure?

Yes.

He paused. I'm her son, he began.

I was told.

Does she—does she ever talk about her family?

A look of commiseration. No, sir.

Not to you?

And not to anybody else.

Is she—in your opinion is she happy here?

We take very good care of her. She's a little . . .

Yes?

A little hard to please.

He couldn't help smiling.

But I think she's happy.

She has friends? he asked.

Oh, yes. Sylvia. They get along the best. They're like little girls together.

All right, he said. He handed her seven one-hundred-peso bills.

What's this for? No, sir. Please. She tried giving them back.

Take it.

No no.

Please.

No I can't.

Just take it.

She looked down at her feet. The money was balled up inside a fist.

He moved back to his mother. Another golf ball whizzed past, landing right at her feet. She looked down as if somebody had brought her a gift.

It's dangerous here, he said.

I like it, she replied, smiling.

CHAPTER 4

'T'HE BIG NEWS during the six months he'd been away was
the death, by landslide, of the inhabitants of a mountainous
garbage dump on the city's outskirts. Hundreds of recovered
bodies did not even account for a full tally of the missing. Those who
remained unaccounted-for, it was believed, were buried beneath tower-
ing piles of trash that had to be left alone because digging would set
off more landslides. There was also the danger that the fuming piles
(nitrogen and other gases, released from the compression, would sometimes mix with each other and spark miniature fires), when raked
through and further disturbed, might finally make an inferno of the
whole village.

But Christmas was the season of hope, and many began to believe
that some of the missing were in fact alive. They had been awakened
by their near-death to forsake life in the city and return to native
provinces to face down the judgment of failure from those they'd left
behind.

Up and left, without having been sighted during the confusion of
the rescue attempts.

Collections continued to be taken up to help the survivors rebuild their homes and lives. The new photographs glutting the rags were of faces from the recent tragedy: a new resident of Smoky Village every other day, and below the photo of him or her, a capsule story of hard luck and dim prospects.

Christmastime, a season of genuine and prolonged merriment, beginning as early as the first day of December, provided the excuse to turn every available surface into a canvas for florid, abundant decoration: the walls of churches; the interiors of every school room; the windows of apartment houses, specially those visible from the streets; the insides and outsides of already overembellished jeepneys; the pillars of street kiosks selling Christmas-themed gifts, which sprouted up all over the city. These were all festooned with *parols,* crepe and tinsel and shiny foil streamers, angels of infinite variety and mangers showing the infant Jesus being lifted by Mother Mary, as Joseph and the three wise men looked on. Billboards advertised gifts for loved ones on "this special season."

Michael Jackson singing "Give Love on Christmas Day" was heard at least five times every hour on the radio, alternating with Mariah Carey trilling "All I Want for Christmas" and a slew of other infernal, appropriate tunes.

It would be a lie to say that Caracera never once thought of Pitik Sindit. Even had he been able to resist the strong lure of picturing the boy's improved life, he would sooner or later have succumbed to the seasonal imperative of "thinking of others" to wonder about the skinny creature who, when last seen, was hugging his own shiny reflection in the hallway of the Petal Towers.

But his friend Benjamin Goyanos did not know what had happened to the boy. Not once had the mother and son tried to reach him through the accountant or the bank.

He waited until the day before he was scheduled to leave. He and Gochengco drove to the apartment building on Magdalena Street. Six months, surely, would be enough time for the boy to come to the conclusion that Caracera's desertion was a blessing in disguise. Caracera did not expect to find him in the apartment, having instead left his mother to live with the American Feingold, besotted pederast. Caracera would, paying the mother a visit, ask after the boy and relay his regards. He wanted to see what three million pesos and enough time settling had finally wrought.

Nobody came to the door even after the bell was repeatedly rung. It was nearly ten minutes before he gave up. Downstairs, he asked a resident about to get into the elevator, and the resident gave a shrug, as much ignorant as indifferent.

He had Goyanos call the accountant, who called the bank, only to relay that exactly a month after Caracera left, a last withdrawal of a few thousand pesos was made on the Sindits' account. Since then there had been no activity whatsoever. More than two million pesos remained.

Late in the day found him being driven by Gochengco to the last known residence of the American Feingold. He approached with great trepidation. What if the boy was still in love with him or, worse, if the love had curdled into an irreversible hate, as black and focused as the love had been frilly and farcical? A young woman wearing the starched whites of a maid informed the visitor outside the gates that the American had departed in advance of the termination of his lease. Where to? The maid had no information, and neither did the owners of the gated residence. Perhaps Caracera wanted to make an appointment to inspect the premises at another time, when the owners were around? No, he replied, he wasn't interested in renting.

It was dark, early evening, by the time Caracera's car pulled up outside the Santa Ana outpost of Madame Sonia, entrepreneur, entertainer, enslaver.

Answering the door in her usual silly outfit of short shorts and clingy T with holes pocking one underarm, the proprietress stood glumly considering the stranger for a minute, before she recognized him: it was neither the Aider of Dreams, nor the American Deserter, but rather, the Angel of Death. The fear Madame Sonia tried to control referred to the last visit Caracera had paid at Santa Ana: overturning the furniture, beating the *bakla* with fists turned pistonlike with righteous rage, capably extorting information on the boy's whereabouts. Sonia knew, looking at the man at the doorway, what he wanted.

Come in, she said, making sure to put the proper distance between them and making sure too, by the glumness of her voice, that the man should know that she was fully willing to cooperate. Also she wanted to give an inkling of bad news ahead.

Even Madame Sonia's did not escape the pagan ornamentations of the Christian festival. The *calesa* wheel flashed Christmas lights, purple and red and green and blue. There was even a tinfoil Christmas tree whose branches looked like elongated toilet brushes, decorated with hanging balls and, at the top, an electric star that went on and off at irregular intervals.

Sonia thought it best to get to the point. You don't knowing? she asked.

The man's heavy chest sank. What, what happened? he mumbled, though he didn't want to know. He saw the man Feingold taking off one animal mask—a docile lamb or a moony, blank-eyed cow—to reveal the feral visage of its true opposite: a fox, a wild dog, a hunter with flame-colored, dripping strips of the boy's flesh in its mouth. He saw himself, Roger Caracera, drawing the animal near with the bait of the boy's flesh, himself giving the animal an encouraging pat on the head.

He is dead.

Caracera couldn't speak.

He is killed.

How? The question was asked against his need to be protected from the information.

Running over by a car.

Who did it, who ran him over?

Nobody knew, could tell. It was a hit-and-run. After which the mother, grieving to the point of near-madness, left for her hometown, to be taken care of by relatives.

Sure, there were eyewitnesses, but, contradicting each other, they had as good as produced no description at all.

The boy was given a lovely burial. Caracera's money, pronounced Madame Sonia with barely suppressed glee at the irony, turned out to be of some use after all.

Caracera had a vision: the final withdrawal on the family account: a few thousand pesos. And then no more activity.

With the money, the mother had bought a simple coffin, an unvarnished pine box which had the distinguishing embellishment of a crucifix, to ensure, she pronounced, that the Angel of Death could easily determine the allegiance of the deceased's soul and know where to send him.

I was at the apartment in Binondo, said Caracera. It's empty.

How can she going back there? asked Madame Sonia.

Which province is this?

Nueva Ecija, said Madame Sonia.

Do you have the address?

She is not giving it to anyone.

But the tale was not quite over. And Sonia's tone, only temporarily pitched at the tone of truce. There was more irony, more pain to inflict.

The boy, having been left behind, returned to the routine of his life with a vengeance. He went back to school, his new school, St. Jude's, that is, applying himself with increased dedication. Announced to his mother that education would be his ticket to America. He would show up the American, whose lack of faith in his abilities would be revealed as racist simplification and oversight. He'd come by Sonia's, who had still not found a replacement and who, impressed by the boy's drive, dissuaded him from taking up his abandoned duties at the House of Beauty and Pain. There was no more past to be loyal to, bound by, assured Sonia, who herself had given up on the profession of her past twenty years.

Sonia encouraged the boy to go back to the other American, Mr. Feingold, giving him another chance. And the boy had. It seemed he had finally recognized the value and advantage of being loved, of being the partner who had the upper hand in the transaction.

The boy and his mother had decided it was best for him to live with Feingold at his walled compound in Fort Bonifacio, leaving the mother at the Magdalena Street apartment. The pair checked up on her periodically and made sure she was not alone during the weekends. The boy could be seen with her at church on Sunday and one or the other of the couple would take her out to the movies on a Friday night, and to walk, on a Saturday afternoon, along the seawall on Roxas, taking in healthy salt air for her stricken, recuperating lungs.

For three weeks, this was the routine adopted by Blueboy, whom Sonia still called by the name of his former occupation, but only as a fond reminder of their early life together, and to acknowledge their lasting bond, regardless of changed circumstance. It seemed this was the unexpected and lasting gift of the American: the boy's long-slumbering anger stirred and used for fuel to drive his journey toward an assured future. A previously unrecognized possibility had opened up for him: yes, America was still the final destination, but in the end it had been Pitik who was solely at the wheel.

And then, on the fourth and final week of his life, the boy seemed to disattach from this new striving self.

He'd burst into tears for no apparent reason, raging against Fein-gold, who had been unable to calm him down even with assurances that they would soon depart for the States. Sonia never knew if this was a lie devised by the American, since she too knew of Feingold's great love for the Philippines.

And then the rage had been transferred onto the boy's mother. He refused to see her, have anything to do with her, saying again and again that she was the culprit for his lasting unhappiness. She was the rot, the rust in his young life. Crying and crying, matching the boy tear for tear and convulsion for convulsion, she had still been unable to bring him to reason. Up he flew into the stratosphere of rage for an unknown—or perhaps, since the American Caracera was still on the minds of everyone involved, an undisclosed—reason, and would not come down.

He quit school. Refused to eat or bathe. Would stare at the wall in his bedroom at the Petal Towers for hours, seeing movies which only he could see, stoking his wrath, sweating as in a fever.

Yes, he had given up living with Mr. Feingold, whose heartbreak—even this second time around—was undimmed.

Not even the latest Nora Aunor film could draw him out of his mis-ery—that was how far gone the boy was.

And then he got it into his head to track down Roger Caracera's re-lations. Somehow or other, he found out where one of them lived. So-nia didn't know the name of this Caracera. Only that it was a woman, an aunt-in-law, one of the wives of the Caracera brothers. Perhaps, wanting to appease the boy, Feingold had helped to track her down.

Outside this woman's house the boy camped. Every time the gate was opened, he screamed at the top of his lungs. Arriving or departing, the drivers learned to roll up all the windows. First the drivers, getting out of the cars, threatened to rough him up. Even when the threats were backed up with decisive action, the boy would not relent. And then the cops were called.

Twice the American Feingold had to bail Blueboy out of jail.

And still he returned. What was it that he screamed at the cars, at the closed gate, hoping for his voice to pierce through to the inhabitants?

Where is Roger Caracera? Where does he live? Give me his address! He owes me his address! He loves me, I know he does, he knows he does, why are you keeping us apart? Roger Caracera, a member of your family, loves me! We can't be parted! Don't try to separate us! Where in America does he live? Where in New York City? You know me! Don't pretend you don't know! You saw me! At his play! At Roger Caracera's play! I was sitting beside him! With my mother! That proves that he loves me! Three million pesos—he bought me with three million pesos! That proves everything! And he helped us buy an apartment! Our love nest! I won't stop until you tell me where he is! I know about your family! First Eustacho Caracera, and now Roger!

One day he did not show up. But peace was not about to descend, the boy was only taking a break.

The next day he renewed his efforts. The vituperativeness in his voice was matched by a look of utter, of absolute masochism; he wanted to show how low he'd sunk, proud to have attained such depths. Sonia had shown up outside the woman's residence in Quezon City to take her turn talking sense into the boy.

The day after that, the boy was dead. Run over, either on his way from or to the house. It was hard not to credit the rumors which sprang up immediately. Perhaps the boy's mother had started them or, hearing them started, had enlarged upon them, eager to confirm details inflammatory to the Caraceras.

The car was dispatched by the woman whose house Pitik had haunted like a vengeful ghost.

Or a friend of the woman.

Or an employee wanting to ingratiate himself or herself to the wealthy family.

The car was dispatched by Roger Caracera himself.

Who knew but that, if the boy's mother hadn't left for the

provinces and given up her role as scourge and accuser, she might have suffered the same sad end?

Other rumors were started. The American Feingold—though of course the rumormongers never knew him by name—had grown jealous, enraged at the loss of the boy to a phantom lover, and had himself run the boy down. Soon enough, he abandoned his residence and did not leave a forwarding address. To this day he could not be found.

Or better yet, a tragic twist of fate: the man Feingold had not intended to run the boy down, only to drive up and offer to take him back home; it was only that his vision was clouded by tears and his reflexes made slow by exhaustion that he had slipped up. In other words, an accident—but one whose cause could be traced back to the boy.

He had willingly walked into the path of a car, along busy EDSA.

Or on Paseo de Roxas.

Or on Ayala Avenue.

He had wanted to die, had been happy to, intending to show up the man who had scorned him. The boy had been willing to carry his spite to such a disastrous, perverse end.

The boy had become insane, and death, the active seeking, courting of it, had become his last, enlivening mission.

The boy had been sentenced to death by the curse floating over bad money he'd supposedly inherited from a deceased lover—whose death from heartbreak the boy had himself caused.

Almost all the theories were ruled by the pleasing, circular, Catholic logic of being done to as one has done to others. Also, of an eye for an eye, tooth for a tooth. The boy was either paying for crimes he'd committed himself, or for the crimes of others for which he'd become the sacrificial lamb, taken by death as a substitute, in place of the actual culprits who, the theories went, remained out of death's reach because of the life-giving properties of the wealth they owned.

Strong feelings animated the face of Madame Sonia in the telling of this story, and the strongest, it struck Caracera, was pleasure. The pleasure of an anger cooled and turned into a curio, a thing of "interest" to be petted and showed off, its sharp points polished for decoration.

Was, was, was . . .

Madame Sonia, in this instance, was the deliverer of the blows, and her opponent Caracera, short of staggering, could be seen to absorb the impact: the blanched face, the suddenly active hands, the stuttering.

Was the car a Mercedes? A silver Mercedes?

Like Sonia already said, cars of all descriptions had been sworn to in front of the police.

And another rumor that she'd almost forgotten: that the police's ineptitude—and the multiplicity and variety of witness testimonies—was bought and paid for by the guilty family.

Where had the boy been buried?

A pauper's grave in a mass cemetery somewhere south of the city, in La Loma.

He was a smart boy, claimed Sonia, eulogizing. Full of promise. Not smart in the way of grammatical English, which Mr. Feingold and the American Caracera—so the boy had told the proprietress—had been constantly trying to instill in him. They gave the boy to understand that appearance, not substance, was the preferred commodity in America.

His teachers at St. Jude Catholic School had known better. During the funeral, one of them had read from an essay which the boy had adapted from a speech given during Religion class. It was a draft achieved after four revisions, which Miss Acevedo had guided him through. He had applied himself particularly to the final draft, the polishing of this work. This was signal evidence of the boy's improvement after Caracera's desertion.

The essay spoke of Jonah, the ordinary man who, by being swallowed by the whale, by enduring this signal, novel hardship, had become extraordinary, living into legend. From the recapping of the story, the writing moved into the lesson learned, which, after all, was the point of Religion class. Difficulty, wrote the boy, was essential to living. Difficulty marked the path through life and was responsible, more so than the passing of time, for turning a boy into a man, and a man into a legend. Flashes of humor, perhaps unintentional, were shown: how the man must have had to endure, along with darkness, the whale's bad breath. Imagination too: every so often, the man found himself knee-deep or neck-deep in swallowed seawater; and how too the man must've had to fight to not end up being turned by the whale's stomach and intestines into food. It showed his ability to look at one thing deeply and in the flesh, and yet be able to abstract it into useful principles for living: in other words, said Miss Acevedo, a talent for looking "from above and beyond" was clear.

This was what Madame Sonia had meant when she called the boy smart, when she mourned the boy's promise, lost.

Part of the reason why the essay had taken four drafts to complete was that the boy's English and spelling had to forever be turned back, relearned. But even from the start, the boy was given to know that what he already possessed—imagination, comprehension beyond the facts and vigor—no school could hope to teach.

The only thing Roger Caracera could add to all this was the meek apology: He was too impressed with me.

To which the proprietress unfailingly concurred: Yes, he was. Putting the fault not on the boy but on the man.

Caracera looked carefully at the family Mercedes—the bumpers, the headlights, the driver's-side door, the back fender, the tires—before getting back in. Of course there would be nothing to tell. Not by this time.

On the way to the airport the next day, he could not stop thinking about Aunt Irene pressing his hands with feeling during the blessing of his father's crypt.

CHAPTER 5

*F*iesta *of the Damned* opened in the second week of December 2000, following Steven Spielberg's *Saving Private Ryan*, which had been released the previous year. Both were poised to extend what Caracera disparagingly called "Gunsmoke Chic": exotic soil as a staging ground for American cowboy antics. Asserting dominion and moral rights which may no longer be applicable.

Even after all that he had gone through, Caracera did not see himself as guilty of this same trend. His defense was stunningly literal-minded: he did not have a gun, what he had was money, and deploying it, he had brought improvement to many lives: the boys of Father Shakespeare's ministry; the slum-dwellers of Frannie Prusso; and most of all, Donny Osmond, the tennis player. Caracera was as far from the Antic American, the Dashing Devil as could possibly be.

It was another seven weeks, in the middle of a mild, though still exasperatingly drawn-out winter, that he finally went to the movie.

By now, attendance had trickled to a few handfuls, and as he watched, he tried to imagine the warm, audible reverence and even the hooting and cheering said to accompany screenings during the first, busy weeks. The movie was a hit not just because of the groundwork laid by the Spielberg picture but, Caracera had to admit, because of the clear skill of the young neophyte director. From beginning to end, the action, as promised, was paramount, and exciting. Teary scenes, sparing in screen time, were doubly effective.

The long Death March to Bataan was a thing to behold. Everywhere, amplifying the torturousness of the soldiers' plight, could be seen the tropical heat rising from the ground in vertical waves to bend and transform vision.

Photographed in what he later learned was "low-contrast film stock," with a gel over the lens that brought out and emphasized blues and cobalts, Filipino flesh became a natural wonder: bronzed for contemplation. This was to make up, of course, for the Filipinos' placements in frame after frame: parts of bodies or heads cut off at the edges; or given no more moment than a medium shot; or given a quick close-up to underline the one trait they possessed that most served the plot, helplessness; or seen always to crane their necks upward at the taller Americans.

This, he conceded, was a prosecutorial fancy of his—getting the goods he fully expected. It made him register the movie's ample virtues with a cool, if not wan, appreciation. Elsewhere in the theater was the total engagement of a true captive audience.

Among the movie's virtues was the casting of Harvey Keitel, whose aura of moral dubiousness brought a welcome touch of contradiction to a hero otherwise frequently associated in the popular imagination with the likes of John Wayne: pushy to a fault, and victorious by livelihood. Keitel, though filled still with a conquering sense of mission, was seen to come by some military decisions with ambiguity, doubt.

Something nagged at Caracera.

It followed him into class and superimposed itself, impishly, over the handsome and pretty faces staring back at him, almost always at the most inopportune moments: when his students were reading aloud from their compositions, or when they were phrasing earnest, confused questions, which he often ended up asking them to repeat, comical when the question turned out to be a simple "May I go to the bathroom?"

Finally he went back to the movie three weeks later, fearing it might be pulled from the theaters soon.

And in the scene which had been the cause of disturbance, in which he thought he saw the dead boy—or rather not the dead boy, he was not that far gone, but some other Filipino who looked like the dead boy—standing, yes, at the side of the main action, there was instead a boy who was robust, thuggish even, with a face that looked as if it had never learned how to smile, posed stiffly and staring straight ahead. This not-Pitik was dressed in crisp whites and an overlarge pair of pants that were a castoff from one of the American soldiers. He looked beyond the camera at Caracera, or whoever would've been seated in his line of sight, with a personal plea. Or a curse. It was easy enough to guess that he might've been transfixed by the lights of the setup, mesmerized by the cameras, the bustle, the attention being paid, the commands in a stern foreign language he probably did not understand. Or perhaps it was not the language itself but the terms, the technicalese.

All right, so Caracera'd been crazy. No Pitik as he'd thought.

Yet a few scenes later, in the undulations of the clear threads of heat, was another boy-creature who was (cut away from too quickly to be contradicted) the dead boy. Or rather, the dead boy's twin.

Again, looking as if he'd never learned how to smile in his entire life. The skin bronzed as a special distinguishment, but the eyes jaundiced and staring ahead, unblinking, to impart a message implacable and unscripted.

After that sighting, the action continued unperturbed.

No more boy to the sides of the picture. None either at the center. Only Filipino men and women aggrieved by losses in the war and, later, seen briefly to share in the refracted glow of the American triumph.

Still, afterward, as the credits rolled, that stare kept compelling itself into the foreground of Caracera's memory. It moved ahead of the throngs of suffering American soldiers, who had been seen to be stranded on an island of fatherless boyhood, not men at all. Touching in their bravery.

It moved past the gunfire, frequent and musical, and which had rearranged the Philippine topography with a reliably wayward hand—shredding straw huts; causing dust to fly up to create illusory figures that disappeared as quickly as they appeared; making fowl and other assorted animals dance and flap around or, less entertainingly, burst forth blackish blood.

It moved past the better-lit, carefully photographed faces and bodies of the stars: John Travolta as a lieutenant stranded by MacArthur; Samuel L. Jackson as Travolta's right-hand man; Robert de Niro as a military tactician, on the boat with MacArthur on his victorious return; James Caan . . .

Out Caracera went into the sludgy streets, having to pull his jacket collar tight. No waves of heat but instead plumes of steam emerging from his mouth, his nostrils and even, as he looked down, from his ungloved hands.

The next day he took his seat in the near-empty theater again. And then the day after that. It turned out they didn't pull the movie from the theaters, despite the fact that on some nights it was solely Caracera who was paying for it to be screened.

Each time he went back, there was a new sighting of the boy (or the boy's twin) at the side of a previously innocent shot. The boy made a mockery of the movie by appearing at the periphery of a different shot during subsequent viewings. The same boy, over and over, skinny, fey even, though unsmiling, eyes dull in the manner of things vacated by hope, as one with the infernal heat and always, always demanding correction for the huge injustice of his plight: he did not belong at the side, and would not be shunted there, forgotten. His haunting was hate-filled, as much hate as there was heat emanating from the screen, and in each appearance he fought and succeeded over the fact that he was placed at the edge of the screen, and only for a few seconds, and he fought and succeeded over Roger Caracera, the angel of his, the boy's, death, using his inexhaustible, implacable, industrious hatred, saying: *Do not come here ever again for you are not welcome anymore.* Even though he knew the man would come back again and again. Death had turned Pitik Sindit into a second, more lasting, more gifted gremlin, finally beloved and courted and welcome.

A NOTE ABOUT THE AUTHOR

HAN ONG was born and raised in the Philippines. At the age of sixteen, he immigrated to the United States, where he spent just one year
in high school before dropping out. He began writing plays almost
immediately afterward, eventually creating nearly three dozen works
for the stage. In 1997, he became one of the youngest MacArthur Fel-
lows. His first novel, *Fixer Chao* (FSG, 2001), was named a *Los Angeles
Times* Best Book of the Year and was nominated for a Stephen Crane
First Fiction Award.